TIGER ISLE
A GOVERNMENT OF THIEVES

E.S. Shankar

TIGER ISLE
A GOVERNMENT OF THIEVES

E.S. Shankar

Gerakbudaya Enterprise

Published by:
   Gerakbudaya Enterprise
   No 11, Lorong 11/4E, 46200 Petaling Jaya, Selangor, Malaysia.
   Email: sird@streamyx.com
   Website: www.gerakbudaya.com

Shankar, E. S.
   Tiger isle: a government of thieves / E.S. Shankar.
   ISBN 978-967-5832-70-3
   1. Malaysian fiction (English). I. Title.
   823

Cover design and layout: Paul Choo
Illustrations by Ridhwan Ahmad, Ritchie and E.S. Shankar.

Printed by Vinlin Press Sdn Bhd
2, Jalan Meranti Permai 1,
Meranti Permai Industrial Park,
Batu 15, Jalan Puchong,
47100 Puchong, Selangor, Malaysia.

TIGER ISLE
A GOVERNMENT OF THIEVES

E.S. Shankar

Gerakbudaya Enterprise

Published by:
Gerakbudaya Enterprise
No 11, Lorong 11/4E, 46200 Petaling Jaya, Selangor, Malaysia.
Email: sird@streamyx.com
Website: www.gerakbudaya.com

Shankar, E. S.
    Tiger isle: a government of thieves / E.S. Shankar.
    ISBN 978-967-5832-70-3
    1. Malaysian fiction (English). I. Title.
    823

Cover design and layout: Paul Choo
Illustrations by Ridhwan Ahmad, Ritchie and E.S. Shankar.

Printed by Vinlin Press Sdn Bhd
2, Jalan Meranti Permai 1,
Meranti Permai Industrial Park,
Batu 15, Jalan Puchong,
47100 Puchong, Selangor, Malaysia.

To Cheryl, without whom nothing would have been possible, and of course Rekha, Prasad who wants to write, and Mrs. Chong, Mrs. Vaz, Terence, and Mrs. Yiap who inspired me all those years ago in Victoria Institution.

Lord Ganesha Chathurthy

Vaakkundam, Nalla manamundam,
Mamalaral nokunddam,
Grant me purity of mind and thought, expression
and eloquence of speech, and of learning governed by
Goddess Saraswathi. And blessings from the goddess
Mahalakshmi, whose feet rest on lotus flowers,

Mayni nudankathu pookondu thuppar thirumayni,
Thumbikkai yanpatham thapparmal sarvar thammaku.
And I shall unfailingly worship daily at your feet,
O Lord Ganesha, with fresh flowers.
  - St. Avvaiyar

CONTENTS

Location & Map of Tiger Isle

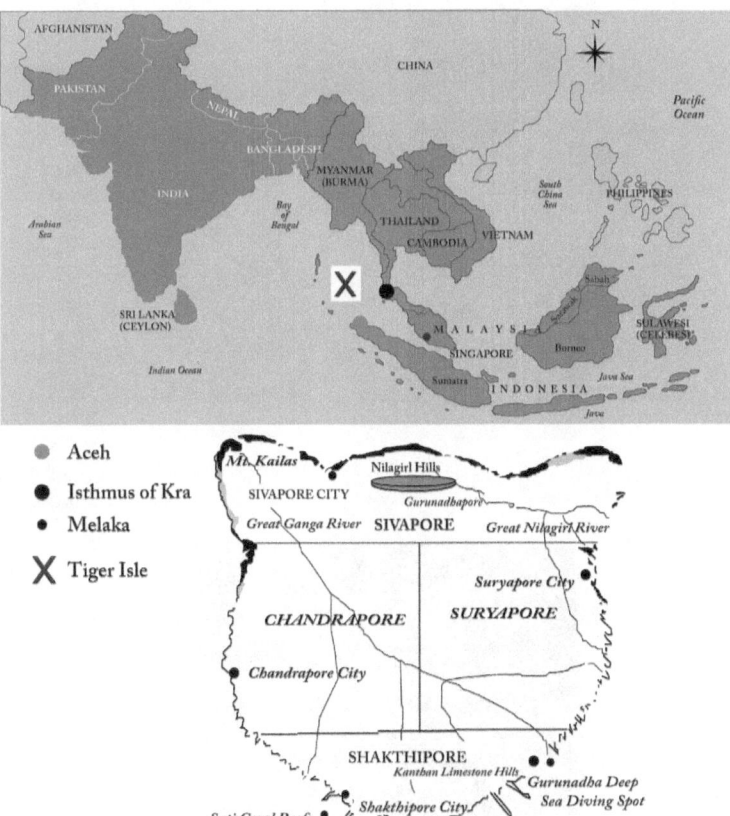

"What Color Do You Want?"
Paper Game

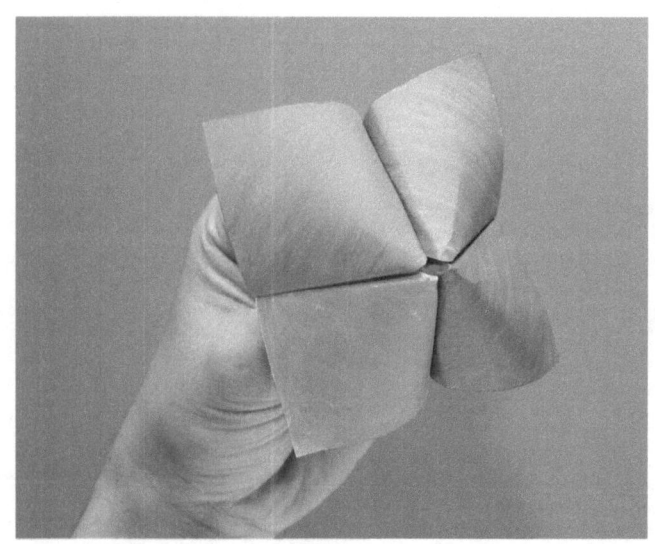

Canna.
Tiger Isle Flower

The Cremation

It began with a death and ended with another. In between many more, millions, perished; yet more lived than died. As Maha Adhi Sri Jagad Gurunadha had once remarked, "What is death but a quick shower, change of clothes, a new venue and a fresh start?"

Rekha's body was cremated at the ancient city cemetery in open air in accordance with Hindu rites, late evening on Tuesday September 4, 2012. The ceremony and prayers were performed and overseen by Hindu priests from the Pillayar (Ganesha) Temple at Indian Settlement near the golf course.

Rekha had not been a Nobel Prize winner, All-England Badminton Singles Champion, or world squash or bowling number one. She had not pocketed a million dollars as the Pulipore National Television Station 4 (PNTVS4) Idol or a reality show winner. She was neither a corporate Ali Baba *fraudtrepreneur*[1] billionaire nor even a titled *Sri*,[2] with which even mere railway gatekeepers, dentists, and gangland bosses were knighted nowadays.

Her corpse had not been found floating headless in the river behind police headquarters after several days of police interrogation. Neither had it been discovered brutally battered

[1] A person illegally fronting for a political party as a major shareholder and/or president/director of a public unlisted or quoted listed company.

[2] Sri: Sanskrit for "radiant," used as an honorific for a titled personage, equivalent to a knighted "Sir" in England.

and bruised in a holding cell after being investigated by police for alleged involvement in a so-called international auto-theft ring, while later a death certificate mysteriously pronounced the cause of death as pulmonary edema, and amidst public uproar a "rogue cop" was charged with causing "grievous hurt not amounting to homicide." Nor had it been gathered in bits and pieces in black polyurethane plastic bin bags due to spectacularly being blown up in a secluded forest, while she was still half alive with dynamite strapped to her chest, for which the courts decided it was not necessary to determine the killer's motive.

Her broken body had not appeared frozen in rigor mortis mysteriously on the roof of a high-rise office complex, where she had gone to "voluntarily assist" in a piddly two-hundred-dollar alleged corruption case, and anticorruption officers later swore her death was due to "sudden voluntary suicide" in which they had no hand.

Yet thousands arrived at her home and at the cemetery to catch a glimpse of Rekha before she was gone forever. First to arrive were seven of her best friends from her schooldays. Bloggers Zorro Unmasked and Desiderata, from ASEAN countries like Malaysia, hastened their way to the cemetery. Evenhanded commentators like Purple Haze rushed before the feral thunderstorm struck.

Shakila, Amanda, Chermaine, Zhi Yan, Nadine, Nelson, Rama, Indran, Jalil, Hamid, Kong Voon, Patel, Darwis, Foo Chi, Jaccob, Jayabalan, Tan Chai, Morzali, Raymond D'Silva, Viji Martin, Shubon, Thiru, Thayala, Kang Hwee, Teong Choon, Zul, Abdul Rashid, Hari, Harjit, James Kui, Mano, Beng Yew, Billy, Balraj and Balraj Singh, "Sarge," Daya, Kim Chuan, Kian Fui, and Paul Nah, the "Old Boys and Girls," marched forward in their alma mater ties. Jaspal, Ket Chong, and Mike Nettleton from London and Seng Tee from Sydney were understandably absent. The "Old London Gang" of Sitsa, Prem, Morgan, Chandru, Wilfred, "Steed" Subra and Robert drove up in two battered Beetles after downing a few lunchtime "one for the road" at the Hilton bar. Rekha would have approved of it. The doctors' brigade of Pathma, Mahendran,

Mohan, Sarmukh, Sivandan, Krish K, Yoong Fong and Cheah forced their way through the mid-afternoon traffic gridlock.

Women are not allowed at Hindu burial sites, but wild horses could not have stopped them. Many wondered why Rekha's husband Roshan and her children, Lakshmi and Karthik, were not there. Her father Krishnasamy explained that regretfully, a terrorist bomb alert had shut down Melbourne Airport, and they were stuck in the departure lounge. The cremation could not wait due to planetary movements and Hindu astrology.

The next morning the sobbing Krishnasamy and his younger brother Ramasamy sifted through the ashes at the funeral pyre. They retrieved the special asthi bones that were placed in a sanctified terracotta earthenware pot filled to the brim with Rekha's ashes. As willed by Rekha, the bulk of the ash was emptied, with the pot following it, into the flowing waters of the river that ran through the city, after the tenth-day prayers to send the soul toward the invisible. Ramasamy packed a sachet of his niece's ashes for the Shradda ceremony at Benares and the Ganges in India.

Rekha passed away early morning at six o'clock while peacefully asleep in her bed at home. Just like that. No heart attack, sudden stroke, or a long bout with cancer. It had been a good half century, a good innings indeed. She was just another ordinary Tiger Isle citizen who died, albeit before her time. It was just another case of an ordinary soul returning to her creator, so testified the death certificate dated Tuesday September 4, 2012. It was just another ordinary death.

Or was it?

2211

"Like Plato's Atlantis in 10,000 BCE? Are you sure?" Pariksith Sequoia Sivan quietly asked.

"Yeah, I'm sure!" shot back Janaki Redwood Rekha, sounding a little exasperated and annoyed.

"What? Like *Chingachgook and Uncas*?"[3] Pariksith asked.

"Yeah, just like Chingachgook and Uncas," replied Janaki.

"And, er…you have what proof? Wikipedia'd it. There's nothing there," he countered.

"You won't find it on Wikipedia or anywhere else even if you Googled or Yahoo'd it forever and a day," retorted Janaki.

"What, Area 51, Roswell, and Hangars 18 and 54 all over again, Jan?" Pariksith asked as he moved his naked body closer to her right side, cupped hand on chin, and smiled as he danced arched eyebrows at her.

"There was no mystery in Roswell, and you damn well know it, Par. There weren't any UFOs or spindly-shaped aliens from Mars with green blood and pigeon-toed feet. Washington and the White House covered up a disastrous crash where they lost several experimental air force planes and their pilots. Of course, they didn't want Congress and the taxpayer to find out and have their 'research' funding cut, so they let the "aliens" story be milked to glory.

---

3   Chingachgook/Uncas: Last Native American chief and his son in James Fenimore Cooper's classic book Last of the Mohicans.

And before you start on it, crop circles, Nazca lines, The Pyramids and the Wiltshire Horse were all manmade. Yes, we are alone in this universe. That's the way it was always meant to be," Janaki protested vehemently.

"And you know all this because which God avatared before you and let you in on it?" Pariksith laughed.

Janaki moaned. "Arrgh! Stop it already. Don't mock things you're clueless about."

But Pariksith would not stop. This was just too bizarre. "There are no records of it anywhere. No Remembrance Day. No archives, Discovery documentary, movies, books, or YouTube videos. All gone, poof, like some illusionist whisked off the cloth, and viola, the Statue of Liberty's disappeared?" he sniggered.

"Sez who? I know! I weep, Par. And it was more like New York vanished," Janaki spoke in hushed tones.

"Come on, Jan. You know exactly what happened two hundred years ago?" he laughed.

"Yeah, what the hell would you know?" Janaki responded as she sat up in bed.

"Who? The Americans? Bullshit! The Commie rats, Iran, North Korea, the Taliban and the Muslim Diaspora would have exposed them. And if it were the Ruskies or the Chinese, Uncle Sam would have gone to town. You think India, Britain, and France would have let it pass? You're out of your mind!" Pariksith bellowed.

"It was all of them, together. For the first time in human history, every single nation on the face of the earth came together and decided collectively what the best course of action was. So, they blanked it all out. It never made its way into any history books or official archives. The greatest cover-up of all time!" fumed Janaki.

"There was a huge island in South East Asia you say just plopped into the ocean without a trace, and no one's heard of it since? And the thirty million people of Tiger Isle?" Pariksith inquired as he gaped at her in disbelief.

"Dead, all dead," she whispered as the tears rolled down her cheeks.

Janaki Redwood Rekha

No one will ever know whether Rekha's husband Roshan Prasad, son Karthik and daughter Lakshmi were spared from the annihilation of Tiger Isle by divine intervention and design. After the Tiger Isle Holocaust, Roshan immediately started a family tradition. They would all, whether male or female, carry "Rekha" as their last name in honor and remembrance of Rekha's heroism.

Interpol investigations showed that Roshan, Lakshmi, and Karthik had left Chandrapore for Melbourne at 1:00 p.m. on Pulirajaputran Airlines flight number PJ 13 on Wednesday, August 8, 2012. There their trail vanished forever. The three who landed in Melbourne were paid impersonators carefully selected for their close resemblance to the Prasads in all aspects.

The real Prasads were in disguise and carried stolen and expertly doctored Malaysian passports, for which they had paid a small fortune. They sneaked off, travelling under the family name of Subramaniam, to Singapore via a specially chartered speedboat. They breathed a sigh of relief after clearing Singapore immigration and its numerous luggage, body, and passport scanners at Keppel Harbour. If their plans were going to be scuppered at all, it would be in superefficient and security-paranoid Singapore.

They exited at the Harbour Front end, a sprawling shopping mall-cum-office complex and mass rapid-transport island hub. They queued up dutifully at the designated taxi stand and soon hopped on to a roomy yellow CityCab taxi to Queen Street Bus

Station. There they hired a spanking-new, fully air-conditioned taxi. Their Singapore taxi driver would not, with a sitting fare, dare light up a cigarette, risk winding his window down, and stick his hand out. If he did, he would be in very real danger of being immediately pulled over by the most vigilant of traffic cops in the world.

As soon as they got in, after the driver had hauled their Samsonite roller-suitcases and backpacks in the taxi boot, the driver engaged them in that most favorite of Singapore cab drivers' pastimes. "You like our variety of food, chicken rice, prawn noodle, rojak, beef ball special, and sea food?" He then moved on to complaining about the Singapore prime minister, his octogenarian father, their politics, and about how much more freedom Malaysians enjoyed in their country and how "cheap" everything there was.

They headed for Larkin Bus Terminal in Johor Bahru at the southernmost extremity of Peninsular Malaysia. The twenty-dollar taxi fare and tip included charges for the Second Link toll highway and bridge over the waters of the extremely busy Johor Straits, from Tuas in Singapore.

At Larkin they were inveigled by hustlers and touts into boarding a spanking-new, fully air-conditioned "pirate" taxi. This was a third-hand, reconditioned, rickety, old, smoke-belching, malodorous Mercedes Benz W123. It was a sweatbox with the air conditioner barely functioning. Its driver wound his window down and stuck his hand out in between taking massive puffs on his cigarette throughout the journey, with absolutely no fear any city or highway cop would stop him. As soon as they got in, after the driver had hauled their Samsonite roller-suitcases and backpacks in the taxi boot, the driver engaged them in that most favorite of Malaysian cab drivers' pastimes.

He started off with, "You like our variety of food, nasi lemak, char kway teow, chendol, Indian banana leaf lunch, roast and barbecued pork, Chinese five-spices marinated roast duck and seafood?" He then moved on to complaining about the Malaysian prime minister, his octogenarian predecessor, their politics, and about how much more freedom Singaporeans enjoyed and how "cheap" and efficient everything there was.

What was it about these Malaysians and Singaporeans, Roshan mused, who thought that the main reason foreigners arrived on their shores was to taste their food, most of which, like anywhere else, was of a local bias? Tourist advertising campaigns there continued to blare various myths. One of these was that Singaporeans and Malaysians always greeted each other first with "Sudah makan?" ("Have you eaten?") and not "Selamat Pagi/Selamat Tengah Hari" ("Good morning/Good afternoon") and the like. What Roshan had noticed on previous trips there was the ubiquitous and meaningless McDonaldspeak of "Have a good day." The Americanization of the East was humming along in full flow.

Their outstation taxi headed northwest for Gemas, some two hundred kilometers away. The journey took exactly two hours on the smooth and fairly well-maintained eight-hundred-kilometer-long north-south blatantly toll-overcharging highway. Most drivers casually ignored the highway speed limit of 110 kilometers per hour imposed on all vehicles.

Gemas, a small town located in Negeri Sembilan (translated as Nine Districts State), was the junction from which train tracks branched off west and north, and east and north. This was forced by nature, as the Main Range Rainforest Mountains formed a central spine that divided Peninsular Malaysia into not quite equal eastern and western halves.

At Gemas they boarded a Keretapi Tanah Melayu train for the six-hour scenic journey, which stretched to eight. The train stopped at numerous stations on its slow east-coast chug to Kota Bahru, capital of Kelantan State near the Thailand border. The fare was about U.S. $15 per ticket for a second-class, air-conditioned, comfortable compartment seat in this slow but hugely popular daytime jungle train.

The shattered and spent Prasads checked into a nondescript, cockroach-infested, "Chinaman"-owned hotel in Kota Bahru. They whiled away the next day riding around the pleasant town in bechas (trishaws). Thankfully, the Kuala Lumpur madness of the "house in the sky" concept of condominium living and skyscrapers had not invaded the air space here.

Kelantan was Malaysia's only completely Islamic state, ruled by Opposition Parti Islam Se-Malaysia, PAS, or the Pan Malaysian Islamic Party. Rantau Abang in Terengganu, Kelantan's immediate southern neighbor state, was world renowned for the turtles that still made their annual pilgrimage and laid their eggs on its hot, sandy beaches. Farther south was Pahang state, home to Club Med. Stretching from Kelantan, in the northern part of the east coast, to Pahang in the south are some of the most beautiful beaches and island resorts in the world.

Later in the evening they headed for Pantai Chinta Berahi, or Beach of Passionate Love, where they sipped mixed-fruit cocktails and stared at the glorious sunset.

The Prasads checked out of their hotel at 2:00 a.m., accompanied by their Thai/Malay/Chinese runner-guide, Abhi, and his assistant Anat. They crammed into Abhi's black and dusty ten-year-old Malaysian-made 4WD Perodua Kembara. Anat drove them all to a secluded spot at Rantau Panjang near the Thai border at Sungai (River) Golok. Anat parked the car in the shadow of trees and bushes and waited there in the jeep with the Prasads, as Abhi alighted and headed for the brightly lit immigration-bureau building. Roshan had paid him U.S. $1,000, with which he was now going to be a little generous.

Five minutes later, Anat's handphone lit up with a sms, which simply said "Go." Anat escorted the Prasads across the Golok River, which at its narrowest point had shriveled up in the high blazing summer to the width of a small drain. Anat and Roshan shared the suitcases and small backpacks between them. They crossed over and walked to the small lawless town of Golok with the kids in tow, while Malaysian and Thai immigration officials went to sleep for a few minutes.

Anat checked them into one of the numerous cheap but air-conditioned hotels that mainly plied the flesh trade. Golok was also one of the main border towns for smuggling rice, petrol, and stolen cars from Malaysia into Thailand. Besides its red-light business, it was littered with pubs, bars, and karaoke lounges. At 2:00 p.m. the next day, Anat loaded the Prasads onto the train to the popular seaside resort town of Hat Yai, from where they caught the connection for the sixteen-hour ride to Bangkok.

Anat had given Roshan a small envelope, in which was a key for a locker at Bangkok Suvarnabhumi (Sanskrit for "Land of Gold") International Airport. In the locker, Roshan found three fairly well-used U.S. international passports and tickets for San Francisco via Taipeh. The travelers were apparently Raman Chandrasekhar, his sixteen-year-old daughter Neeraja, and his thirteen-year-old son Prashant. Roshan carefully tore up all their Malaysian passports into small pieces and flushed them down the airport toilet.

The real Chandrasekhars, among whom the father was a physicist with NASA, had left Washington D.C. a month earlier for a retreat to an ashram in Rishikesh, the yoga center made world renowned by the Beatles. They did not know their passports and return air tickets had been stolen from the safe of their family home in Chennai or that they would soon find themselves victims of identity theft.

All the trouble Rekha had meticulously taken to expose the Tiger Isle conspiracy was undone swiftly. Email accounts of her friends and sympathizers had been hacked, and thumb drives and hard-disc backups intercepted, smashed to bits, and then torched. Those in London, Paris, and Washington, whom Rekha had relied upon, were kidnapped, threatened with dire consequences to their lives if they chose not to remain silent, and had their PCs and laptops destroyed.

The five permanent and ten nonpermanent members of the United Nations Security Council met, considered, and approved it. Then, a unanimous resolution was passed at the UN General Assembly for an international moratorium on the Tiger Isle Holocaust. There were no absentees or abstentions for that motion.

They began with any online information or reference to it, followed by archives maintained by newspapers, television and radio stations, and cinematography organizations. The UN sent out wrecking crews, auditors, and oversight committees to the Smithsonian, British Museum, and official archives in Malaysia, Singapore, Thailand, Indonesia, Philippines, Portugal, Holland, India, and China. NASA scientists raided the offices of Google, cleansed Google Map, and moved on to all known satellites and their computer banks.

Every nation checked and double checked the job was complete, as they destroyed old history and geography books and atlases, and they printed new ones. Led by the UN, it was not until ten years later that the world was satisfied that Tiger Isle was history, as if it had never existed. The UN enforced its mandate and strong-armed internet service providers in every country to block and suspend all forums, discussions, and blogs on Tiger Isle. There was very real fear worldwide that tinkering with the unknown force behind Tiger Isle's destruction might result in Armageddon. Fifty years later, few could recall Tiger Isle, while many thought it was mere legend. A hundred years on, and it was finally obliterated from human mind and history.

Or so they thought.

Two hundred years of UN, U.S., China and India-led surreptitious investigations had not made a single dent into unraveling the mystery surrounding the Tiger Isle debacle.

I am not married, and I have not decided whether I will give birth to any child. I do not take my life and existence in frivolity, for I am Janaki Redwood Rekha, fifth generation after Lakshmi Roshan Prasad Rekha, daughter of Rekha Krishnasamy Roshan Prasad, who saved the world.

I should know, for I am among the last of the Tiger Islanders.

The Father

The Old Man, Adhi Sri Dr. Bhairav Oak Broad Leaf Sivan, LLB (Hons), former president of Pulipore, or Tiger Isle, gazed in awe at the magnificent 180-degree panoramic Indian Ocean view from the ceiling-to-floor French windows of his penthouse office. There was five thousand square feet of it on the eightieth floor of the Pulipetro Corporation Tower (PPCT), headquarters of Pulipetro Corporation (PPC). And why wouldn't he? After all, were it not for his inspirational idea, resolve, push, and cunning, the once tallest tower in the world would not have been constructed, albeit at a hugely inflated cost.

"Why bother, Dad? We have all the money in the world to last thirteen lifetimes. Your place in the history books is assured. You're famous on all four continents. Our people, as well as the Arabs and Palestinians, adore you. Travel. Write and publish that eagerly awaited second volume of your autobiography. Why, if you're up to it, take on a new trophy wife. Enjoy! Everyone will admire and love you all the more for it. Hmm, Dad?" Duryodhana spoke as he interrupted his father's reverie in a rather careless manner and somewhat rude tone.

Bhairav laughed loudly to mask his disappointment. Trained politician that he was, he nevertheless struggled to suppress anger and bile that threatened to leap out and scorch his eldest son like a shower of searing coal sparks. He could not bring himself to chastise his last great hope and legacy. He still saw Duryodhana in his mind's eye as the baby who had induced awe and an outpouring of love the instant he had witnessed him taking his first faltering steps all those years ago.

Two remarkable features of Bhairav's visage were his moustache and goatee that when combined with gold-stemmed rimless glasses, made it a close resemblance to a cross between comrades Vladimir Ilyich Lenin and Leon Trotsky, and Hitler. Though his passport stated he stood five feet six inches in his socks, he had shrunk and looked a good two inches shorter. At eighty-one, his hair had thinned and his hairline receded, gracefully. He did not slouch when sitting or have a stoop. He still moved with more vigor, energy, and purpose than many men half his age.

He was famous and infamous in equal parts. The Americans, Tiger Isle's main trading partner since independence in 1960, despised him for his "look East" rhetoric and "but export West" hypocrisy. The CIA had pondered his quiet exsanguination when Bhairav promoted the "avatar virtual world" version of 9/11 conspiracy hypotheses. The British were always on the back foot from Bhairav's constant "colonial plunderers and murderers" speeches, while the Zionists had their hooks in him as the "International Jew Baiter."

"You don't understand do you, my dear boy? In this universe, only change is constant. Nothing is assured permanency in a creation where entropy, slow decay, is an inbuilt mechanism to safeguard against inaction, sloth, and complacency. That's why I financed and bought our way to make it doubly sure you were elected a member of Parliament. Leave it to chance, and Maitreya and his Democratic Justice Party will seize power in the blink of an eye," Bhairav calmly replied.

"You have no confidence in Kapalin as president then? That's rich. After all, you anointed him your successor," Duryodhana said.

"That was one of my biggest mistakes. A disaster of Aceh Tsunami proportions. Then again, I had no clear alternative. I am afraid our United National Tigerists Association, which has been in power the last fifty years, resembles the once Austrian Hapsburg

Dynasty. Too much elitism and inbreeding has resulted in weaker and weaker leadership. All indications are that Kapalin will be a one-term wonder."

"You reckon?"

"It's a certainty unless we act. He is weak and does not have the courage or willpower to see through unpopular but absolutely necessary social, political, and economic reforms. One week he announces poorly fleshed-out policies, the next he does a U-turn, all in the face of fire from Maitreya, who has made major inroads into our heartland.

He does not realize it, but his wife Natasha has also quickly become his Achilles' heel. She has no constitutional position but fancies she's a Princess Diana or Hillary Clinton. She's antagonizing everyone here, traipsing all over the globe on illegal junkets and passing the exorbitant bill to taxpayers. The scandal sheets are full of photographs of her wining and dining with American movie stars. Why, she even secretly strong-armed that young merchant banker of dubious origins and reputation from Morgen McKinzy Merryk Whoreton Saks to take out a full-page, million-dollar advertisement in the London Times proclaiming her first lady of Tiger Isle. What a shameless hussy. Wait till Adhi Gurunadha hears about it."

Then again this was Tiger Isle, population thirty million or officially Pulipore, derived from "puli," Tamil for "tiger," and "pore" from the Tamil word "oor," meaning any of town, city, or even country,. Located in the waters of South East Asia, north of Sumatra and west of Peninsular Malaysia, it was the corruption capital of the world.

At $4 billion, double its true cost, PPCT was still an architectural wonder. Up to $1.5 billion of inflated construction cost had been siphoned out and flowed thick like sweet honey into secret offshore tax-haven bank accounts maintained in Guernsey, Channel Islands, by UNTA. Another $500 million from interior fit-out works had trickled into similar Panama bank accounts operated by nominees handsomely rewarded by Bhairav.

There was nothing unusual with all that, since it was now a matter of government culture. Taking home office notepads, paper clips, pencils, ballpoint pens, and staplers for personal use, teeming and lading of petty cash floats, or even indulging in petty larceny was wholly acceptable, good. Daylight robbery you say? Even better, for which a knighthood or Sri awaited the daring.

The entire fabulous construction contract for PPCT was awarded after seemingly due consideration. But actually it was by virtue of the direct negotiation, or "direct nego," business model absolutely favored in Tiger Isle. The beneficiary of it was Empire Office & Interiors Limited. It was a newly incorporated two-dollar company owned by two unknown individuals with no business track record whatsoever. Empire fronted for Bhairav and UNTA.

There was nothing unusual in that, either, in a can-do country. In Tiger Isle, an entrepreneur was defined as a visualizer and actualizer of a massive 100 percent government-guaranteed contract secured with an advance gratuitous "mobilization" payment of at least 50 percent of the contract sum. These homebred Ali Baba fraudtrepreneurs did not have to stake one cent of their own capital in any commercial venture. The government insured them against failure of any kind. Were any of these cronies to abscond with the advance payment and disappear to the Middle East, China or Africa, that would be the usual end of that matter.

Again, it was a matter of government culture never to prosecute a crony, especially one who had a lift up the greasy pole through affirmative action policies meant for the benefit of the poor, the backward, and the underclass. If by public pressure any had been charged in court, a rarity in Tiger Isle history, no conviction had ever been recorded against one.

Of the two Empire nominee shareholders/directors, one was a Form Three educated Tigerist homemaker. The senior accomplice was his Form Five dropout Tigerist wife, who chauffeured the latest Mercedes for the Old Man's son's uncle-in-law. A disturbing trend in Tiger Isle was the increasing number of men who failed to complete high school and practiced kitchen and home economics instead. Surprisingly, it did not seem to affect their performance in sexonomics.

With so many direct nego billion-dollar government contracts floating about, and they were all for a billion dollars or more (true cost, half to two-thirds less) spewing out daily from the president's office, the net for nominees had to be cast far and wide. Having virtually exhausted the pool of candidates from close relatives, blood or otherwise, it was sad they had to rope in masseurs, drivers, maids, security guards, cooks, kitchen help, garbage collectors, milkmen, old newspaper collectors, and the like. At least relatives with college diplomas or university degrees looked genuine on paper.

To be fair, these diplomas and degrees were not bought in a country where anyone and anything could be bought; everyone and everything here did indeed have a negotiable price. They were given away as of right under affirmative action programs in favor of the majority. Corruption and cribbing in examinations was thus checked, the minister for education claimed quixotically.

How could cooks and drivers be revealed as such in publicly accessible statutory declaration forms filed with the Registrar of Companies for awards of direct nego billion-dollar contracts and projects? The real (bent) creative geniuses beavering away at the Economic Planning Directorate (EPD), a division under the purview of the president, hardly broke sweat with that one. The new underclass of nominees was all declared "businessman" or "company director."

All these abuses were in direct contravention of government standing orders that demanded open tenders, especially for billion-dollar contracts. The cowed citizens of Tiger Isle hardly dared protest.

The Son

Shortly after the $4 billion PPCT construction contract was awarded to the anonymous Empire, it was acquired as a 100 percent wholly owned subsidiary of Harbour Maritime Plc. Harbour was one of the stable of public listed companies "helmed" by the Old Man's son, Sri Duryodhanan Acacia Broad Leaf Sivan. He was regarded as a genius of an Ali Baba fraudtrepreneur, even in a nation of superb Ali Baba fraudtrepreneurs.

It did not matter there was no "synergy" between the businesses of Harbour and Empire. Merchant bankers, investment gurus, market researchers, and "informed analysts" were prepared to make an exception, given who Duryo was. In any other situation, they would have ignored this lack of "synergy," the industry buzzword and alarm bell, only at their own peril.

Harbour was a serious loss-making concern whose quoted ordinary stock price hovered miraculously around three dollars a share against its initial public offering price of one dollar. It was close to being classified a PSE 04 company and in danger of being suspended and delisted from the Pulipore Stock Exchange (PSE). Several years of trading losses had virtually wiped out its share capital of $250 million. But that did not faze investors, who knew the real power behind Harbour was their ex-president.

News of the Empire and Harbour deal was leaked. As is usual all over the world, the culprits were sworn to probity and secrecy, insiders. Manipulating majority and controlling shareholders, their conniving corporate presidents, CEOs, directors, and an armada of merchant bankers, lawyers, and their staff working on the "numbers," all played this game. Where government too had a stake, the directors of bodies like the EPD joined in the planned fleecing. Everyone knew the real suckers would always be the mom-and-pop retail investors that formed the masses.

Family members, cronies, close friends, lovers, mistresses, and would-be conquests of these bloodsucking velociraptors all made a quick sizeable buck. Insider trading was punishable by stiff fines and prison sentences. No one gave a damn since the chairmen of the Pulipore Stock Exchange and the super-watchdog Pulipore Securities Council (PSC) themselves broke the rules with impunity, employing nominee share-trading accounts. Did not Wall Street know way in advance it would always be able to shift blame to guileless Main Street investors and scare and bully them into footing the bill as well? Government was only there to make sure Main Street did not respond with something like the 1917 Russian Revolution.

Duryodhana, more popularly known as Dan, bore an uncanny resemblance to the square-jawed Desperate Dan of the British comic book The Dandy. He had Dan's six-foot, two-inch height, and girth as well. Some referred to him as Jay L. Dan played his part in quickly spreading the news that Empire was "in the pipeline" for several more government construction and fit-out contracts "worth a billion or two." Furious handphone calls were made and texts sent to other "captains of industry," market players, movers and shakers, and politicians. Harbour's share price rocketed to six dollars in a day before it was suspended, pending a "probe" by the authorities.

The PSE's query to the board of directors of Harbour began with the usual pompously worded and obsequious "If we may be permitted to inquire about the unusual market volume activity and share price movements affecting Harbour." It was answered by return fax with the stock reply, "The directors and management of Harbour are not aware of any reasons for the irrational exuberance." The stock exchange promptly consigned the reply to the rubbish bin and went back to sleep.

Even if they wanted to, they would never, never cross swords with a son or daughter of the Old Man. They simply did not have the spine or guts for that kind of trench warfare.

The Unholy Ghost

Bhairav glanced at his $250,000 diamond-encrusted, perpetual day-date Omega wristwatch. The inscription on its back indicated it was a gift from a Saudi Prince. It ought to have been registered with the Government Treasury Department and deposited in the Pulipore National Museum. It was 9:00 a.m. sharp. He had arrived at 8:00 a.m., but that was his nature. His intercom buzzed right on cue. His secretary's sweet voice, belonging to the shapely fifty-three-year-old married mother of six, Tigerist Chandrika Morning Glory Chandran, broke through.

"Adhi Sri, Sri Mahamaya Lion's Mane Jellyfish Chandran is here," she said.

"Show him in, show him in," shot back Bhairav. "Ah!" thought Bhairav to himself, "Quasi is here." He chuckled to himself at the image of Quasimodo flitting in his mind as he walked toward the door. "Time to turn on the charm," Bhairav reminded himself again and again even as he shuddered at the thought of doing business with slime.

"But how could a simpleton like Maha help us Tigerists, Dad? I mean, he would embarrass the Three Stooges, Gomer Pyle, and Bozo the Clown all in one go," posed Duryo aloud.

"Oh, don't be stupid, Duryo," Bhairav replied irritably. "We don't need conning, cunning, conniving, or clever. I've had enough of the trio of Kapalin, Natasha and his nephew Kethu Desert Fox Suryan. Let me be frank. We want a patsy. We'll pull the strings, and he'll jerk into action."

"Oh, I don't know. It may backfire on us," Duryo countered lamely, fully aware that he was no match for his father's Machiavellian mind and machinations. "I'll see myself out the concealed door and private lift. I've changed my mind about sitting in with you on this meeting. Maha might not be at ease in my presence. Bye Dad," whispered Duryo as he bolted.

"I'll brief you in full tomorrow then, son. Take care," Bhairav tenderly bade his son farewell.

But make no mistake. Like the deadly Golden Frog of Tiger Isle, he was pure poison. For was not Bhairav, one of the manifestations and 108 names of the Hindu God Siva, the Lord of Terror?

When Sri Mahamaya Lion's Mane Jellyfish Chandran was born eight weeks premature, his parents had wept at the sight of their shriveled infant. They instinctively bestowed upon their baby a name beginning with the word "Maha," meaning "Great" in Sanskrit. It would certainly fool those who never met him; in reality it would cause those who did to pause and wonder if there was less to him than met their eyes.

The Lion's Mane is the largest of the invertebrate jellyfish, which is not a fish. Mahamaya's father, Eswara Sea Urchin Chandran, a fisherman, knew all about the power of the huge Lion's Mane. One had landed in his net while he was once out deep at sea. It had taken him three full days to recover from the nausea, vomiting, and high fever induced by a lash from its nematocyst-laden tentacles, the marks of which he still bore on either forearm.

If ever a man were a walking caricature of his name, it was Mahamaya. His head, neck, and shoulders all seemed to be one continuous mass, while his bug eyes bulged out even more through thick, fishbowl bifocals. He wore his hair shaved close to his scalp, had long sideburns, a mousy moustache, but no beard. He stood very round at five foot, two inches, but looked taller in calf-length handstitched expensive cow's leather boots that had an extra inch of heel, much to his liking. He had a slight stoop, hence Quasi. He was never seen in public without his grey bush jacket and trousers of the kind once popular with car park supervisors, electricity meter readers, colonial officers, and even now, district officers.

To top it all he squawked in a Donald Duck voice.

It was opposition leader Maitreya who, recognized as a wit, drew guffaws in Parliament when Mahamaya slagged him with, "You are uglier than a toad" and received the quick repartee, "It's fortunate your face ran into a truck. At least now you look a little human."

Yet at forty-three, Mahamaya was a survivor in the tiger-eat-tiger world of Tiger Isle politics. He was one of the first beneficiaries of Bhairav's New Economic Agenda (NEA), without which he would not have enjoyed tertiary education, having failed his Pulipore Certificate of Education (PCE) examination. In 1981, Bhairav had replaced the colonial School Certificate Public Examination with PCE, the papers for which were set and marked locally, instantly creating a thousand new jobs for teachers and educationists. The medium for teaching right up to university level was switched in phases spread out over five years, from English to Pulish, creating yet another thousand jobs.

This was all pretty much a farce since the reference textbooks were all in English, and Pulish, being an underdeveloped language, had to borrow heavily from English, Tamil, and Sanskrit to extend its vocabulary. To secure a place in the National University of Pulipore (NUP) or get a job in the civil service, a student had to garner a minimum-credit pass in Pulish. The Pulish experiment was extended to the courts, and as in schools, so too the farce was extended. The only time anyone spoke Pulish was when a teacher or judge walked into class or court and said, "Good morning" in Pulish before switching to English. As the pro-English lobby put it, "We don't mind as long as Pulish is taught in English." But all public examinations were set and had to be answered in Pulish. Broken Pulish, dubbed Puglish, proliferated. By the time Bhairav called it off fifteen years later, the damage was done. The information, computer technology and internet revolutions had bid Tiger Isle farewell.

By virtue of a credit in Tigerism, Mahamaya secured a place in university and graduated by a hair's breadth with a Bachelor of Arts degree, majoring in Theology. Over the next thirteen years, Mahamaya indulged in nothing more than seat warming in the civil service. From the day he graduated and enlisted, he never put in an honest day's work. It did not matter an iota. Tigerism was all he needed to propel himself up and up.

By forty-two, he was sitting pretty as the government nominee for the minister of energy, alternative resources and green technology, as non-executive director at the Pulipore Electricity Corporation (PEC), when he ran into Sri Sanatkumar-Yoh.

First Crony Among Equals

Sri Sanatkumar Mutthiah Muralidharan-Yoh was a half-Tamil, half-Chinese Tiger Isle Ali Baba fraudtrepreneur whose ancestors on his father's side were originally from Trichi in Tamil Nadu, South India, while his father himself had been a Ceylonese (Sri Lankan) national. His mother was a second-generation daughter of a railway immigrant worker from Fujian in China. The "*Kottai*"[4] and the Chinawoman had the coolie lines of Tiger Isle to thank for

---

4 Literally meaning "nut" as in coconut but a common reference in Southeast Asia to a Sri Lankan Tamil.

their chance meeting and marriage.

Sanat-Yoh had been prowling the corridors of power for a direct nego independent electricity producer (IEP) contract. It wasn't that Tiger Isle was short of electricity or would be for the next fifty years. The odd national blackout once a decade due to unforeseeable quirks of nature and Murphy's Law was no more than that experienced by Malaysia, Thailand, Indonesia, Singapore, and even the USA.

Tiger Isle had surplus electricity reserves of 50 percent above projected consumption, unheard of internationally, against norms of 15 percent. The surplus in Tiger Isle arose from construction of twelve stratospherically priced hydroelectric dams built along its east coast. A couple of billion dollars were sloughed off from construction of these "dirty dozen damned dams," as referred to locally. The money was utilized to illegally finance UNTA's election campaigns, not to mention the extravagant lifestyles of several of its Ministers, Chief Ministers, MPs and well-connected party members.

PEC, however, had $8 billion in cash reserves earning 3.5 percent per annum in bank fixed-deposit accounts. This Bhairav deemed criminal, and he planned on something infinitely more larcenous to rectify this apparent financial mismanagement. He awarded direct nego independent power producer contracts to five of his cronies.

The kilowatt-rate-per-hour charge was guaranteed on a "take or pay" basis with a 100 percent cost-escalation pass through clauses at three times what it cost PEC to produce its own electricity. More than that, the cronies armtwisted PEC into selling them "surplus" power generation plants, equipment and land at way below market and book values.

Within five years, with all the unused surplus electricity going straight into the ground, PEC was in debt to the tune of $20 billion "subsidizing" these IEPs. The cronies responded with a spending spree, buying $250 million renovated and restored castles in Vienna, Geneva, England, and Bavaria for their new holiday homes. Bhairav and UNTA's offshore bank fixed deposits too prospered by several hundred million dollars. One IEP crony even celebrated with a free concert for Puliporeans by the internationally renowned Three Tenors in an island where they knew not the difference between opera and Winfrey.

In the early 1980s, Sanatkumar-Yoh, then an expatriate beancounter with Exxon Petroleum in Dubai, fortuitously bumped into Bhairav at an OPEC-sponsored conference on oil and energy. Bhairav had been exploring avenues to spend his way out of global recession and jumpstart Tiger Isle's sluggish economy.

"President Sri Dr. Bhairav, I presume?" Sanatkumar-Yoh introduced himself.

"Stanley?" Bhairav quipped humorously, glad for some recognition and a friendly face in a sea of Arabs at a time when he had not quite made his presence felt on the international stage, yet.

The duo hit it off instantly notwithstanding one was a Tigerist and the other a Hindu Tiger Islander. This was not least because Bhairav was desperate. Or that Sanatkumar-Yoh, despite his much envied expatriate's remuneration package, was humiliated and depressed at being considered a pauper in a foreign land where sheikhs routinely presented Mercedes Benz motorcars to their servants as birthday gifts.

Tiger Isle did not have its own oil. It imported it 100 percent. But With Sanatkumar-Yoh's urging and Exxon and Saudi support, Bhairav took a leaf out of Singapore's book and set-up Pulipetro Corporation, a fully owned government-linked company (GLC). A huge oil refinery, petroleum-cracking plant, and chemical factories were set up in the northeast coastal area of Suryapore. They proved a resounding success, with Pulipetro contributing annually some 40 percent to Tiger Isle's coffers.

Sanatkumar-Yoh's reward for bailing out Bhairav was a government-secrets act (GSA) classified, exclusive commission contract to market Pulipetro's products internationally. This was achieved through a maze of companies with well-compensated, Bhairav-approved Tigerist nominee shareholders and directors. It would not do to have non-Tigerists seen heading these lucrative monopolistic concerns. This was the much touted "Win, Win" Bhairav concept.

The oil corporation's financial and business dealings, however, did not come under the purview of the Government Audit Department (GAD), the Pulipore Audit Report Council (PARC) or Parliament. It answered only to the president of the day, and Bhairav set the bar by treating it as his personal bank.

When Tiger Isle once again faced a severe financial crisis in the late 1980s, this time brought on by a steep U.S. dollar decline, Bhairav turned to his think tank of one.

"Any bright ideas Stanley?" Bhairav asked.

"Strange you should ask me just now. But there is a 150-acre piece of prime real estate in Chandrapore City that has come to my attention lately," Sanatkumar-Yoh replied.

"There's only one piece of land of that size in the heart of our capital. Surely, you're not suggesting we mow down Chandrapore Botanical Gardens for development? The environmentalists would have you and me for breakfast if we replace such a huge green lung with glass, steel, and concrete. That's suicidal, Stan," Bhairav shouted.

"There's a way to go about it, generate about $160 billion of economic activity, and satisfy the greenies as well."

"How's that? $160 billion! Come on, that's way over the top even for you," Bhairav sneered.

"In reality, we will need about $20 billion cash for what I have in mind. As you are well aware, one dollar of real estate development will generate eight dollars of economic activity, so there's your eventual $160 billion economic flow through. But, I don't have $20 billion in loose change, and in these hard times no sane bank will finance me. That's your department, I'm afraid."

"Carry on," commanded Bhairav.

"Phase One, we move the entire Botanical Gardens fifty miles away from the city center. There's oodles of government land out in the boondocks that goes for under one dollar per square foot. The greenies can't really protest."

"Okay. Phase Two?"

"We'll need something iconic for that kind of money. I've had some perspectives sketched for a world-class, eighty-story skyscraper office block. It will be the tallest tower in the world, resting on a two-million-square-foot shopping mall. We'll need about one hundred acres for that. Road widening, landscaping, a small eco and children's playing park, fountains, a lake, etcetera, will take up the balance of fifty acres."

"And we'll sing High Mass for the Botanical Gardens? Who'd make the effort to visit that far away from the capital? "

"That's where Phase Three comes in," Sanatkumar-Yoh smugly announced.

"Phase Three? There's more?" asked a clearly surprised but interested Bhairav.

"Phase Three should actually start soon after Phase Two commences. It will be the fifty-mile light-rail transit system that will link the skyscraper and mall site to the new Botanical Gardens. I reckon that in time we'll have to upgrade it to a full-blown mass rapid-transit and people-mover system and expand it to cover the entire city as the roads become gridlocked with cars."

"Do the math," Bhairav demanded.

"Ten b in total. Two b for skyscraper and mall, one for Botanical Gardens and seven b for LRT. Before you ask, much of the seven b will be for one-off infrastructure, compulsory city land acquisition that will command a huge premium and for elevated rail tracks and coaches. But we can leverage on it for future expansion throughout the city."

"So, times two gives us $20 billion. There's lots of fat there, Stan. Billy Bunter would look positively anorexic by comparison. You'd better deliver," warned Bhairav as he thumped his stamp of approval.

Thus, Bhairav's "personal bank," Pulipetro Corporation, once again swung into swift action. It gave birth to Pulipetro Corporation Tower and its two-million-square-foot underbelly, Chandrapore City Centre Plaza (CCCP), with a real cost of $2 billion, inflated cost, $4 billion.

And once again profits creamed off the top flowed offshore to Panama, Guernsey, Geneva, Singapore, Maldives, and beyond.

Ali Baba Civil Serpents

Sanatkumar-Yoh had, of course, done his homework. When he eventually met Maha face to face, he sized him up in a second. He invited him for lunch at Le Cordon Bleu restaurant at Shangri-la Pulipore. Maha was stunned, to say the least, that he had been so honored by Sanatkumar-Yoh, whose reputation preceded him.

At Le Cordon Bleu, Sanatkumar-Yoh had reserved a private dining room, and to start off proceedings he referred the drinks waiter to Maha, who did not know the difference between wine and vinegar. Nevertheless, Maha would not be upstaged by Sanatkumar-Yoh, whom he, despite his admiration for his success, regarded as a second-class immigrant.

Maha had seen Bourdain do it on the Travel Channel. So he picked a Mateus Rosé that looked safe, sniffed it, rolled it around in his mouth, gargled noisily, swallowed, and said, "Yes!" in triumph. One sip of it and Maha was a goner, floating deep in astral space.

The classy menu in French, with no Pulish or English translation, stumped Maha. But Sanatkumar-Yoh saved him the embarrassment and ordered escargot for hors d'oeuvres, followed by potage du jour aux oignons and entrees of tender filet mignon viande chevaline well done. Maha thought the garlic-masked snails were prime fresh mini oysters, but the small shells puzzled him.

In between juicy morsels and mouthfuls, Sanatkumar-Yoh and Maha chatted about the economy and Bhairav's "Win, Win" and de Bono out-of-the-box "paradigm shift" brilliance.

"Let me share something with you, Sri Sanat. Last week, the chairman of the Pulipore Chamber of Commerce complained to me that it was all really paradigm shafting. Ha, ha," Maha laughed.

"That's preposterous, if not seditious," Sanat-Yoh replied, tongue-in-cheek. "How they backbite."

"Yes, yes. Of course. Preposterous. Traitors," Maha agreed, a little too quickly perhaps.

They dug into superb horse steak with chopped garlic, onions, mushrooms, potatoes, and brown gravy. It tasted like chicken. They washed it down with a bottle of fine red Australian Merlot.

Just when Maha was ready to pass out, Sanatkumar-Yoh ordered crepe suzette flambé topped generously with Grand Marnier liqueur, ice cream, and rich chocolate sauce. It was whipped up and served at their tableside by the hotel's four-star Michelin chef. As they tucked into their delicious dessert, Sanatkumar-Yoh turned on his magic.

"Ah yes, Sri Mahamaya. As you may be aware, I'm bidding for an Independent Electricity Producer license."

This was a blatant lie since the deal had already been struck with Bhairav, and there were no competing bids. All other competitors who may have harbored notions of an open tender had been paid off or neatly checkmated with a visit from the Pulipore Special Branch (PSB) police officers.

"I need a strong, mature, highly intelligent, experienced and independent chairman for my Tesla Power Corporation to lead my first foray into the electricity and energy industry. Someone I can trust, someone of great integrity and industry. I've asked around, and even Sri Bhairav thinks you may be the right man for the job."

Maha's ears pricked up. This was news to him. Especially that bit about Bhairav. Now he was fully awake.

"Sri Mahamaya, I know I cannot match your government remuneration package. Besides, soon you will probably be Chief Secretary to the government. What with pension, gratuity, and eventual chairmanship of Pulipetro Corporation waiting in the wings, I can only appeal to you to consider the big picture. I am planning to take Tesla global.

So, I can only start you off on permanent employment with no probation clause and a monthly salary of forty-five thousand dollars, rising to fifty thousand dollars after twelve months. In addition, a minimum of three month's equivalent bonus a year and forty-five days paid annual vacation are guaranteed. Class A fully company-paid medical, hospitalization, and personal accident-insurance coverage also applies. The perks for a position of such paramount importance include chauffeur-driven latest BMW seven-series car, your own office and personal secretary on the forty-ninth floor of Tesla's HQ. The penthouse suite at the deluxe Highland Towers Condominium is available rent free for you and your family if you wish. All corporate travel and hotel stay will be at first-class rates, and you will have an unlimited entertainment allowance. When do you think you could join me?"

"Yesterday!" Maha wanted to scream.

He nearly fell out of his chair. As a government nominee director at PEC, they paid him six thousand dollars a month salary plus director's fees of twelve thousand dollars a year. That was hardly sufficient to keep a mortgaged roof over his head and support his wife and six children. He hadn't seen a bonus in five years and drove a ten-year-old secondhand Toyota Vanette to office. He recovered his composure.

"Could you consider forty-eight thousand dollars to start with? It will make it a little less burdenly. You are right. They will consider it a bit odd my designing for something that pays less. But as you say, there is the big movie to consider, and a man's graps must exceed his breach, or what else is a tax haven for, don't you think?" Maha squeaked in his excitement.

"Brilliant! Consider it done. Oh, I missed mentioning the usual stock option of $1 million, which you can pick up after serving Tesla for twelve months," Sanatkumar-Yoh added slyly, as he stood up and began to pace up and down the private dining room. "In all honesty, I can't go higher now. But rest assured, I'll take care of all your needs in the future, once you're on board. Can we shake hands on that?" he asked in his most obsequious and unctuous tone and manner.

Maha was in a daze.

"Million dollar stock option? Is this a dream? Am I dead?" he wondered as he pinched himself. Once again he recovered admirably.

"In principle, I think we have a deal, Sri Sanatkumar. But I'll have to consort my wife first. You sir, are a man of the world, and you know how wifes feel if their husband make bilateral, frivolous decisions which could hurt the family finances advicely. But the roof, as THEY say, not me, is in the puddling. When can I expect something in black and decker?"

"Ah, you drive a hard bargain, Sri Mahamaya. I'll have my secretary hand deliver your letter of offer of employment by five this evening. Is that too slow for you?" Sanatkumar-Yoh continued in his most servile and toadying of manners.

"Oh, that won't be necessary. I'll follow you back to your office to shave time," was Maha's quick reply. A little apprehension too had crept into his voice. Gone was "consort my wife."

Later that evening, Sanatkumar-Yoh played back to his secretary, Mastura, and fellow directors the entire recording of his lunch charade with Mahamaya at the Shangri-la. They laughed till they collapsed on the floor.

For once, Maha returned home at 3:00 pm and lay down on his bed. Mahani, his wife of twenty years, rushed in flustered, shaken and white as she observed him rubbing the shirt over his heart with his palms. The tears were streaming down his face.

"Ma, what's wrong? Why so early? Is it your heart? Are you having an attack, darling? Oh, how can I manage the children without you?" she cried as she moved on to the bed next to him and replaced his palms with hers and continued rubbing in a circular motion.

"My dearest," answered Maha. "You remember that holiday you always wanted to take to Melbourne to see the little penguins on Phillip Island, and the kangadingoes and coca cola bears? Well, I'm going to book it tomorrow. All of us are going!" he shouted, as he suddenly leapt up and jumped up and down on the spring-worn mattress of his ancient and squeaky queen-size bed.

"What? What? Have you gone stark raving mad? Where's the money? Did you rob a bank?" she queried as she tried to grab his hands and bring him back to earth.

Mahamaya stopped and snatched the letter from the bedside table. He flipped it to where it said, "Monthly salary of forty-eight thousand dollars" and pushed it in her face. "It's the usual million-dollar stock option," he belted out at the top of his voice to Tom Jones' It's Not Unusual.

That got the neighbor's wife worried, as she could not fathom what Mahani ever saw in that gloppy hydrozoan. It sounded like a murder was underway next door.

Husband and wife hugged each other, laughed, wailed and cried together. Fortunately, the children were all still away at school. Hunter-gatherer and homemaker made love for the first time in five years.

A sleeping giant had been awakened. The professional Ali Baba Director/Chairman was born. Word got around that Mahamaya could be "trusted." Tigerist, Chinese, Indian, and Malay fraudtrepreneurs courted him. He had to reject many. The top 5 percent of civil servants, only yesterday referred to as civil serpents, now sped eagerly to work every morning with a spring in their steps. Before, they would have clocked in lethargically at 8:00 a.m. and slipped out to the golf course for a "short tea break" till 2:00 p.m. Now, they waited anxiously till 4:00 p.m. for the businessmen and Ali Baba fraudtrepreneurs, who hastily headed to their office doors, creating a deeply lined and worn path to it.

These new ex-civil service multimillionaires would now confidently march out at the end of each month, after early or post-retirement, with a little black notebook in their hands to remind them of collections to be made. At a minimum of $250,000 of fees per annum per directorship/chairmanship, they settled for ten public listed companies and top private companies and had to stave off the rest. It was nice to be a Tigerist civil servant or just plain Tigerist, if you knew and played the game as it was meant to be played.

And of course, the Sri Sanatkumar-Yohs of Tiger Isle tittered and salted away their one-sided "government secrets act"-stamped and fully government-guaranteed IEP contracts in their office safes. As did the Sri William Van Tang Trangs with their casino and lottery licenses, the Sri "Rambo" Jamal Omars with their airline-monopoly contracts, the Sri Charlie Chan Chin Chais of Euramerica Realty Ltd. Plc. with their real estate and development constructions contracts, and the Boothesh Lin Liong Tans of Everich Construction Plc. with their toll-highway monopolies. There were others, like Hisham Yellow Leopard Rudra, who came of age with sewage and water-treatment plants and who also cornered bus-transport contracts.

A once somnambulant part of the bowler-hat-and-brolly brigade had finally woken up. The party was truly on.

Mahamaya's popularity in the business community soared, as did his ambition. In 2001, he entered politics and stood as the UNTA candidate for a Parliamentary seat at Rahupore constituency in Chandrapore. The by-election at Rahupore was brought on by premature demise of its incumbent. He had succumbed to a massive coronary attack, which was now the number-one silent killer in affluent Tiger Isle, where conspicuous consumption was the norm. The voters did not know Mahamaya from Adam, but all he needed was a Tigerist ticket.

Nevertheless, Mahamaya, never one to do anything by halves, spent $20 million, financed by Sanatkumar-Yoh, buying votes in blatant violation of election rules. The Election Council, long regarded as the fifth arm of government after Parliament, the executive, the judiciary, and the police, declared "clean elections" after "in-depth investigations" that lasted three years.

However, Mahamaya's love affair with UNTA was short lived. As soon as Bhairav appointed Kapalin president, he demanded Maha vacate his lucrative Tesla chairmanship in favor of a retiring crony army general. Maha balked, politely refused, and left UNTA. He did not, however, resign his Parliament seat, which is what any gentleman would have done.

But Maha had no pretensions to sporting or genteel conduct, and after briefly courting Maitreya and being rebuffed, he reinvented himself as a reforming independent MP. That was only in name, as he never went to his constituency unless elections were brewing.

He spent most of his time blindly signing documents that ensured Tesla received more fully government guaranteed contracts.

Otherwise he would be off on overseas jaunts, purportedly to do "PR work" with Tesla's principle suppliers and multinational corporation partners, who performed most of the work in Tiger Isle under cover of Tesla's name and umbrella. In reality, these were carefully planned junkets Sanatkumar-Yoh organized to keep his frontman Ali Baba from inadvertently tripping things up in areas he knew nothing about.

At fifty-three, Mahamaya had finally arrived, and he wasn't about to leave without an almighty scrap.

Project Tigerism - *p to q4*

Bhairav warmly hugged Mahamaya, much to his surprise. Mahamaya was in total awe of Bhairav. He could not believe he was actually standing next to the ex-president, who was a legend in his own time.

Mahamaya's feet sank an inch in thick Italian carpet that must have cost a couple of million dollars. The walls were festooned with the most exquisite of hand-woven, hundred-year-old silk Tabriz Persian carpets imported directly from Iran. Rare paintings and collectors' items of ancient and modern Tigerist art and calligraphy worth a large fortune hung from the office walls. Oil money and paintings mixed well. Dealers and consultants wrote their own checks for objets d'art displayed beautifully on exquisitely fashioned mountings and tables and in glass-topped cabinets.

As he moved toward the conference table, Bhairav hooked his arm and whisked Mahamaya away in the opposite direction.

"Come, come, young man, there's lots of time for business. Let's have some tea and cakes first," oozed Bhairav, as he led him to the sumptuous spread of freshly made local and foreign delicacies laid out in style.

There were branded Italian coffee and British tea machines, freshly roasted Blue Mountain coffee beans, and Darjeeling tealeaves flown in from Jamaica and West Bengal. Mahamaya stared in astonishment as Bhairav brushed aside the pretty miniskirted waitress, Kim, and began to make tea for himself.

"And what will you have, tea or coffee?" Bhairav graciously offered.

"Well, really Adhi Sri, you shouldn't be infussing all over me. Some warm water will do, please," replied Mahamaya, still unable to make himself at home.

"Oh bosh and nonsense. Don't be shy, Mahamaya. I know you are a coffee man. Here, let me grind the beans and brew it for you. Did you know this is just about the best coffee bean in the world? I thought not. The most expensive is the Kopi Luwak from Indonesia. But you don't want to have anything to do with a berry that's passed through the alimentary canal of a civet, do you?

And don't touch that caramel or vanilla-laden poison at Moonbucks Coffee & Tea. What's the other joint called? Ah yes, Longoria's Tight Jeans or something, absolute gallons of swill at twelve dollars a whack. You might as well drink ditch water! And soon their small Styrofoam cup will become "economy" and "regular" will be reclassified "grande" as they mug you for another three dollars. You did not notice that kind of marketing Bernie Madhoffism happening already at that soggy burger and extruded fries place fronted by that stalking clown in yellow?"

Mahamaya could not believe it. Was the Old Man really indulging in small talk with him? Bhairav's short fuse (after all he was a short man) and impatience had been his presidential hallmark. But Bhairav was right about the Jamaican beans. They were heavenly. The cups, saucers, plates, and dishes were all of the highest quality Wedgewood China. For a similar quality buffet spread and setting with a view of the world, Shangri-la Pulipore would have charged $150 per pax.

There was also something about Kim as she kept brushing up against him here and there while serving pancakes and maple syrup. Was Bhairav testing him? Mahamaya made mental notes of everything. After all, nowadays, he had access to corporate Lear jets, and if he left early Friday morning, he could make Jamaica and back by Sunday night. Darjeeling? A day trip. He had to talk to Sanat about that breakfast spread.

When they finished about forty-five minutes later, Bhairav guided him into the plushest and softest of leather armchairs imaginable. The leather seemed to mold itself around his somewhat ample buttocks and suck him into its cool center. After a heavy breakfast like that, all his brain could contemplate was forty winks. Bhairav walked around, wheeled back and positioned his chair next to Mahamaya's, so as to be able to stretch his legs out fully and at the same time look Mahamaya in the eye.

"A specter is haunting Tiger Isle," announced Bhairav, who looked dead serious. Gone was the smile and host's charm.

That startled Mahamaya. The words were faintly familiar. He knew Bhairav was well-read and a good speaker who could quote from any number of famous orations and writings.

"Did you hear me, Mahamaya? A specter is haunting Tiger Isle, the specter of our recolonization. If we are not vigilant, we will end up second-class citizens in our own land. We will no longer be Lords of the Land of Pulipore, Tiger Isle. The social contract will be broken.

People like you will end up back in the Ministry of Land and Mines, where you started, and after thirty years of service, retire as assistant chief clerk. You will be answering, "Yes sir, no sir, three bags full sir," to Chinese, Indian, and Malay bosses. You will be working fifteen hours a day to make these immigrant bosses billionaires while they toss you crumbs. Is that what you want? Is it?"

"No! No! Of course not, Adhi Sri. But are we not in control? Tigerists constitute 60 percent of the population. We control everything. Parliament, government, army, police, appointment of judges, government-losing, er...no, I meant, linked companies, everything, even the triads, I hear. Where's the treat?" asked a genuinely concerned Mahamaya, mindful of the rip-roaring time he was having. He and his family of seven had just returned from a two-week vacation in Disneyworld

Florida and the Rocky Mountains. They had travelled first class all the way there and back.

"Yes, but UNTA no longer has two-thirds control of Parliament. Surely you know that? Kapalin gambled with early elections in 2006 and paid the price for playing the race, sex scandal, and religious card," spat Bhairav.

"Huh? UNTA has been playing the same race, sex scandal, and religion cards ever since Bhairav came to power in 1980. That had always been Bhairav's stragedy. So what's he talking about?" thought Mahamaya to himself.

"Well, do you know secretly conducted polls show that UNTA and Kapalin will be lucky to get 40 percent support in the next general elections? All due to DJP, that rat Maitreya who is a traitor to his own race, and his Punjabi sidekick, Kirpal. They are forging ahead. The Treasury is almost bankrupt supporting the three million-strong bloated civil service and government-losing concerns, and from wantonly splashing out billions of dollars on submarines that can't dive, jet planes that don't fly, and rifles that can't fire.

The economy will underperform, and Tigerists will suffer the most. Do you know that Tigerists make up the majority of the 55 percent who are poor here? The Chinese, Malay, and Indian rich and middle class have prospered and own 80 percent of the economy. What stake do we have in our land and the country that bears the name of our race? Kapalin is screwing it all up," continued Bhairav vehemently.

Now Mahamaya sat up. "Bankrupt Treasury? Is that possible?" he wondered. If there were secret polls, how did Bhairav get wind of them? And if Tigerists figured among the poorest after thirty years of the New Economic Agenda, who else was there to apportion blame to? And Pulipore was named after a tiger, not a human, he mused.

"Yes, you are right about that traitor Maitreya." weighed in Mahamaya, still smarting from the insult in Parliament and that rebuff from DJP. "Well, Adhi Sri, in that case you must squeak up. Your poise must be heard so all Tigerists can receive advance global warming and act before it's too late."

"That's where the real problem is, my son. They have conspired and shut me up for good. No one can hear me anymore," moaned a forlorn-looking Bhairav.

"Who has shut you up? How is that possible, Adhi Sri? You built this Metropolis from squatch. You are our first Adhi Sri, leaving aside Adhi Gurunadha. How could anyone bring himself to step you in the back, you of all our heroes?" Maha asked.

"It's Kapalin, his wife Natasha and his young Harvard graduate and ambitious nephew, Kethu. They replaced all my men in the New Pulipore State Times and other mainstream Pulish, English and vernacular newspapers and news agencies, in television and radio stations and in the government and GLCs. Everywhere! Now no one reports what I say. Media moguls and editors have been warned of dire consequences to the supply of oxygen to their brains if they give me an inch of space or publicity.

Yes, I have my blog. But even that they hack and desecrate with their vile language and comments. Then again there are the DJP bloggers who counter and spin everything I write. They openly call me a racist and religious bigot and tell me to go back to India. I, who put Tiger Isle on the map of the twentieth-century world!" roared Bhairav bitterly.

"Shameful, that's really shameful. That's not very airy fairy at all," enjoined Mahamaya, as he tried to show great empathy. He owed it all to Bhairav—his university degree and that hugely overpaid sinecure position in Tesla courtesy of his liege, Sanatkumar-Yoh. "Thats mean we must do nothing," he added in his peculiar English.

"What?"

"What?"

"I have an idea," whispered Bhairav. He looked a little unsure, as though it had suddenly dawned upon him.

"Here it comes," thought Mahamaya to himself, as he sat up, leaned forward, and put on his most attentive and earnest expression.

"Ours will not be a fight of class or oppressed versus oppressors or that of the rich minority bourgeoisie. It will be that of the majority which owns this land for all time taking back what belongs to it by birthright. I will take Tiger Isle back for all Tigerists, not for my own selfish interests, you understand? What say you?" asked a clearly excited Bhairav.

"How will you do it? What's the plan?" wondered Mahamaya aloud, clearly aware from years of sitting in at Sanatkumar-Yoh's board meetings that the devil was really always in the details.

"I have Adhi Gurunadha's blessings. He's part of my plan and has agreed to give us his full backing. Our first step will be to take control of the media. Next we'll form a new force that will start off as a nongovernmental organization. I have found a name for it—PRAKASH, meaning "shining" in Sanskrit. Adhi Gurunadha will sanctify and bless it at the public launch of PRAKASH.

We'll champion Tigerist native rights, extend the NEA for another fifty years and legislate that the private sector will allocate a 50 percent quota of Tigerists into their workforce at all levels. Tigerists will also aim for a minimum 50 percent share of the economy. Other quotas in government service, education, etcetera will continue indefinitely until we have a clear and level playing field.

It will be a warning to Kapalin and Kethu. If they heed us and toe the line, we'll remain an NGO. If not, we'll reregister as a new political party and stand for elections head to head against Kapalin and his sycophants. Kapalin and Kethu will then be history."

"Us? We? I haven't agreed to anything," thought Mahamaya.

"Ahem, Adhi Sri, can you expend on who will leak the PRAKASH movement, please?" asked Mahamaya aloud.

"What?"

"What?"

"Why, I have none other than you in mind, Mahamaya. You have all the qualifications, and most importantly, you are an independent MP who is not tied to any of the isms and party politics. Don't worry about money. I have a huge budget. We'll commence with infiltrating the mainstream media and buying the loyalty of the editors, especially at NPST. I will instruct them on what to write and print, and what not to. Officially, I will not be a member of PRAKASH, but I will support you volubly and publicly, while pulling the strings from behind the scenes, as it were. Why, are you game? How much money do you think you will need to start off with?"

"Hmm, assuming I am interested in a change of poetical direction, perhaps for the media owners, heads and editors, for about a year, I'll need monthly fifty or one hundred t..." paused Mahamaya, as Bhairav impatiently cut him off midstream.

"Yes, yes, $50 or $100 million for a year for sure. Let's make it $100 million. I'll have that TT'd to your bank account by noon tomorrow. I'll speak to Zara at Pulipore Federal Reserve to keep it hush hush. She's one of us. You sure that will suffice? You pay peanuts, you get monkeys. You should know that. Anything else?"

"Well, vacuum-packed Toe brand peanuts go down very well with Carlsberg Special Brew, doesn't it?" wondered Maha to himself. But he controlled his excitement superbly. He now realized that with Bhairav he had to think in the hundreds of millions and billions of dollars.

"What happens in the bend? Where do you really finger in all this?" Maha said.

"As I said, if Kapalin cooperates, he and Kethu can continue in office. Otherwise my son Duryodhana will take over. He's an UNTA MP, and of course, he will have the benefit of his father's experience firsthand. Depending on the situation, I may take the presidency back for a while myself to set things straight before handing it to Duryo. I still have loyal generals in the forces. We'll play it by ear. Are we of one mind on this?"

Mahamaya gave a long silent whistle to himself as he smiled like a thousand suns at the Old Man.

"Brilliant! What else can we suspect from the Master? I'm with you. When do we start? I will publicly bleed PRAKASH."

"What?"

"What?"

"That's a huge relief for me you accepted. You can pay yourself $1 million a month. If you are running low, sound me out early, and I'll TT more funds. I think that's it for today. But we'll have to spend more time planning, strategizing, and fine-tuning to the last detail. We'll meet from noon to 8:00 p.m. here every day for the next month. Leave your bank-account details with Chandrika on your way out. She will also issue you a specially encrypted handphone, which is the only one you will use to contact me from now on. Oh, and always use the code word PT for Project Tigerism."

Mahamaya was thus dismissed by Bhairav, a meticulous planner who left nothing to chance. He would go over the draft plans a thousand times till it felt right. He was not known as a psychotic perfectionist for nothing.

After Mahamaya left, Bhairav made a call to the EPD.

"Peter?" Bhairav said. "Listen carefully. Chandrika will call you with details. Get $200 million ready; a hundred immediately and another hundred on standby. Got that? Call me when it's all done. Bye."

Sri Peter Weller Brown Mole Suryan, referred to as "that Nazi Kraut" behind his back, was president of the all-powerful EPD, often referred to as the Economic Plundering Unit. It was by a long and circuitous route that he had gotten to that position. In the mid-1980s, Peter, son of a German immigrant engineer and his secretary Tigerist wife, had nearly bankrupted the PFR to the tune of $10 billion. He had gambled feverishly in the forex market against the rise of the U.S. dollar.

He was sacked forthwith from his job as chief forex trader, but he returned quietly to government service with the EPD on a contract basis. In the intervening years he had languished as forex advisor to a chain of Indian Muslim moneylenders and moneychangers. These were the "Havala" usurers whose business footprint extended from India, Pakistan, Burma, Tiger Isle, Thailand, Malaysia, Singapore, Indonesia and Dubai to Australia and the UK. Bhairav had arranged that as he did the job at EPD. He needed someone to secretly advise him on the intricacies of the forex markets, in particular the future of the U.S. dollar, euro, Indian rupee and the renmimbi.

"Set a thief to catch a thief," Bhairav had reasoned.

No one had ever thought fit to grill Peter where exactly all that $10 billion he had frittered away had vanished to, least of all the comptroller of GAD or the PARC. But Bhairav had a fair idea.

When he'd finished with Peter, he buzzed Chandrika to get Kapalin on the line.

"Let's call his bluff," Bhairav whispered to himself as Shanita Ho Say Wan put him on hold at the other end.

Meanwhile, as Mahamaya left the eightieth floor of PPCT, he could not contain himself. His hands and fingers shook so much that he had to dial the number thrice before he got it right.

"Ooh, is that my honey bear Lion's Mane?" cooed back the sexiest voice in town.

It was like sweet musical bells chiming softly in his ears. Mahamaya trembled in anticipation.

"Listen Jaqui, how about dinner at 8:00 p.m. tomorrow? You off Fridays, right?" Mahamaya said.

"No, I am not OFF. But I can get a medical certificate for a good cause. Where to, Manny Janny?"

"Jamaica!"

"Arrrrhhh!" shrieked Jacqui, "Big foot, six foot, seven foot bunch. Stack banana, daylight come, I wanna go home, Mr. Tally Man," she calypso-joked with him.

"The limo will pack you up at 6:00 a.m. You can catch up on your beauty sheep in the Lear jet. We return late Monday morning. Ciao," he signed off.

Jacquelina Roxana Angel Fish Chandran was the incredibly sexy 9:00 p.m. newscaster on PNTVS4. She read the daily English news as fifteen million Tiger Isle men desperately tuned in to catch a glimpse of her and dreamed of ravishing her body in every possible way imaginable, and then some.

Jacqui was twenty-three and single, and she would have been Tiger Isle's and the world's choice for Miss Universe had she entered the competition. She lived life in the fast lane and needed burn money. That, only the Sanatkumar-Yohs and their ilk, which now included Mahamaya, could provide without worrying about the bank balance, since the fully guaranteed money supply would arrive from the government's treasury.

Intellectually, she was Mahamaya's match, which meant it never mattered. She had God's gift of that husky, inviting voice and Marilyn Monroe looks that made mice of men, and an attitude and skill in bed that enslaved them.

For Mahamaya it was the perfect time in his life for a trophy wife, and he was damned if, like many of his age and Ali Baba class, he was going to buy a stud horse farm as consolation. Besides, he took to horse like cobra to mongoose. Mahamaya had to fight off hordes from Tiger Isle's fraudtrepreneur and Ali Baba director/chairman corps who would engage in bloody pitched battle to conquer the latest female TV newscaster, financial program host, weather forecast presenter, program announcer, actress, or chanteuse.

Those femme fatales who made it to the big screen were the sole preserve of government Ministers.

While Tigerism demanded monogamy, and adultery was in theory punishable by stiff jail sentences, the rules for the elite were always different. Many in Tiger Isle maintained mistresses in the penthouses of exclusive high-end $5 million and $10 million condominiums. They would quote at length from history about their ancestor kings who had ten wives each and extended families of hundreds. If you can afford it (on fully government-guaranteed money), why not, they would argue and present their cases sincerely and artfully.

It had been a long day when he got home. Mahamaya showered and jumped straight between the sheets, pleading to Mahani that he had to get up before sunrise for that arduous trip to Jamaica to reconnoiter for satellite launch sites for Sanatkumar-Yoh's new communications business.

He tossed and turned in bed all night long and sighed as his thoughts turned to how he was going to break the shocker to the old goat and the kids that he was going to dump her for a woman half her age. He sighed and moaned some more at the thought of Kim's handphone number that he had discovered neatly printed on a scrap of paper in his briefcase. He wondered about the wink that attractive Chandrika had flashed him as he gave her his bank-account details for that $100 million TT.

It never rains but pours were his last thoughts as he finally slipped into a deep sleep.

And long after Mahamaya and Bhairav left, Chandrika made sure no one else was around in the office as she flipped open her handphone, dialed, and left a voice message.

"Listen Rekha, we have to meet tonight," she said. "Have I got a humdinger of a tale for you or what. Tigers at eleven. Kim will be there too. Ciao."

Tiger Isle

Pulipore was originally called Pulioor. But when the British colonized it completely in the nineteenth century, they could not resist changes, and the name Pulioor disappeared forever.

Pulipore or Tiger Isle lay in the tropics at a most important junction in the maritime trade between East and West. It stood at the gateway to the pirate-infested waters of the Straits of Malacca, just north of the equator between the tip of Sumatra and Peninsular Malaya on the opposite side, as the crow flies.

Ships entering the narrow funnel of the straits had to go around the eastern or western ends of Tiger Isle to make their way to Singapore. From there it was north and northeast to Cambodia, Vietnam, and China, or south to Sumatra and Jakarta and then east to the Spice Islands of Borneo, Celebes, and the Moluccas. Further north and east stretched the seven thousand islands that make up the Philippines. Beyond them lurked the headhunters of Western Papua, the swaying beauties and paradise of Bora Bora and Tahiti, and the Pacific Ocean.

Pulipore did not exist two thousand years ago.

It is nowhere mentioned in the first-century CE Periplus Maris Erythraei or Ptolemy of Alexandria's Geographike Syntaxis on what lay beyond India and the Indian Ocean. It mysteriously emerges in South Indian Tamil lore and temple inscriptions from about 200 CE as part of the conquered lands of their marauding kings.

Legends pieced together from etchings on ancient pottery, clay tablets, pillars, and copper plates found in the peaks, hills, and foothills of Kailas, the tallest mountain in Pulipore, spoke of a violent undersea storm and quake that rent the seven seas. Out of the churning of the oceans rose an island. Sometime later a strange celestial craft, Vimanam, in the shape of a white bull, landed on the peak of Mount Kailas in the northwest.

Four Indian demigod warrior princes, led by Sivan and followed by Suryan, Chandran, and Krishnan, accompanied also by their priest Gurunadha, emerged from the Vimanam. The first living creature they encountered was that most ferocious of big cats, the tiger. The Hindu God Siva is often pictured wearing a tiger-skin waist wrap or seated on tiger skin, signifying the radiant power of the mind. What the demigod warrior princes faced was an unusual tiger of thirteen stripes. It inspired the country's name, Pulipore, the emblem for its national flag, and the evolution of Tigerism religion.

The party of five was met in awe and wonder by indigenous natives. The origin of these Animist natives, whose gods were those of natural objects and phenomena, was unknown, as was the name of their land before the arrival of the four Indian demigod warrior princes. There were numerous hypotheses later about it, based on their south China Yunnanese DNA, but nothing that was definitive or conclusive.

Many among the natives were already cohabiting and intermarrying extensively with migrating groups from Sumatra, Jakarta, Malaya, Borneo, Singapore, Brunei, Celebes, Moluccas, the Philippines, and later with the conquering hordes and immigrants from India and China. This mixed group outnumbered the natives within the next two hundred years. The demigod warrior princes married four daughters of the chief of Mountain River Pulipore. Each of the demigods then picked one of the four main compass points and sojourned to rule as king of that part of Pulipore.

Pulipore was one country split into four provinces, which became the states of Sivapore, Krishnapore (renamed Shakthipore), Suryapore, and Chandrapore in the north, south, east, and west, respectively. There existed a fifth region within northern Sivapore that had no real defined borders. This was Gurunadhapore, the holiest city in Pulipore.

The seat of political power originally lay in Sivapore with Sivan, to whom all paid homage and pledged total loyalty. When a series of earthquakes, floods, and tsunamis struck Krishnapore repeatedly, causing a great number of casualties, deaths and destruction of property, the priests were hastily consulted. They determined there was an imbalance in nature between the universal forces of the north at Sivapore and that of the south at Krishnapore. The priests pored over their almanacs, did their calculus, and made their recommendation.

Krishnapore was subsequently renamed Shakthipore after the God Siva's consort, and the name of Krishnapore was largely forgotten thereafter. For the next fifteen hundred years, Shakthipore was spared serious natural calamities.

Pulipore, unlike Malaya, Sumatra, or Jakarta, had no natural resources or spices of its own to trade with. No gold, oil, silver, tin, iron, rubber, porphyry, precious minerals and stones, aloe, or camphor. But its strategic location, natural beauty and landscape were everything.

Ships and their crews from Alexandria in Egypt (carrying wares from as far as Rome and Athens), Persia, the Hadramaut region of Arabia, Calicut, Cochin and Nagapatnam in South India and Nanjing, Canton, and Shanghai in China would dock in the natural deepwater sheltered harbors on its west coast at Chandrapore City, Pulipore's capital, the largest city, and the main port. Its east coast doppelganger was Suryapore City. Pulipore's harbors provided much needed respite from the shifting northeast and southwest monsoon winds, sudden driving rains, and thunder and lightning that heralded blinding thunderstorms, typhoons and violent squalls.

The Chinese Muslim eunuch, Admiral Zheng He (Cheng Ho) and his crew of twenty-eight thousand sailors from 317 ships are reputed to have set foot at Suryapore City in 1421 CE on their way to India and as far as East Africa. The presence there of a five-hundred-year-old, still-active Sam Po Chinese Temple honoring Cheng Ho stood testimony to that. Zheng He recorded his impressions of Pulipore (Fou-li-mo-lo-ti) and Suryapore (Cho-li-liu-lo-ti) as "this heaven on earth" in his Travels of Eunuch Sanbao to the Western Ocean.

The ancient Chinese, next to the Greeks, probably had some of the most phonetically challenged professional scribes in their travelling ranks. They described Java (Yavadvipa or "barley island" in Sanskrit), Sri Vijaya, and Temasik (Water Town or Singapore) as Ye-po-ti, Che-li-fo-che, or even San-fo-tsi, and Tan-man-hsi, respectively.

Early Chinese travelers like Fa Hsien and I Tsing of 400 and 600 CE had travelled west searching for original Buddhist scriptures and texts in India. They had rested in Suryapore on their way back to China, while waiting months for the monsoon winds and rains to abate, shift gears, and change direction in their favor.

Explorer Marco Polo in 1300 CE, and traveler Ibn Batutta in 1347 CE, both noted the sailor's identifying landmark promontory of the Kanthan Limestone Hills in Shakthipore. Their ships had hurried past it westwards to Venice and Morocco with the prevailing winds from Java and Sumatra. Kublai Khan, who sent an expedition to attack Java and Sumatra in 1292–1293, had demanded tribute from Pulipore's King Kaundinya III and been haughtily rebuffed.

Magellan, feverish with anxiety and searching in 1511 CE for the mythical gold of Ophir, said then be to found in Malacca, gave Pulipore a miss. The English "discoverer" of Australia and New Zealand, Captain James Cook, sailed the southern route through the Sunda Straits between Sumatra and Java in his two global circumnavigating voyages between 1768 and 1779 CE. He avoided Pulipore altogether in his hurry. On his third expedition in 1779, he sailed even farther south and then north toward Hawaii and death.

Pulipore was also the ideal place for ships to stock up on fresh water, vegetables, fruits, salted and dried meat, fish and produce before heading elsewhere. More importantly, it evolved as the entertainment capital of South East Asia. The spice wars and trade brought to Pulipore the slave trade and the all-important flesh trade!

Pulipore transformed itself into the greatest bazaar in the near and far East, where anything and everything was sold, bought, and enjoyed. It also had some of the most glorious beaches in the world on all four sides of the island, the world-famous Sati Coral Reefs off the southwest coast, the Gurunadha deep-sea diving spots off the southeast coast, and rich marine life and fishing grounds.

Later came the colonizing Europeans from Portugal, Holland, and finally England, before which Islam had already arrived, driven by Arab saints and Ulama. But it, like Christianity, could not make a serious dent in Tigerism, the main religion of Pulipore. The proselytizing Europeans further drove bands of Animist Pulipore natives into the jungles and the mountains from which they never retreated, even as their numbers dwindled.

The English, in particular, brought indentured and conscripted laborers, "coolies," from Madras, Kerala, Fujian, Canton, and Shanghai to open up the island with roads, highways, railways and airports. The two sheltered harbors at Chandrapore and Suryapore were expanded into full ports capable of handling the ever-increasing larger, wider, and bigger ships, and their wares and trade from Asia.

This altered Pulipore's demographics forever. By the time of independence from the British in 1960, the population breakdown was the following:

Puliporean Tigerists	40%
Largely business-oriented immigrant Chinese	40%
Manual labor, administration, and professional-class South Indians	9%
Farming, fishing, trading Malay Muslims from Malaya and Indonesia	7%
Non-Muslim Malays, Sri Lankans, Punjabis, Gujaratis, Arabs, Turks, Indian Muslims, Portuguese, Dutch, Pakistanis, Filipino, Aborigines	4%.

Most of the Chinese embraced Buddhism, Christianity, or ancestor worship for their religious needs. The Indians and Sri Lankan Tamils had Hinduism, with the main gods being Ganesha (Pillayar), Siva and Murugan (Lord Subramaniam), Ganesha and Murugan being Lord Siva's sons.

Tiger Isle had been sailing along smoothly before 1980. Its people were happy. They celebrated the diversity of their origins and reveled in their multicultural, multireligious, multiethnic, and multiracial society. "Many Colors, One Race," they would joyfully chant at National Day parades.

From an economic standpoint, Tiger Isle had the highest GDP and per capita income in Asia. It had no external debt, its balance of payment was in surplus, and its currency was strong. All the economic indicators were positive. Issues such as affirmative action for the poor and the underclass were genuinely and successfully tackled. Every Puliporean had command of a minimum of three languages. The main medium of instruction in schools, colleges, and universities had been English, with Pulish the national language and "mother tongue" of Tamil, Chinese, Malay, or Punjabi.

Then disaster struck the nation in 1980.

The last of Tiger Isle's post-independence Founding Father presidents, Sri Devadeva Chola Mountain River Suryan, of Indian, Turkic, Arabic, Malay, and Puliporean mixed origins, resigned. He pled terminal cancer. Puliporeans walked the streets in shock, stunned by news of the impending loss of the leader they tigerised as the "Unifier of Pulipore." Worse was to follow. In a moment of inexplicable weakness, probably induced and compounded by severe pain from the ravaging malignant disease, Sri Devadeva nominated Sri Dr. Bhairav Oak Broad Leaf Sivan LLB his successor, which came to pass sooner rather than later.

Thereafter, Tiger Isle was sent hurtling downhill on a course of self-destruction from which it was never to recover.

Krishnasamy s/o Murugayasamy, Rekha's Father

Krishnasamy s/o (son of) Murugayasamy was born in 1915 in Peramboor, Madras, to parents who were poor by any classification and standard. They were only a rung or so above those categorized as pariahs, the lowest of the castes, and the untouchables who were below caste and completely banished and isolated from all of society. Indians did not normally pass on a common surname. The British, typical of those with an insular nature, found it all so confusing with so many Muthus, Krishnas, Murugayas, Murugans, Subramaniams, and more. So they introduced the s/o for some sense of paper identification.

The Murugayas lived in a ramshackle of a village, Idumbangramam, in a ramshackle of a hut about fifty kilometers from Madras city center. Fourteen adults and children shared the two rooms in the hut. There were Krishna's seven younger brothers, his parents Murugayasamy and Valliammah, and Murugaya's four younger jobless brothers. Murugaya and Valliammah's five baby girls had all perished shortly after birth to smallpox, dysentery, and cholera.

About twenty meters from the back of the house were an outhouse and bathroom-cum-toilet with buried pipes that led to a river some fifty meters beyond a small hill. These were shared by the occupants of several other huts in Idumbangramam. There was piped potable water but no electricity. The water supply was intermittent, interrupted frequently by burst pipes and plant shutdowns from electricity outages and contamination.

Their only means of transport was a rickety old bicycle. Anyway, they rarely left the village. If they had to, they would head for Madras or the Sivan shrines in Mahabalipuram, some one hundred kilometers south, by bullock-cart or a smoky old inter-city bus that cost a few precious rupees and annas.

The family survived with the men attending to growing vegetables in a patch at the back of the hut, doing odd jobs in the village and nearby, and working as laborers for public works subcontractors to the municipal administration. Such work was seasonal and sporadic. Valliammah, who had aged beyond her years from giving birth to twelve children, nevertheless provided love and care for her sons. More importantly, she ensured that nutritious food was cooked and rationed according to the needs of the children and adults.

Survive they did, held together by Murugayasamy, who would not stray from the straight and narrow. They were clearly held together by their religion, gods, temples, ceremonies, and festivities. They were fatalists whose religion, to some extent, as in all over India and the world, demanded they remain poor for their salvation.

When Krishna was eighteen, the standard oily-faced, sweaty, and BO-stinking but smiling and optimism-laden agent arrived in Idumban. He had with him the de rigueur black notebook and pencil to recruit workers for Pulipore. The British were in full flow, opening up Pulipore with railways, roads, and ports. New towns and cities were springing up everywhere, and infrastructure was struggling to catch up with that and the population explosion. Work, hard work, was guaranteed. But at what price?

The agent painted a happy picture of coolies owning their land and homes and raising families and children in paradise. They would even be able to remit money back to support their fathers and mothers in Madras. Many suspected that hard work and abject poverty at home were infinitely preferable to hard work and probable poverty in a foreign land. At the worst, if you died in

Idumban, your body would be cremated according to Hindu rites, and the soul would receive salvation. In a foreign land of mlecchas and chandalas, barbarians and casteless, soulless devils, there was no hope.

Krishna took a different view. It wasn't as though he really had any reference point to compare his status and station in life with anyone anywhere, since he had hardly stepped out of Idumban. He had never attended school, but he could read, write, and speak passable Tamil due to a little effort from his mother and Gopalsamy, his eldest uncle. They had all heard about the fabulous wealth and palatial bungalow home and land of Perambur district's jhamindar or zamindar, the tax collector, the wealthiest man in these parts.

But at eighteen, Krishnasamy had no real future, female companionship, secure job or career, or business acumen, and he felt hemmed in. He was not a particularly bright young man. But he could not see how it could be worse in Pulipore than at home. After all, the British would have to, at a bare minimum, provide a roof over his head. Besides they promised secure paying jobs, notwithstanding that it would all be manual labor.

Murugaya, surprisingly, did not object for long to Krishna's constant pestering. In fact, when Ramasamy, Krishna's younger brother by two years, also pitched in, he gave them both his blessings to sign up with the agent. Murugaya, tired and worn out from years of staring at hopelessness, could see no reason to hold back his children. If there was even one chance in a million of a better life for them in Pulipore than he'd faced, and that his children were also likely to face in Idumban, he wanted them to take it. Something prodded Murugaya into the realization that poverty bred poverty.

They sailed to Chandrapore City with hundreds from the collection point in Madras harbor. From here they were dispatched to various parts of Pulipore by military trucks to report to the Public Works Department (PWD) in the five provinces. Their final destinations were the worksites in the cities, townships, and villages. The agent kept to his word that the two brothers would not be separated. Krishna and Rama were initially contract coolies, laborers, and they signed up with Chandrapore City PWD as road construction and maintenance workers.

Fortune favored the innocent, the desperate, the damned, and the brave. They were housed in PWD semi-brick house line-quarters. These came with shared outhouse-bucket toilets and separate and enclosed male and female shower areas. Married couples with and without children, and single ladies and bachelors, were all segregated by quarters with fenced compounds. Oh, miracle of miracles, there was piped potable water AND electricity and even ceiling fans.

The women were really mostly girls below the age of sixteen who either had no birth certificates or had forged ones, as was also the case with most of the bachelors. The ladies worked not only as drain and road sweepers. They carried sand-filled baskets balanced on cushions, made from their work sari wraps, on their heads for dumping at road surfacing and construction sites. They also worked as public building cleaners.

A fourth group, which the other three shunned, comprised those who cleaned public toilets and latrines in schools, hospitals, and government offices. They also collected and disposed the night soil from outhouses, government quarters and private housing estates.

Many supplemented their income by working on Saturday afternoons and Sundays, their off time. They washed and ironed clothes, swept and mopped floors, washed dishes, cut grass, and even did some babysitting at the homes of the island rich, the Chinese Taukehs, Indian Mudaliars, and Malay Orang Kaya. What they took home, though decent, was not quite the Midas barrow loads the agents had promised. Most had to service the usurious and extortionate interest the agents charged on their loans on top of the huge bribes they had paid for jumping the queue in Madras.

The Brothers Samy had little to complain about. They worked hard, supplemented their income at every opportunity and saved every cent they could. They kept to themselves and kept out of debt and out of trouble. They avoided the weekly gathering for toddy- and "Tiger" beer-drinking sessions at the common workers' mess, which often ended with quarrels, fights, a knifing or two, and an occasional killing. They remained teetotalers (all their lives), sold their toddy coupons at a discount, and salted away the money in their post office savings accounts.

These minor altercations and more serious incidents at the mess hall were prompted by caste and ethnicity and further exacerbated by racial and religious differences. Much else could not be expected. Not from a workforce that comprised Indian Tamil and Sri Lankan Hindus; Christian Keralan Malayalis; Sri Lankan, Hakka, Cantonese, Hokkien, and Teow Chew Buddhists; traditional Chinese Taoists; Muslim Malayans; Indonesians and Sri Lankans; and non-Muslim Indonesian and Malayan Malays.

Five years later, the brothers had saved enough money to put down a 10 percent deposit for a twenty-five-hundred-square-foot piece of agricultural-status land. Surplus farm land compulsorily acquired by Government to build highways had been freed up for other development. As contract laborers, they could not legally acquire land or property in their own names and did what others in their situation did. They signed an illegal power-of-attorney agreement with the trusted local Indian Nattukotai Chettiar.

These Chettiars were some of the biggest landowners in Pulipore. The Nattukotai Chettiars from Karaikudi district in Madras Presidency were wealthy moneylenders who charged less than the Madras immigration agents for their loans. They were also more sophisticated and just as efficient and ruthless as the mafia in collections and repossessions and in pursuing bankruptcy cases in the courts.

A year earlier, Krishna and Rama had started sending their mother five hundred rupees a month through the same Chettiars, who offered their customers a better exchange rate than the official banks. The Chettiars guaranteed next-day remittance confirmation to anywhere in South India. This was much better than one having to sacrifice one's lunch hour or getting wages docked to go to the Indian United Bank. There they would have to tolerate the hassles of filling forms, queuing up and being sneered at by bank clerks and tellers. Then again there were those ridiculous bank-draft and

TT charges, one-week remittance duration and the three months it took to clear up any bureaucratic delays by the bank.

It was also the year, 1938, when Krishna married Rasammah, a drain sweeper and washerwoman who was twenty to his twenty-three years. He did not marry her for love, looks, status, money, intelligence, or carnatic singing and dancing ability. He married her for sex, and that was the plain and simple but awful truth of it. She lived in the ladies' quarters, was fair, skinny, and of average height and passable looks. Her family home in Madras was in the remote village of Andigramam, about a hundred kilometers north of Perambur.

Mostly he lusted after what her femininity promised. When he eventually plucked up courage, he proposed to her after one of many encounters at the mess hall. She knew the score and readily accepted, a little too casually it first appeared to even guileless Krishna. But long before that, she had surfed the grapevine and discovered his straight and dependable nature.

As for Krishna, there was only so much holding back any young man of twenty-three could do with so many single and eligible young women literally a stone's throw away from his shared quarters. If truth be told, any woman, or as Haniff Hassan, chief of police, had once said of President Kapalin, "even a skirt around a coconut tree" would have sufficed for Krishna's bursting loins.

Among the young men in the quarters and the squatter area were those who were known now and then to engage in a bout of rape. They would do this sometimes alone and sometimes in small gangs. They would usually be emboldened after a long night of heavy toddy drinking, singing and dancing at the end of the month, after pay day. There was no excuse for it. Those caught and convicted were always whipped, made to serve long prison sentences and were eventually deported to their motherland. Krishna and Rama's fortitude and restraint owed much to their father's character.

Yet, what exactly were these young men supposed to do? Especially, superbly built, muscular, and bucking young men who worked eight to eleven hours a day, most of it under the burning sun? Those who had little means or opportunity to buy or freely court the opposite sex, how long were they supposed to use their hands? There's no doubt the sex instinct and drive are fused into human genes and DNA. The continued survival of the human race depends on it. But how long was youth expected to hold on?

So marriage was the only way out. They did not have a formal wedding or a honeymoon. One Friday evening after work, Krishna, Rama, Rasammah, and Angammah, her best friend and bridesmaid, made their way to the local Sivan temple. Half a dozen each of their men and lady close friends from the line quarters accompanied them. Krishna was attired in brand new beige silk jubbah and vashti (waist-to-ankle-length wrap). Rasammah was bedecked in pattu, or a silk sari and blouse imported from world-renowned Kanchipuram, Madras. He had a broad swath of vibuthee, or white holy ash on his forehead, and in its center, a dot of yellow santhanam or fragrant sandalwood paste.

She had oiled and combed her hair into a single, waist-length plait and scented and adorned it with jasmine flowers. In the center of her forehead was a dot of round, dried red kungumam or tilak powder, made from mixing yellow turmeric powder with slaked lime (calcium hydroxide). It was often also made from saffron, the costliest spice by weight in the world, mixed with red kusumbha (safflower)—Carthamus Tinctorius—seeds. Her palms, fingers, forefoot and toes were beautifully hennaed.

Both of them had also liberally doused themselves with No. 4711 Eau De Cologne. In South India, Pulipore, Singapore and Malaya, consenting clients would receive the "special treatment" from their Indian barbers. Following the normal haircut, the barber would shave off the tiny hairs at the back immediately below the hairline with a stropping sharp, long razor. Then only would follow that special service. After applying No. 4711 Eau De Cologne to the back of the neck for a stinging sensation, the barber would massage and crick the neck for an invigorating experience.

Rekha never tired of teasing her parents about "barbershop perfume." She heard about it from Rasammah during a moment of heart-to-heart weakness between mother and daughter.

The priest, who had been consulted a month earlier to peruse through the Tamil almanac for an auspicious date and time, recited the wedding prayers. At its conclusion, bride and groom exchanged garlands and cheap gold rings that Krishna had purchased at the local patther, or goldsmiths. Lastly, Krishna tied his maternal grandmother's solid gold thirumangalyam, or thali, and kodi his mother had entrusted to him around Rasammah's slender neck. Then it was all over as they prostrated before the shrine and made three circumambulations around the temple before returning to Krishna's quarters.

There their friends had prepared a superb wedding dinner of fried chicken, briyani and sticky white rice, mutton curry, and fried fish. They had not forgotten traditional cucumber and buttermilk pachadi (watery salad), some traditional wedding cakes, vadai (fried lentil patties), and sweet payasam drinks. There was no best man's speech or wild drinking and dancing. Presents were not expected. There was no wedding registration book to sign, marriage certificate issued or even a photograph taken as evidence of any wedding.

Such marriages among immigrants often proved to be convenient, especially for men who planned to discard their wives for another, later. Such common-law weddings were fairly common in Tiger Isle, and not just among the poorer segment and lower class of immigrants. In ancient times in India, honorable and dishonorable Rishis would sometimes impregnate the wives of their frequently absent (to war) kings. Occasionally, noblemen and the rich who entrusted their daughters to these Rishis for education would face the same dilemma. There would then follow a ghandarva or "marriage by mutual consent" shorn of all rituals.

After the sumptuous meal, Krishna and Rama's mates diplomatically departed to spend the night at their accommodating neighbor's quarters. Krishna and Rasammah, both virgins, promptly and in a quivering, throbbing state of anticipation, consummated their marriage. But all did not end well. Rasammah could not conceive. The times, their lack of education, financial circumstances and embarrassment precluded their consulting any gynecologist. Being god respecting and fearing, they left it once again to fate.

They survived the difficult war era. Tiger Isle did not suffer Japanese attack and occupation. The Japanese had certainly wanted to. But a combination of the island's mystique, the lack of general knowledge and intelligence about it coupled with strange rumors, tales and legends of giant tigers and gods kept delaying Japan's plans until it was too late. It was Krishna and Rasammah's good fortune they did not have a baby during the war years when fresh milk, infant food, and supplements were scarce.

Both the Samys slowly rose up from the ranks of laborers in Chandrapore. They were never going to make it to the director level at the PWD. But their diligence and honesty were recognized and appreciated traits. They could speak and converse in fluent Pulish. By listening to their superiors and British site engineers, they had even slowly accumulated a smattering of English words, albeit of the pidgin variety. They would eventually retire in the 1970s as grade-A road construction supervisors, the very pinnacle to which they could reasonably aspire.

Rama married Angamma in 1948 at a grand temple wedding organized by Rasammah and Krishna and attended by almost everyone from the quarters. That was a love marriage. Had it not been for the war, they would have been married in 1940. Much to their disappointment, Angammah too was barren.

In early October 1957, Krishna received a telegram from his uncle Gopalsamy that Murugaya, sixty-eight, and Valliammah sixty-five, were seriously ill. That was when Krishna, Rama, and their wives made a highly emotional return to Madras after a hiatus of twenty-five years. Other than the monthly remittance of five hundred rupees, increased to one thousand from the 1950s, contact between sons, parents, brothers and uncles was irregular. Both sides comprised people who bottled their emotions and were poor and lazy at putting down their thoughts on paper.

Nevertheless, genuine love and affection flowed between the two parties at their reunion. Daughters-in-law showed great respect to their in-laws. They did not hesitate to address them as

"Appa" and "Amma" (father and mother) or prostrate before them to receive their blessings.

Certainly, Murugaya and Valliammah's health recovered considerably as Krishna and Rama took them to Madras city for the best medical attention they could afford.

The brothers also accompanied their wives to Adigramam, where another emotional reunion took place between the girls and their families. When Muniammah, Rasammah's mother, heard of the childless duo, she advised all four to make a special trip to the Kamleshwar Mahadev (Siva) Temple in Srinagar, capital of Kashmir, in conjunction with the Vaikuntha Chaturdashi celebrations and prayers, which advice they took. Legend still has it that childless couples who pray at midnight at that temple honoring Lord Vishnu on that day would be soon blessed with a child.

After a month and a half, it was with a heavy heart that the Samys and their wives returned to Chandrapore. A month later they received a telegram from Gopalsamy, informing them that Valliammah had passed away followed by Murugaya a day later. It would have been pointless for them to return to Madras. The brothers wept with deep regret and wondered what more they could have done for their poor parents and why they had not stayed on in Madras for a few more days.

The truth was that despite their wallowing in poverty back then, they had still been happy by grouping in numbers. Few sons kept to the regular remittance of money back home that kept their parents alive far longer than would otherwise have been the case.

Yet grief and unjustified guilt overwhelmed the Samys. Krishna and Rama took a couple of days of compassionate leave from work to attend to prayers in the temples and talk about the old days. Like most immigrants and even non-immigrants separated from their parents for years, they reminisced about their childhood days.

Rekha Is Born

Almost to the day of the Indian New Year in April, both Rasammah and Angammah reported to their husbands that they had missed their menses. Husbands rushed wives to the general hospital. The GP there confirmed both were with child.

Rekha Krishnasamy was born in January 1959, and a week later, her first cousin Gemini Ramasamy arrived by natural birth as well. Krishna was forty-four years old then and Rasammah forty-one. The parents ensured their children were endowed with more modern and shorter names. There were many Hindi and Tamil actors and actresses to choose from.

Krishna underwent a major transformation with the arrival of Rekha, regarded as a miracle child, (as was Gemini, her cousin), her brother Shivaji that December and sister Sharmilla two years later. For the first time in his married life Krishna saw his wife in a different light. He had never been deliberately unkind to Rasammah, abused or mistreated her otherwise. Or stinged on money, gold, and jewelry, which every Indian girl would accumulate and hoard wherever and whenever she could.

Slowly, the early years of treating her purely as a sex object had given way to genuine friendship, if not a little husbandly affection.

He had quietly observed the exhaustion the late age of her first childbirth wrought on her. Yet, she had not wavered in her maternal duties a jot. He watched as she showered unrestrained tender care, love, and affection on their children.

His heart melted.

There was some sense after all in the old adage about love after, and not before, marriage.

Krishna often wondered if Rekha had been born during the first few years of his marriage whether he would have been ready for fatherhood. Or as was so common in the quarters, he would have become a tyrant to a child who interrupted a one-sided, demanding relationship with his wife.

Independence for Pulipore in 1960 presented the Samys with a new dilemma. The government had generously offered full citizenships to permanent residents, work-permit-holding foreign workers and illegal ones who registered by the end of

1960. Yes, he had kept abreast of developments in India by reading the national Tamil dailies. He understood colonialism and what Gandhi had achieved for India. Yet he figured the British and Tiger Isle had brought him luck and fortune, not to mention a loving wife and family.

He could have perished in poverty in Madras. Had India remained under Mughal Muslim or even French rule, he was not sure if he would or could have left India. It was his and Rama's lucky stars they did not end up in the rubber estates and coconut plantations of Malaya. There, thousands of indentured laborers and coolies had succumbed to the usual and unusual tropical diseases and atrocious working conditions. Many more had expired due to the evil and cruelties inflicted upon them during the Japanese occupation of World War II.

So the Samys trusted their instincts which had served them so well. They applied for and received full citizenship and new passports. Their umbilical cord to Madras and India was severed once and for all time. They proudly saluted the island's flag and sang the national anthem to usher in the independence proclamation at National Stadium in Chandrapore City. Rekha, Gemini and Shivaji were too young to remember all that later.

The brothers applied for and were allotted adjacent, more comfortable and spacious married men's quarters in a government housing area. The monthly rental there was a token ten dollars. Electricity and water charges were for their account. Their land by the highway had appreciated very nicely indeed. They sold it and reinvested their profits and capital in two brand-new double-story linked houses in the newly rising suburbs of the city. They moved to their new homes in 1970, five years before Krishna's retirement from government service.

Their children skipped kindergarten and started attending standard one at a nearby government school. None of their parents were able to assist them much with their homework and studies. They could only emphasize reading, writing and conversing grammatically correctly in Pulish, Tamil and English.

Nevertheless, the children blossomed, as the homes they grew up in were extremely happy ones.

Their lovely houses were situated in a mixed-population area. Here the children played, fought, quarreled and made up with other children of Tigerist and non-Tigerist, Malay, Indian and Chinese descent. The lawns and gardens in front of their homes were unfenced, unguarded and ungated.

Bhairav, who had lived through that era too, could not have failed to notice how this racial harmony had galvanized and united the new nation with genuine positive patriotic fervor. Yet when he was elected president in 1980 he embarked with a vengeance on modernization with the clear intent of polarizing the people.

While Rekha grew up loving her father unconditionally, there was always a part of her that questioned the fates. She could not forgive the gods for her inheriting her father's almost black skin and not her mother's fair features. Neither could she accept that Gemini and his sister Rakhini should take after their fair-looking father and not their dark mother. From an early age, Rekha was recognized as a black beauty. But slights from insensitive and immature neighborhood play pals and schoolmates continued right through to her senior year in school, where she learned to cope with it.

Rekha's final two years in school, in lower six and upper six, were spent at Victoria Academy, or VA, in Chandrapore. VA was founded in 1900 by the British, as was NUP and for the same reason too. It was one of a dozen such premier government schools named after Edward, George, Elizabeth, Henry, Richard, James and the like. Until, that is, Bhairav was appointed minister for education. After which you could not pay parents to have their children admitted to these schools which practiced Bhairav's concept of egalitarianism by Tigerist quota.

For most girls, lower six was their first real encounter with boys and sharing classroom and school activities with so many of them. As all over the world, a few of those boys linked up with a few of those girls who became their high school sweethearts, whom they later married and settled down with for life. Most were shy and reserved and found it easier for self preservation to stick together in small cliques. That is exactly what happened to Rekha and her seven friends. There they formed the Gang of Eight, as they were famously recognized and known in their senior years. They were:

1. Rekha Krishnasamy.
2. Simran Kaur, a Punjabi Sikh who was Rekha's best friend and classmate from primary one.
3. Ho Say Wan, who added Shanita to her name in the 1990s (based on Shania Twain and Anita Baker, her favorite singers).
4. Chandrikha Morning Glory Chandran, a Tigerist.
5. "Kim" Catherine De Silva-Wong, of Sri Lankan-Chinese mix.
6. Suryani Frangipani Sivan, a Tigerist.
7. Mastura Mokhtar, a Malaysian Malay Muslim.
8. Fahrizat Shariff Hamid, of a Malayan Muslim father and Madras Indian Muslim mix.

The first five were from the science stream and the remaining three from the arts. The common factor between the two groups was that they all made it to VA's 1st eleven girls' hockey team from the lower six year.

They came from as varied a background of class, wealth, racial, ethnic and religious backgrounds and personal preferences as any in lower six. Over a period of some six months they gelled and became inseparable friends. The girls joined VA after completing their PCE at various all-girls' schools in Chandrapore. VA was all boys between forms one to five, and then mixed. None of the girls had a tertiary education even though their Pulipore higher certificate of education (PHCE) public examination results were better than that of most of their Tigerist classmates.

They were denied places in the NUP. Perhaps it was the first-generation syndrome hypothesis, someone mooted. Undeniable and successful geniuses would only emerge in the third generation of immigrant citizens. Only then would the DNA algorithm have had sufficient time to mutate. Then again, the contrarian Chinese view was that it would take three generations for the family fortunes to be completely destroyed. The two Tigerists in their midst had turned down places in the NUP medical faculty even though they had only applied for a BSC biology degree course. Realistically, they had felt it was beyond them. Bhairav's experiment in replacing education with paper certificates was slowly unfolding.

So, at age nineteen, they joined the workforce and struck their way up. They had youth, optimism, looks and gritty determination on their side. More than that, they had that indefinable je ne sais quoi that separated the innocent, witless and naive school graduates from the subconsciously confident ones. It came from their wholehearted participation and involvement in extracurricular school activities while keeping up with their studies and grades.

Hockey was one such activity. But they did not shy away from choral night or selling flags to the public to raise money for the Red Cross Society. They baked cakes and fried curry puffs for Teachers' Day, organized the annual Arts Union Ball and more. They were the survivors who could, like Pisces, swim either way with the flow. They would form the backbone of many a successful business enterprise and government administration.

At age fifty-three, they were all attractive and in good shape, and they looked ten years younger than that. Simran was the exception. She looked another ten years younger and was still easy on the eyes. Rekha, tall for the average Tiger Isle female, stood at five feet five inches in her socks. She had a lovely oval face with knee-length double-plaited hair but was dark as hell. Over the years she had maintained her slim-on-the-skinnier-side figure.

They met every Wednesday on Hen's Night at Old Town White Tigers Café, when drinks were half-price, to catch up on their personal lives, work and gossip. The eight did not give two hoots about the Tigerist religious snoop squads, and they drank whatever alcoholic drink they pleased. They smoked like chimneys and when high would spew forth dirty jokes and swear to glory, except for Simran, who did not need an excuse for it.

They would even occasionally, when on cloud thirteen, fart loudly and scream with hysterical laughter.

The Princes and Names

For a thousand years, from 200 CE or so of its history, Pulipore and its four provinces were ruled by adventurous South Indian princes, scions of kings from Kerala and Tamil Nadu. These were the princes from the famed Chera, Chola, Pandya and Pallava Dynasties who maintained their lineage in Pulipore by "importing" royal wives from the motherland. Thus, King Kaundinya III of Pulipore was pure South Indian as was his queen, and Kaundinya IV who succeeded him. After him began the reign of the Hinduised kings of mixed blood who gained power after a major revolution in the mid-thirteenth century CE.

Each of these early Pulipore kings had several other wives, all daughters of native chieftains. These were of course marriages of a certain convenience. Their very survival in a foreign kingdom depended on forging strategic alliances through marriages to maintain a firm grip on their rule. Nevertheless, these native queens would match their Indian counterparts in beauty, charm, intelligence and matters of a private nature associated with the royal bedchambers.

Preceding the Cherans, Cholans, Pandyans and Pallavans were the Kalingans. They were the "Kelings" of Malaya and the most renowned of traders and merchants in South East Asia. They were the earliest "Westerners" from Kalinga in the central east on the Coromandel Coast of India. They trekked through Burma and Thailand through overland routes to the rest of South East Asia.

Kalingans experimented with rudimentary sailboats, then larger ships for over five hundred years before they understood and mastered the secrets of the periodicity of the winds and rains of the monsoons, enabling Indians to reach Sumatra, Java, Bali, Borneo, the Philippines, Celebes, Moluccas and possibly, the South Seas.

At the time of independence in 1960 the peoples of Pulipore counted themselves as one. Their nationality was Puliporean, full stop. Puliporean society was structured along patrilineal lines. "Pure" native Puliporeans all had names like Mountain River, Broad Leaf, Lotus Flower, and Willow Leaf. These were the Animists.

Those who claimed direct descent from the four demigod Princes who married the four native princesses, since they were of mixed blood, had the following:

1. A male first name derived from the 108 names each of Lord Siva (e.g., Aja, Bhairav, Nilakantan), Chandra (e.g., Vivasan, Shasha), and Surya (e.g., Kritha, Sanatana), and occasionally others.
2. Or a female first name derived from the consorts of Siva, Surya and Chandra, like Parvathi, Tara, Rohini, Usha, Chhaya, Sanjana and other Indian deities as well as others associated with the deities like Ganga, whose sacred waters flow from Siva's matted hair as the Ganges River in India.
3. A male middle name that was native, personal or familial, such as Raintree Jagged Lightning, meaning Raintree of the original Chief Jagged Lightning clan. Some tagged on Chola, Pandya, etcetera, as a proud reminder of their "royal" blood. The scurrilous tagged it on especially when planning a flotation of their company on the stock market or a major Ponzi scheme.
4. A last name from one of the three demigod warrior princes (i.e., Sivan, Chandran or Suryan).

Thus, Sanatana Blazing Comet Suryan claimed direct descendancy from the second demigod warrior prince Suryan, who took one small step for Indiankind on Pulipore land and also married a daughter of Chief Blazing Comet. So did Parvathy Lotus

Jagged Lightning Sivan, from the ancient marriage of demigod warrior prince Sivan to a daughter of Chief Jagged Lightning. These were the Tigerists who embraced Tigerism and the Tiger Puranam. Non-Tigerist Puliporeans like James Limestone Hills, Mohamad Thunder Cloud and Prakash Great River were names that announced their "other" religiosity AND native ancestry.

There were of course Chinese, Malay, Indian and other Puliporeans who were Taoists, Buddhists, Hindus, Christians, Muslims, Atheists, Agnostics, Free Thinkers, Universalists and even Satan Worshippers. The Malays of Pulipore were as eclectic as those in Indonesia in their choice of religion, which included Islam, Hinduism, Christianity and Animism. The Indians were mainly Hindus or Christians, and the Chinese, Taoists, Christians or Buddhists.

Many maintained the languages, dialects, customs and traditions of their "motherland," although this faced serious erosion as their third and fourth-generation children could only converse, read, and write in English and Pulish! Most from this band settled in the great commercial provinces of Chandrapore and Suryapore, where the Chinese merchants, traders and entrepreneurs stalked supreme. Sivapore in the north and Shakthipore in the south were the heartlands of the Tigerists and native Puliporeans who grew rice, vegetables and fruits and raised livestock in farms on their ancestral land.

There slowly developed in Pulipore a fifth force whose influence permeated every aspect of life there - Tigerism, led by the Adhi Gurunadha.

Adhi Gurunadha

In ancient times, no party of Indian warriors sailed overseas to conquer, pillage, plunder and rape without the presence of a high priest in its ranks. He was indispensable for conducting ceremonies for untimely deaths on board the ship or in a foreign land, for no Hindu soul could be left hovering in limbo between Earth, and

Shorgam or Narakam (heaven and hell).

Only he could beseech and invoke the gods for guidance in treacherous seas amid jutting, jagged rocks and coral-strewn unchartered waters. He held power over life and death with his Ayurvedic knowledge of plants, herbs and minerals, from which he concocted life-restoring elixirs and medicines. In a foreign land, the high priest would unleash his magic on ignorant natives and Aboriginal tribes. He could predict the movement of the sun, moon, stars and planets. He could foresee eclipses, forge steel from iron, extract gold from rocks, cast bronze and erect monuments, temples, towns and cities. He brought with him the art of reading, writing, communication and the sundial and the calendar to keep time and record history.

Gurunadha was all that and more. He and his priests were the bedrock on which a more advanced civilization was constructed. He brought culture and the higher arts, science, mathematics and numerology with him. But when that Jagad Puli of thirteen stripes crossed his path that fateful night of their landing, Gurunadha knew this was a sign from God. He put away all his Brahmanical Vedic and South Indian philosophies and religion and departed at once for the most remote and open space at the peak of Mt. Kailas to meditate in yogic trance.

The Gurunadha of 200 CE was, in time, elevated to the position of Maha Adhi Sri Jagad Gurunadha. The masses continued to fondly call him Adhi Gurunadha. He was Pulipore's first "pope," who received, developed, spread and secured Tigerism throughout the island.

He set up the Council of Thirteen High Priests, one of whom would be elected by common consent as the next Adhi Gurunadha when the time came. Succession as Adhi Gurunadha was based on seniority, ability and merit, and not necessarily nepotistic connection. The Adhi Gurunadhas, like the princes to whom they were indispensable, married wives from India and Pulipore. It was also mandatory throughout the island for all Tigerist priests to have Gurunadha as their last name.

In recognition of his loyalty, services and religious work, the princes gifted Gurunadha an elliptical-shaped area of land in the foothills of Nilagiri Hills in northern Sivapore. It was developed as Pulipore's Holy City. At first, Gurunadha's task was an uphill one. The four princes were pure Indian Hindus who allowed Gurunadha his indulgence in Tigerism as they were too busy with their forays to all parts of the island and conquests, both of Pulipore and the daughters of chieftains. The pickings were too rich, and the land, too generous and bountiful for the princess to be overly concerned with Gurunadha, who was reputed to have lived for over two hundred years.

As time went by and the links with South India became more and more tenuous, the Gurunadhas found it easier to lead the succeeding kings, queens, princes and princesses toward Tigerism. By 700 CE, Hinduism had all but faded. Tigerism was firmly entrenched as the main religion of Pulipore, although the reign of South Indian-named kings continued for much longer.

Gurunadhapore was the Vatican, Jerusalem, Mecca, Amritsar, Benares/Varanasi/ Kashi, Bodh Gaya, Sarnath and Lhasa of its people. The Maha Adhi Sri Jagad Guru Gurunadha, or Adhi Gurunadha, was the equivalent of the pope. He was non-celibate and presided as the guardian and protector of Tigerism from his seat of power at the Maha Jagad Puli Kovil (temple) complex. The Adhi Gurunadhas maintained an unbroken chain of succession from 200 CE to present times.

This Puli Kovil, a wonder of the ancient world, was constructed between 200 CE and 210 CE entirely from marble quarried and cut from the Nilagiri (blue) Hills and transported a hundred miles by river and oxcart to Gurunadhapore.

Tigerism and the Holy Tiger Puranam

"WE were before and after the beginning of time. WE are, and WE shall be for all time to come. We shall always be your ONLY God, for there are or were none others. WE are Time itself. From the beginning WE were the only Truth and OURS the only true message that was ever revealed. OUR ONLY guide for humankind shall be Gurunadha and his descendants. All other gods and prophets who claimed to be so before, now and those who may lay claim otherwise in future, shall all be false gods and prophets. There is no beginning and there is no end. There are no upper or lower or lateral limits. WE are infinite and WE are eternal. WE have no birth. WE have no death. WE are male and female. WE are non-male and non-female and half male and half female. WE are love, hate, the devil and all else. OUR existence and power are sustained through OUR creation of YOUR Universe. WE are the primal base radical matter, substance and force of atoms, molecules and compounds that make possible the worlds, suns, moons, stars, comets, objects, creatures, plants, phenomena, the Human species and more. WE are beyond any human or other understanding. WE are a substance and force like the Puli of OUR creation.

The Universe is for your enjoyment. Look not elsewhere for your salvation. The truths and perfection of the Puli Puranam are contained and proven herein! The followers of the Puli Puranam shall not endure ANY who question OUR existence, OUR truths or OUR purposes. Neither shall graven images be made nor pictures drawn of US for representation or to be worshipped or mocked. There are no errors, mistakes or contradictions in the Tiger Puranam

The Universe IS. The Cosmos IS. WE ARE. Your worlds ARE. You ARE."

These were the opening lines of the Holy Book of Tigerism, the Puli Puranam, known to the outside world as The Holy Tiger Puranam, or just plain Puranam. It was inscribed simultaneously in Tamil and Sanskrit through divine inspiration as stated in the main text of the holy book itself, by Gurunadha, the fifth man to alight from the celestial Vimanam on to Pulipore soil high on Mt. Kailas in 200 CE.

It was written on Palmyra leaf parchment. Both versions stored in the vaults of the Maha Jagad Puli Temple in the holy city of Gurunadhapore at the foothill of the Nilagiri Hills in northern

Sivapore were said to be the exact ones crafted by the founding Gurunadha.

The precise date the Puranam was created was based on the solar Tamil calendar, and as stated at the foot of its last page, was equivalent to April 13, 200 CE. Several Indian historians disputed these findings, while carbon dating tests proved inconclusive. The Tamil New Year, or Varusha Pirappu, falls every year in the month of Chittirai on April 13 or April 14 during the vernal equinox. Tigerists, however, celebrated their New Year on the fixed date of April 13.

The Puranam comprised 371,293 words made up of thirteen chapters of thirteen subchapters, each divided into thirteen pages of thirteen lines of exactly thirteen words each. The chapters, subchapters and pages were all numbered sequentially and in chronological order.

The Tigerists claimed it was the most perfect holy book ever delivered by any god, and by extension theirs was the most perfect religion on earth. It was meant for all humans for all time. The number thirteen therefore could not be overemphasized in Tigerism as a lucky number. However, as $1 + 3 = 4$, or tsei, meaning death in Chinese, it proved to be a stumbling block for them. They avoided it like the bubonic plague.

Thirteen followed by four, for the warrior demigod princes, were deemed the luckiest and most propitious of number combinations by Tigerists. Eight ($13 + 4 = 17$; $1 + 7 = 8$) was good, while they were neutral about one, five (one Gurunadha plus four princes), seven, and nine. Six was to be avoided at all costs as it could not be derived from any combination of thirteen, four and eight.

Next in the Puranam were these startling lines:

"In the beginning there were thirteen. The word, the explosion and sound were US."

There followed a treatise on the thirteen equal entities that made up "WE," "OUR," and "God," who never acted without consulting each other or were ever in conflict. It almost seemed to mock the established religions of Hinduism, Judaism, Buddhism, Christianity and those yet to arrive.

"By what law do you presume that in the beginning there was only one?" it posed. The best philosophical and theological minds of the twentieth and twenty-first century could not find any really logical arguments to refute the Tiger Puranam's revelation. They conceded that the concept of a single undifferentiated omniscient, omnipresent, and omnipotent god responsible for everything was just as arbitrary a notion as any other. In a famous debate between Tigerists and others at the UN-sponsored International Symposium on Comparative Religions, the then-Adhi Gurunadha had shut up everyone else with a simple question:

"Were you there in the beginning to know any better?"

The "WE" of the Puranam was named only once in the entire book as "Ampa," mother AND father, derived from "amma" and "appa" in Tamil. In 400 CE, Tigerists clerics, philosophers and Adhi Gurunadha had gathered in Sivapore city to pray, meditate and debate whether any significance could be attached to the fact that "mother" in Ampa came first and if a female bias applied to God. They came to the conclusion that had the Puranam referred to "Apma" instead, there would be endless unresolved disputes about a male bias to God. So the arguments ceased that day, forever.

The Puranam then went on to narrate the thirteen days of creation, the thirteen dimensions, the thirteen worlds and the thirteen pairs of first men and women, the "Adam and Eve" of the Holy Bible. They were created by Ampa and placed in thirteen lands on Earth. So much for the "Out of Africa" hypothesis.

There was no concept of a "tired" God who needed rest after creation, nor of paradise, heaven, hell, or original sin. Right from the beginning, men and woman were created by the same process and materials and as equals. Given the differing cultures, races, religions and philosophies extant in Pulipore, there were persistent questions by men over equality between the sexes. Surely men who were leaders, conquerors, hunter-gatherers, innovators and providers were superior to women, they would claim.

Adhi Gurunadha settled that one when he challenged the doubters with, "Show me first how to create one without the other?"

One suspects too that any Creator would have paused a little, stepped back to observe the unfolding scenario, read the progress reports and taken action to rectify the bugs in as complex a project as the Universe: Version 1 of a billion light years across, before continuing.

The Puranam borrowed heavily from Hinduism but differed significantly from it, as it:

1. Made no distinction between an absolute God and a relative God of the human universe.
2. Made it absolutely clear there were no greater or lesser or other gods, and there had been none in the past and no new ones would emerge in the future.
3. Gave no credence to Yugas, cycles, dissolution, or the "End of Days."

The Puranam then traced the migration of the begetting thirteen Adams and Eves, details of all their descendants, prophets and saints up to Adhi Gurunadha. None of the names connected with any historically known names anywhere from any nation or their legends. Adhi Gurunadha's origins, however, were clearly traced to India, the Aryans and Brahmins from Vedic times.

Other chapters of the Puranam dealt with morals, ethics, do's and don'ts, parables, and rewards and punishments. All Tigerist children had to learn the Puranam by heart and recite it loudly and flawlessly in the graduating Tiger Cub Ceremony, when they attained the age of thirteen. This was possible in ancient times and done over several days in groups, but almost impossible in the modern era.

Therein lay the beauty of the Puranam.

There was no compulsion about entering or leaving Tigerism, other than the Tiger Cub Ceremony, which applied to new initiates and converts as well. How it all changed later is another story. Rites, rituals, ceremonies and punishments could be modified to suit the times. This was permitted so long as the essence and spirit of Tigerism and justice was preserved and not compromised.

It is a strange thing to say, but the God of the Puranam was indeed far sighted! Thus, stoning to death, cutting off limbs, flogging, flaying the skin off the back and beheading as punishment for adultery, robbery, blasphemy and murder were proscribed by the twentieth century. They were replaced with appropriate counseling, community service and prison or life sentences.

Contrary to popular opinion, Tigerism was NOT about worshipping the tiger. The Puranam clearly forbade idol worship of Ampa, even the tiger.

The Puranam gave a precise formula and architectural plan for a basic Tigerism temple constructed with thirteen columns, the primary material being pure white marble. In the sanctum sanctorum of the temple would be a copy of the Tiger Puranam, held vertical in a sanctified recess in the chamber. Worshippers were encouraged to pray once a day, preferably early morning at a temple before they went off on their daily labors, or they could do it at home and no other place!

Priests would lead worshippers in prayers, clasping their palms and reciting the prayers while looking up at the sun and sky, or the moon and stars in the evenings, visible through an opening in the ceiling. The junior priest would ring two hand bells, no more, as the simple and to-the-point words prescribed in the Puranam were recited loudly, as follows:

"Our God who created us, we are guided by your love and compassion. Amen."

Many would silently add their requests for boons, favors, lottery winnings and rescue acts, and then prostrate themselves on the floor still in contemplation of God. There were no lengthy orations invoking or praising Ampa, the heavens, the 108 names of each of thirteen gods, or announcing to the world one's religion. Tigerism was a religion virtually shorn of myriad ceremonies, rituals and holy festivals.

Solomon Benjamin, a sea-faring merchant and trader from Jerusalem, had landed in Pulipore in 1100 CE. He had been so entranced with its religion, culture, people and inclement weather that he stayed on, converted to Tigerism and married a Pulipore lady.

Solomon had suggested to the then-Adhi Gurunadha he might consider introducing circumcision as a formal, mandatory practice in Tigerism. He had waxed lyrical about the benefits of circumcision among the Semitic races. Adhi Gurunadha then suggested to him that he take a sojourn into the jungles of Pulipore, and if he should come across a circumcised tiger cub or adult in nature, then he might consider tabling this request to his inner council of priests.

Among the holy relics displayed in the temples of the Maha Jagad Puli Temple were a thirteen-centimeter-long tiger's tooth and a ten-centimeter-long tiger's claw. They was said to belong to the Jagad Puli that Gurunadha and the princes had encountered. In its honor, Gurunadha had overseen the erection of the remarkable seventy-foot tall sandstone pillar Puli, or Tiger Thoon, capped with four huge back-to-back bronze tigers with thirteen stripes each on Mt. Kailas at the spot where they first landed. Primarily, the tiger was an imperial Chola symbol.

Opposite it stood the equally tall and imposing Sivan Lingam, mistaken by many outside of India as a phallic symbol. The Hindu God Siva is regarded as the creator and destroyer of the known universe, the lingam being a symbol of his powers.

Tiger New Year was ushered in at Gurunadhapore and throughout the island with great pomp and ceremony, emphasis being placed on reenacting legends involving tigers. One of these, from India, is about a male child conceived by Siva and Mohini, a female avatar of Vishnu. They appear in the original Churning of the Oceans fable in Hindu mythology to charm and seduce the demon Asuras from partaking of Amirtham, the immortality-conveying food of the gods.

The child, born with a gold bell around his neck, is gifted to King Rajashekaran of Kerala and his barren queen who name him Manikanthan, derived from Mani for "bell" and Kanthan for "neck."

Some years later the queen unexpectedly conceives and delivers a son. She plots with the king's youthful chief advisor, the diwan who had ambitions to succeed the once-childless king, to have Manikanthan killed so that her son would become the next king. The queen feigns severe illness and her doctor, who is in the pay of the diwan, informs the king that she suffered from a rare disease for which the only cure was tigress's milk.

The king finally succumbs to Manikanthan's entreaties when the queen's condition appears to worsen and no other volunteer steps forward for this dangerous and almost certainly fatal task.

The boyish Manikanthan, with his divine powers, returns riding a tigress, followed by a whole ambush of tigers and tigresses after engaging in an epic battle and slaying the demoness Mahishi. The plot is foiled and Manikanthan returns to God after advising the king to have a temple built at a hilltop site with exactly eighteen steps leading up to it, where his flaming arrow lands.

A temple was erected a thousand meters up in Sabarimalai, or Sabari Hills, in honor of Manikanthan, renamed Lord Ayyappan the Ascetic. Every year some fifty million Hindus visit this holy site and chant "Swamiye Charanam Ayyappa," or "Seek refuge in Lord Ayyappan," as they trudge their way up the hill. Women are not allowed into the temple, possibly due to the queen's plotting in the legend.

The Chinese too have a legend about the tiger which was not among their original zodiac signs. The insignificant tiger was sent by their God to battle the lion which had begun attacking humans on Earth. The tiger successfully routed the lion, regarded even then as the king of animals, on four occasions, after which God honored the tiger by drawing three horizontal lines on its forehead, followed by a vertical connecting one, which today is the Chinese word and symbol for "king."

This logogram can apparently be discerned on any tiger's forehead, if you can get close enough to view it! Every tiger has a unique pattern of stripes, a white spot, or ocellus, behind each ear and yellow irises, except for the white tiger, which has blue eyes.

The Puranam ended with the cryptic words:

"As there was no beginning, there shall be no end. All is with you and within you."

It took days and weeks of solitary meditation on that before the first Adhi Gurunadha received the words, "There are none others. You are the masters and mistresses of your own fate." While Adhi Gurunadha's various thoughts, meditations and commentaries were indispensable to acolytes and scholars, and preserved in a compendium, the Puranam remained the supreme source of Tigerism and in resolving theological disputes.

For nearly fifteen hundred years, Tigerism remained shrouded in secrecy, as its practitioners made no attempt to export it elsewhere. Although the world came to Pulipore and Gurunadhapore, many places like Mt. Kailas remained out of bounds to foreigners. In turn, Adhi Gurunadha deemed that a perfect religion needed no advertising or trumpeting overseas.

All that changed when the British entered the arena in the late eighteenth century.

They mapped Pulipore accurately and discovered its uncanny resemblance to a tiger's head! The British anglicized everything they came into touch with. The religion of Pulipore, Puli Bhakthi and their holy book, Puli Puranam, were translated and popularized as Tigerism and Tiger Puranam. Pulipore achieved international fame as Tiger Isle.

Oddly, the British hunted Pulipore tigers to almost extinction. They had an insatiable appetite for tiger skin, stuffed mounted tiger heads and whole tiger trophies, creating many a millionaire taxidermist. In early 1900, the Prince of Wales led a hunting expedition where two hundred tigers were shot dead in one frenzy of a late afternoon party, to the horror of Pulipore. "Like shooting fish in a barrel, what ho," he had been quoted as having remarked.

Puliporeans Tigerists worshipped a spirit whose physical embodiment had nearly vanished from their land and was slowly disappearing off the face of the earth as well! Was it portentous of things to come?

Rengasamy Muthu, Bhairav's Grandfather

Adhi Sri Dr. Bhairav Oak Broad Leaf Sivan, the fifth president of Pulipore, referred to universally as the "Old Man" even in his youth, was a lawyer turned fulltime politician.

His Tamil grandfather of Dravidian origins, Rengasamy Muthu, was an enterprising and fairly well-to-do cotton and textile trader from Madras City in India. His father and grandfather before him had all been local Tamils who worked as sewers in the rag trade. The hours in the sweatshops were long and the pay meager. But father and grandfather were frugal men who saved every penny to invest in land, build and own their homes, and afford Rengasamy a high school education.

The uneducated womenfolk in such families were always homemakers. Rengasamy, like his father, was the sole survivor of his generation, as many as a dozen of his siblings having succumbed in early childhood to cholera, smallpox and diphtheria.

Located in the south along the Coromandel Coast of the Bay of Bengal, Madras, renamed Chennai in the twenty-first century, was the largest, most populous city and capital of the British Madras presidency. Renga, as he was known in the business circles, sourced most of his trading stocks from the thriving cotton farmers, textile mills and wholesale marts in the Coimbatore district, some three hundred miles away to the extreme west.

The energetic and workaholic salesman that he was, Renga contrived to have two families. In Madras he had his legal, traditional Tamil wife, Sita and six daughters. In Coimbatore town, he stashed away Rambha in his "chinnaveedu," or "small house." Rhamba was a stunningly beautiful and mature seventeen-year-old widowed and childless, poor Indian girl. She had been abandoned by her in-laws after her husband died prematurely from a severe bout of malaria. She had no other family or friends to turn to.

Renga had spotted Rhamba doing odd jobs in a remote Coimbatore village textile co-op sweatshop, looking aimless, desperate and close to exhaustion and death. He handed Rhamba a lifeline in exchange for thrilling, experimental and insatiable sex. A healthy Rhamba, an ever-willing partner, was as inventive as the Kamasutra. She bore Renga two illegitimate sons, Mahathevan and Mahabalan, named after her long gone father and grandfather.

Rengasamy was fifty when the strain of supporting two families began to worry him. Most worrying was the staggering fortune of dowries he would soon have to start conjuring up like widgets on a production line to get his six daughters married off to respectable and honorable young men of substance and wealth. He had saved diligently, but the demands of prospecting in-laws were unpredictable.

He decided to make an exploratory trip to Pulipore, having heard from returning sailors and traders of the fortunes to be had there for the asking. He departed for Pulipore by sea with eldest son, ten–year-old Mahathevan, in tow. Mahathevan was escorted separately aboard ship by Rhamba about half an hour after Renga had boarded. It was a precautionary move to avoid the gaze and suspicion of prying eyes.

Undoubtedly, Renga had wandering eyes and was a philanderer, as his business took him the length and breadth of the Madras presidency most days in any month. Left sequestered in Madras were Sita and six daughters, ensconced in the warm company of his in-laws. Rhamba, Mahathevan and Mahabalan fended for themselves in the comfortable chinnaveedu in Coimbatore, with funds made available by Renga to last them a lifetime if they watched their budget.

There was every reason for Renga to worry about the safety of his women as he left them temporarily. In ancient times Hindus practiced Sati or Suttee, whereby a widow was expected to join the body of her dead husband in the blazing funeral pyre. In the days of the British Raj and even before that and a little after, widows could only remarry on pain of death. Widowed mistresses? Renga was playing with fire.

Had Renga kept a check on his libido and stuck to the straight, narrow and virtuous path of his illustrious ancestors, he would have done what any Indian would have before venturing forth to the land of the "mlecchas," or barbarians. He would not have dared leave Indian shores before consulting an astrologer. When you break once with millennia-old traditions, it's like diamonds; it's forever.

Rengsamy Muthu and his bastard but much loved son Mahathevan boarded the steamship from Madras for Chandrapore City on June 27, 1914, the eve of the assassination of Archduke Ferdinand Franz of Austria.

With World War I, it was some five years before Renga could make the return trip to Madras. Fortunately, he had brought with him a good deal of hard currency, gold, textiles and fabrics. The textiles and fabrics he had pretty much to write off, but he survived the war buying and selling fresh and canned food he purchased on the black market with his gold.

In his second year in Chandrapore, Renga met Parvathy Lotus Jagged Lightning as she sought him to purchase fresh fruits and vegetables for her family. Within a week he proposed marriage to her and she accepted without her father's consent. She was seventeen, good-looking and a virgin. With the uncertainties of the war, she decided to take her chances with him. After all, he had money, food, a decent roof over his head and connections everywhere. If she was going to survive the war and not die of starvation, Renga was her safest hedge.

Renga would lovingly invite her to bed as Lotus, or sometimes he would slip into Tamil and woo her as Thamara. She was the daughter of Parameswara Jagged Lightning Sivan, Chief of

Kalagramam, a fairly large village of some fifteen hundred Tigerist Puliporeans on the northern outskirts of Chandrapore City. Parameswara readily accepted the marriage proposal. While he was not the most intelligent of men, he recognized the situation for what it was and relented without insisting on a traditional three-day wedding bash.

By the end of World War I in November 1918, Rengasamy Muthu had found time not only to marry Lotus (Thamara), but also father a son, Lingamraja Jacaranda Jagged Lightning Sivan and daughter, Lalitha Dewi Sirikit Hibiscus Jagged Lightning Sivan. Their names bespoke also of Lotus' Indian, Malay and Thai mixed origins on her mother's side. Renga was quite happy to consent to his children being named in the Pulipore tradition and custom without interposing his Indian name anywhere.

Renga returned to India alone, not wanting Mahathevan to be spotted together with him when landing in Madras or for him to spill any beans yet when back in Coimbatore. Besides, he expected to return to Pulipore soon, as he gauged the potential for business and super profits there to be unlimited. Mahathevan too was comfortable with his stepmother and stepgrandparents, and enjoyed playing elder brother to his half-brother and half-sister. He resumed his schooling, which had been interrupted by the war, and found Pulish a breeze. He had already picked up a smattering of English in primary school in Coimbatore.

But Renga never returned to Pulipore. While in Madras, he succumbed during a rampant cholera epidemic. Only on his death bed did details of triple-barrel Renga and his womanizing ways slowly emerge, much to the disgust of Sita and her parents. But they did the decent thing and sent word to Rhamba and Parvathy Lotus of Renga's untimely demise.

After Rhamba established contact with Parvathy Lotus and Mahathevan by mail, she reasoned that no practical purpose would be served by her going to Pulipore. Her wealth was adequate for the survival of herself, Mahabalan and Mahathevan. But she, now "widowed" once more, had lost all desire to raise another son. She decided Mahathevan was better off (for her convenience) staying put in Pulipore. So she encouraged a heartbroken Mahathevan to stay put in Pulipore with his stepmother. The two brothers were raised apart and did not meet again until Mahabalan visited Pulipore twenty years later.

Mahathevan, in turn, developed such an intense hatred for his parents that he never again communicated with Rhamba or visited his motherland the rest of his life. When he turned sixteen he burned his birth certificate in a fit of rage. He had his stepgrandfather officially adopt him, changed his name to Aja Teak Jagged Lightning Sivan and embraced Tigerism. The Sivans lay claim to being direct descendants of the demigod warrior prince who landed on Mt. Kailas in 200 CE.

Mahathevan /Aja Teak Jagged Lightning Sivan, Bhairav's Father

As was only to be expected, Aja shunned society and developed into a classic introvert. He buried his nose in books and eventually graduated with a Bachelor of Arts (Honors, First-Class) history degree from the NUP at Chandrapore.

NUP was then Pulipore's sole university, having been commissioned by the British administration in 1900 to commemorate the new century and long reign of Queen Victoria in England. It was rare for any Puliporean of Tigerist or native origins to be admitted to NUP. This was part of British policy to keep the masses as ignorant as possible and to divide and rule them.

But Aja was too bright a student to be ignored. He was one of a handful of students in the British colonies in South East Asia to secure all A's in the form-five school certificate public examinations, for which questions were set and marked by examiners based in London. The subject for the SCPE comprised English, English literature, geography, history, general science and maths one and two. After that, Aja had enough of learning. There was that fatal flaw in him despite his brilliant mind. Whether it was a kink in his DNA sequence or whether his antisocial nature was shaped by events beyond his control, we'll never know. He researched his options meticulously. He did not wish to work in the private sector, as much as it paid better. Money was not his priority. He scrutinized the newspapers and the notice board at the government-services HQ for openings. He was in no hurry.

After some six months he found a vacancy for the newly established post of Patents Administrator at the Ministry of Trade. Aja's odyssey was calculated to secure a job where interaction with his fellow homo sapiens, especially ladies and children, would be kept to the bare minimum. The Patents Office hardly attracted two applications a month. The pay was the same as any for entry level into government service; it was bearable with perks such as free medical treatment, pension and most importantly, secure tenure of office for malingerers.

Aja happily slipped into a settled groove at the 8:00-to-4:00 routine in government service. He had few interests outside of books and crossword puzzles. Not for him football, hockey, cricket, politics, cinema, travelling, bicycling, exploring nature, mountain climbing, sailing, swimming, going to the beach, fishing, painting, music, or drama-nothing. He was a bookworm who read without purpose. Rarely did he step outside his family home unless he had to-to get a haircut, buy new shoes or shirt, be measured up for made-to-order long pants, watch a movie at the local cinema, attend family weddings and the like.

Aja would have been extremely content to drift on as Bachelor of Patents Office for life. Pulipore was an island of shopkeepers. Puliporeans made their fortunes too from the R&R business catering to sailors, mariners, divers, tourists and gamblers who congregated here from all over the world. Many also flocked to the temples and monasteries of Pulipore to observe and study the religion and culture of the only people in the world who practiced Tigerism. It was hardly the place for the nurturing or blossoming of a Euclid, Dickens, or Einstein, though Aja did masquerade as an enterprising civil servant at the Patents Office.

However, Chief Parameswara was not going to allow Aja to drift through life a bachelor. That would have placed too onerous a burden and stain on his family, personal reputation, tradition and preeminent position as village chief. One could not have the sexuality of a member of a Sivan chief questioned, adopted grandson or not. Never. So, word was sent out to the community and horoscopes received and forwarded to the village Chief Priest Jatin Ironwood Gurunadha for evaluation. A suitable girl and match were found and the wedding arranged.

Mahathevan, now known as Aja Teak Jagged Lightning Sivan, age twenty-five, married sixteen-year-old Uma Oak Broad Leaf Sivan, daughter of a Kalagramam village elder. Chief Parameswara owed his community one Tigerist temple wedding at least and he made up for the remiss over Parvathy Lotus with much joy and festivities.

Uma was a classic beauty. Her family had settled for Aja since he was their chief's adopted son and had a steady government job with a fixed monthly salary. The couple, if they could not afford luxuries, could at least live in better circumstances than most villagers.

If one were to judge by old sepia-stained Eastman Kodak Brownie Box Camera and magnesium-flashbulbs-lit snapshots of the couple on that glorious day in Kalagramam, one could be forgiven for thinking that Aja was not a willing participant. He appeared moody, withdrawn and unsmiling. Secretly, he was stunned by Uma's charms and looks. But he froze in the presence of the female of the species and reacted in zombie fashion. It was she who held his hands and guided him to the guests and showed tenderness and affection.

In the same year, on December 8, 1929, the year of the Wall Street Crash in America, Uma delivered the first of her six healthy sons, Bhairav Jagged Lightning Sivan. Again and again, Uma had been forced to take the lead, this time in bed, where Aja lay like a piece of petrified oak.

Aja once again settled into a routine of office, home and a few social visits prompted by having a wife. He showed little affection for his sons. It was Aja who suffered from postpartum depression and not Uma. He could not stand the babies' crying and would shut himself up in his study with his crossword puzzles and books. Increasingly he became impatient. As the children grew up, he would resort to the rotan to inculcate rote learning of the Puli Puranam and English, Pulish, nature study and other school subjects. Bhairav, as the eldest son, bore the brunt of his father's silent rage even as he tried to please him by topping his class. He never forgot that all his life.

When the Japanese invaded Malaya on December 8, 1941, on Bhairav's twelfth birthday, Aja returned home from the office at 5:00 p.m. sharp in an even greater funk than usual. He immediately disappeared into his study den without acknowledging anyone. Uma, Bhairav and the children waited on tenterhooks for about two hours for him so they could cut the birthday cake she had lovingly prepared. She never ever forgot to celebrate the children's or Aja's birthday.

The kids were anxiously waiting to wolf down the birthday and special cupcakes and jelly and quaff the Coca Cola, Orange Crush and lemonade served in glasses with crushed ice. The drinking straws especially fascinated the children no end. Equally anxious were their neighbors' fifteen children, who had also been invited for the party. Uma had put up bright decorations and strung up balloons everywhere. That was another focal point for all the children.

When finally Bhairav plucked up the courage to knock on the study door and open it a fraction, the sight that greeted made him swoon immediately in a dead faint. There, dangling from the oak crossbeams of the high-ceilinged study was the still and lifeless body of his father. He had finally bowed out from a world that had treated him cruelly and unfairly in his formative years, and from which he had never really been able to see the light or rise to claim the inalienable happiness that was his birthright.

And if Aja had hated his parents and never forgiven them, then Bhairav's abhorrence and loathing for his father bordered on homicide. He did not count his fortunes and blessings in having at least one loving and caring parent alive to nurture him through the dark days that lay ahead. He was too young then to appreciate it.

He refused to be associated in any way with his father and that side of his family. When he turned eighteen, he changed his name by deed poll to Bhairav Oak Broad Leaf Sivan, after his maternal grandfather. A timeline had diverged as one of the many worlds collapsed in the probability-driven quantum subverse. It altered Pulipore's fate forever.

Rekha, Demon Auditor - Part 1

When Rekha and her friends could not secure places in the NUP despite having better results than many of their Tigerist friends, they were forced to curtail their ambitions. Those of their peers who could afford it went overseas. Others worked and saved money to go overseas or applied for more affordable second and third-choice degree courses in Australia, New Zealand and the UK, where they illegally worked part-time to pay for their education. By dint of sheer effort too, there they secured half and full bursaries and scholarships.

The New Economic Agenda, implemented in a totally biased manner by an administration that was now almost entirely charged to the trust of Tigerists, was in full flow with a vengeance. Failures and grade-three PHCE Tigerist students were allotted places in pre- and first-year university courses in medicine, law, pharmacy, biotech and IT.

Bhairav did not give a thought as to the quality of graduates such a system would produce. He did not ponder what they would be passing on to their children, the crutch dependency mentality that would inevitably evolve and the long-term multiplier effect on the country of embracing wholeheartedly a society of inferior minds. Yet another problem was the brain-drain from Tiger Isle, which Bhairav dismissed as inconsequential, as that was part of his master plan to drive non-Tigerists out by denying them meritocratic rights.

The state was nevertheless forced to employ these Tigerists at a huge cost to the economy to keep unemployment numbers low for electoral gains. All of this produced two types of young Puliporeans. There were the angry Tigerists who felt they were not being accorded any respect by "unfair" non-Tigerists. Then, there were the non-Tigerists who simmered in anger that they had been denied their rights to higher education by a truly racist government. Both types of youth were so angry and disillusioned with their government that it would eventually translate into a loss of votes for Kapalin.

It was in such a setting that Rekha found herself looking for a job. Schools then did not have career-guidance counselors. The education system had not prepared her to be thrust so prematurely into the world of adults. All she had was a distinction in mathematics, good credits in biology, physics and chemistry and a pass in general paper in English. She had applied to the NUP for a Bachelor of Science degree course, not being keen on maths, and been rejected.

She was not offered an alternate course, unlike Shanita who had a distinction in chemistry, had applied for pharmacy and been offered business studies. Fahrizat, who had A's in bookkeeping, was counteroffered geology studies in place of business studies. All this was deliberately done at the Ministry of Education to frustrate these candidates into forgoing tertiary education so their places could be offered to more Tigerists.

Her parents, with little education to speak of, were not much help in assisting Rekha secure a job. They advised her to be patient, scour the ads in the newspapers and not to be too choosy. They kept keep her morale up by not harping on the fact that she, like her friends, was pretty much sponging off parents.

She dashed off a few applications for bank clerk and account executive openings though she had no idea what the work entailed. She went ahead anyway since it said, "No prior experience required. Training will be provided." She responded to recruitment advertisements for teachers and laboratory assistants at the Palm Oil Institute Research Centre. She responded immediately to a "earn a six-figure sum within twelve months!" screamer for insurance agents.

In her third month in a state of limbo, Ramasamy brought over a cutting from the local Tamil newspaper for an audit executive with the Office of the Comptroller of Government Audit Department. She applied because her uncle told her that in India everyone had great respect for auditors. The perks of a government job included fixed wages, automatic annual salary increments and bonuses, free medical benefits, annual leave, subsidized government housing, car loans and pension for life on retirement. She applied out of respect and love for her uncle and darn it if the following week she did not get a letter in the mailbox from the GAD inviting her for an interview.

She was one of a handful of women, ten out of a total of four hundred male and female applicants, who had written in for forty vacancies at the GAD. The interview at GAD HQ in Pulijayam, conducted by a three-man panel comprising the comptroller, his deputy and the director of staff, seemed headed nowhere. The DS, who regarded the audit profession as the sole preserve of men, flipped through her application and certificates.

"What do you know about auditing?" the DS questioned her.

"Accounts and checking it, sir?" she answered, which was not that bad an answer considering the previous interviewee had said that it was the job of an auditor.

"Any previous experience? Did you study bookkeeping in school?"

"No, sorry sir."

"Hmm, any questions from you, sir?" the DS directed at the comptroller after passing Rekha's application and documents to him.

"Any involvement in extracurricular activities in schools?" he asked her without looking at the documents.

"Oh yes!" she exclaimed, "I played hockey for the Victoria Academy First Eleven."

"Really?" shot back the comptroller, showing sudden interest. "VA? You know Chandrika or Suryani?"

"Yes, Yes! They are among my best friends. We were in the championship team that I captained. Chand was a fantastic left winger and our most valuable player last year, while Suryani was rock solid in defense," Rekha gushed excitedly.

The comptroller put down the papers, smiled and replied, "You know I was in VA myself all those years ago, played in the Boys' First Eleven Hockey Team and was the MVP in my senior year too. Like father, like daughter, eh?"

"Oh, you are Chand's dad? I didn't know that. You must have been a fabulous player to win the MVP," she flattered him.

"That's right. I wasn't just a bookworm. Not one sided like many youngsters these days. Heh, heh, heh!" he laughed. "So, you were the captain, eh? That's good, yes, very good." So saying he brought the interview to a close as he pushed his grading sheet, where he had scribbled "hire her" over to the DS, got up, thanked her for making the interview and walked out.

On such slender threads and quirks of chance did government-job opportunities exist for non-Tigerists. Rekha's PHCE results were even better than those of the comptroller during his time. They had both started their career in the GAD at the same audit executive level reserved for PHCE qualifiers. Twenty years into his career, the comptroller sat pretty as king of the heap. He had been at the right place at the right time when Bhairav was in power and looking to name the first Tigerist comptroller of GAD. The fact that he was a nephew of Adhi Gurunadha did his prospects no harm.

Twenty years into her career, Rekha, although she was a fully confirmed government servant and an outstanding performer in GAD, would hit the glass ceiling. She would not be promoted beyond the position of acting auditor. Her gender had nothing to do with that at all. Not for her were any of the positions of full auditor, senior auditor, district auditor, state auditor, or director of audit. Of course the prize of deputy comptroller or comptroller was beyond the reach of any non-Tigerist, female or male.

Her starting salary of $750 a month was considered a fair wage for 1980, given that a fresh non-relevant graduate at the senior audit executive entry level drew $1,000 a month. An accountancy or economics-with-finance graduate would collar $1,200. The fact that, unlike their Western counterparts, most single and working youth continued living in their parents' homes also helped make the relatively low wages bearable.

The different and unfavorable treatment of non-Tigerist employees did not stop only at the bar on promotion prospects. All new non-Tigerist employees would, without fail, be posted to the provinces and remote districts and towns away from their home base for a minimum of three years. The government did not support them with outstation cost-of-living allowances. Rekha had to fork out the additional four hundred dollars a month for half board and lodgings from her eight hundred dollars a month in salary when she was posted four hundred miles away to the Shakthipore State Education Department for her three-year outstation stint.

It did not mean that once the non-Tigerists completed their three-year outstation stint they were exempted from it thereafter. GAD reserved the right to transfer any employee any time at its own discretion and often did that where non-Tigerists were concerned. The government did that even when it caused chaos in families, where both husbands and wives were breadwinners who had children to shepherd.

What was good about the GAD, though, was that it had a superb training department. It had to since it recruited a large number of audit staff that had absolutely no idea of what a debit was from a credit. Equally, many had never opened a bank account or prepared a bank reconciliation statement. They had to be brought up to the mark within a very short period of time. The tyros at every level were not allowed to touch an accounting voucher for inspection until they had been through the rigors of a very comprehensive month-long initial training course.

That took them from the civil service structure and system, basic accounting, finance and audit acts, government, civil service and treasury rules, regulations and circulars, auditing and accounting standards, IT and computer systems and basic microeconomics and macroeconomics. There were also mandatory civil service confirmation examinations that had to be cleared within three years of enrollment, followed by periodic refreshers, new techniques and audit courses scheduled throughout one's career.

Auditing attracted the three standard types:

1. The born snoop-sleuths,
2. The workhorses and,
3. The ones who had nowhere else to go.

In turn, they gave rise to the performers, the sloggers, the shirkers and the sinecures.

The quantity-over-quality policies of Bhairav increasingly produced a GAD overrun by low-grade Tigerist Puliporeans. Born auditors were the exception to the rule. Admittedly, much of auditing must rank side by side with accounting and data entry. They are among the most boring of mind-numbing repetitious work, responsible for creating legions of the brain dead even in an era where computers had rendered such work more tolerable.

Much of standard government auditing work consisted of audit clerks and executives perusing payment voucher after payment voucher to ensure compliance with authority, authorized budgets and codes backed up by valid receipts, contracts and other supporting documents. The more interesting work was to be found in investigating, appraising and evaluating tender-board decisions and award of contracts in the various Ministries. These were the fertile grounds for corruption and looting on a national scale.

There was a time when Ministers and their Chief Secretaries would wait with trepidation for the publication of the GAD's annual report. The GAD AR was the equivalent of the school report card. A red mark in it could mean reprimand, demotion, fine, transfer, or the sacking of a Chief Secretary or senior officers at a Ministry. Occasionally, it would sound the death knell for a minister's career.

The public may have once regarded the comptroller of GAD as its bulwark against wayward government procurement of:

$200-apiece screwdrivers,

$1,000 toilet seats,

$5 packets of instant noodles for the army, navy and air force,

$15,000 personal computers,

$25 per-square-foot compulsory acquisition of private land when valued at $10 psf by professional real estate valuers,

$5 million beds for a $1 billion hospital project undertaken by the Pulipetro Corporation,

$20 billion direct nego privatization contracts for navy patrol boats and,

$4 billion contracts for secondhand reconditioned submarines passed off as brand new to Bhairav's and Kapalin's cronies.

Not anymore.

If the new-millennium GAD AR and the PARC investigations were to be believed, Bhairav and then Kapalin ran the cleanest government in the civilized world. Even the most basic of frauds, teeming and lading of petty cash, were nonexistent in government departments. In fact, the GAD and PARC submitted a joint proposal to Parliament that, given the low incidence of frauds and corruption, the public would be better served if the GAD reports were to be submitted once every three years as opposed to annually.

Yet, Rekha knew better, as did everyone else in GAD and government. Where once auditors were told they were watchdogs and not bloodhounds, Bhairav and Kapalin demanded they be mere poodles and lapdogs. From meek submission to total capitulation of auditors in the public as well as the private sector, it was merely a natural progression of events. They became accomplices with the government in fraud and deception.

The majority of Tigerist Puliporeans in GAD and government service comforted themselves that their annual bleating and begging at the temples in Gurunadhapore and India would erase the slate. Then, they would return to work with greater zeal in further robbing their fellow tax-paying citizens in tandem with their government.

Rekha's career in the GAD began in 1979, when standards were still high and all civil servants feared the GAD. All was, however, laid to waste within ten years of Bhairav becoming president in 1980. Every arm of government was compromised to become a mere tool to achieving Bhairav's planned racist ends.

Rekha was a natural auditor who could smell a rat a mile away. She had an almost photographic memory that could link payment vouchers to contracts and government budgets and codes, detect duplicate payments, or spot the groundwork being laid to test the system for a big sting. She had an intuitive and innate ability to ferret out the false claim artists and the chief accountant who worked hand in glove with the HR manager to make salary payments to nonexistent staff. The stores manager who falsified stock records after selling off office stationery, and check forgers, paid invoice reusers and fake-invoice claimants would cringe upon her arrival.

After fifteen years of service at the GAD, Rekha was recognized for her speed and thoroughness. She was even much admired in the GAD, where she was referred to as the Demon Auditor. The rise of women in the civil service had always been notoriously slow and almost ground to a halt in the Bhairav era. Mere Tigerist clerks and lowly qualified executives saw a meteoric rise in their careers, as they were hastily promoted over the heads of their non-Tigerist colleagues. Even an exceptionally outstanding performer like Rekha would finish her career in GAD only as an acting auditor, as she failed from the viewpoints of gender, religion, skin color and from being brighter than most of her Tigerist Puliporean colleagues.

Adhi Sri Dr. Bhairav Oak Broad Leaf Sivan, LLB (Hons)

Adhi Sri Dr. Bhairav Oak Broad Leaf Sivan, the Old Man, was sworn in as Pulipore's fifth President on January 6, 1980.

He was also chairman of the United National Tigerists Association, the country's ruling political party since independence in 1960. Membership to UNTA was open to any Tigerist citizen, regardless of ethnic origins. Pulipore ostensibly practiced a Westminster-style Parliamentary system with a written constitution.

The opposition to UNTA in a two-party political system was the Democratic Justice Party, DJP, led by Bhairav's nemesis, Sri Maitreya Blue Dolphin Suryan and his chief strategist and lawyer, Kirpal Singh. Some twenty years Bhairav's junior, Maitreya was a charismatic leader and gifted orator. His leadership qualities were nurtured from far back, when he was elected head prefect in his final year in school. He was a liberal arts graduate who had been a firebrand student leader and socialist in his days at NUP, fighting causes ranging from the plight of starving farmers to the abuse of Vietnamese in refugee camps to overcrowding in prisons.

He developed an international network of friends and contacts among students, student movements, scholars, religious groups and top officials at the IMF, World Bank and the United Nations. He was on a first-name basis with Prime Ministers, Presidents, Senators and politicians across the globe, especially those from the USA, for which Bhairav and UNTA branded him a Zionist and Jewish sympathizer. But Maitreya had once been part of the very system that produced dictators like Bhairav and it required the intervention of a higher authority to free him from the stifling shackles of a gulag.

Bhairav would have scaled any mountain, swam any ocean and bribed any god if that would have conferred upon him 100 percent pure Puliporean Tigerist or Pulirajaputran, Prince of Pulipore, status. All his life, especially during school days, his enemies and political foes had taunted him as a half-breed. That cut, rankled and chafed at his ego like sandpaper on rock. Beware the man with a permanent chip on his shoulder.

When younger, Bhairav had applied for a full scholarship to study undergraduate law at the prestigious Madras University. To his chagrin he discovered the British Administration only offered scholarships to non-Tigerist citizens. So Bhairav had filled in the scholarship application form stating he was an Indian and that his father, Mahathevan, had been an Indian national.

This was of course the absolute truth, which he never referred to again in his life and was blanked out from all official records. He hated himself for that subterfuge. Rumor had it that Maitreya had secured a photocopy of Bhairav's original scholarship application form from Madras University and had confronted him with it. Bhairav had apparently threatened to lock him up under the all-encompassing Patriot and Security Act (PSA) in Shakthipore Prison and throw away the keys. "Patriot" itself was an acronym for Providing Appropriate Tools Required to Intercept and Obstruct Terrorism.

After Bhairav graduated from Madras University with an LLB Hons, Bachelor of Law degree, he returned immediately to Chandrapore. In Madras, contact or socializing with his fellow students and Indians were kept to the minimum, and concentration on securing his degree as quickly as possible, kept to the maximum. The proximity to his father's motherland frightened him and he never let on to anyone there about his Indian origins.

In Madras he maintained the fiction that he was a pure Pulipore Tigerist. He studiously ignored any attempt by his fellow students to get him to open up about Pulipore and especially Tigerism, about which many were more than merely curious. By all accounts he was a brilliant student, but few of his peers remembered him when he ascended to the Pulipore presidency some thirty years later.

On returning to Chandrapore he served his pupilage with a leading local firm of solicitors and advocates, Compton, Dexter, May and Robert in Chandrapore City and was soon called to the Pulipore Bar. Robert of CDMR was actually Lee Wing Loong, grandson of Hokkien immigrants who arrived in 1850 from the Fujian province in China to work as coolies at construction sites. His father, Lee Wing Yang, whose formal education stopped at form four, owned a chain of prime seaside resorts and hotels, having started off with a small Travelers Inn, the seed capital for which came from the elder Lee's hard-earned savings.

Lee Wing Loong was not a Christian. He tagged on "Robert" while at Oxford University, but everyone there called him "Bob," which stuck for life. He eventually rose to become the first non-Caucasian to be promoted to partner in CDM. The two locals in CDMR, Bhairav and Lee, clicked instantly and till his last days Bob Lee handled all Bhairav's defamation lawsuits.

Following a short stint in CDMR, Bhairav earned another scholarship to successfully pursue a doctorate in international law at NUP. It was there in 1956 that he came to the notice of the likes of law professor Sri Devadeva and other Pulipore nationalists seeking independence from Britain after World War II. Bhairav was not exactly the easiest of persons to get close to. But Devadeva was a master at pressing all the right buttons to get the best out of the most introverted of personalities and psyches. He recruited Bhairav to their cause and introduced him to the other Founding Fathers of independent Pulipore, who served as the first four presidents of Pulipore between 1960 and 1975. In order of succession, they were the following:

Ravilochana Chera Wise Owl Sivan
Varuna Pandyan Honey Bee Suryan

Nisha Pallava Black Panther Chandran
Anantha Chola Brown Bear Sivan

He thrust Bhairav into writing propaganda material and editing UNTA's broadsheet, The Tiger's Roar. Bhairav was at first not much of an orator; he shone more at writing in a fluid, uncluttered, uncomplicated and easy non-bombastic style that got the message home to the masses. He was part of Devadeva's campaign team, though not at the forefront of it, being so much younger than the Founding Fathers. But it all rubbed off on him. He developed a similar style of oration as his writing when Devadeva ordered him to stand for election as a member of Parliament for Soma District, Chandrapore, in 1969.

The first four presidents were all law graduates too. But they all came from old, connected and moneyed families that could afford to send them on "family scholarship" to Oxford or Cambridge. They were accepted as members into one of the Inns at Lincoln's, Gray's, the Middle Temple and Inner Temple in London. They wined and dined there, attended moots and participated in debates. They were put through the rigors of the fine art of socializing and hobnobbing with the elite. They learned how to hunt with the hounds and run with the hares, essential experiences for securing political and survival acumen.

Therein lay the difference between them and Bhairav. They had international exposure and respect for the "enemy." Bhairav had only hatred for the British and the West, which showed up throughout his presidency. He was a plain and blunt-speaking man who never minced his words. His parochialism and his shame and hatred of his Indian ancestry were his Achilles' heel. His penchant for Mein Kampf and his detailed research on the Holocaust and the writings and philosophies of Lenin, Stalin and Mao were troubling.

It was later palpably apparent that in those years, Bhairav wore a mask that carefully, successfully, concealed his true fascist, dictatorial and totalitarian leanings.

Glowing Reddish-Orange LP

Bhairav and UNTA had a two-thirds majority representation in Parliament. So the stage was set for the emergence of one of the worst dictatorships in the history of the world. A Westminster-style Parliament manipulated racial and religious tension and sentiments to divide and rule. The tyranny of the majority became UNTA's secret agenda, weapon and credo.

The first step the Old Man took to "change the world" and "to make a difference" was to amend sections of Article 6 of the Tiger Isle Constitution, whereby:

"A Pulirajaputran shall be defined as any Pulipore Tigerist citizen whose mother tongue is Pulish, adheres to the customs and traditions of Pulipore and has at least one parent of pure Pulipore origin.

Notwithstanding Article 6.1 of the Federal Constitution, it shall be illegal for any person to marry a Tigerist Puliporean without converting to Tigerism."

It was not perfectly worded but it sufficed for national policy. Article 6 also dealt with important issues such as the inalienable rights of individuals to life, liberty, the pursuit of happiness, freedom of speech and their rights of free and public association. The amended constitution was silent on two very important issues:

1. The rights of Animist aborigines who were THE original settlers of Pulipore
2. The marital status of non-Tigerists Puliporeans already married to Pulipore Tigerists and the legal status of their non-Tigerist children.

As for converting out of Tigerism, while freedom of religious affiliation was constitutionally guaranteed, in practice, as one cleric put it succinctly but brilliantly, "You can check out any time you like, but you can never leave."

"Pure Pulipore origin" was not defined in the amended constitution. Neither were "customs and traditions." Were the originally Muslim Bugis from the Celebes and Moluccans who migrated to Pulipore some three hundred years earlier "pure Pulirajaputrans" because they were now Tigerists? But not Chinese Puliporeans who could trace their roots back to the time of Zheng He and Hindu Indians even before that? What about more recently immigrant Chinese and Indian indentured laborers and their second- and third-generation children, spouses and grandchildren who were full Pulipore citizens?

What the Old Man's tinkering about and tweaking of the constitution did was to immediately create a New Race defined by its religious affiliation as opposed to DNA. Census statistics broke down Puliporeans as Pulirajaputrans, Chinese, Indians, Malays and Others. This effectively pitted religion against race. Of course, Bhairav, when questioned by Maitreya in Parliament, proudly claimed he was a "Constitutional Tigerist Puliporean."

He found his way into the annals of Pulipore history as the first to identify himself by his religion and only then, his nationality. That remark, flung at Maitreya with an air of defiance, dare and arrogance, was soon parroted by many a Bhairav sycophant and crony "purist." While they proudly wore Tigerism on their sleeves, their hopelessly mixed ethnic origins would not have stood up to the close scrutiny of daylight. The Constitutional Tigerist Puliporeans seized control of Tiger Isle.

A national registration exercise followed. Tigerist Puliporeans were issued reddish-orange local passports (LP) that glowed in the dark. "Others" were issued black ones. Anyone—Pakistani, Anglican English, Bangladeshi, Protestant Irish, Iraqi, Iranian, Syrian, Bosnian, Catholic French, Arab, Indonesian, (Burmese) Rohingyan, Malay and others who spoke not a word of Pulish or adhered to any known Pulipore customs and traditions—who married a Pulirajaputran (and now had to automatically convert to Tigerism by order of the constitution) could secure a reddish-orange LP. They were automatically classified as Pulirajaputrans. After all, could any snoop squad infiltrate the sanctum sanctorum of people's homes to gauge what language they spoke at home or what passed for customs and traditions there?

In summary, a Pulirajaputran was now, first, a LP-holding Tigerist. Only after that did his ethnic origins matter, if at all. Of least relevance was his Pulipore nationality, which the Old Man would have abolished had it not been for international relations and passport requirements.

More than that, by virtue of the new constitution, a Pulirajaputran could not legally marry (in Pulipore) another Puliporean or foreigner who did not convert to Tigerism. Converting out, while technically possible, was in practice a virtual impossibility, as the most cowed, compliant, biased and corrupt judges limped along the corridors of justice like wounded, lame tigers. They were mocked by Maitreya, who was quoted everywhere when he said, "In Pulipore, we have some of the best judges in the world whom money alone cannot buy."

The Old Man now promoted the concept that the birthrights of Pulirajaputrans, like that of the Native Americans of North America, Aborigines of Australia and the Maoris of New Zealand, had been usurped by British imperialists. He reveled in stoking up his controversial notion of a "social contract." It was his pet thesis that all those "Others" who were granted full citizenships at the time of independence in 1960 had agreed to recognize Pulirajaputrans literally as lords of the land. Their "special-class" rights as to licenses, job quotas in the civil service, scholarships and rule in perpetuity, regardless of their excesses, was inherent.

Part and parcel of creating this new race of Pulirajaputrans involved the wholly "necessary" exercise of rewriting Pulipore's history and addressing how and what was taught about it in schools and institutions of higher learning. Where legends and earlier history books clearly indicated the arrival and rule in early Pulipore history of Indian Hindus, history books now spoke of "Hinduised" kingdoms led by Pulipore Tigerists.

Extant revisionism blatantly popularized the idea that these were brief aberrations in Pulipore's eighteen-hundred-year past. Tamil and Sanskrit words that constituted some 60 percent of

Pulish, and Indian culture that was at the root of all Pulipore customs, had apparently flitted in by mysterious osmosis and not by the once actual presence of large numbers of Indians from the subcontinent.

Archaeological discoveries and excavations now came under the tight control of the Ministry of Antiquity. Public announcements of the discoveries of ancient Indian settlements were couched in brilliant civil service PR-doublespeak. "Historic discoveries" were announced without a single mention of their origins. The formation of the Ministry of Truth was just a step away.

Affirmative action policies, or the New Economic Agenda, now applied completely in favor of the majority Pulirajaputrans. International opprobrium and condemnation of it was studiously ignored. It grated the Old Man when accused of practicing a kind of, if not actual, apartheid. He dismissed it peremptorily, even though all the NEA produced was mainly substandard graduates, rent seekers and a few crony Pulirajaputran millionaires and billionaires. The enormous gulf in income and standard of living between the haves and have-nots widened dangerously.

The failure of the well-intentioned but massively financially abused NEA programs was apparent to all Puliporeans but the Old Man. He judged success solely by GDP and per capita income at the macro level. The dangerously skewed distribution of it was not his concern.

The rich had gotten richer and the poor, poorer. Oh, there were gleaming new futuristic towers, airports and cyber cities. But the toll-highway concessionaires, independent electricity producers, water, electricity and telephony monopolies and the heavily subsidized Pulirajaputran Motor Works, Pulirajaputran Airlines and Pulirajaputran Shipping Lines sucked dry the national coffers and citizens' savings.

Swathes of Pulirajaputrans were only marginally better off than they had been in 1980. Most Chinese and the middle- and upper-class Indians and others, had prospered by dint of hard work and entrepreneurial endeavor. The underclass of Pulirajaputrans and rural Puliporeans stagnated, which actually meant they were going backwards as inflation pummeled them into submission and surrender.

Puliporeans numbered thirty million in total; the island could easily sustain twice that number. Their prosperity languished in the doldrums. The Old Man, blinkered by spurious statistics and fed and lulled into a false sense of achievement by the elite, cronies and hangers on, fell victim to his own megalomania.

Through a surfeit of chauvinism, misplaced patriotism, jingoism and downright racism, Bhairav managed to systematically dismantle all the advantages they had over their neighbors in South East Asia. Pulipore's GDP and per capita income were now among the lowest in Asia. Literacy and the numeracy and command of English, the lingua franca of the world, were way, way below that of Singapore, Malaysia, Indonesia, Hong Kong, Taiwan and Korea. Where once Puliporeans had reigned supreme, producing scholars of international renown, it now produced legions of crutched duds. Pulipore was unable to take advantage of the internet revolution, losing out dismally to Bangalore and Tamil Nadu.

The system churned out a hundred thousand graduates a year. But the deliberate lowering of education standards and examination pass marks meant most were substandard graduates whose degrees were no better than the grade-three SCPE students of Bhairav's youth. The private sector would not, could not, accept such low-quality graduates. So as Bhairav put it, "We have a duty to provide a safety net lest these graduates become robbers, thieves and rapists." What followed was an obscenely corpulent civil service workforce of three million. Many of them clocked in for work and then disappeared to their second jobs selling local food, delicacies and drinks in the bazaars.

Criticism of Bhairav, his policies, or the government were met with mass arrests of his detractors under the PSA, income tax investigations into their financial affairs and businesses or defamation lawsuits that neither Bhairav nor the government ever lost. The Police and Anticorruption Commission were as compliant to Bhairav as the judiciary. The concept of separation of powers, deemed sacrosanct by the Founding Fathers, was openly discarded.

The rewards of unquestioning loyalty to Bhairav were huge. At a bare minimum, a Puliporean Chief Judge, Chief of the Armed Forces or a general, the National Director of Police and Security (NDPS) and the Director-General of the Pulipore Anticorruption Council could be quickly worth a minimum $10 million post-retirement. Waiting in the wings were cushy $1 million a year nonexecutive chairmanships of public listed companies or Quangos.

All the top positions and 90 percent of other jobs in government, government-linked companies, the army, navy, air force, judiciary, police, universities, colleges and schools, nominated positions in the United Nations and elsewhere and promotions within were reserved for Tigerist Puliporeans, without exception. Eighty percent of all government scholarships were not based on merit. Of these, three-quarters were said to be awarded to Tigerist Puliporeans. In actual fact it was 90 percent, as the official statistics deliberately did not include awards by GLCs. Chinese, Indians, Malays and others were offered the crumbs.

Not surprisingly, many opted for the private sector or migrated overseas far away to escape the stench of Bhairav's toxic fumes.

What was one nation in 1980 was now a nation without a cohesive force. Bhairav's social engineering maneuvers were no different from those once sanctioned in apartheid South Africa or the Ku Klux Klan's white supremacism. So blinded was he by his detestation of his father's and grandfather's origins, so hurt was he at being taunted as a half-breed in his childhood days and so warped had his thinking faculties and process become that Bhairav seriously contemplated partitioning the island into a Tigerist majority portion and a tiny enclave for the others. Or offering them cash to be repatriated to India, China, Malaysia, Singapore, Indonesia and anywhere they pleased.

Racial and social polarization was his secret desire, which permeated every single policy he repeatedly rammed through Parliament with his two-thirds majority control there.

It was only his fear of the devastation that would be wreaked on an economy so dependent on foreign tourists and investments that kept at bay more overt Stalinist or Mao-style pogroms and mass ethnic-cleansing programs. Bhairav had not been happy at all with the nature of this external restraint on his predatory instincts.

The Little Hitlers

During the last five years of Bhairav's twenty-year dictatorship, the worms, the Little Hitlers among right-winged Tigerists, emerged and began to turn. Those who warmed seats of power in city halls and local councils refused to issue permits for the construction of new mosques and Hindu, Chinese, Sikh, or Buddhist temples. Mosques, temples and churches were compelled to move to shop lots and warehouses. Representative committees were offered remote land on the outskirts of the city for their houses of worship, far, far away from any Tigerist temple.

New Tigerist temples were constructed, entirely funded by taxpayers' money while centuries-old temples of "nonbelievers" were bulldozed without warning to make way for yet another unnecessary housing estate or gated and guarded condominium. Tigerists mounted feverish protests against the mere suggestion of erecting a mosque in or near their mixed-population neighborhoods. "Not for those unclean, pariah, Taliban, five-times-a-day warbling terrorists. Like hell, we'll allow it!" they would scream. "Pariah" was the universal honorific used by Tigerist extremists and fundamentalists in reference to non-Tigerist unbelievers.

In 1998, Parliament passed the Beef Consumption Act. In line with classic governmentspeak, it was all about eradicating beef consumption by fiat. By law all cafeterias in universities, colleges, schools and government buildings were banned from preparing, cooking and serving beef dishes at their premises. Staff and students were also prohibited from consuming beef dishes bought elsewhere or from home anywhere in these buildings.

Restaurants serving beef dishes were ordered to have clearly partitioned seating areas separating beef eaters from non-beef eaters. Their food had to be cooked in segregated kitchens by segregated chefs and kitchen help and served by segregated waiters. Kitchen knives, knife sharpeners, can openers, strainers, spoons, ladles, pots, pans, oil, herbs, condiments, sauce, stove, roasters, serving dishes and cutlery could not be shared. Cutlery could not be stored in the wrong kitchen or, once used, cleaned in common dishwashers.

The Beef Enforcement Squads conducted surprise checks throughout the island. Offenders were issued with summons threatening stiff fines, jail sentences and closure. No one went to court or paid any fine since members of the BES were not above being at the receiving end of palm greasing. Beef-eating Chinese and especially Malays and other Muslims, since pork eaters were not segregated, seethed privately in anger.

Aberdeen, Angus, San Antonio, Texas, Arizona and Kobe Beef steakhouses put up the shutters. Fortunately for McDonald's, their India experience gave them the depth to rejigger their menus. But revenues were never the same as soya vegetable patties and lentil burgers never really caught on. "No bite," customers used to Chateaubriand, T-bone and sirloin beef steak and hamburgers well done (steak rare or medium being rare in these parts) would complain as they abandoned their favorite haunts. That and the fact that soya and lentil induced wind, big time.

Protestors were arrested and jailed under PSA and accused of being Nazis. While the constitution guaranteed the right of citizens to peaceable assembly, the home minster insisted that police permits were required for any such association of individuals. Any public gathering and often even private ones involving opposition party members, of more than two persons, was deemed by the police as prima facie show of intent to overthrow the government. It was worthy of arrest and remand detention for seventy-two hours in a police lockup without right of access to a lawyer. This reached absurd levels when twenty lawyers who had assembled outside a police station to visit their incarcerated clients were themselves arrested for "illegal gathering with intent to cause affray, riot, mayhem and public disorder."

Newspaper editors and reporters who wrote about a racist rant by a Bhairavite MP who labeled Malays, Indians and Chinese as third-class immigrants and an opposition MP who raised that issue in Parliament, were arrested. The Minister of Domestic Security explained that it was done "for their own safety and protection" as the police had been besieged with many anonymous telephone calls from Tigerists threatening to kill the journalists and the opposition MP.

A Tigerist Race Relations Commission (Qango) Chairman, appointed by Bhairav, delivered his inaugural elevation address, which was posted on YouTube. He spoke at length about "Pulipore Malays sponge off the state. What else can we expect from those whose mothers and fathers had immigrated from Malaysia as whores, sodomizers and mendicants." He was predictably not charged in court with stoking racial tension. But after resigning his position, he was punished by being appointed a Justice of the Peace.

Bhairav slammed thousands in prison under the PSA and the Sedition and Publishing Acts for legitimate dissent against him and his government. The last signs of the evolution of a complete police state emerged soon enough. Hangings and deaths in custodies in police stations, prisons and other government detention centers, such as those for drug addicts and in UNHCR-sponsored and monitored refugee camps, proliferated. These numbered some five thousand deaths, for most of which statutorily mandatory postmortems and inquests were never held. These were cataloged by the Pulipore Parliamentary Commission of Inquiry, which documented the atrocities. The national director of police and security and others in charge were never held accountable for the criminal negligence under their watch. But all were rewarded with Sris close to or upon retirement.

Unsolved snatch thefts, armed robberies, rape and murder rates soared. But the NDPS chipped away at it with the assistance of U.S.-based PR consultants engaged on a $100 million retainer per year. They spun their way from public concern with spurious statistics that Tiger Isle crime busters had a better record than their counterparts in Singapore, Malaysia and Hong Kong. The NDPS lamented they could not solve many crimes as a result of public apathy, ignoring completely the preventive aspect of policing.

In 80 percent of serious crimes, the accused were discharged without their defense being called in court due to poor police investigations or insufficient evidence. Many were acquitted, causing widespread suspicion that government prosecutors had been "taken care of." The police continued to measure success by arrests and not convictions in court.

The signs of a collapsing country were seen everywhere. Billion-dollar investment followed by billion-dollar fraud and embezzlement was a quarterly affair, both in the public and private sectors. Judges pronounced strange rulings and provided no written judgments. They ruled one way where it favored the government and the other way where it did not. It was especially so when it involved toppling an opposition-controlled constituency, province, or state.

The Twenty-first Century

The Founding Fathers had concentrated on uniting the fledgling country behind one flag, one anthem, one language and one people. They had been confident the economy of over a thousand years would take care of itself. But it was Bhairav who dragged a somewhat laidback Tiger Isle kicking and screaming into the new millennium. Previously undreamt-of infrastructure, oil refineries, soaring skyscrapers and computer-chip and other manufacturing factories spurred the new-age economy. Tiger Isle appeared to compete with India and China for an almost first-world developed-nation ranking.

But there was a price to pay for progress measured by standards and parameters dictated by the very white men Bhairav detested, while consigning to the backburners the moral dimension of accumulating wealth anywhichway. Not the least of this was an increasing core of more educated and aware people who knew their rights and demanded them.

Bhairav's predictable response to legitimate dissent was more mass arrests and playing the race and religious cards more frequently. Bhairav was therefore a politician of two halves. One was a modernist where the economy was concerned; the other, a reactionary where "my people" were concerned. Many thought he was devil spawned, but like the devil too, he was God's child just like any other. Unlike his father, he had genuine love and affection for his wife and children and showed it publicly too.

But he could not, try as he may, see Puliporeans in any other way but as "us" and "them" and as Tigerist Pulirajaputrans and immigrant second-class usurpers.

The Chinese, Malay and Indian tycoons who bankrolled his extravagances in a wonderfully symbiotic relationship for so many years slowly began to distance themselves from his never-ending overtures to finance yet another mega hydroelectric dam, cyber city or airport.

"It doesn't matter if it's overpriced. No one will ask questions about a product they can see with their eyes. What say you?" he would ooze as they felt a cold chill descend over their wallets and check books. In his first years as president, Bhairav had tried the stick method on these tycoons and found he could not land a stroke on this extremely nimble-footed species. They could move money around the globe with a magician's and illusionist's panache. No amount of banking laws and Central Bank controls could contain their wheeling and dealing finesse.

All that changed when he met an up-and-coming fraudtrepreneur, William Van Tang Trang. William was the happy result of a Vietnamese "boat people"-fleeing university professor from Saigon meeting a plump, matronly looking local Chinese cook at the United Nations Human Commission for Refugees camp in southeast Shakthipore. He had class and she had pots of money from selling toiletries and prime cuts of nourishing meat on the side to paying refugees. He wanted his freedom; she, a life.

Van had boldly bid for a new $5 billion casino, resort and horseracing and greyhound-racing tracks on Suryapore's east coast. His Feng Shui Gaming, Resorts and Hospitality Plc. was the darling of stock market punters. Van's agent in China had "guaranteed" procurement of twenty thousand high rollers a week from Guangdong, Beijing and Shanghai. He described them as frothing at the mouth to be fleeced in Tiger Isle, if but Van could engineer it.

The casino part of the bid was, of course, a major money-laundering proposition. The Chinese apparently had billions of black money renmimbi hidden in pillow slips and underneath the mattresses of their beds. More than that, they had, sitting in bank safe deposit boxes overseas, hard U.S. cash earned from underinvoiced exports, illegal commissions and kickbacks from defense and other state procurements. The government of PRC routinely executed those found indulging in such traitorous illegal activities and conduct.

Runners and agents would transfer into Van's dedicated bank accounts in Malaysia and Singapore money for their overseas holiday airfares, hotel, food, entertainment and travelling expenses. They would then be extremely fortuitous at Van's casino and return to China with bank drafts or photocopies of checks offered as proof to the income tax officer that their huge tax-free winnings were genuine. Van and his agent took a swingeing 30 percent cut on these transactions.

But the betting-license part of it was workable. There was World Cup Football, cricket, hockey, badminton, the Olympics, Grand Slam Tennis and golf. Horseracing could be beamed in live thrice a weak via super deals with the BBC and Sky Network. There were races from Ascot, Epsom, Chepstow, Doncaster, Cheltenham and more from the UK as well as Australia and Hong Kong. The illegal bookies were raking in $30 billion in bets and during the year of a world sporting event, it could peak at $50 billion.

"Two plus two equals five," Bhairav smugly computed and concluded in his zippy brain at his office in Pulijayam. He promptly demanded from Van a $750 million one-off license fee, a $250 million refundable security deposit and a 5 percent annual royalty over and above the corporate and gaming tax to be paid to the Treasury. Van had politely sniggered and suggested they adjourn to his private meeting room at the Athenaeum Golf and Country Club Resort, which he owned.

In the plush surroundings of his private room they snacked on fresh Iranian Beluga caviar on toast, sipped Dom Perignon White Gold Jeroboam Champagne and smoked the best and most expensive Cohiba Havana cigars. Van explained the rules of engagement:

1. If any tycoon had a billion dollars he would only consider handing it over to the government on pain of death and on reconsideration, never.
2. Money sitting in the vaults of the treasury and under the control of the Mandarin Mafia was as good as dead money.
3. You have to spend money to make money. But if you have to spend big money, then you use other people's or the government's money; never, never yours. Never!
4. The only way a $5 billion project of this nature could be successfully implemented was if they had a zero-upfront cost. A compliant Stock Exchange, Securities Council and auditors would have to be told in no uncertain terms to look the other way or not look too closely or, to look at all.
5. With much misgiving, he was prepared to place a $10 million security deposit with the Treasury for appearances' sake, refundable after one year. This was conditional upon receipt of approval from his chairman, board of directors and especially, foreign shareholders and investors. The chairman, board of directors, foreign shareholders and investors were a figment of the quick-witted Van's imagination. It sounded sincere, genuine and impressive to Bhairav.
6. The license would be issued for an initial period of twenty years and renewable for another thirty years at his option. There would be no annual license fee or special royalties. "After all, I will be providing gainful employment for

thousands and generating billions of dollars for tourism and Pulirajaputran Airlines. Not to mention forex for the economy and paying crippling gaming and corporate tax. Capisce?"

7. There would be no open tender for what was, after all, an "original" proposal from him. It wouldn't do to stifle entrepreneurial spirit by inviting competition. The services of the Chief Justice would be required to stymie any attempt to tie the government's hands.

8. The entire deal was to be protected from prying eyes by classifying it under the Pulipore Secrets Act.

9. He was prepared to offer UNTA 30 percent of the profits.

"Leave the number-crunching and paperwork to my beancounters and shark shysters. Oh, of course that includes 10 percent for your children and grandchildren. It will come in handy when they go to Harvard or MIT, wouldn't you say?" Van announced. That was an audacious stroke. But it clinched the deal.

Bhairav was not naive. But equally he had not really been exposed to the commercial world of mega deals or the mechanics of it all before this. Van proved an excellent tutor in this methodology, known throughout Asia as the "Ali Baba Direct Negotiation Contract" or just plain direct nego contract. It became Bhairav's preferred route for all future contract dealings, which never slipped below the billion-dollar benchmark with these tycoons.

Corruption was not conceived during Bhairav's time; it had always been there. It was only a question of degree, which attained its zenith with his full blessings. He did not hate the amoral and apolitical tycoons to whom even charity was a business run by their appointed trustees. They made no gift or dispensation unless the tax-exempt nature of the transaction was confirmed by the Pulipore Treasury. He did not like them either and was forced to play a dangerous game. Without these fraudtrepreneur Chinese, Malay and Indian tycoons, Bhairav and Tiger Isle would have perished much earlier; with them, they were doomed and damned forever.

Then exactly after twenty-four years of iron-fisted rule in iron gloves, the Old Man suddenly announced his retirement from office and active politics on January 5, 2004. Had he jumped out the windows of one of the numerous skyscrapers he had commissioned, he could not have produced a greater seismic shock in local politics. Many suspected and feared their gravy train would come to a screeching, sudden halt. The sycophants, cronies and UNTA begged him to stay on. Few realized that he had quit while he was ahead.

He proudly boasted he personally did not pocket one cent of corrupt money. That was of course predicated on how one defined corruption. His four sons and two daughters, beneficiaries of munificent direct nego NEA contracts, had all become billionaires within ten years of him taking office. They cornered monopolies, including:

- The supply of coal at above-market prices to the Pulipore Electricity Corporation
- The mandatory government-approved "security seals" on all bottled alcoholic and non-alcoholic drinks and cigarette packets for a fee
- The approved vehicle permits issued to them free by the Ministry of Transport and Vehicles that they tagged on to imported cars at fifty thousand dollars per vehicle
- The import and manufacture of fiber-optic cables
- The licenses for taxi and bus services at all airports and in major cities
- The purchase of pinball and gaming machines
- Internet and handphone services
- Toll highways
- Landfills
- The Independent Electricity Producer license
- Water-treatment plants

None of it required these cosseted and mollycoddled Pulirajaputrans to get their hands dirty. They collected these licenses and contracts, issued to them no questions asked by the EPD, as they applied under special-class affirmative action policies.

They did not know the difference between a simple toggle switch and a transformer. But that did not matter a jot. The more complicated high-tech contracts were farmed out to foreign MNC giants. The formula was simple: 10 percent upfront fees, 10 percent free equity held in overseas nominee names and 10 percent fee on mobilization and unlimited entertainment budget. Masters-degreed and PhD managers and accountants did all the work. Their primary job was to ensure the cash came pouring in on time every month and that the bank balances were reconciled to the penny, offshore.

Unlike other megalomaniac ex-leaders elsewhere who also wished to rule from the grave, the Old Man did not secretly bargain with Kapalin for a fabulously paid sinecure post-retirement position as Advisor Minister to the Cabinet or Pulipore Ambassador-at-Large to the Universe. He had expected his successor would "do the right thing."

That expectation of course proved fatal in his eventual undoing.

The Old Man's successor as president was Kapalin Blowfish Black Panther Chandran, a short, broad-faced, podgy and portly sixty-year-old scion of Tiger Isle's third Founding Father president, Nisha Chola Black Panther Chandran. Kapalin had an ancestry that stretched from Thailand to India and China. But he preferred to boast only of his "fearless Moluccan warrior" and Tigerist heritage.

The Old Man was honored by Kapalin as the first Puliporean recipient of the title of Adhi Sri, which ranked higher than Sri. The perks of an Adhi Sri title included:

- A (secret and illegal) usage for life, rent-free, $10 million bungalow house on ten acres of government land

- A fully government-sponsored, functional, ultramodern, state-of-the-art, permanent Pulipetro Corporation Tower penthouse office with staff, chauffeur-driven latest Mercedes Benz
- An unlimited entertaining expense account
- A monthly tax-free stipend of twenty thousand dollars over and above his government pension.

Kapalin had assumed Bhairav would retire quietly to pen his keenly awaited autobiography and support him and his government with inspirational words of wisdom to the electorate and the younger generation of Pulirajaputrans.

That silly assumption of course proved fatal in Kapalin's eventual undoing.

False Claims and Fraud 1.01

It was a truism among the elite, the Ali Babas and other fraudtrepreneurs, the captains of industry and the towering global corporate czars from the ranks of Pulirajaputrans that their expenditure always increased to meet and exceed their income by a factor of two to one. The higher they rose, the more rapidly they achieved this ratio. Like the Parieto Principle or the 80/20 rule, this was yet another of those mysterious universal laws no one could explain.

There were only two ways for these Putrans, as they were popularly called, to bridge the gap between spiraling, runaway debts and their salaries. It was either through self-realization and scaling back all unnecessary expenses or by willfully embracing deceit, corruption, downright fraud and thievery. Many opted for the latter course of action.

It had to do with laboring under the illusion that local schools and universities were not good enough for their normal-IQ children. Perhaps they thought they belonged to a kind of royal-blood group that should not be allowed to mingle freely with the "peasants" when they returned to rule over them. So they would pack their children off to England and Switzerland and their public schools, which so strangely were all privately owned.

That would set anyone back a minimum of $250,000 a year per child. The Putrans were a very fecund lot with no fewer than four children per family. They would tweak the government scholarship system so their children would be awarded full or half scholarships meant for the brightest and deserving minds or the 10 percent minority affirmative action candidates. Official records were falsified to show the awards had flowed elsewhere.

If that was insufficient to balance their fantasy personal budgets, as was always the case, they would look to the companies for which they worked for as President, Chief Executive, Operating Officer, or General Manager. They would always refer to it as "my company." They would pack the board of directors of "my company" with compliant cronies and "independent nonexecutive" directors.

The "independent compensation committee" derived from this group would go through the proposal for "rationalization of the Chief Executive's remuneration package" with "a fine-tooth comb." They would, within five minutes of the proposal being tabled, rubberstamp the Putrans' fabulous salary plus allowances, stock options, bonus entitlements and golden handshake/parachute clauses for early termination and retirement or in the event of a takeover. This would happen in a year during which the company registered record losses and half the workforce was laid off. The bonus and increments of general staff would also be frozen indefinitely. The Pulipore Confederation of Business and Industry would then crown the Putran "CEO of the Year."

Their final remuneration packages would only be confirmed after making comparisons and evaluating against local and regional corporate and relevant industry practices and standards. That is, with those in London, New York, Paris, Tokyo, Munich and Sydney. That would, by pure coincidence, mean benchmarking against the salaries and perks of the likes of Warren Buffet of Berkshire Hathaway, Bill Gates of Microsoft, Steve Jobs of Apple, Michael Bloomberg and the presidents of Ford, General Motors, American Airlines, British Airways and similar laggards.

If that did not solve the problem, which it usually did not, they would start padding and falsifying expense claims. Their one-year corporate planner would be filled with overseas travel at the rate of one trip a week to London, Korea, Detroit, Tokyo, Beijing and Sweden in search of cheaper manufacturing components, outsourcing possibilities and general R&D.

They would purchase their own tickets through an entity not on "my company"'s list of approved travel agencies. They would travel alone after dispatching a technical team a day or two ahead. They would travel economy while disguising themselves with wigs and dark glasses. Later they would submit a fake invoice for first-class air fares that would be procured through the 10 percent generous services of the self-same unofficial travel agency.

No one would query the president. But if internal audit did by chance raise the question and ask for the ticket stubs and boarding passes, the president would throw a tantrum. He would threaten to sack his personal secretary and claims-processing clerk for "misplacing" the original supporting documents.

If he travelled to Paris for ten days, he would on his return submit a claim for a 2,000 a night suite at the Royal St. Georges Hotel on Rue St. Honore. Actually he would have put up at the nearby St. George Hotel at 200 a night. Once, the original hotel logo and stationery had been so artfully scanned and copied, even the corporate chartered accountant finance controller with twenty-five years of experience had been completely fooled. The drop of genuine red-wine stain in the upper-right-hand corner of the hotel bill and what appeared to be the tiny part of a cockroach's leg and blood in the lower-left-hand corner of it was a work of art. Here was a fraudster genius without equal.

If the invitation to visit BMW's Regensburg plant included an official dinner, the president would be obliged on that trip to leave his wife at home and take along his mistress. She would be presented to everyone in Germany as his wife. He would have fooled nobody since she wore miniskirts, chewed gum while wearing earphones hooked at the other end to an iPhone, held his hand in public and called him, "Honey," all of which behavior no self-respecting wife of thirty years would ever indulge in.

To cover her shopping excesses in Hamburg, the president would submit an "unsupported" cash claim for 10,000. That would be explained away to the "independent" check-signing director as being karaoke and Munich red-light district entertainment expenses for his generous German hosts (in reciprocation of their dinner invitation), which would be too embarrassing to query.

This was all really petty cash, which only the novice or desperate executive would indulge in. The more experienced ones would play the corporate-rebranding or corporate-revamp game.

Thus, Pulipore Telecommunications Plc. was re-branded as PTC with the name in canary yellow and in small cap italics. The concept-and-design cost for the new corporate logo alone would reach $10 million, while another $200 million would have to be spent on new signage, corporate stationery, calling cards and TV and newspaper advertising. Ten percent of that, or $21 million, was deposited in PTC's new president's bank account in the Cayman Islands by Scatchi, Scatchi, Rubicon & Mother International (SSRMI).

It gave you the impression SSRMI had offices in London and Rome, and New York as well. However, SSRMI was actually owned by Kapalin's son Jaya Sea Cucumber Black Panther Chandran. He left the running of it to two Tigerist ad executives, Richard Chan and his mother, a one-time model, who registered SSRMI in Monaco to claim international affiliation for her fake ad agency with a client list of one name.

Pulipore Electricity Corporation's total corporate revamp was first discussed in a private meeting room at the members-only Chandrapore Lake Gardens Club. PEC's new president, Sagara Kingfisher Great Ape Suryan, gave an overview of what he had in mind to the president of Berkshire Global Management Consultants (BGMC), Warren Edward.

Warren, an American who had settled down in Pulipore, was a close friend of Haniff Hassan. Ninety-nine percent of those who saw the full name of BGMC and its president were convinced they were affiliated and linked to Berkshire Hathaway's holding company in Omaha, Nebraska, USA and Warren Buffet. In actual fact, Warren had concocted the name from Berkshire Gardens where he lived and a fairly large globe of the world placed as a marker on the landscaped lawn outside the guardhouse to his exclusive housing estate.

The other one percent comprised those who never went anywhere near a consultant, because they knew here was a class of men who were the masters of a thousand ways to make love to the female of our species, but had never known any.

Sagara had explained to Warren that five years earlier his predecessor had made a "huge cock-up" by centralizing all PEC's operations and administration at its head office in Chandrapore. This placed a huge strain on him and his executives. It had further resulted in increasing the costs of purchasing parts and maintenance, and there were undue operational delays. Warren was asked to come up with an initial study and report to PEC's board of directors, justifying complete decentralization. The fee for the initial study would be $10 million. If the recommendations were accepted, there would follow a more detailed countrywide "in-depth" consultancy contract to BGMC that "could be in the region of $100 million."

This was all complete nonsense, since PEC was doing just fine and centralization was saving it hundreds of millions of dollars a year in bulk purchasing. Some of PEC's excess land had also been utilized to build warehouses for storage. Their IT department was manned by a single lady from Bangalore, India and her pet poodle. That department had huge computer banks that kept track of everything and could deliver a bolt, nut, or even a spare transformer at a moment's notice to anywhere in Tiger Isle. This was possible via the extensive network of Pulipore Railway, with which PEC had a long-term contract for bulk-shipment discounts.

Decentralization would mean four of everything, which is exactly how Sagara hoped to profit from the situation.

"Well, I have some ten or twenty immediate supportive answers in mind for you, and certainly my office will add more, refine and add flesh and substance to it. But just so I can confirm them and in case your board members query you, could you run through your thoughts with me?" Warren inquired.

Sagara was an old hand at this bluffology and quickly jotted down on the back of a paper napkin twenty points that he could think off-the-cuff to justify decentralization. Warren carefully folded the napkin and transferred it to his solid leather briefcase. BGMC received its appointment letter by local courier two days later. Within a month it tendered its beautifully drafted, printed and bound five-hundred-page report titled, PEC—A Case for Decentralization.

Minus the:
- Ten-page introduction on BGMC
- Its mission statement
- Consultancy services range
- Long list of clients
- Preamble
- Fifty-page disclaimer
- Photographs of all PEC plants and offices,

BGMC's report was nothing more than a regurgitation of Sagara's twenty-point off-the-cuff reasons he had scribbled on the paper napkin.

They had "beefed up" the report with charts and diagrams of management structures, chains of command and tree charts that branched everywhere. No one noticed because they never read the report except for its last paragraph.

The concluding paragraph strongly urged PEC to seriously consider the international trend toward decentralization without providing any specific statistics or case references. It read, "We fully reiterate that if PEC were to accept our recommendations and implement the total revamp, it could book in savings in the region of $2 billion." That was underscored in bold with double lines. They had not said that previously anywhere in that report. But "reiterate" gave the impression that a case for decentralization had been made and emphasized at least ten times and only an imbecile would not concur with their findings.

When questioned by a PEC board member why there were no detailed analyses of the areas of savings, Warren had leaned back in his chair, grinned widely and replied, "Heh, heh, heh! Come, come gentlemen, I was not born yesterday and neither were you shining captains of industry and guardians of your shareholders. If I gave all that information without the contract for the full in-depth study in hand, why, one of your beancounters or general managers, not you honorable men of course, may photocopy it and implement the changes. Where will I be then?"

They liked that, being sucked up to as "captains of industry," and their chests puffed out as they heard the ringing tone with which Warren had knighted them "guardians of your shareholders."

BGMC received its $100 million contract by special courier the next day, following which Warren made a call to Siemens in Germany. Six months later, PEC announced to the stock exchange its $3 billion decentralization plan that would "over the next five years, based on discounted net present value cash flow computations, save PEC at least $2 billion all of which will go straight to the bottom line." Most of the inflated contracts for new offices, furniture, provincial warehouses and IT computerization costs went crookedly to Sagara, his cronies and his relatives.

Eventually, PEC lost $4 billion over five years due to the loss of bulk-purchasing discounts, and from additional warehouse rentals, electricity, water, air-conditioning charges, pilferages and the massive increase in head office administration staffing costs in keeping an eye on the provinces, all of which went straight to the bottom line.

Sagara grew wealthier by $200 million within twenty-four months of his walking in through the doors of PEC's HQ.

Pulirajaputran Tiger Motors (PTM)

PTM was yet another "must not fail" national project mooted by Bhairav and supported by his deputy Kapalin.

To be fair to Bhairav, the idea of a national car and auto industry was not without some merit. Billions of dollars flowed out of the country every year to pay for imported Datsun, Toyota, Mercedes Benz, BMW, Jaguar, Fiat, Ford, Volkswagen Beetle, Citroen and Volvo cars. Per capita, Tiger Isle had the highest number of Porsche, Ferrari, Lotus and Maserati cars in the world. They were mainly owned by the children, grandchildren, nephews and nieces of the likes of the Bhairavs, Kapalins, Haniffs, William Vans, Rambo Jamals and Bootesh Lins.

That exerted huge pressure on Pulipore's balance of trade and currency-exchange rate. Of course the rising import of cars signaled a galloping economy. However, the opportunity cost foregone in accumulating know-how to industrialization, technology spinoffs and sustainable long-term jobs for Tiger Isle were huge. All this Bhairav had noted while on an official trip to South Korea and its Hyundai and Daewoo car plants, which were giving Detroit, the Fatherland and the Land of the Rising Sun a run for their money. That was all it took for Bhairav to aim for the stars on his return to Tiger Isle. To say that he was excited would have been an understatement.

He knew he needed an accelerated start and signed a twenty-year joint-venture agreement with Toyonda Motors of Japan for design, manufacturing, technical and management services, as well as for technology transfer. The Japanese ran the show from A to Z, but Bhairav appointed Mahashiv Electric Eel Octopus Sivan, his wife's favorite nephew, as his puppet and sinecure president for the car project. Prior to this Mahashiv had been the sinecure president of the Pulipore Secondhand Car Dealers Association. That was all it took to have him knighted Sri and be hailed "Towering Global Auto Czar" by NPST.

The project cost was to be borne entirely by the Tiger Isle government, financed by cheap loans from Japanese banks. Interest rates had gone south and negative in Japan and while 2.5 percent was a bargain for Tiger Isle, it was a lifesaver for the Japanese banks.

Thus was born Pulirajaputran Tiger Motors, or PTM.

If logos and emblems were all it took to guarantee success, PTM should have conquered the world with its imaginative and evocative reddish-orange leaping tiger of thirteen stripes.

That logo and emblem mounted in front on the car's bonnet won numerous international design awards and became a collector's item that outsold Ferrari's neighing-horse emblem and Manchester United's Red Devil jerseys.

Houston, We Have a Problem

Bhairav assembled a team from the Economic Planning Directorate, Ministry of Transport and Vehicles and Ministry of Finance. Their remit was to come up with technical and financial models for PTM independent of Toyonda's proposal. An interesting meeting unfolded at the conference hall of the $20 billion Pulirajaputran government complex in Pulijayam.

"Gentlemen, what say you?" asked Bhairav.

All the directors and VPs there unanimously agreed that PTM should go ahead. They made PowerPoint presentations that strangely seemed to mirror Toyonda's simulations almost word for word, number for number, graph and chart for graph and chart, recommendation for recommendation and conclusion for conclusion. Not surprising at all since Sri Meiji Nakamoto, PTM's director of production and marketing, seconded to them by Toyonda, had given a "briefing" to EPD, MoTV and MoF a month earlier. After that meeting, he had accidentally on purpose left under his table in EPD's conference room a copy marked "Top Secret" of Toyonda's final proposal to Bhairav for the setting up and running of PTM.

"Well," concluded Bhairav after three hours, "it looks like we have lift off. If anyone here today has any reservations, speak now or forever hold your steering wheel."

That had them laughing and relaxing. After that, there was a short silence. Just when Mahashiv was about to bang the gavel on the table to adjourn the meeting, there was a bit of commotion and a rustling of paper as a goggle-eyed, grey-haired gentleman stood up.

"We have a problem," a nervous Ramanujam Charya, PTM's cost accountant, nervously, softly and apologetically announced in a broken and faltering voice.

You could have heard a pin drop.

"What am I, Houston?" Bhairav shot back, eliciting another round of whooping and laughter.

"No, Sri President. What has not been finalized is how much we are going to sell a PTM car for." There was a rustling and turning of pages everywhere as many directors and VPs rifled through their briefcases, files and reports.

"Hmm, that's true," said Bhairav after flipping through his notes. "But I can't see the problem. It should be fairly simple. Take the production cost per car, marketing, administration and finance expenses and multiply it by a factor of, hmm, say, two and a half times to get a margin of 60 percent, adjust it for the market price of similar competitor's models and you should be home and dry."

"Yes, Sri President. If we were to do that, we would have to sell our basic Tiger Alpha, TA 1600cc sedan for one hundred thousand dollars. Our competitors like Toyota, Hyundai and Kia are selling their equivalent car for fifty thousand dollars," informed Ramanujam.

Bhairav blanched.

"Really? That's very, very interesting. I didn't know that," admitted Bhairav. "Why is that, Mahashiv?"

"Uh, er, hmm, Ramanujam may not be comparing apples with apples, Sri President. We have double checked Toyonda's market survey and simulations using GM and Ford's auto industry yahgooplex supercomputer models. We think we have more leeway that that," waffled Mahashiv.

"Well, since Ramanujam's brave enough to speak up, let's hear him out," ruled Bhairav.

"I have expressed my reservations before, Sri President. I sent many detailed memos to the PTM Project Review Committee. I think realistically we will not achieve 95 percent production efficiency within twelve months of commencement of assembly. Nor market penetration of 80 percent within two years of rolling out the first car. To achieve decent sales we will have to price TA at about forty thousand dollars. Also, the cost for the thousand acres of land annexed by the government for the plant and manufacturing slated to take place is not known and its amortization cost has not been accounted for."

There was absolute silence.

That was the precise moment at which Bhairav realized he had to nip things in the bud then and there. To him, the launching of the PTM project was a foregone conclusion. Equally, he could not allow his pet project to be sunk by shoddy planning, financial tweaking and oversight. He, personally, would not survive that kind of a fiasco. His real genius as a man who could extemporize, think on his feet and dazzle others with his innate De Bono lateral thinking ability came to the fore.

He pulled out a small, AA-battery-powered, thirty-dollar Casio calculator from his shirt pocket, grabbed a ballpoint pen and drew the writing pad closer. Everyone else pulled out their ATT scientific calculators, which cost a few hundred dollars each, or powered on their seven-thousand dollar Apple, IBM Thinkpad and HP laptops. Bhairav didn't really need the Casio; he could churn the numbers all in his head, but did not want to appear to be showing off.

"Thousand acres of land, say at twenty dollars, psf amortized at 2 percent for fifty years as per international accounting standard... 30 percent starting efficiency rising to 90 percent over thirty-six months, finance cost 2.5 percent, another two years for market penetration, starting at 20 percent and rising to 55 percent over the next three years...plant, labor cost, manufacturing, marketing and administration overheads of..."

When he'd finished, he looked up and asked, "Any volunteers?" Even Ramanujam didn't dare.

"Oh, if all you tigers in heat won't take a stab, let me ask the only lady in our midst," Bhairav smiled and pointed at Chandrika Morning Glory Chandran, Mahashiv's attractive and shapely steno. You could have heard a feather drop.

She stood up, smiled back at Bhairav, put one hand on her hip and reeled off, "Thank you for the number crunching, Sri President. Basically, the TA will have to be sold for no more than thirty thousand to start with, subsidized by the government. That may necessitate considering a 1300cc car as opposed to a 1600cc one. There are no alternatives. The initial startup cost will be, give or take, $2 billion, excluding land, which with interest will be another $1 billion.

You don't have to build the whole production line in one go. It can be staggered to suit demand. The worst-case scenario is $20 billion capital over ten years. Forget gear shift, make it auto. You might consider an all-in-one standard package. Let's give the competition a run for its money—warranty, road tax and insurance, power windows, power steering, air bags, front and rear seatbelts, windshield wipers, child lock, auto-lock with remote control and stereophonic radio and hi-fi—should all be included.

Oh and personally, as a woman, I would recommend you consider a two-door 1000cc smaller model with adjustable seats, wide windscreen and dipping bonnets so lady drivers can see the whole of the road in front of them.

Where will we find the money to pay back the Japanese banks? Float local-dollar-denominated Patriots' Bonds. Many will subscribe out of a sense of national pride even if yields are lower than 5 percent. As a sales strategy, offer ten-year 20 percent:80 percent cheap and subsidized hire purchase loans, which is the only way middle- and lower-income citizens, who are the masses, can afford it. Yes and why not methane for controlling pollution. Brazil and India are doing it. Hmm, that's it, I think."

She giggled as she sat down in her chair.

Bhairav blinked. Then he took a long stare at her before he spoke.

"The lady makes absolute sense. Perhaps you have been too ambitious with a 1600cc model right off the bat and leaving out what millions of ladies need. I'll give you all exactly one week to relook at the works and come up with completely realistic plans and projections, or else heads will roll. Let's take a fifteen-minute break before we come back and I run through the checklist with you."

As he left the conference hall, he nodded and motioned to Chandrika to follow him to his office.

"Very impressive. I didn't see a calculator in your hand," Bhairav complimented her.

"Thank you, Sri President," she gushed.

"Who do you work for and how much do they pay you?" he queried.

"I'm Sri Mahashiv's personal sec and steno, have been in government service for over fifteen years. Oh, I draw five thousand dollars a month," she fibbed, going for broke.

"I'll get you transferred to my office within a week. Your specific portfolio will be the PTM project, but I also want you to review for me special projects and proposals that land on my desk and I pass over to you. You think you can manage that for me, my dear? I can't pay you more than seven thousand dollars plus a government car and petrol allowance to start with. You game?"

Bhairav recognized talent where and when he came across it, even though he was a bit of a misogynist, if not a misanthrope. He had just made an offer.

She wanted to faint, recovered fast and blurted, "I think I can handle that. I'll give it a go," she answered, then involuntarily giggled. She had accepted.

The next afternoon, she received a letter of offer of employment signed personally by Bhairav. She did not care what else it said but scribbled her dhobi mark on the dotted line after verifying the figure of seven thousand dollars a month was in there. That was honor.

Offer, acceptance and honor in print, signed, sealed and delivered.

She had a gorgeous, valid, beautiful contract she hugged and kissed and danced with.

She immediately called her seven friends and threatened them with serial murder if they did not turn up at 7:00 p.m. that evening at Tigers. When they got there, lined neatly on the bar top were eight tequila shots.

"Guess who's going to get stinking drunk tonight, you tippling mothers?" she forewarned them.

The Engine of Growth Stalls

If it had been as simple as that, Bhairav would have left office much earlier. World Trade Organization rules meant that Tiger Isle's auto industry faced ever-increasing competition from Eastern Europe, South America and other startups. India's Maruti was beginning to flex its arms in the international arena. But once again, the biggest threat came from China. Few could challenge its labor cost and up to a point, productivity. Bhairav had not done sufficient homework.

The repeated crises at British Leyland, Detroit and Dearborn and all over Europe were clear indications that the cyclical nature of the auto industry deserved closer study. Even in the West, supported as they were by a car-crazy populace and large corporations that regularly changed their fleets, the big four were all bleeding badly. There were of course broader economic issues. Ten-year boom-and-bust economic cycles impinged on the car market. That only meant closer attention had to be paid to planning.

Toyonda, while transferring huge management fees, billions of dollars of it, back to Tokyo, stalled and stymied on technology transfers to Pulipore. They gave excuse after excuse. Puliporean workers were slow and not motivated. There were insufficient local engineers to handle the complex design issues. New models could not be rolled out because of the soaring costs of retooling.

But monopoly was at the heart of sloth and lack of innovation. To protect PTM, Bhairav imposed a 100 percent duty on all imported cars. But even that did not help. As Puliporeans became wealthier, they would only drive a Tiger Alpha, a carbon copy of Toyonda's Samurai, on threat of torture and death. Even with the swingeing import duty, they still flocked to Mercedes, BMW and Volvo. The two-door 850cc Tigress Man Eater, or TME, for ladies, while it complied with Chandrika's input on enhanced road visibility, was rejected as a tin-can coffin; so poorly did it stand up to even the slightest of collisions.

So TB, Tiger Beta, was only different from TA with the inclusion of an additional ashtray for rear-seat passengers. TG, Tiger Gamma, came with drink holders at the front and rear. Soon-to-be-launched TD, Tiger Delta, had key chains and key slots that glowed in the dark. Frequently, auto-windows seized up, exhaust pipes and doors dropped and steering columns snapped off brand-new PTM cars. Exports never really took off and PTM car owners were incensed their models were being sold for significantly less in the Middle East.

The ink ran red, as "production line realignment and rebalancing" became "minor management reshuffle" that spilled over as "voluntary separation scheme" to full-blown government bailout. Increasing demand and production did not translate as economies of scale, as a 30 percent wage rise secured by union-led strikes, poor productivity and monopolistic contracts for parts and spare parts awarded to cronies all strangled PTM.

Bhairav and his close advisors recommended creative accounting as the patient slipped into a coma. Huge operating losses were masked by hundreds of millions of dollars of "government research-and-development grants." PTM claimed these grants for fictitious new models and fuel-efficient and cost-effective revolutionary engines.

It wasn't just a case of another Tigerist "project that must not fail." PTM was listed on the PSE, which meant the public owned 25 percent of PTM. Another 60 percent of shares were held by four fully government-owned financial institutions, while Toyonda Japan held the balance of 15 percent in its own name. In actual fact, 10 percent of the public's 25 percent and 10 percent of Toyonda's 15 percent were secretly owned by Bhairav and his sons via nominee agreements.

Miraculously, PTM's share prices hovered at five dollars per share, even though the daily volume of shares traded did not exceed ten lots (ten thousand shares). This was achieved by the four state-owned institutions forming a cartel and through friendly brokers, buying and selling the shares daily among themselves. The brokers were happy to earn the commission, while the PSE refused to investigate the poor public float and lethargic trading of PTM shares. When Morgan Stanley International discovered the sham, they downgraded PTM shares to "sell."

Eventually PTM was diagnosed with terminal cancer.

Bhairav decided enough was enough and initiated a famous meeting at Pulijayam with Toyonda Japan President Hideki Yamashita.

The Real Art of the Deal

The real art of the deal, however, lay in taking nothing, making something out of it, running it to below the ground to nothing and then selling something for several billion dollars without anyone being aware of it, all tax free. This was the safari adventure for those wielding elephant guns, the big-game hunters like Bhairav and Kapalin.

Yamashita, a Zen Buddhist who loved to negotiate in koan mode, had near-perfect command of English and was an orator as well. Equally he knew not a word of Pulish. Bhairav wanted a buffer of sorts to slow Yamashita down and deprive him of his elocution and oratory skills. About fifteen minutes before Yamashita left his hotel for the meeting, he received word from Bhairav's office that they would have to employ the services of a translator, Kenji Omahe, from the Japanese Embassy for their meeting.

Yamashita was surprised but did not suspect anything. He was mollified and did not protest at this last-minute change, especially since the translator would be from his own embassy. Little did Yamashita know that for years Kenji was in Bhairav's pay and secretly advised him on all negotiations with the Japanese government and Japanese corporations. But Kenji was a double-agent who reported to Toyonda's nonexecutive chairman as well.

The meeting was reported some years later in Omahe's international bestseller Conversations with Bhairav. Yamashita spoke in Japanese, Bhairav in Pulish and Kenji translated.

(After the usual welcome and exchange of pleasantries):
Yamashita: The autumn leaves fill the pond.

Kenji: Toyonda is in the crap house. Up the shit creek without a paddle.

Bhairav: Can't believe it. He's bluffing. Tell him, yet the koi nibble at the worms.

Kenji: PTM is in the crap house. Up the shit creek without a paddle.

Yamashita: Can't believe it. He's bluffing. The share price is still five dollars. PTM made $200 million profit last year. Tell him, yet the koi nibble at the worms.

Bhairav: Koi do not eat worms.

Kenji: PTM is dead meat.

Yamashita: How is that possible? Does not a koi or a worm have a Buddha nature?

Bhairav: Does a car have Buddha nature?

Kenji: PTM will be filing for Chapter 11 next month.

Yamashita: Good God! Is that true? What is the sound of a one-legged horse running?

Bhairav: Clip...Clip...Clip?

Kenji: PTM is really tottering on its last legs.

Yamashita: How fast can a one-legged horse run?

Bhairav: What is it with this damn lame-horse fixation? We have a hundred stables of wholesome Arab stallions if he wants them.

Kenji: The money part is no problem.

Yamashita: Ah, now he's talking! Why did Bodhidharma go east to China and not the Buddha too?
Bhairav: Because the flights were full?

Kenji: We need independent consultants and negotiators. Yamashita's son is available.

Bhairav: So is mine.

Yamashita: Good. Agreed. The sun and the moon shine at the same time. But where does the rainbow meet the earth?

Kenji: There's a huge pot of gold and treasure.

Bhairav: Seventy/thirty.

Yamashita: Sixty/forty

Kenji: Forty/forty and twenty for me. Yamashita concurs.

Bhairav: That's highway robbery! Forty-nine/forty-nine and two for you. Take it or leave it!

Yamashita: What is the sound of one hand clapping?

Bhairav: God help us from these "the frog goes plop in the pond" Zensmen.

Kenji: It's the sound of $2 billion in the right palm of your hands.

Bhairav: Satori!

Yamashita: Satori!

Six months later, when they returned to work after a ten-day break brought on by New Year celebrations that covered two weekends, PTM's eight-hundred-strong workforce were shocked to find the gates to their factory secured by chains and huge padlocks. The perimeter of the entire thousand-acre fence was guarded by camouflage-green face-painted elite commandos toting machine guns. After protracted negotiations lasting two hours, PTM's union head was allowed to enter the factory alone.

What he saw there shook him to the core. The place was as clean as a whistle. Gone were the assembly lines, robotic welding machines, paint sprayers, engine hoists and paint-set ovens. Not a single spanner, screwdriver, screw, bolt, or nut could be seen anywhere.

Over that ten-day period, Bhairav and Yamashita, through their consulting sons, flew in two planeloads comprising four hundred Japanese car engineers, technicians and packing crew. They cut, dismantled and packed machines and crates and loaded and unloaded equipment. They even brought their own cooks, food in refrigerators and cleaners.

They got down to working in shifts as soon as they arrived and by the eighth day they had completed their job after numbering and labeling every component and compiling a very detailed master packing and shipping list, which included every office file, computer, car design and factory blueprint. On the morning of the ninth day, the chief engineer had all four hundred Japanese, including cooks and cleaners, assembled in ten lines to load everything onto a fleet of shipping trucks for Pulirajaputran International Airport (PRIA), where awaited four jumbo cargo planes.

By the evening of the tenth day the last crate had been delivered to Toyonda Siam Plc. in South Thailand, where the assembly line had already been expanded to accommodate PTM's new home.

A year later Toyonda Siam rolled out the world's most sought-after 4W-drive car, the 3.0 Litre Road Terrorist Tiger 1, or RTT 1. It combined the power and solidity of a Mercedes with the acceleration of a Honda Civic, the ruggedness of a British Jeep and the sleek, sexy look of a Ferrari. It ran on methane.

The White House and Homeland Security in the USA protested and were only pacified when the USA model was renamed Road Warrior Tiger 1. Half of PTM's laid-off workers ended up in southern Thailand. The remaining workers, who had always been surplus to requirements, received letters generously offering retraining in Thailand.

Toyonda took over PTM Pulipore, lock, stock and barrel for one dollar. The one thousand acres of land was revalued at forty dollars psf when it was really worth one hundred dollars psf. They wrote this off against their outstanding consultancy fees inflated by false invoices for "other consultancy work," interest, late payment and penalty charges and $500 million of the Japanese bank loans of $2.5 billion.

Toyonda used their industrial might and influence in Japan to strong-arm the Japanese banks to also agree to a "haircut" on the remaining $2 billion PTM loans for a full and final settlement at $1 billion "in the interest of bilateral relations with Pulipore," and $500 million of that ended up in the Bhairav, Yamashita & Sons account in Geneva as consulting agents as well as another $250 million from a very grateful Pulipore government.

Toyonda next sold 250 acres of PTM land at $250 psf to a Japanese real estate tycoon, Tetsuro Aoki Tanaka, for development into the very exclusive Zipangu Golf and Country Club Resort. Membership was restricted to five hundred of Japan's top corporate presidents and chairmen, who all agreed that land at $250 psf and transferable membership fees at $1 million was a steal. They would fly in from Tokyo early Friday morning, get in seventy-two holes and return to Tokyo Sunday night after a beautiful message and relaxing day at Zipangu's spa. The day after the balloting and allotment, Zipangu membership was traded on eBay and the black market at $2 million.

The remaining 750 acres was leased out at a whacking rental by Toyonda to Tiger Cub Patrol Motors on a ninety-nine-year lease. TCPM was wholly owned by "Sterling Mo" Loh Boon Chong, an immigrant Puliporean from Shanghai. He concentrated solely on 1.3-liter four-door cars that closely resembled the Golf GTI. He captured 50 percent of the Pulipore car market within two years.

PTM shareholders were given shares in Toyonda Siam, albeit at the rate of one TS share for ten PTM shares. It was either accept or tear up their PTM share certificates. They all accepted. Many of PTM's main subcontractors, like Ibrahim Nazar and Yahya Sulong, who manufactured and supplied shock absorbers and steering columns, when faced with crippling debts and zero settlement from PTM, committed suicide.

PTM Patriot Bondholders, who ranked second to the Japanese banks, also received nothing and threatened a mass gathering of millions to protest in the grand eco-park attached to the grounds of the Pulipetro Corporation Tower. They were supported by Maitreya, Kirpal and DJP. Bhairav relented and they were also offered one-for-ten shares in TS and here was somewhat of a happy ending. Like PTM's shareholders, they all began receiving 3 percent dividends from TS every year without fail, which slowly increased to 8 percent.

When the accounts were drawn and cash squared, Bhairav and Yamashita ended up with a billion dollars each in their palms and the taxpayer, $20 billion of irrecoverable losses. This was the prescient "worst-case scenario" number Chandrika had boldly announced all those years ago in Pulijayam in front of those blind and spellbound PTM executives.

With his ill-begotten spoils, Bhairav, who already owned a stud-horse farm in Argentina, joined hands with Yamashita to start a koi-breeding farm on one hundred acres of land in the hills of Chandrapore. They were ready to list that fishy business on the stock exchange four years later.

It did not have to be koi-breeding; it could have been anything. After all, their money had to be laundered somewhere, somehow.

Infinity and Beyond

By that time Bhairav was no longer interested in PTM. He had moved on to his next national project that must not fail.

He was literally shooting for the stars as he struck a deal with NASA of the USA. Bhairav engaged World Lobby Corporation International (WLCI), a shadowy U.S.-based lobby and PR outfit, as a consultant to select a Tigernaut for NASA's next manned space mission to carry out maintenance work on its orbiting space station.

"We have to embrace the space age," Bhairav thundered in Parliament and added in that bit that was his favorite. "The spinoff from technology will be tremendous. IT IS ROCKET SCIENCE!"

WLCI indicated NASA had asked for $1 billion. Bhairav did not flinch. He, however, suggested to NASA, "that so as not to put too fine a point on it, you might consider restructuring the financial module and proposal." The White House agreed without hesitation to Bhairav's proposal to an official fee of $20 million for accommodating a Tigernaut and $980 million of defense contracts for Pulipore. They switched to the latest American M16i combat rifles and machine guns to replace AK-47 Soviet ones.

NASA advertisements to find Tiger Isle's first Tigernaut drew tremendous response. Bhairav had rejected a proposal to make it into a TV reality show, calling it "tacky" and "typical crass Americanism." The short list comprised three women and two men, only one of whom was a Tigerist. Bhairav bust a gut, as this had materialized despite the test papers being leaked to several Tigerist male candidates. His disquiet was conveyed to NASA by WLCI, which set up a conference call.

"Well, how would you like it, Neil, if your 1969 moon men had been Jose, Fidel and Estefan instead of Armstrong, Aldrin and Collins?" Bhairav asked angrily.

"That's the way the chips fall, that's the way the chips fall, the American way," Neil, NASA's chief, chirpily replied with a smile.

"I can give you ten million reasons why that might not work for us," Bhairav subtly offered.

"I'm sorry Sri President. I wish I could help you. You can offer a hundred million reasons. It still won't change the transparent manner in which this selection process will be personally handled by me," Neil retorted, visibly upset.

Bhairav was toying with two hundred million reasons when Neil's "personally handled" struck a bell.

"You are absolutely right, Neil. It would be remiss of me to interfere with NASA's process systems and integrity. I'll leave it with you then to do what's right. Thank you for setting me straight," he suddenly concluded and switched off.

As Neil cursed for playing the wrong card, for he would have succumbed to "two hundred million reasons," Bhairav called Haniff Hassan and gave him very precise instructions.

Four Tigernaut candidates accepted five million reasons each to pave the way for the fifth, Jothi Saltwater Crocodile Suryan to fulfill his destiny as Pulipore's first Tigernaut. The four had reasoned that with the possibility of expiring in space always there, what they had heard of Bhairav and what this offer really hinted at, they could do worse than say "showmedamoney!" So Haniff had submitted to NASA blood, tissue and fluid samples, cat scans, electrocardiograms, X-rays and complete medical reports that showed four of the five Tigernaut possibles enjoyed the perfect health of eighty-year-olds.

Yet another obstacle was placed in Bhairav's way when Adhi Gurunadha and his fundamentalists objected to the project.

"How can he pray in space?" they asked a stunned Bhairav in another video conference call.

"I suppose the way we have always prayed, with hands clasped and reciting the simple prayer we have been uttering for eighteen hundred years. The Puranam says we can pray anywhere, anytime. No?" Bhairav trod carefully, as it would not do to have Adhi Gurunadha on the wrong side.

"Yes, we all know that," replied a very agitated Adhi Gurunadha. "But the palms must be in contact, skin to skin. Don't you see?"

"Aah," remarked Bhairav as the stultifying nature of the problem dawned on him and nearly caused him to reach forward and choke Adhi Sri by his neck. He was saved from a long stay in prison by virtual technology. "Yes, yes, you are wise indeed, Adhi

Gurunadha. Forgive me. Good lord, after my death my soul could be lingering in limbo for eternity. Thank god you are here."

When the question was put to NASA, they replied that it was really up to Bhairav. But if they insisted on exposing Jothi to frying by cosmic radiation or cancer, they wanted written waivers, warranties and guarantees. So as an acceptable compromise, they proposed Jothi's wife, Kumari, be allowed every morning at 8:00 a.m. to recite the prayers aloud with her palms clasped, led by Adhi Gurunadha on national TV via satellite linkup.

Bhairav bust another gut as Kumari refused. She, it transpired, was actually a Muslim convert, who though forced into Tigerism by law, prayed five times a day in the safe confines of her bedroom at her home. Eventually the daily prayer session was televised live. The transmission showed a cardboard cut-out silhouette of Kumari with her palms clasped, with a voiceover by Chandrika.

Maitreya attacked Bhairav in Parliament.

"You call this space tourist a Tigernaut? Why, pray tell us what exactly will his mission be?"

"What do you Luddites know? You are always negative about anything I propose. NUP science professors have designed several clever, original and world-class experiments that will be carried by our own Tigernaut Jothi, in space. His contribution to science and the future of the world could help earn someone here a Nobel Prize for physics, chemistry, or biology one day soon," Bhairav replied. But Maitreya's deliberately provocative "pray" had set his teeth on edge. "Even that's been leaked already," fumed Bhairav silently.

"Oh, pray do tell us what these experiments will be so that our children, the children of our children and of theirs can all worship at the altar of science and not God or Mammon," Maitreya mocked Bhairav. He twisted the knife in farther with, "I'm sure Adhi Gurunadha would be most interested to know."

"Why, there will be experiments on the singular and multidirectional effects of the G factor, or the lack of it, on organic cellulose and chlorophyll, lipase molecular bonding and hydrolysis of esters in organic chemistry, the effects of cosmic radiation on carcinogenic cells and tissues and Hodgkin's Lymphoma,

Escherichia coli anaerobic toxicology in yeast and the lower colon and lastly, capillary action in polymer tubes vis-à-vis viscous black and colored fluids, the shape of their meniscus and surface tension," Bhairav reeled off to a standing ovation from his UNTA MPs.

For once Maitreya was taken aback, flummoxed by jargon, gobbledygook and verbosity. Just as he cleared his throat to continue the onslaught, Bhairav pushed with his elbow on Maitreya's blind side and a load of files, books, resolutions and proposed draft bills crashed to the floor. In the resulting melee and confusion, the speaker of the house got the message and adjourned the sitting for the day.

When Hansard was eventually published, there was only a reference to Bhairav's "world-class and revolutionary scientific experiments that may bear comparison with the works of Galileo, Newton, Max Planck, Einstein and Hawking," on that day's proceedings for the "Tigernaut Supplementary Bill for $1 billion."

NASA and Soviet Roscosmos had conducted the first four experiments on plants, cancer, the liver and food poisoning several years ago and it was ongoing. The fifth, "capillary action in polymer tubes vis-à-vis viscous black and colored fluids, the shape of their meniscus and surface tension" was for a plastic ballpoint pen that American astronauts could use in zero-gravity space. It was a joke Bhairav had actually fallen for after reading an anonymous email forwarded to him by his son. The story circulated that the Russians had solved the problem using the common fifty-cent lead pencil attached by a string to the writing board. NASA had expended a billion dollars before they cottoned to the Russian solution, which they had kept secret for several years.

On his return from outer space to Chandrapore, Jothi, a dentist and not a medical doctor or astrophysicist, was given a ticker-tape parade by the city and knighted "Sri." Little did anyone suspect Jothi was yet another illegitimate child of Adhi Gurunadha, who coupled and dropped litter like cod, which lay five million eggs in a single sitting every winter.

After the initial euphoria, nothing more was heard of Pulipore's "Space Age Tourist." Bhairav did consider that something had been achieved. After all, they had close to a billion dollars worth of American rifles and machine guns. Surely the nation slept better? Furthermore, a $200 million contract was awarded to President Kapalin's wife, Natasha, for new climate-controlled storage warehouses for these national assets, along with the old Soviet AK-47 Kalashnikovs, which were in perfect working order.

Once again, Bhairav moved on as his think tank reported the national education system had deteriorated to a point where there was insufficient paper for the chase. Even Puliporean Harvard, Oxford and Cambridge PhD-holding professors at NUP never wrote research papers.

Bhairav flipped through their two-thousand-page report and spat, "Don't attempt to dazzle and confuse me with verbal diarrhea and numbers. What's the recommendation and bottom line?"

Natasha's plant in the think tank, Sai Nithyanathan, cleared his throat and said, "We have to privatize education. Let the rich private companies, public listed companies and wealthy individuals take over. Let's create more public schools and public universities, as in England."

"Let me get this right. What you are saying is we take all these schools, colleges and universities that were all built, funded 100 percent by taxpayers and that are already owned by the public through the government, and flog it to a few people in the private sector. We can then call them public institutions of learning," roared Bhairav.

In for a penny, in for a billion pounds, thought Sai Nithyanathan to himself, as he charged in where angels feared to tread.

"Not exactly, Sri President," he continued and gulped as an image of being strung by his scrotum flitted across his mind. "We are proposing they list these higher institutions of learning on the Pulipore Stock Exchange. That way the public can buy shares and truly be the owners of their alma maters. We can reduce government expenditure by billions of dollars a year, still set standards and control the quality of education and graduates from the Ministry of Education."

"Stop!" cried out Bhairav as he held out his hand in front of him. "What is the damage, quick?"

"Our initial estimate, using supercomputer simulations and methodologies rigorously tested by the leading universities in the world, indicate a ballpark figure of $100 billion," Sai Nithyanathan announced. He then seemed to shrink into a turtle shell as he saw Bhairav stiffen in his chair, then stand up and thump his table top.

In actual fact, to back up Sai Nithyanathan's presentation to Bhairav, the Ministry of Education had six months earlier sent a three-hundred-strong delegation of educators and their spouses on a fortnight-long "fact-finding" study-cum-travel trip to Morocco and Bangkok, sponsored (read as armtwisted) fully by Pulipetro. The party they had there was used to justify the "methodologies rigorously tested by the leading universities in the world" claim. This in fact was the norm and modus operandi for Ministers, Chief Ministers and directors in government, government-losing concerns and local councils to wrangle free overseas holiday trips on the taxpayers' account.

Many in government would otherwise have never visited Disneyworld Orlando, USA, the Pyramids, the Taj Mahal, Paris, London, the Great Wall of China and other wonders of the world and traveled first class all the way. On one such Pulipetro, PEC, PTC and PTM jointly sponsored trip to Tahiti and Bora Bora, Kapalin and his wife even took along their two Indonesian and Filipina maids. They were accompanied by five hundred civil servants purportedly to study tourism and the preservation of natural coral in the face of onslaughts by resort developers.

Sai Nithyanathan, who had already slightly wet his underpants, pulled out a writing pad and began drafting his last will and testament.

"Brilliant! That's the kind of big thinking I, no we, no, Tiger Islanders, need," a clearly animated Bhairav shouted. His eyes glazed as he looked up far, far away for a few minutes, as far as Mars and Jupiter, and then returned to Earth as the permutations criss-crossed in the left cerebrum of his brain.

"No, Sai Nithyanathan, you have underestimated by at least half the potential money involved! Come see me Monday!" he thundered and then walked out, lost deep in his thoughts.

Thus was born the MOTHER of all national projects that must not fail, ever.

The future of Tiger Isle children, the children of their children and of theirs was in safe hands, guaranteed.

That year alone a million more Puliporeans took to second and third moonlighting jobs or opened hamburger, hot dog and other eatery stalls outside their homes, along the shoulders and verges of roads and highways, or in night bazaars.

If Hong Kong was the Asian New York, the city that never sleeps, the people of Tiger Isle had evolved into South East Asia's perennial, psychotic insomniacs.

Tiger Isle parents stayed awake so they could sponsor their children's education as far, far away as possible from the island, at whatever effort and cost it took.

Rekha, Demon Auditor - Part II

The fast evolving police state did not stop conscientious workers like Rekha from gathering information on the duplicitous nature of Bhairav and the government she once served willingly. She stumbled upon it first at the Income Tax Department. The comptroller had taken no action against Tigerists, especially Ministers, UNTA leaders and their cronies who persistently failed to submit tax returns or pay any taxes.

The opulent lifestyles they all led clearly indicated they had income and assets running into the millions, if not billions of dollars far, far in excess of their known salaries. This created much concern among other Puliporeans, who contributed some 80 percent of all income tax collected in the country. They woke up to the reality that they were being duped into bearing the brunt of the cost of Bhairav's affirmative action NEA policies applied largely in favor of the wealthiest Tigerists and cronies.

It was at her stint with the Ministry of Finance that Rekha finally woke up to the truly breathtakingly racist aims of the NEA. It became clear to Rekha that Bhairav's real aim was to rid Tiger Isle of non-Tigerists. The Chinese who had accumulated vast wealth through hard work as well as successful exploitation of the Ali Baba system were the main target.

Over a hundred billion dollars of loans disbursed to Tigerist "businessmen" and students under the ill-conceived entrepreneurship fund and study-loan scheme remained unserviced. Yet the MoF took no legal action whatsoever against loan defaulters. They resorted to creative accounting to classify these uncollectible loans and accumulated interest thereon under "long-term assets" in the government's balance sheet.

Commercial banks and financial institutions sat on billions more of such toxic loans they were forced to disburse. Bhairav and the MoF applied relentless pressure and strong-arm tactics through the PFR. All banking licenses and appointments of chairmen and directors of all financial concerns, whether government or privately owned, came under the purview of the PFR.

Ministers, their relatives, party leaders and their cronies took up staggering sums of bank loans, totaling billions under the entrepreneurship fund. They used this easy money to acquire private islands, palatial homes and fleets of prestigious sports cars. They speculated wildly on the PSE and even reeled in trophy wives and mistresses. They did so with the full knowledge they would never have to repay one cent as long as UNTA remained in power.

The smarter ones hid their ill-begotten loan money in off-shore tax havens. They would move the cash around a few times to different locations to make it impossible for any repo investigator to trace it. Of course no auditor who valued his life would dare look below the surface at these transactions, which in most cases were not even documented well enough for any chance of a successful prosecution in the courts.

Zara Mother Hen Sivan, president of PFR, was as well brought up, highly educated and god-fearing as anyone could have wished for. Her parents had been equally well brought up, highly educated and god-fearing as one cared to name. But she did the nation a great disservice by adopting a "see no evil, hear no evil, speak no evil" attitude. In Tiger Isle, the sins of deliberate omission were as mountainous as the sins of deliberate commission.

Rekha had written several memos to her comptroller about capital flight from Pulipore and the illegality of it all. The comptroller did not even extend to her the courtesy of acknowledging her memos.

A very worried and frustrated Rekha discussed the politics of massive plunder, in contravention of the Government Secrets Act, with her gang of friends. It was Simran who persuaded and arranged for Rekha to meet with Kirpal and Maitreya. Rekha discussed it first with her husband Roshan, a business studies graduate who, like Rekha, had reached his glass ceiling as acting deputy director at the Ministry of Trade and Commerce.

Roshan had kept away from politics all his life. He was a "realist" whose aim was to salt away as much money as possible so their children could afford an overseas education. If in the process they could secure jobs in the UK, Australia, or the USA, that would fulfill his "one leg abroad" Plan B should the situation in Tiger Isle become untenable for non-Tigerists.

He reasoned they were secure in government service. By the time they retired, their government-subsidized car and housing loans would have been fully paid off. Thereafter their savings and pension would be more than adequate to afford them a comfortable lifestyle. So they saved, scrimped and stinged and led an extremely frugal life. They earned extra money from conducting maths and bookkeeping tuition classes for O, A and London Chamber of Commerce Industry lower and higher diploma-level students.

Rekha's increasing political stridency worried Roshan, who tried hard to persuade her to focus and stick to their long-term goals and plans.

"Yes, yes, I know, dearest. You can't sleep over how the country has changed. I've stopped counting the number of days you've been pacing up and down our bedroom at 2:00 a.m. But we saw it clearly before we even got married. We did discuss it in detail. We agreed we'd stay away from politics and just concentrate on creating a better future for Lakshmi and Karthik and being able to retire in comfort. Don't be sidetracked by emotions, or we may end up losing everything we've worked so hard for," Roshan pleaded.

"Rosh, don't for one moment think I don't understand the issues and tradeoffs involved or the consequences of taking on the system. What I see is like cancer. No, it's worse. It's like an uncontrollable alien disease that's reached epidemic proportions.

It's happening right in front of our eyes and I just can't ignore it anymore," Rekha lamented.

"You think it's not happening at MTC? If a start fingering the looters, they'll have to close down the whole Ministry. I mean it because they won't be able to find any clean replacements either. The Tigerist male and female elite realized some time ago they only have a small window of opportunity to become zillionaires before the curtain comes down. So, they are not going to relent or back off. But can you afford to be hauled up before the courts for breaching GSA regulations or be locked up forever without trial in Bay of Pigs under PSA? How would you expect me to cope with the situation then?"

"Listen, Rosh, we've heard all those quotes and clichés about standing idly by when Rome is burning. I, we, cannot allow them to win by doing nothing. Neither of us are particularly religious Hindus. But we have a responsibility from being members of a civilization that's withstood the test of time for over five thousand years. We are not necessarily better than others, but the good men and women must not turn their backs. We must not allow evil to destroy everything we've worked to achieve. I'll go so far as to say we have to fight even if it means sacrificing our children's future."

"What! Have you gone mad? Are you prepared to lose Lakshmi and Karthik to these beasts? What for? Let them have whatever they want as long as they leave us alone."

"No, Rosh, that's precisely where our thinking and logic is all wrong. We have to mount a challenge because of our children. Say they end up on foreign shores and get walked all over by another bunch, this time some white supremacists or other religious bigots. What lessons are they are going to draw from to defend themselves? Lie down in supplication and be sodomized? No! If we don't engage the crooked Tigerists openly, discuss, negotiate, agree and ensure equitable treatment, then the only option left is to bring them down at the ballot box. If that doesn't work, I'm afraid we'll have to engage in subterfuge to destroy them. It's as simple as that, my dear."

Husband and wife danced, argued, lunged and parried for long hours and days. They could not resolve the impasse over their children.

"I mean, what's our life without Lakshmi and Karthik? What are we slogging our guts out for?" he asked.

"Rosh, I care as much for the children as you do, if not more. After all, I gave birth to them. But you and I had a life before the kids came and we'll have one after they've gone in their own directions later, as they surely will. Don't delude yourself that they will be staying with us forever. But seriously, there are very big issues and principles here. If we walk away as though it does not matter, it will affect their lives adversely as well. I don't know how to express it better. I feel it in my bones. It's important our children know we stood up for our rights. What the consequences will be of our stand and actions, I cannot predict. But if justice is not merely another ephemeral concept and there's a God out there, I believe we'd have done the right thing."

So Roshan and Rekha drew up new plans and strategies. They agreed that Roshan would not get involved in Rekha's activities involving Kirpal, Maitreya and DJP. He would steer clear of it and stay clean so that the children would not be deprived the caring company and leadership of at least one parent who was financially independent and secure. They made sure all their assets were jointly owned and they drew up wills making each other the primary beneficiaries of their respective estates. It did not amount to much beyond their house, cars, some bank shares, one hundred thousand dollars or so in fixed deposits, insurance policies and jewelry.

The children were likely to inherit whatever property and cash, and that was by no means insubstantial, their grandfather would leave them and their cousins. There was one other intangible reserve they could not quantify. Maitreya had assured them, after leaving them with no illusions as to the danger they all faced, that DJP would take care of the children should anything happen to Rekha or Roshan. So began Rekha's double life as fulltime government auditor and on-the-sly part-time spy to stem and reverse the tide of a wave of evil that drew bigoted Tigerists to it like moth to flame.

In the late 1980s and 1990s, her job was made that much simpler. Most government departments and Ministries did not employ even the most basic of security measures for documents classified "top secret." Secret number, word, or letter markings, which when photocopied would lead to the source of leaks, were not in usage. Later, when mass computerization became the rage, WLCI coordinated most of the billion-dollar contracts. It created bogus consultancy corporations in Bangalore, Singapore, Silicon Valley, Moscow, Sydney, Auckland and across the globe. This created the facade of international consultants having been engaged to propel Tiger Isle into the twenty-first century with state-of-the-art hardware, software and IT systems.

The truth also was that the major computerization contracts had been divvied up among the children and family members of Bhairav, Kapalin, government Ministers, Haniff and top police officers and army, navy and air force top brass and the like. WLCI thus created another layer of nominees comprising Pulipore IT Service (PITS) companies. These were awarded the major contracts by various "independent" international consultants. WCLI of course claimed that "no stone was left unturned" in evaluating the experience, capability and resources of PITS in carrying out the contracts in accordance with global standards.

PITS, in reality WLCI, would then subcontract most of the work to its Israeli management staff in partnerships with IT-specialist individuals and companies in Bangalore, Chennai and Singapore. Hence, the son of a former minister for foreign affairs would corner most contracts in the $50 million to $100 million range and immediately put the squeeze on local Chinese, Indian and Malay-owned IT companies. They would accept these thin-margin subcontract jobs for 30 percent or less of the total contract sum on a "take it or leave it" basis. There were no other avenues for them to secure lucrative government IT contracts under the NEA.

All this meant that national secrets and sensitive information could be freely bought as the Ali Babas put the squeeze on the workhorses, especially the Puliporean ones, who comforted themselves with revenge. Occasionally, the rewards from selling GSA information exceeded the net income from overinflated and squeezed IT contracts. Besides, as auditor, Rekha had access to most GSA files in the MoF and knew how to work the system where higher levels of security clearance were needed.

She used tiny two-gig thumbdrives to download passwords and information long before they were introduced in the local market. A mysterious team of unknown high-tech DJP beavers, anonymous even to Rekha, hacked government computers by regularly breaking into the homes of, Chief Secretaries to the various Ministries and top Mandarins. They used these home PCs and laptops to access government computers, with passwords and answers to security questions accessed by Rekha. The government eventually caught up with technology and introduced more secure and advanced anti-hacking and anti-copying systems.

But DJP and Maitreya's loyal and savvy sympathizers in the USA, the UK and Europe did not let Rekha down. They had moved on to an advanced version of Roland's device, as so stunningly revealed in the TV series Prison Break. Dubbed the RDPB13, it was a darling of an electronic data-copier gizmo that could access and download any electronic information from close quarters and relay it back to a PC, laptop, or external hard-disc storage device. It could not be detected, as it did not it leave an electronic signature or trace.

A very clear picture emerged from piecing together the pattern of information stolen from government computers, files and employees and from paid informers and volunteers. Huge sums of money, billions and billions of dollars of taxpayers' money, were being siphoned out of the government's consolidated fund through overpadded procurement contracts. Most of it was remitted overseas, mainly to off-shore bank accounts across the globe.

It was obvious to Rekha that WLCI played a huge role in this fraud and money-laundering operation. That may not have been obvious to the casual onlooker or even many a top civil servant insider. However, the same WLCI officers kept cropping up in one-to-one meetings and negotiations at Kapalin's office in Pulijayam, EPD and various Ministries.

They were spotted at the PFR where special authorization was required from Zara for remittance of foreign currency to offshore-destined bank accounts. The same group of WLCI directors and managers appeared in closed-door meetings across Asia wherever Pulipore IT and other contracts were discussed and negotiated.

Middlemen such as WLCI, cronies, nepotists, top UNTA leaders and close cadres creamed off up to 15 percent of the excess by Kapalin's consent. The bulk of it flowed back to a UNTA- and Kapalin-controlled nominee master bank account in Zurich. Like tiny droplets of mercury, the cash coalesced together to form one massive reservoir and reserve. Of late, the mercury droplets appeared to be flowing more frequently and quickly to the mother dam.

The new Department of Yardsticks, under Kapalin's purview, was headed by his new blue-eyed boy, John Cobra Fang Sivan. It saw a flurry of activity in appointing all sorts of international management-consultancy firms that were going bust in the USA, the UK and Europe. The governments of these foreign consultants were increasingly finding out that they could not trust these economic pundits and gurus anymore. Among them numbered several Nobel Prize winners who could not forecast in which direction the sun would rise in the sky the following morning. Yet, they found a ready home for their roulette-wheel-spinning and dart-throwing expertise in Tiger Isle. They milked it for all it was worth.

Cobra's DoY, dubbed the "Department of Fiddlesticks" was set up with a whopping annual budget of $8 billion. It was entrusted with setting, measuring and evaluating the key performance index for all government departments and government-losing concerns. The exception was, predictably, the assessment of the president's and Fiddlestick's own performance.

Kapalin and Cobra politely ignored the question of "quis custodiet ipsos custodes," or "who guards the guardians?" Cobra and his coterie of foreign consultants soon held press conferences. There they "explained" the "paradigm shift long-term economic transmutation transformational metamorphosis master plan" they were formulating. They hoped for Puliporeans to attain per capita income levels comparable to the USA.

They held numerous $5 million per-workshop sessions up and down the country. This was the new all-inclusive consultative process approach where "all stakeholders give their input." Once again "no stone was left unturned" in identifying viable policies and projects that would see this major miracle materialize "in the foreseeable future."

Soon after this charade was completed, Kapalin announced the same old barrage of billion-dollar contracts awarded by direct nego to the same old barrage of cronies. The almost universal clamor by Puliporeans for income tax cuts, more aid for the poor, downsizing of the lard-laden civil service, total revamp of the education system, return to the open-tender process for government procurement contracts, etcetera were completely ignored in the new government budget that followed.

Had it not been for Adhi Gurunadha's timely subtle advice to Kapalin and Cobra, they would have introduced an annual $100 Tigerist temple worship tax, applicable to every man, woman, child and foreigner who worked in Tiger Isle. They were brought to their senses, in what would have been suicidal folly, when Gurunadha telephoned Kapalin and asked, "Is there any rumor to the truth that you and Cobra are working for the Taliban, have converted to Islam and are planning to make Islam the official religion?"

When Rekha finally got wind of Kapalin criss-crossing the globe furiously and of his scheduled meeting with Bhairav, Quasi Mahamaya and Adhi Gurunadha, the small hairs at the nape of her neck stiffened.

Rekha often wondered if God was Greek or Hindu and if it was really all a game for His own amusement. Would it all end exactly as God planned and was said to be predicted? What would it matter if she did not lift a finger against what she perceived was evil incarnate? After all, if she was careful and minded her own business, her family could still continue to live in relative comfort all their lives on Tiger Isle. If push came to shove, she could join her brother and sister in Melbourne and still survive.

The question that nagged her most was whether Hope, or "Elpis" in Greek, had remained in Pandora's Jar for mankind's benefit or to be kept away from mankind forever. It was all really quite hopeless. Created by Zeus from earth and endowed with all sorts of seductive gifts by the gods to torment men, Pandora and her ancient legend involved a jar ("pithos" in Greek). Not Pandora's Box as it is now universally known. Was it a story to explain the existence of evil in this world and if so, what was the relevance of Hope contained by itself? Or was it about Hope being mankind's greatest ally and weapon on Earth?

Rekha knew one thing deep in her soul. The Titan Prometheus had stolen fire from the gods for the benefit of the human race. His brother Epimetheus had accepted the poisoned gift of the gods, Pandora, thereby releasing evil into this world. She knew she would rather suffer the fate of being chained to a rock and having her liver pecked at by a white eagle for an eternity than allow Kapalin's and Bhairav's Tigerist extremists prosper for one second longer on the face of Earth.

Rekha constantly searched and reached for that image of Pandora's Jar in her most depressing moments.

She knew without a shadow of a doubt which version of the legend she believed in.

Kapalin Blowfish
Black Panther Chandran

What Bhairav bequeathed Sri Kapalin Blowfish Chandran was not so much a disjointed nation as a recipe for self-destruction.

Kapalin took office as the sixth successive Tigerist president on January 6, 2004. His fate and that of Tiger Isle was already sealed by that most unfortuitous of Tigerist numbers: six. Most Puliporeans referred to him as Ed, a nickname derived from Warren Edward Buffet's middle name. Kapalin and his wife had this annoying habit of portraying themselves as gurus on the economy and government investments.

Scurrilous bloggers and online news portals took special delight in writing about his numerous U-turns on policies under column titles like "Ed the Talking Horse." He had $2 billion in unaccounted-for wealth, some of which was in cash in his children's and wife's bank accounts. Mostly, it was invested in high-end condominiums, palatial estates and land registered under nominee companies in London, the south of France, Dubai and Sydney.

His wife, Natasha Pink Hippo Suryan, a Filipino Malay on her immigrant grandmother's side, was his third. His two previous marriages had ended in highly publicized bitter divorces where Ed had been cited for adultery. She had been nothing more than a two-bit but very sexy, sultry, seductive actress, both on stage and in real life. However, at age thirty-five, she appeared at the right moment in Ed's life, when he was forty-eight.

This was about the time most titled Sris had illegally accumulated at least $100 million during their government careers and were contemplating trophy wives, failing the acquisition of which they would have bought a horse farm and raised studs. The fact that she was exactly thirteen years younger than Ed meant wild horses could not have convinced him she was not right or meant for him. "Kismet," he had boldly declared.

She masqueraded as the nation's first lady in London and Paris during Ed's official visits there, although such a position was constitutionally reserved for the wife of the presiding Adhi Gurunadha. She had insisted on singing her favorite selection of Pulish songs at the official dinners there in her naturally high-pitched and off-key karaoke voice, much to the amusement of the queen and the Fifth Republic. A power failure had to be faked to pull her and her microphone off stage. Such a breach of protocols and brazen gaffes meant nothing to a woman of astronomical ambitions.

But, Natasha was also a two-bit billionaire actress. What she lacked in formal education, and many discounted completely her (fake) online-earned MBA degree, she more than made up for with cunning and by being pushy. When Ed was minister for education, she had, through various nominees, cornered contracts for construction of new schools; at the Ministry of Health, construction of new hospitals; at the Ministry of Road Transport and Vehicles, maintenance of all government vehicles; and at the Ministry of Defense, construction of new army barracks and training centers for the new Pulipore National Service Program and the purchase of army uniforms, t-shirts, boots, socks and caps. This was all justified under Pulirajaputran affirmative action policies and the NEA.

But it was chicken feed. Two billion dollars was hardly the financial base from which to launch a permanent ruling dynasty. Her target was $50 billion, at the very least. After all, Kiyosaki and Buffet had spoken to her to "THINK BIG."

Natasha was caricaturized everywhere as Big Porka.

Years of wining and dining at posh restaurants and never sparing on her favorite dish, combo mutton-chicken-pork with potatoes, or Muchipo, had done her body irreversible damage. Muchipo was always served submerged under a generous inch-thick layer of chili and curry oil, in a bowl. That had widened her hips, enlarged her bosom and shelfed out her derriere beyond repair. Muchipo was always consumed with fragrant oil rice, which added to the massacre. The online newspaper puliporenow@soros.con.pp referred to the couple as the BotoxEds—her as the de facto (for her now blubbery lips) President Botox who wore the pants, and her husband Ed, the talking horse who minded the till.

She astutely set her sights on defense procurement, for anything could be justified under national security. No price was too high where chauvinism and outright fraud were the logic and intent behind the cover of right-hand-over-heart patriotism, while the left hand rifled through someone's, usually the citizens', pockets.

The New Pulipore State Times, owned by UNTA, carried numerous articles and opinion pieces about China's threat in the Spratly Islands, underneath which were rumored to lie the world's largest deposits of oil and precious minerals. China, Vietnam, Malaysia, Cambodia, Singapore, Philippines, Taiwan and Brunei all claimed sovereign rights to the alleged fabulous undersea wealth. Hawks in all these countries played it up because, in a region where peace had reigned for thirty years, they needed a damn good excuse to fan the flames of the arms race and military buildup.

If truth be told, none could muster enough arsenal, given even an eternity, to counter the might of China or India. So an exercise in deception and fraud was enacted as though for real. A commission agent for a Soviet submarine could earn half a billion dollars, if successful. Many were prepared to slit their mothers' throats for that kind of money. These agents did not know the difference between periscopes, protoscopes and stethoscopes, often referring to the submarine's peniscope.

The NPST played up the "China String of Pearls" hypothesis, which they said was not only to strangle and neutralize India, but the rest of Asia too. China had never hidden its anger against India for providing asylum to the Dalai Lama. Thus it courted Pakistan and Sri Lanka. More than that, many suspected that in the longer run, China would use its importing and outsourcing strengths to render vassal states of many South East Asian countries like Taiwan, Vietnam, Cambodia, Thailand, Burma and Singapore. Malaysia alone had naturally bountiful resources of rubber, oil palm, rice, coconut, cocoa, pepper and timber with a nice balance of manufacturing and a tourism base. How they would fare in a straightforward invasion by China was a foregone conclusion.

It was all meant to play on the nerves of the USA, which was already neurotic about China's 10 percent compounded average annual growth and massively expanding economy over the last decade. And that's precisely where the think tanks in Washington and New York misread the signs and why, due to myths and fears created and fed by their arms industry, the Americans and Europeans floundered from a crisis of confidence.

One of these myths was that the Chinese were a harder-working people than any other. Does the history of the world for the last thousand years support that proposition? To whom do we owe the gigantic strides taken by humankind as a whole in the twentieth century? The Chinese have an unparalleled work-ethic culture, so the gurus spout. Hard work is a Confucian virtue. So for the Vietnamese, Thais and Laotians, hard work is a vice or an indulgence?

To add more to America's neuroses was the Indian lobby. If it was not China, then it was the hard-working Indians and India they should all fear.

What are the great inventions of China and India so we can honor their scientists and mathematicians for ushering in the modern era? To the Chinese, time is money. What then is it to Burmans, Thais and Indonesians, horse manure?

Then again, time is not money. Time is the span of human consciousness and conscience with a bare minimum of two participants who are aware of each other's existence. Time has no meaning for any entity that is alone in the universe.

But few understood that and so they would offer bribes and promise kickbacks, for there could be no corruption without a willing giver and a willing recipient to compromise themselves for lucre or power or both. Non-Chinese Puliporeans were not innocent either; they caught up fast and played loose and played hard. The Johnny-come-lately Bhairavs could teach their Chinese, Malay, Indian and Indian Muslim masters a trick or two about the art of the crooked deal. They could, as the expression goes, "put them in their trouser pockets, shake and give them change."

But if the truth be told, the main reason why many fraudtrepreneurs and businessmen who controlled the economy and stock market were prepared to pay their way under the table for any deal, any contract and any money-making venture was pure, unadulterated greed.

Another myth posited was that those in power never asked for bribes. It was forced upon them so persistently they had to accept it for peace of mind.

Yet, at the very first encounter to schedule a meeting with the Minister for the direct nego proposed $30 billion sea-bridge link to Aceh, Sumatra, the senior personal aide to the Minister of Public works fired a salvo at the president of Everich Construction Plc. with "How much?" He was only interested in the contract cost to benchmark the quid pro quo. Its necessity, viability, financial cost and environmental concerns never preyed on his mind, as it did not the Minister's.

What most do not seem to understand is that with the rise of the giants, China and India, the size of the world economy must also logically expand. Those who will gain most will be those who know how to compete on merit. On that score, the West had little to fear and should have encouraged Asia to move it.

Do not also forget that giants cannot be tamed; they must be contained or controlled. Every legend we know tells us they must be cut down to size and have their wings clipped. The Kraken was either chained, or when unleashed, destroyed.

If Adhi Sri Bhairav had raised government thievery to an art form, the BotoxEds had turned it into a science. They transformed

Tiger Isle into the Corruption Capital of the World. Crooked Pulirajaputrans, middlemen, the Mr. 10 Percenters and the rent and license seekers and agents pillaged, robbed, plundered and raped the national coffers with unabashed gusto and glee. So did the Sris and Adhi Sris in government, as a matter of habit and policy.

Plain Ponzi scheme artists, corporate raiders and asset strippers, poorly educated men and women with bought and fake PhDs, the lazy, the blind, the deaf and the dumb were knighted "Sri" and "Adhi Sri" for only one quality: their unwavering membership to and support of UNTA.

It was a country in which failure and fraud were rewarded with promotions, the larger the failure or fraud, the higher the elevation. On that score alone, Ed had ascended to the position of Chief Executive of the highest public office on Tiger Isle by sheer overwhelming weight of solid qualification and credentials.

When the writing was clearly emblazoned on the wall, only a fool would hesitate to reach in and haul out the television set from within the display cabinet of the shattered shop window. So they say.

For it was clearly a government of thieves.

The BotoxEds

Ed, as he was popularly known, was an Oxford University first-year dropout. He was described in press releases and in his official resume as a "trained analyst." It was the practice in Tiger Isle that, without exception, the sons and daughters of all elite and top Pulirajaputrans would be carted off on government scholarships to the West to further their studies and education. They would do this while bragging to all and sundry about the world-class and affordable education system on Tiger Isle.

They were sent even if they secured only a grade-three result with no distinctions in any subject at SCPE, for graduate courses in public administration, sociology and human resources. They were sent on full scholarships with all expenses paid, even if their parents were multimillionaires, which they all were. When they returned, they would all be referred to as technocrats even if they failed to complete their degree programs.

You could become a "trained accountant" by signing up for a four-year apprenticeship with a firm of accountants. But "trained analyst" could have been the most foolish of games to play. "Trained in analyzing what?" would be the naturally expected question. This had prompted a lot of waffle from Ed about his experience with the Federal Reserve and Pulipetro Corporation. He had spent all of six months in total there before he and his employers realized he had catapulted in record time to his maximum level of inefficiency. He had been posted to these exalted government institutions to beef up his credentials before being appointed Chief Minister of Sivapore at the tender age of twenty-two. Thereafter his rise up the corridors of power was guaranteed.

But in fact "trained analyst" was a bold and calculated move because the press apparently practiced voluntary censorship. After all, UNTA owned all the large mainstream media (MSM) organizations anyway. The few remaining independent newspapers were harassed and muzzled by annual licensing restrictions.

Under the 1980 Publications Act, the Minister for Communications and Media could and did issue "show cause" letters almost every day on "unfair" or "biased" news reports and articles criticizing the government, its Ministers and UNTA. The law did not require the Minister to state specific reasons for issuing show-cause letters or his decisions banning any publication. There was no right of appeal to any court.

The MSM had carefully constructed a portrait of Ed as the most trustworthy of presidents to whom you could divulge details of your innermost personal and family secrets, health complaints, financial worries, and about the fur balls coughed up by Toby, your cat. Reams of articles were published about body language and how a broad face signaled honesty, probity and integrity. Ed was short, fat and prematurely balding as well, but the negative aspects of such a lethal combination as Napoleon's features were not touched upon.

More than that, with his thick brush moustache and broad face, he bore a remarkable resemblance to that vilest of all dictators, Joseph Stalin. Tiger Isle was crumbling under the weight of leaders, Ministers and fraudtrepreneur robbers who all bore uncanny resemblances to the infamous dictators and/or genocidists of the twentieth century. It was like a "Who's Who" of mass murderers as Hitler, Mao, Tito, Enver Hoxha, Radovan Karadic, Sukarno, Suharto, Ne Win, Idi Amin, Bokassa, Pol Pot, Pinochet, Saddam Hussein, Mussolini and Slobodan Milosevic were more represented on Tiger Isle than anywhere else in the world. They were either drawn to it like iron filing to a magnet, or sprang from sovereign soil as they once did in the fields of Ares in Colchis, as Earth-born men whom Jason encountered in his quest for the Golden Fleece.

The public had a perception that "trained analyst" meant Ed had a PhD in a discipline, if not in several and that he was a polymath. An image was created and crafted that it was the misfortune of Obama, Cameron, the IMF, the World Bank, the EU and the United Nations that they did not consult Ed on how to overcome global recession, secure world peace, resolve the Israel-Palestine conflict, save the whales and of course, rescue the little children in Ethiopia and Somalia.

Thus at the Ministry of Education, they reckoned Ed was a trained educator, at the Ministry of Agriculture, trained agronomist and at the Ministry of Defense, trained Arnold Schwarzenegger.

No one becomes con man or crooked overnight. It becomes easy after the first fall, easier as you accumulate baggage and the fraudtrepreneurs at home, England, France, the USA, China, India, Canada, Argentina, Japan, Singapore, Indonesia, Taiwan and Russia have noted the soft underbelly and added to its increasing girth. If it was true now for Kapalin, his presidency and his wife, it was equally true before, that Kapalin and his wife sagged under the staggering weight of a whole mountain of accumulated baggage.

What else could anyone expect from a man whose name translated as "The Wearer of a Necklace of Skulls."

Hens' Night

The girls were already into their second round when they heard the loud screech of brakes and the powerful brand-new midnight blue 3.0 Liter BMW 3.18i whrrump into the parking lot reserved for the cafe owner and stop there. The driver turned the F1-type small, compact steering wheel until it clicked in the lock position. She opened the door, slid out of the sports bucket seat and stood on the tarmac, all in one motion.

The men seated inside the cafe near the tinted windows gave appreciative whistles at the flash of Angie Dickinson legs and slim, shapely white thighs as the BMW owner pressed the remote control and walked straight in without a backward glance. She stood six foot in two-thousand-dollar red Ferragamo stiletto high heels.

The rest of her attire, and there wasn't much of it by yardage, was a tasteful combination of Dior and Chanel. Together with her hairdo it came to another mind-blowing ten-thousand-dollar outlay for that day alone.

She hip-swinged up to Rekha and the girls, pushed her shades to the tip of her beautiful nose, looked down, smiled and said, "Shall we adjourn to the back, comrades?" Without pausing or missing a beat she looked up at the bar and added, "Oh piss off, Farid. Mick's not in town and he's not going to keel over from a heart attack if my BMW's parked there, is he? Get me my usual, double rum and coke with ice and a twist of fresh and don't forget, fresh lime peel, dearie. Chop, chop!"

Poor pony-tailed and double-earringed Farid slid back behind the bar with his cute tail between his legs and complained softly about foul-mouthed bitch-lesbians to his boyfriend, lover and soul mate, Jaimie Chin. The girls got up quietly and carried their drinks to one of the tables in the open-air, but fenced up and magnificently gardened area at the back of the Old Town White Tiger Café, or Tigers. Special air conditioners mounted on to the roof and programmed on timers swivel-sprayed a fine mist of cooled water that made it very pleasant indeed in the garden.

This was Chandramandalam Avenue in the heart of Chandrapore City. It was distinctly not the Avenue des Champs-Élysées in Paris. In the height of summer no one here sat at sidewalk tables hoping to get a decent tan. Besides, there was serious risk of catching bronchitis or contracting lung cancer from the fumes of passing Pulirajaputran Motors 850cc Vimanam cars. If that did not get you, surely the high humidity would drain you of life.

They made themselves comfortable before simultaneously, as though on planned cue, slipping out their compacts to paint and brush.

Rekha arched her eyebrows and said, "Well, Jesswindler Kaur, new BMW, new Chanel miniskirt, new Dior low-cut blouse, Ferragamo stilettos and that ice on your non-wedding finger and around your neck looks real. What, one hundred thousand dollars? Robbed a bank, shag bag?"

They all laughed at "Jesswindler" and "shag bag."

"Fuck me!" exclaimed Jess. "About time, innit? That skinflint Rambo finally got around to releasing my $5 million check for the balance of that Pulipore Air Force 1 refit out contract. The bastard made me wait a whole year, and did that check burn a hole in my Aigner handbag or what? I banked it in last Thursday and it cleared Monday. Tuesday morning I paid cash and collected the BMW. The rest of it was shopping, shopping and shopping till I dropped, dropped, dropped. Anyway, I got each of you something as well," she announced in a matter-of-fact tone as she fished in her Aigner and pulled out the tiny boxes.

The girls opened their presents and oohed and aahed at the genuine diamond earrings that must have set Jess back a thousand dollars a pair at least.

"Don't say I go cheap on my best friends," enjoined Jess, fishing for more compliments.

"Never," said Rekha as she and the others reached out and hugged her warmly and with genuine affection. "You are the best friend anyone could wish for and no one's been more generous to us then you."

Jess hadn't always been like that. The seven had known her most of their lives as Simran Kaur!

She'd always been pretty, but shy. When she was twenty-one, her parents had gotten her into an arranged marriage with Tiger Isle's most famous human rights lawyer and Punjabi Sikh politician, Kirpal Singh, older than her by ten years. She could not have asked for a better husband. When she turned forty, she went from riches to rags within the space of six months. Bhairav had been gunning for Kirpal, who proved to be the biggest thorn in his flesh in failing to put Maitreya behind bars with a series of fabricated illicit-sex charges and high-profile court cases. They had offered him land, big money, sex, boys, kinky sex, chairmanship of a company and even ambassadorship to the USA. But nothing would tempt Kirpal.

Then they fixed him up. When he returned to Chandrapore from Amritsar after attending a first cousin's wedding in the Punjab in India, immigration impounded his passport at the airport. The Police Special Branch, or PSB, an elite department under the control of the national director of police and security, whisked him off that very night to Suryapore Bay Maximum Security Prison on the east coast, popularly known as Bay of Pigs, reserved for suspected and known terrorists.

The Minister of Home Affairs, Bhairav's cousin, had signed a detention order accusing Kirpal of consorting with known Punjab separatist terrorists and detained him under the PSA. Various surveillance photographs were produced showing Kirpal sitting next to Punjab terrorists in various bars and parks in Amritsar.

These were clearly doctored by the PSB, but as there was no right of appeal to the courts for PSA detentions, the evidence could not be legally refuted.

Maitreya's lawyers had filed for Kirpal's habeas corpus and failed all the way to the Supreme Court, which upheld there was no right of appeal against the Minister's signed detention orders. The Chief Justice and the Supreme Court also refused to entertain any motion that any conferment by Parliament of absolute power to any Minister during peace times was ultra vires the constitution. That was a dozen years ago. Since then Kirpal had been detained "at the minister's pleasure" in solitary confinement in Bay of Pigs.

As yet no charge had officially been filed against Kirpal in the courts. They did not stop there. With Zara's and PFR's assistance the PSB traced all of Kirpal's bank accounts and share investments and froze them, including joint accounts with Simran and their children's savings accounts. Among the favorite tactics of the PSB was to have the Income Tax Department conduct frequent audits on anti-UNTA lawyer's clients' account statements and bank accounts.

Lo and behold if five cents of a client's money should be discovered in the wrong bank account. The solicitor would be charged with criminal breach of trust and put away for five years at a stretch. It was unfortunate for Bhairav, but fortunate for Kirpal, that he was as straight as a die.

Maitreya and DJP organized candlelight vigils outside the prison gates of Bay of Pigs to pressure the government to release Kirpal. Simran and her seven alma mater friends would drive three hundred kilometers there in a convoy of rented vans with sympathizers and activists. They would stand arm-in-arm in pouring rain while singing, We Shall Not Be Moved while the PSB made mass arrests under the arbitrary "not more than two people" assembly rules.

After six years of misery, Simran finally made up her mind. Her parents and in-laws supported her with money for the children's education, but the stress was simply too much. Her eldest son, Ranjit, twenty-one, was thrown out of NUP for "involvement in undesirable activities" when he was spotted at a candlelight vigil. The Universities and Colleges Act forbade any student from enrolling as a member of any political party or taking part in any political gathering or activity.

Kirpal's law practice, facing huge debts in his absence, had been wound up, with encouragement from Bhairav. Creditors had threatened Simran with physical harm when they found that her fully paid house was registered solely in her name. So Simran made a decision. She sold the house and had half of the money TT'd to her paternal uncle Karamjit Singh in London. He used it to cart Ranjit off to the London School of Economics Law School and to pay for the schooling and living expenses of Ranjit's younger brother and sister, Harcharan and Meera.

With most of the balance she bought a small flat under her mother's name far away from the city and secured through Maitreya's network an LP with a fake name and identity. As a homemaker for twenty-five years, in between caring for the family, she had kept herself trim and fit and mostly studied fashion magazines and the Tatler.

She had a fair idea what she needed to do for a complete identity makeover. The innocent, dutiful, simple and ambitionless Simran was out. In place of her there emerged the metamorphosized Jesslinder Kaur, single, of indeterminate age and sexy and desirable as hell. She spent a year attending a secretarial course before applying for and sailing through the interview for a 9:00-to-5:00 job as junior secretary to "Rambo' Jamal Omar, president of Pulirajaputran Airlines.

All this, Kirpal and Simran had discussed, planned and agreed to mutually. Kirpal instinctively knew that the tension and stress of the week in-week out six-hundred-kilometer journey to Bay of Pigs and back would get to her sooner or later. Kirpal himself had spent his youth in London and been a student activist. He had charted the goals with Maitreya and was fully aware of the risks and dangers involved.

He, Maitreya and DJP were playing a no-holds-barred, winner-take-all game with the Bhairavs and Kapalins. If he failed, there would be others to carry on. But if Simran tipped over, the future of his children would be at stake. So he released her, told her that one visit a month or even one in two would suffice. He comforted her that while she would always be in his heart, he needed her whole and strong for the continuity of their family.

The Kirpals of Tiger Isle were men who hadn't gone to London to merely earn a law degree. They went there to find about more about Gandhi, Mandela and the real art of war, for freedom is never given but earned.

Simran's newfound freedom took her in another direction as well. If Punjabi women are known to be naturally "hot," Jess was the core of Helios. That had not gone unnoticed by her boss, Jamal Omar. Jamal had been handpicked by Bhairav to head Pulirajaputran Airlines (PRA), which was listed on the PSE. It was 55 percent owned by the government, which divested 30 percent to Rambo, who financed it 100 percent with a "friendly" bank loan.

PRA was Tiger Isle's sole airlines and prior to Jamal's arrival, it trumped Singapore International Airlines as the most punctual airline with the best in-flight service, food, stewards and stewardesses and the friendliest of crews on the face of the planet. SIA had now and then been unfairly and unjustifiably accused of favouring "ang moh" or Caucasian passengers, and of sneering at those from South East Asia, the Indian subcontinent and the Middle East.

Jamal Omar, whose grandparents were Malaysian Indian Muslim and Malay immigrants, had up till then made his mark as the sole million-dollar loss-generating agent and distributor of Humley Toy Shop of London products. Among Humley's range of toys were fantastic aeroplane assembly kits for kids and adults. That was all that was necessary for Bhairav to proclaim Jamal Omar as a towering global-aviation czar worthy of being sat next to the Wright Brothers.

Even earlier than that, Jamal had been granted a twenty-year monopoly license to import wheat and flour as well as to set up and operate Tiger Isle's first privately owned satellite TV station with interactive services.

Market talk, probably of apocryphal origin, was that Jamal had been jogging in Hyde Park in London when he literally ran into a startled Bhairav taking a leisurely evening stroll there. Bhairav had just that very afternoon achieved the rare treble at the Commonwealth Conference. He had insulted the queen by greeting her with "Good afternoon, Lady Liz," created an international furor when he described Blair and the UK establishment as "lackeys of Israel," and caused apoplectic fits in the White House by asking if Blair's bosom buddy Bush had secured his retirement home in Tel Aviv.

Now he was out basking in the warmth and glory of his own estimation, by which he had struck a real blow for freedom and democracy. The Palestine Liberation Front hailed him as a hero and nominated him for the Nobel Peace Prize. The Middle East could not quite figure out Bhairav's interest, but they were not going to look a gift horse in the mouth. They flogged it for all it was worth. "Bhairav Bumps Bush!" their headlines screamed.

Bhairav, The International Jew Baiter, had an axe to grind ever since he was fed the rumor (partly true) that the Israeli government and air force had secretly agreed to train Singapore and Malaysia's Top Guns and Mossad would train their internal and regional espionage networks.

Jamal had apparently helped Bhairav over to a park bench after apologizing profusely, when he experienced a "eureka" moment. He lectured Bhairav on how Puliporeans were being exploited by Chinese merchants who, through their secretive and close-shop guilds, trade associations and chambers of commerce, had a stranglehold on the import of wheat and flour. He proposed that Bhairav allot a twenty-year monopoly license by which his Triticum Industry would create a level playing field.

Bhairav had asked him what experience he had in an industry that stretched from Canada, the USA, Russia and China to India and the Chicago Mercantile Exchange. Jamal spoke fondly and nostalgically of his youth, when he had helped his father and grandfather sell wheat flour by the kati in the night markets of Sivapore City. Bhairav expressed some misgiving at the stumbling block of Jamal being a Muslim Malay. Jamal assured him that he had already divorced his Malay Muslim wife via sms of "Talak, Talak, Talak," converted to Tigerism and taken on a Tigerist wife.

All of which he actually attended to when he returned to Sivapore.

Thus was born Tiger Isle's Towering Global Wheat Czar.

Astral TV's main selling point was its twenty-four-hour transmission and interactive service. A subscriber should have been able, on his Astral TV screen, to read and answer his email and dial and answer telephone calls with caller ID and built-in webcams, all activated by voice-control technology. While lying in bed he should have been able to download pay-on-demand versions of his latest and all-time favorite songs, videos, movies and TV serials and specials. Consumers especially looked forward to Discovery, the Miss Universe contest, the World of Wrestling and Boxing Classics channels from Astral's digital bank, all on their plasma screens, for a supposed pittance. That was the theory of it, anyway.

Triticum Industry failed, as the Chinese merchants, distributors and traders declared war. When threatened with the shattering of their "wheat bowls" they first cut prices to rock bottom before their stocks ran out. Next they imported tons of wheat and flour to bonded warehouses in ports at Aceh, Singapore and Port Kelang in Malaysia. From there, they smuggled them into Tiger Isle with the help of well-compensated rogue boat and ship operators. If they took the official route, the manifests falsely declared the cargo as rice, powdered milk, mangoes etcetera. Government officers in Customs and Excise were only too happy to connive for all the "right" reasons.

The well-connected Chinese tycoons also nudged the "Big Dragon," People's Republic of China. They in turn quietly expressed to Bhairav "our concerns" about anti-WTO practices and of the dangers of "creating an uneven playing field," through ever-so-diplomatic channels.

Astral TV tanked even more rapidly. After paying $300 million to Nigerian promoters for the revolutionary "N'con Box," pronounced "En-tson" as though it was French, they discovered the technology did not work. When finally Jamal's chief engineer prised open an "En-tson Box" with a screwdriver, he found inside it three AA batteries of the brand where the bunny still marched on long after others seized up.

The batteries had been hooked up to an intricate circuitry design based on a PHCE physics practical-examination paper. The inventive and resourceful Nigerians had faked their expensive and glossy brochures and beautifully printed project manual. They had downloaded German and Japanese research papers from the internet and fooled Jamal with videos shot in Pinewood Studios in London and virtual demos beamed in by their comrade-in-arms at the HQ of PNTVS4.

Both projects cost the government plenty. Astral TV Limited and Triticum Industry Limited were fully guaranteed by the government. They quickly wrote Jamal checks for $2 billion dollars for all his worthless shares. Rambo paid $1.5 billion to his bankers and pocketed the balance. Other creditors and suppliers were left to salvage what they could from rotting gunny sacks of wheat and carton boxes of leaking AA batteries.

For his bull-in-china-shop forays Jamal Omar was duly christened "Rambo" by the business community. Bhairav duly rewarded him with a 'Sri' and the presidency of PRA. Shortly thereafter, PRA began to register its first business loss.

Rambo's first question before he cleaned up was to ask his management team of engineers, stewardesses, stewards, pilots, marketing men and women and accountants what sounded so sensible and reasonable that they all fell over themselves agreeing with Rambo's "I'll tell you like it really is" rallying call.

"What business are we in? Flying and delivering passengers for an excellent experience to secure repeat customers, or selling pork chops and lemon chicken with cute award-winning designer salads and desserts? Are we here to sell Chanel, Oil of Olay, Dunhill and Scotch, or to concentrate on the safety and comfort of our paying passengers, who are our real employers and business partners? Your job and salary depends on them, not the pencil and paper pushers in the Ministry of Aviation and Space Industry. You agree?"

They famously and joyfully agreed, unanimously. After that meeting they were all fully charged up to take on SIA, MAS and Emirates and rub their nosecones on the runway tarmac. Rambo's masterly zero-based budgeting approach and total reorganization of PRIA sounded the death knell for PRA, not SIA, MAS and Emirates. Everything—air cargo, in-flight meals and entertainment, hand soap, hand towels, toilet paper, perfume, hand moisturizer, kiddie handouts, duty-free alcohol, cigarettes, souvenirs and collection items, aircraft maintenance, luggage wrapping, loading and unloading, airport limos, taxi and bus service and ticketing agencies—was carved up and outsourced to companies owned by Rambo through his brothers, sisters-in-law and Bhairav's and Kapalin's children.

The cost of in-flight meals doubled and the cost of other services increased by anywhere from 30 percent to 50 percent. The price of air tickets could not be correspondingly increased due to competition from SIA, MAS, Garuda, Emirates and Thai Airways. PRA was further undermined by the rise of low-cost carrier flights (LCC) led by Malaysia's Air Asia.

Exclusive fuel-hedging contracts awarded to Rambo's crony oil men went drastically wrong. Rambo got wealthier as the agents kicked back 30 percent to him. The government's investment arm that bought aircrafts and leased them to PRA, sat on two mountains of debt. One was in the form of sovereign guaranteed ten-years-to-maturity international bonds floated to pay Boeing, MacDonald Douglas and Airbus Industrie. The other sat as "receivables" from PRA for aircraft-leasing charges, which due to cash-flow constraints, correspondingly sat smugly in PRA's balance sheet as "payables."

Rambo and PRA were now approaching their third PRA Total Systems and Hardware Reorganization Master Plan. They gave the impression that it was all due to a conspiracy by those dang Americans or chauvinistic French, their planes, IT systems or computers. Insiders and market analysts simply called it "another monstrous cock-up of a government bailout plan" estimated at a whopping $10 billion.

Like many of his fellow Towering Global Captains of Industry, Czars and Fraudtrepreneurs, Rambo had an indiscriminate and voracious sexual appetite. He called up for Jesslinder's personal file and noted that it said, "Thirty-five, single, previously unmarried and childless. Next of kin—None. Person and phone number to contact in case of emergency—Mrs. Randhir Kaur, Sivapore."

That meant only one of two things to Rambo. Either she was a lesbian, or a mistress of one of his brethren. So he hired a private detective from Singapore to fly in to Chandrapore as a tourist, track her movements for two weeks and brief him. He could have hired one from Kuala Lumpur for a lot less, but there were some significant differences. The Singapore private detective was a thorough and true professional who, after completing his job, filing his report and collecting his fee, would maintain total secrecy about his client and his mission unless his government wanted to know.

Of late, the Kuala Lumpur guy would be a thorough and true professional who, after completing his job, filing his report and collecting his fee, would sell the information to any bidder for fifty dollars and disappear, before which he would have tried to proposition his female trackee for a roll in the hay.

In other words he would be a real dick.

Having established Jess was neither lesbian nor "taken," Rambo found reason after reason to keep her back in the office with overtime work, until one fine late night she accepted his offer to drop her off at home. She saw through him as soon as he said, "It's on the way," as the only way he could have known that was by peeking into her personal file. Her co-workers were too new and she had not divulged that personal information to her colleagues.

But Rambo was not without personal charm, attraction, some charisma, or wit. He followed up every week with flowers and chocolates. One thing led to another and she eventually agreed to a weekend tryst with Rambo at PRA's exclusive corporate condo for entertaining foreign aeroplane manufacturers and local politicians.

Besides, she'd not had male companionship for over five years and she ached.

She enjoyed it, felt no guilt and found the clandestine nature of their trysts thrillingly stimulating, though she did not let that on to Rambo. She was not sexually naive, but sex with Kirpal had been of a different kind where he always took the lead and was predictable. Sometimes, and often she refused to examine her life with Kirpal more deeply, she felt her love for him was based on her awe at his intellectual capacity, strength of character, honesty, tenacity and quest and commitment to justice for all. But she admitted the truth to herself that sexually, she was a little unfulfilled.

She made it very clear to Rambo, though, that she was not his mistress and they were not in any "relationship," temporary or permanent. It was she who would decide when to meet him and where, for which he would pay. She did not want money or expensive presents from him and never invited him to her apartment. This piqued Rambo's curiosity and he toyed with the idea of making another call to that Singapore detective agency, but dropped it..

Hell, he was not desperate. He had more than enough skirts for every day of the week and then some left over. Her attitude was also a pleasant, welcome and refreshing change from the usual trash and gold diggers who thrust themselves against him and drained his wallet. Some even threatened to call his wife and would require additional "incentives."

So when that opportunity came to fleece PRA, this time for a $125 million refit out of the "superjumbo" Airbus A380 for Kapalin, he seduced Jess into cooperating in thievery. He instinctively knew this woman could be trusted to not take him to the cleaners. Had Kirpal been free, Jess would not have touched Rambo or his crooked deal with a ten-foot pole. But money to burn was money to burn. Now she felt footloose and fancy-free. Again, the illicit nature of it, the smell of danger and giving one back to Bhairav, Kapalin and the government that had ripped her tranquil life apart and destroyed her idyllic existence, excited her.

She wanted revenge, badly, and this was as good a start as any.

Captain Jeff Tharma DeSequeira

The affair with Rambo continued for a few months then cooled off somewhat. That was about the normal length of time all his affairs lasted, though her propinquity in the office kept alive his interest in her. She had gotten over the initial thrill of wild sex and found Rambo a bit boring, especially since his mind was always preoccupied with PRA's survival problems. She began to get restless again and felt more so after visiting Kirpal in prison. "So near and yet so far," she had cried.

It was while sitting behind her office desk and dabbing away at the corners of her eyes with soft tissue the day after that visit, that she had that eerie feeling of being stared it. She turned around and spotted Jefferson Tharma De Sequeira staring at her from the half-open door of Jumbo's room.

"Oh, I'm so sorry," he apologized. "But the boss requested another round of black coffee for all. You don't mind do you, please, er…?"

"Jess and I don't mind. That's part of my job. I'll be back in a jiffy," she replied as she got up and headed to Rambo's adjoining office kitchenette.

"Great, super. Thank you. See you. Oh, I'm Jeff. That's me," Jeff babbled and grinned as he closed the door and then disappeared back into Rambo's office.

She'd been arrested by his tall, commanding stature, the crisp navy blue uniform-suite with gold buttons on the jacket, the epaulettes and four stripes. A captain, she noted. She'd seen him before in the cockpit of the A380 when she handled that $125 million contract. She had not really taken notice of him during that brief encounter. Now, she felt a stirring and excitement that made her hands shake and the cups, pot and saucer rattle as she knocked on Rambo's door and walked in with a tray laden also with cookies and biscuits.

Rambo and five others were hunched over volumes of reports. He did not look too happy, with his tie loosened at the neck and shirt sleeves rolled up halfway. She recognized Rambo's financial controller and human resource manager, but not Jeff's colleague Mohamad Isa, obviously also a pilot and a first officer from his uniform and three stripes. She had called in late that morning and missed them as they came in.

As soon as she set the tray down, Jumbo waved her off without a glance or "thank you," although the others did thank her, for which she was grateful and replied, "No problem. Call me if you need anything else." She then turned around and walked away smiling as she knew they were timing the swing of her swaying hips with metronomic precision.

PRA was now being threatened with a pilots' strike. The regular A380 pilots had discovered that Jeff and his first officer Mohamed Isa were being paid a special 30 percent allowance that they were not. A mistake had been made, in that while Jeff and Isa and their four other standbys had been contracted to the government, PRA still wrote out their paychecks and got a reimbursement monthly from the president's office budget. That's how the information was leaked out.

Try as he would, they would not accept Jeff's explanation that his job involved more security and danger, as it concerned flying the president, cabinet members and Adhi Gurunadha. The PRA captains and first officers were all well acquainted with Jeff and Isa from the old days when Jeff had been their union head. They continued to mingle freely in their waiting rooms in PRIA and overseas airports, as well as in hotels were they bunked overnight. It was not personal, but they saw no justification for the allowance differential and demanded equal treatment. Jeff had asked them for a forty-eight-hour stay of strike and volunteered to discuss matters with Rambo to resolve the impasse.

Rambo, his FC and HR managers, together with Jeff and Isa, pored over union collective agreements, recent pay hikes and allowances and the essential services "no strike" agreement all PRA pilots had signed. It wasn't worth the paper it was typed and signed on, as Rambo knew that if they played hard ball, it was a simple matter for these pilots to go AWOL and flee into the welcome, open arms of Thai Airways, MAS, SIA, Emirates, Garuda and even BA. An A380 pilot with a clean safety record was worth his weight in gold. After all, you didn't get to be captain or first officer for the superjumbo unless you had clocked a minimum of 4,500 flying hours.

After four hours of intense research and discussions, they still had no solution. Rambo made it clear there was no money in the kitty for additional allowances. That worried Jeff, who was concerned about the hinted-at financial woes PRA was facing. Anyway, it was not his problem.

Then Jeff suggested some creative accounting.

"What do you mean?" Rambo and his FC both asked.

"We have a separate contract with the government, but our paychecks are written out here. We'll change that. From next month, PRA will issue us a check for our pay excluding the special allowance. We'll get the president's office to issue us another check for the allowance and we'll collect it personally from them. If the pilots ask, the allowance has been withdrawn. There's no way they can find out about our arrangement with Kapalin unless one of us talks. We'll even get a new set of dummy contracts done up and send copies to PRA's HR department, FC and the union. They won't really buy it, but if they can't prove it, they will just have to accept it," Jeff explained.

Rambo, a man of few words in the office, nodded and got up. "Yes, that's it. Get it done," he pronounced and dismissed them.

On his way out, Jeff stopped by Jess's desk, coughed politely, slid a file to her and said, "Excuse me, Jess, very sorry for interrupting your work. But Rambo wants this typed up as soon as possible. Hope you don't mind. Thank you again and bye."

"Oh sure, just leave it in my in-tray. I'll get to it as soon as I finish this letter," she replied without really looking up. After which Jeff took long, easy, elegant strides out the door to the elevator. She watched him all the way to the door and then took out the remote control and pressed the buttons. The security TV slid out of its concealed cabinet. She then tracked him all the way till the elevator doors closed.

"Adonis!" she exclaimed loudly as she pulled out the file from her in-tray and opened it. There pinned to the top letter was a note that had Jeff's handphone number inked in beautiful handwriting. Beside the number was a cute sketch of a folded fist with the thumb and index finger sticking out that conveyed the message very clearly. "Call me."

Her pulse raced when she saw that. 'I'll give you an hour. Then you'd better be ready, pretty boy," she spoke to herself.

Marriage

She had made up her mind she would sleep with him on their first date. She had called him that evening as she had promised herself and he had been very considerate by excusing himself, switching off and calling her back straight away. They went to the coffee bar at the railway station no one went to, sat in a booth, ordered latte and mocha and talked like old friends. She reminded him about that time she had seen him in the A380, but he, honestly, had no recollection of it.

While they got to know each other over pork chops, her mind had only really been on one thing and she quivered inside like Angeline when she first met Brad. When they finished she eagerly awaited that question, "Coffee at my place?" It never came. She felt like someone had poured a flask of liquefied nitrogen over her head. She reckoned perhaps it was her fault in pushing it too much on a first date. She promised to wait for his call the following week, as he dropped her off at her apartment and left after politely declining her offer of coffee.

They drank at bars and pubs, wined and dined, went together to the movies, the parks, museum, shopping malls and even the zoo. It was obvious they enjoyed each other's company beyond that of mere friends. The spark was there, but he would not light the fuse or hold her hands. Their dates always ended with a peck on her cheek until she could not stand it anymore. Jess was not the conservative, innocent Simran of old who would have fainted from merely thinking about any man other than her husband.

Kirpal had hinted, or was it her imagination from their long-enforced separation? She had spread her wings and was enjoying life, albeit discreetly. There was no certainty they would ever reunite again. The Kirpals belonged to a class of humans to whom walking the talk was, everything. Kapalin would only release Kirpal if he played ball and that was something Kirpal would never compromise on. Rambo, although he did not know it, had arrived exactly at the right time in Simran's life and opened up the possibilities. She did not love him and that suited them both fine.

On their eighth date, when they finished their Cointreau liqueur with coffee at Le Cordon Bleu at Shangri-la Pulipore, she looked up at him, smiled, took his hands in hers and said, "Listen, Jeff, we're not little children. I think you know exactly how I feel about you. But tonight it's make-or-break time. You understand what I'm saying, hon?

He in turn took her hands in his and spoke softly and tenderly, "If you hadn't brought it up just now, I would have. You know, and I don't know about you, but it was love at first sight for me. When I saw you sitting there and wiping away those tears, I knew there were only two possibilities. Either your husband had left you or it was the anniversary of his death.

Oh, I'm forty-four and can tell even if they discard their wedding rings, just as I know you are older than me. That has no bearing on the issue. But that morning was the moment for me. It's always a moment for most. A tinkling laugh, sparkling teeth, ice cream trickling from the corner of the lips, a tongue kiss you never knew existed, as she slipped and splashed into the swimming pool, as a gust of wind made a mess of her hair, the way she sympathized with you when the boss gave you a dressing down in front of your colleagues, or you suddenly noticed the elegant way she walked and a thousand other moments when a man falls for THE woman in his life.

But there must always be tenderness, affection and love, even if it was a wild one-night stand with a stranger you found powerfully attractive, or you paid for it in a brothel. There must be that straining and then yielding by both partners. That's something the Bhairavs and Kapalins will never comprehend. Even when they think they have found love, it's not; it's all about conquest, power and domination. I pity Dawn…"

"What, am I hearing it right? You mean…"

"Ssh! Walls have ears. Forget I ever said that. Let me tell you, I was twenty-five when I qualified as a pilot with PRA. I soon realized that I was never going to get married. I had the pick of women. There's something about the cockpit that's an aphrodisiac to most women and not just stewardesses. There was no class or racial barrier. I went to bed with Tigerist, Indian, Chinese, Malay, Portuguese, Dutch, Aborigine and then French, English, American, European and women of just about every nationality, whether they travelled first, business or economy class.

They were super rich, rich, just scraping by, poor and bag-packing students. I had beautiful sex with them on all five continents. Bhairav, the truest and most vicious of all Tigerist racists, hasn't a clue what he's missed his entire life. When it's one to one and you can look into a woman's soul and touch her there and she touches you back in yours, you think white, yellow, black and brown has any substance or meaning? Fools!

I could not see where I would have the time to settle down, have children and be a real father to them. So I've remained single all my life. You see, I can offer you love, companionship and more, but not if you wish to start a family. So that's the real reason I've held back. There you are. I'm usually a man of few words, but I guess I owe you that.

After all that, I have to know, will you marry me?"

He did not spoil it by sliding down on his knees, whipping out a bouquet of a dozen roses and springing open a tiny velvet box, inside which sparkled an expensive diamond the size of a hen's egg mounted on a ring from Tiffany's, while a trio of French violinists (Puliporeans made up to look French) appeared magically and discreetly behind them and beautifully struck up Lara's Theme from Dr. Zhivago.

She stared at him. She stood up, slipped out two hundred dollars from her pink Dior handbag, flung it on their dining table, grabbed his hands and ran all the way down the stairs and out the hotel lobby to valet parking. There she rummaged through her handbag and retrieved and handed the captain her ticket. When her BMW arrived, she looked up at him and rasped, "You drive. Your place. Now!"

As soon as they entered the basement car-park elevator at the exclusive condo, they began kissing and tearing at their clothes. She didn't care how many times it might stop on how many floors. Fortunately for her, it whisked them straight to the private lobby of Jeff's three-thousand-square-foot condo on the thirty-ninth floor, just one below the penthouse. As they tumbled out of the elevator, gasping for air, Jeff punched the numbers on the security lock and the door to his unit opened silently. He had the presence of mind to scoop her up in his arms and carry her over the threshold.

After all, he had proposed and she had accepted, if not by words, then certainly by wild, unrestrained, flailing, uncontrollable passionate action.

What else is a marriage?

A Promise or Two

They never made it to the bedroom. The living room sofa cushions were all they had time for.

When they calmed down after taking a few puffs on her cigarette, they talked about their childhood, growing up and their likes and dislikes. She mentioned her seven special girlfriends. She could not, however, bring herself to confess to Jeff about Kirpal and her children in London. The fate of a whole nation hung in the balance. But she did tell him she was married, was not living with her husband and that their children in London were all complicated issues. She assured him though, her husband and children would not figure in her "marriage" to Jeff and the day the situation was finally resolved, she would make it formal. Jeff played a few scenarios in his mind and figured the husband was away overseas with the children and there must be huge common money and property that would take long years to resolve. Either way, he didn't care, as he had more than enough money and several condos for the two of them for the rest of their lives. Not to mention a couple of million dollars of savings in his pension fund.

"So when are you going to move in with me?" he asked as he caressed her face, neck and breasts.

"Give me some time, my love," she pleaded. "The situation is a lot more complicated than that which I described. My husband has me watched and might use the information to deny me custody," she lied. "There's no problem meeting you here every night, but I have to be very, very careful. Bear with me. But moving in fully will have to wait a few months."

He could not deny her anything in the warmth of the afterglow of their spent passion. That is why she extracted two promises from him. There's not a woman alive who cannot recognize a moment of weakness in any man or when to take advantage of it.

"Promise me," she whispered as she tongued his earlobe.

He would have cut off his manhood for her at that moment. "Sure thing," he croaked.

"One, I want to know everything about Kapalin and Azalea Dawn Gazelle Chandran. Don't hold anything back, or else!" She did not, like every woman and female teenager, track Dawn in the Tatler and every gossip magazine from Tiger Isle to Hollywood for nothing. They lived for it and secretly all wished they were her.

He hesitated. Love and fantastic, beautiful sex was one matter; national security, a long stay in prison under the PSA and solitary confinement and detention, another. He cursed himself for his weakness and reluctantly agreed to it after she had playfully grabbed his testicles in a vice-like grip.

Next she laughed a naughty laugh, took hold of him below and asked, "Two, do you by chance know anything about the Mile High Club?"

"Good Lord, never!" he exclaimed with a straight face. The truth, though, was he had always been conscious of his job and career and had planned well ahead for his captainship and the A380. The last thing he wanted was to answer charges of sexual harassment or be caught in flagrante delicto with a stewardess or a female passenger on board, while on duty or otherwise. So although he knew several colleagues who had done it for fun and bragged about it, he had always steered clear of joining the unofficial Mile High Club.

"Well, there's always a first time. At least promise me a free tour of the A380 with you as personal guide. My seven girlfriends are all keen as well. Besides, I've told them everything about you and they are waiting to hear from me whether you are a closet gay, eunuch, or transvestite," she giggled.

"The tour's not a problem. I'll have to get special clearance and all that. You sure you want all your girlfriends there? I mean, what if one or two or even three of them fall for me too? Don't ever underestimate the power of an A380 cockpit. It packs more wallop than an intercontinental ballistic missile," he teased her.

"Try any funny stuff, buster and I'll castrate you!" Jess screamed, as she simultaneously swung on top of him and began stroking him again.

The Economy

The economic picture was pretty from far, but actually far from pretty.

"Bankrupt? Us? Tiger Isle? Surely not?" the trained economist questioned. He searched Somasundram White Cheetah Chandran's face to see if he was bluffing and scaremongering. Soma was their newly appointed Chief Economy Strategist at the EPD. Aptly, he was not an economics graduate, financial analyst, or strategist. That was par for the course for Kapalin, who labored under the misconception of yet another myth that relevant qualifications and direct experience were not really necessary for top posts.

Thus presidents or directors at the EPD, civil service and GLCs were human resource, public administration, business, or Tigerism degree holders who were regarded as the most versatile of managers in the world. They all gained their "relevant business and commercal experience" in government departments. The newly appointed president of PEC had earned his spurs at the Ministry of Fisheries, the president of Telecorp and Telecommunications Pulipore Plc at the Ministry of Antiquities, and the president of Pulipore Water, Sewerage and Environment Plc, at the Ministry of National Unity and Rural Development.

All these Ministries were cited in the GAD Annual Report for huge overspending and various financial misdeeds and frauds. Soma, a biology graduate, served fifteen year's sterling time at the Department of Prisons and Corrections before he was plucked from obscurity and catapulted to national fame. Of course, the fact that he was Kapalin's pretty sister-in-law's distant cousin had no bearing on any issue.

"The options are pretty straightforward and obvious," continued Soma, wringing his hands like Pilate before washing them. "Firstly, increase direct taxes or introduce indirect taxes or both."

This favorite indirect tax was something like Value Added Price. VAP really was a misnomer carefully, cleverly, cunningly and deliberately crafted and coined by the spin doctors in the EPD to mislead the innocent and ignorant, since it did not augment anything to the value of anything. It was not as though tagging 10 percent on to the price rendered potato chips more palatable or saleable, or baby diapers more wearable and absorbent.

VAP was a plain and simple tax. Some in the EPD would refer to it in hushed tones as a "consumption tax," which it really was since 10 percent was added to the purchase price in any transaction, at every stage. The only things going for it were you could avoid it and secure weight loss by consuming little or nothing at all. It applied to everyone regardless of economic status and the government's cash flow and revenues increased with an improving economy.

Both proposals were suicidal for the trained financial manager's government. Income taxes could not be increased due to election promises of "Watch my lips. NO TAX INCREASE." Besides, Hong Kong and Singapore had cut income taxes to below 20 percent and Tiger Isle acting in contrarian fashion would result in more FDIs fleeing offshore. As for VAP, VAT, Goods-and-Service Tax, or by whatever name they chose to call it, every public poll conducted over the previous ten years clearly showed the government would not last twenty-four hours after introducing and imposing it.

VAP was also an administrative nightmare that would cost ninety cents to collect a dollar and in the corrupt atmosphere and culture of Tiger Isle, it was more likely the price would be $1.50.

"Secondly, we have to completely remove government subsidies for oil, sugar, flour and rice, while scaling back on free education and healthcare services," Soma said.

This completely ignored the fact that there was no nation on Earth that did not subsidize a modicum or dollops of expenditure in education, healthcare, welfare, food, oil and especially, free trade. Free trade was of course an international joke championed by the USA through World Trade Organization, or WTO, rules. It was nothing more than thinly disguised Versailles Treaty all over again. Whenever and wherever the USA and Europe were unable to compete in labor cost or selling price with China, India and Malaysia, they would pull out the bogeyman of "dumping." Crunching anti-dumping levies and tariffs would be exacted and crocodile tears shed over child and labor exploitation. But the imports from Bangladesh, Pakistan and China and from all over the world would not abate. They would weep and campaign over the cancerous effects of palm oil, funded of course by the corn and soya lobby and backed by their faked and spurious "research and studies."

The French were the chief stymieists and consummate masters at playing this WTO game, like Yo Yo Ma his cello. Singapore and Penang Island (in Malaysia) assembled PCs that were unscrewed and inspected individually for authenticity. The French understandably plumbed for overpriced locally assembled ones, while Malaysian and Singaporean manufacturers and exporters asphyxiated from slow strangulation, the three-day week in Calais and Le Havre customs and the extortionate port and warehouse charges, plus VAT at 19.6 percent.

Soma's "complete healthcare revamp" hinged on charging outpatients ten-dollar consulting charges as opposed to five dollars currently at government hospitals, and introducing a crunching 10 percent national health deduction on wages.

"Thirdly, we must reexamine our commitment to the upgrading of our world-class civil service, its enhanced professionalism and competitiveness in the global context," Soma said.

This was government and Somaspeak for downsizing the civil service. If introducing VAP would be akin to the government legislating rebellion, riot and overthrowing itself, then taking a knife to the adipose layer of the three-million-strong civil service and the GLCs (government-losing concerns) was the equivalent of Japanese Seppuku or Hara Kiri. It would be sheer political suicide to alienate the elite six hundred thousand thieving, looting and honors-bribed top Pulirajaputrans in civil service. They happily assisted Kapalin and his government in gerrymandering, downholding the rule of law by rule by law and promoting racial, religious and cultural polarization of Puliporeans as a matter of policy.

"Fourthly..." Soma said and that's when Kapalin put up his hands up. He'd had enough of gloom and doom for one morning of quarterly review.

"Excellent analysis, Soma," he lied. "That's lots to reflect and chew on for a first morning. You and your team must have burned the midnight oil. Good work. We'll reschedule the rest of your presentation for noon tomorrow. Let's look at some big-picture numbers and stats, shall we?"

He gazed at the other two in the conference room. He had excused the Chief Secretary of the Ministry of Finance from attending this review. He would only have regurgitated lies and figures Kapalin fed him as a trained Minister of Finance. He knew it would be an exercise in futility to call to the floor the Economic Planning Directorate's Sri Peter Weller Brown Mole Suryan, who had once lost the government $10 billion. Peter's grasp of economics was as sound as that of an ape's on the missing link and the ascent of man. Kapalin nodded at him anyway since face was everything at this level. "Well, Peter, let's make it quick, but skip the numbers we reserve for the MSM. Tell it like it really is."

"In that case, Sri President, if I may humbly suggest, perhaps, maybe, we should go straight to right honorable Sri Zara, who keeps a daily watch on all the inflows and outflows?" responded Peter in his most bootlicking, crawling and groveling manner. He fantasized he was being astute and cunning as he passed the buck over to the Pulipore Federal Reserve.

Zara Mother Hen Sivan, president of PFR, was one of the very few PhD holders in government service, having written a brilliant thesis in international economics and foreign exchange at Harvard.

The only problem was, she, like Peter, was a Bhairav appointee. Kapalin suspected their loyalties lay elsewhere, although they did their job professionally and seemingly observed the civil service code of service with blind neutrality.

Kapalin knew it was all hopeless anyway. Even if Poseidon/Neptune had stood at the bows of the Titanic, the result would have been the same.

"Good thinking, maestro. However, I went through the executive summary with a fine-tooth comb last night," Kapalin lied again. "And the picture looks pretty grim. Anyway, we are two months into the second quarter and the historical figures are what they are, historical. What I need to know is how we are faring right now, realistic projections for the second half of the year and your recommendations for a quick recovery. We are on the right track, are we not? After all, Bernanke and Obama say it's stabilized?"

All three nodded in unison.

"Hmm, in that case let's adjourn for the day. We'll reconvene at 9:00 a.m., sharp tomorrow morning and I'll expect as usual scintillating input from you all so I can brief Obama when I meet him in Washington DC."

So saying, he dismissed them for the day and could have sworn he heard a collective sigh of relief from the trio. After they left, he banged his forehead several times on his desk and then held it cupped in a vice-like grip between the palms of his hands. Something about the comparative statistics and performances of India, China, Malaysia, Indonesia, Thailand, Philippines, Korea, Hong Kong and Vietnam in that executive summary he had skimmed bothered him. Most of all Singapore bugged him.

What he needed to save them from bankruptcy, which U.S.-led conventional economics and sage wisdom said was impossible, and U.S.-led conventional economics and sage wisdom had gotten it wrong for over two decades, was something way out of the "out of the box" thinking. He needed more than mere lateral thinking and paradigm shifting, something from beyond the thirteen worlds and thirteen dimensions of the Tiger Puranam.

It was clear to the trained globalist that Bernanke and Obama had not understood that "greed is good" capitalism had evolved and mutated to "greed is God."

Azalea Dawn Gazelle Chandran

He needed to unwind a little, stretch, relax and recover from the stress and burnout caused by a sinking economy and society. So he buzzed the intercom and asked his personal secretary, Shanita Ho Say Wan, to connect him to Natasha. She buzzed back to inform him that regretfully the "first lady" was away in Dubai to look into the plight of immigrant Pakistani and Kerala workers' orphans there and she switched off.

Kapalin chuckled to himself. "There goes another hundred pairs each of Jimmy Choo and Manolo Blahnik shoes," he chortled loudly. He knew of her exact whereabouts every second of the day. National Director of Police and Security Sri Haniff Hassan Foxwolf would have received his marching orders had he been remiss on that. But it always paid to double check.

Kapalin pulled out his twenty-thousand-dollar, specially encrypted PSB handphone and dialed that delightful number.

"Hmm, who's that?" came back a sleepy, dreamy, languorous but rich and to-die-for voice. It was midday and she was still in bed. But that only added to his excitement.

"Now, now, don't pretend. You know who it is, Aminah," chided Kapalin. Only he knew the number for her twenty-thousand-dollar, specially encrypted PSB handphone.

She laughed a tinkle that melted Kapalin. He stood up from his chair. He had to.

If you have ever observed a female gazelle in full flight on the Serengeti's Endless Plains of Tanzania and Kenya, there's not a deer, or Russian or Romanian gymnast or ballerina, who could match its grace and beauty, for which you would fall on your knees and thank God for that emotion and experience that cannot be described in human words. All that and more was Azalea Dawn Gazelle Chandran.

Dawn, as she loved to be called, won a Hollywood Oscar for her lead role as the eponymous heroine in a tastefully done brilliant screen adaptation of the Marquis de Sade's Justine. She was bestowed the Legion d'honneur by the government of France for her contribution to the revival of French literature and culture. She was Tiger Isle's diva extraordinaire. If anyone deserved to be called first lady for the sheer class and dignity with which she carried herself in public, it was her more than Adhi Gurunadha's wife or that pretender, Big Porka. The public loved and adored her, as did the international media.

There were, however, a few secrets about twenty-eight-year-old Dawn that only Kapalin was privy to.

She was another of Adhi Gurunadha's illegitimate children. That knowledge alone could have made some newspaper reporter or blogger an instant multimillionaire. She was also Kapalin's secret lover and mistress, which every newspaper and tattle-tale gossip magazine editor knew and could not profit from. She was not Kapalin's only mistress; there were a couple of others besides the one-night standers whom he went through like so much loose change over a career now spanning thirty-eight years in government.

But Dawn was THE ONE, special. Were it not for the fact that Natasha knew all his financial finagling and operated for him many of his off-shore nominee bank accounts, Kapalin would have discarded her years ago in favor of Dawn.

He lusted for her so much, he underwrote the entire $200 million production cost of Justine through WLCI, the Washington DC-based PR outfit. It had been engaged earlier by Bhairav and now Kapalin, outwardly to improve Tiger Isle's relations with the USA. In reality they hoped to thwart Maitreya's influence and blacken his name and image wherever and however possible, at the expense of all taxpayers.

The Mossad secretly controlled WLCI. That was apparent to anyone who tracked the careers of retired Israel intelligence officers, several of whom were planted as country heads in WLCI.

Tiger Isle retained the services of WLCI at a measly $100 million a year. Thirty percent of that was secretly paid by WLCI annually as a co-consulting fee to Alpha Consulting Enterprise, Singapore. ACE was led by Kethu Desert Fox Suryan's crony, Redhuan Ong Tai Kuat, a Chinese Muslim convert who had been Kethu's buddy at Harvard. Redhuan reserved $25 million of the $30 million every year for Kethu's personal budget and entertainment requirements whenever he went overseas.

The system never failed its practitioners. In all his wheeling and dealings Kapalin dealt directly only with one person, Haniff Hassan, whom he trusted implicitly and absolutely. Really, he had no choice, as such extensive systematic corruption and looting could not be executed by the president of any country all alone and still ensure his longevity in office.

So Haniff made all the arrangements through WCLI. Its mission was to secure Dawn the lead role in Justine in the face of murderous competition from Hollywood, London, France and even Aishwarya from Bollywood.

But no one else made an offer to Justine's American producer, Cameron Etruscan Spellburger Polski V, a personal token of $40 million, from which Dawn was paid $20 million. Nude and sexually explicit scenes of Dawn/Justine bordered on hardcore pornography. Kapalin's tasteful contributions ensured that the members of the Academy and public were educated into accepting that it was art, as in Picasso.

The glue that cemented the bonds of Haniff's loyalty to Kapalin was none other than "well taken care of." Haniff was worth a cool and useful $300 million. Justine's cost came in at $125 million, but $35 million more was required for several agents of several actresses who had to be negotiated away.

Mission Impossible became Dawn's Waterloo as she finally succumbed in Kapalin's bed after cat-and-mouse games that stretched, besides Kapalin's pants, over a year.

Dawn was half Mongolian. Her real mother, Aminah Gurragchaa, was the wife of a minor official at the Mongolian Consulate in Chandrapore City. Somewhat a free spirit, she had gone alone to Gurunadhapore to catch sight of the New Year celebrations, take in the sights and understand Tigerism. She was swiftly granted a private audience with Adhi Gurunadha.

Later, Adhi Gurunadha and Kapalin had fixed it all up with Tigerist parents and a reddish-orange LP. Soon after giving birth, Aminah returned to Ulaanbaatar, capital of Mongolia, never to return. It had been a small matter of only $2 million. But Adhi Gurunadha could not forget her and would affectionately coo over Dawn as Aminah. It was her good fortune that she looked European and could easily pass for a French Caucasian. To cap it all, Adhi Gurunadha had made sure she took up one foreign language at least besides English. She mastered French at the Alliance Francais Institute at the French Embassy in Chandrapore City. It was surely fated.

"Give me a kiss," she demanded, which Kapalin eagerly and gladly dispatched over the handphone.

"Oh, I have a headache," she feigned.

"Really?" chipped back Kapalin, making sure his tone of voice showed genuine concern and distress. "I have the perfect cure for that my darling," he offered.

"Oh? What's that, Kap? It's really driving me out of my mind."

"Poor thing. Never mind. I'm thinking of the Aman Kila Resort and Spa in Bali. I know the owners. We can get a whole private villa to ourselves with personal masseuses who are the best in the world. They have aromatherapy, ayurvedic treatment, foot reflexology, Shiatsu and Reiki massages. Not to mention those open-air, flower-filled and scented baths you can laze in the whole weekend while listening to your favorite recordings of Rachmaninoff, Randy Crawford, Stevie Wonder and Billy Paul."

"You sure know how to spoil a lady," she squealed.

The long weekend plans of a couple of Ministers and their mistresses had to be hastily rescheduled as Haniff commandeered PAF One for names and destinations classified "Top, Top Secret."

Before Kapalin, the Presidents, Ministers, their wives, entourage and illicit appendages all flew commercial airlines on official and unofficial business. Kapalin found it a little too laissez faire and proletarian to his liking. The perfect excuse arrived when six Muslim Kashmiri separatists accosted and jostled Adhi Gurunadha on board an Air India flight to Jammu from Chennai. They mistook him for a well-known Hindu Indian right-wing leader. Kapalin lashed out that he would not tolerate such "international incidents" or be held hostage to it. He had summoned the Indian Ambassador to his office in Pulijayam for a dressing down.

"There were six Muslim terrorists? That was surely planned!" Kapalin fumed at the Ambassador. He was visibly upset at that most inauspicious of numbers.

A contract was quickly drawn up to lease a specially fitted out "superjumbo" Airbus A380 from PRA, exclusively for the usage of himself and cabinet members, which included Adhi Gurunadha.

Normally, Kapalin would have been flayed alive in Parliament for proposing such an extravagant supplementary bill. By riding on Adhi Gurunadha's name, the bill was passed unanimously without any debate.

The special fit-out inflated contract for $125 million was awarded to PRA President Rambo Jamal Omar's junior secretary and occasional squeeze, Jesslinder Kaur. She gratefully returned $25 million each to UNTA's coffers and Rambo's fake aviation consultancy company in Guernsey, Channel Islands.

PAF One had its own secluded and totally secure entrance and enclosed boarding and disembarking bay at PRIA. Its pilots were specially selected from PRA, retrained in Germany and contracted to the government, not PRA, to fly PAF One and no other aircraft.

"Ah, this is paradise!" exclaimed Dawn as she gazed through her thousand-dollar Prada sunglasses at the azure sky and turquoise-blue sea and took a drag on her special cigarette.

She was covered up to her neck in rose petals in the Balinese outdoor bath. The facemask peel of papaya and cucumber extract would follow soon, expertly applied by the henna-tattooed hands of her exquisitely graceful Balinese attendants. They made the most mundane of tasks, even sweeping the room or making the bed, seem an art form.

Maya and Madura wore Balinese sarongs knotted a little too loosely, at just the swell of their breasts, as they looked after Dawn's and Kapalin's every comfort. Earlier, Dawn had spied amusingly at Kapalin's eyes, darting hither and tither like a frog's furling and unfurling zipping tongue in a mosquito fest. Now, he lay snoring nineteen to the dozen in an adjacent similar bath. Seductive, sweet, cloying rose fragrances danced in the air. At first Kapalin, trembling, wanted to join Dawn in her tub, but he held back as he was really exhausted from work. Besides, he would need all his energy later that night.

Whatever it was about life at the top and the world of Hollywood hustle and national and international politics, it developed a taste for designer drugs and voracious, rapacious and no-holds-barred sex when politicians met divas. In Kapalin's and Dawn's case, they could not achieve satisfaction by conventional sex. They had figured it out by trial and error, putting it down at first to stress, fatigue, the clandestine preparations, anxiety and guilt.

When they finished that night, she was glowing. Not knowing how to satisfactorily express his gratitude and still unabated with lust triggered by her extraordinary beauty, Kapalin held her in an embrace that threatened to squeeze the life out of her.

"Did you?" he asked tenderly.

"Did I? Did I? Like an atom bomb, several atom bombs," she coyly whispered, as she withdrew a little, arched back a bit, cupped him below and caressed and squeezed gently. "Oh, something's stirring again, I suspect," she laughed her throaty, husky laugh.

"Hmm, yes, ignore him. He has no conscience," Kapalin answered with a trace of triumph, as he hugged her closer and whispered in her ears.

But she would not relent and coaxed him with fingers, arms, legs, thighs, breasts, tongue, lips, cheeks and teeth. She reached back to the top of the exquisitely carved Balinese teak bedside table, ripped the packaging open with her teeth and slipped the rubber over his fully erect penis. She snatched the small tube from the folds of the bed cover, where they'd flung it before and squeezed a few droplets of KY jelly onto her palm and transferred it gently over his length. She gracefully slid over on her belly and waited for him.

Kapalin could not believe he could be ready again so soon. But she knew how to get him there and make him ride the pleasure for another half hour. A couple of minutes after they'd finished and cooled down from the thrusting, heaving and panting, she crashed into deep sleep in his arms.

Strangely, Kapalin could not get to sleep straightaway. Something she said earlier was nudging him awake. He tried to dredge it up, but this time the command performance and pleasant exhaustion defeated him. He slowly and reluctantly disengaged himself from his Aphrodite, Athena, Hera and Calypso all-in-one lover, kissed her lips and breasts, then grabbed his handphone and headed for the bathroom. There he locked the door, pressed the handphone keys and played the recording from the start. There it was:

"Like an atom bomb, several atom bombs."

Kapalin smiled widely as it set off a train of lateral thinking that emerged like a comet blazing out from the fourteenth dimension, if one existed. Instead of returning to bed, he quietly exited the bathroom and sat down at the writing desk in the living room. He took out a whole sheaf of unused stationery and began jotting down the ideas as they flowed in a torrent. He finished two hours later. He read and reread his musings.

When he was sure he had memorized all the salient points, he tore the papers, including the unused ones that bore traces of the ballpoint pen's imprint, into tiny pieces and flushed them all down the toilet. Next he took a stingingly cold shower, dried himself thoroughly and splashed on a modest amount of Bvlgari Pour Homme evenly over his whole body. He crawled into bed and slowly slid his body against Dawn's.

"Hmm, is that you again, dearest?" Dawn asked in half-sleep that sent the blood rushing to all parts of his body.

"Yes, bitch! I'm going to fuck you hard a third time and a fourth tonight," he laughed as she jolted around. She could not understand his unusual strength that night, but his use of profanity and coarse language for the first time had gotten her excited in ways she had never thought possible. She was game and ready as never before.

Kapalin of course knew exactly why and from where he would later summon the energy for a fourth invasion of her body that night.

Later, he lay in bed wondering what attracted goddesses like Dawn to him, deluded by his own sense of megalomania and illusions of grandeur, not to mention short-term selective memory. He lived for the thrill of the chase and the moment of conquest before he discarded them, these goddesses and there were many, like his underclothes. But Dawn was truly the exception from those he tossed like slag onto the scrap heap every week.

Haniff had realized it when he had remarked to Kapalin, "My God, do you realize you have created history? At $200 million, that's the most expensive lay in the history of the world."

Well, if $200 million did not come out of your wallet but that of your fellow citizens', it surely was a steal.

Dawn, in turn, was representative, not of an individual, but of a class of women to which honor, dignity, integrity and honesty in a man did not matter and certainly not looks. They were born with several blind spots. They were galvanized, excited, thrilled and turned on by ambition, greed, fame, money and power. More than anything else, they were born without that most important of character traits: self-respect.

If it were just a few like the Kapalins of our world, it would not have mattered. But the world pays for it through the United Nations. They only appoint stunning Hollywood, Bollywood and Honkywood actresses as their ambassadors-at-large to save the children in Africa. Why, to complete the farce, these divas would adopt one or two of these tots, as though only those with a beautiful body and face are endowed with love and compassion for the unfortunate.

Had Kapalin paused to reflect a little more and longer, taken counsel with one or two of the Founding Fathers or even with the council of priests minus Adhi Gurunadha, the smirk might have been wiped off his lips. Tiger Isle might have been saved.

The seductive nature of entrenched evil, corruption and megalomania had, however, penetrated him to his core.

It was too late even as he climaxed and groaned, "Oh, Aminah, my soul mate, I want to marry you!"

The Seduction

"That's pretty clear, I must say, Mr. President. You have covered every angle. I suppose the next step will be for me to get back to my embassy and contact my secretary of state. She'll be very keen to hear what you have proposed and we discussed the past couple of hours, I'm sure," boomed the U.S. ambassador to Pulipore, John Milton Bell IV, in a baronial voice.

He looked every inch the career diplomat he was. So distinguished did he appear, surely he would eventually have been the wealthy chairman of an American international bank or even of Goldman Sachs, had not the U.S. State Department plucked him soon after he graduated from Wharton Business School. They drafted him into government service and fast-tracked it. Two generations of Bells before him had served in the U.S. Navy as admirals and his father as chief intelligence analyst at the CIA. It was whispered in the corridors of Congress that John Milton Bell IV was destined someday soon for the exalted and much coveted secretary of state's post.

"If I may be so bold as to suggest, John, it may, in the interest of national and international security, be an advisable approach if you were to take the first flight to Washington DC and brief Madam Secretary of State yourself, personally. Why, I can get PAF One ready for you in a couple of hours if necessary," Kapalin offered in a very chummy manner.

"Thank you for your generous offer, Mr. President, but we have the most secure communications system in the world you know. Besides she will want to hear about your proposal right away," Bell smirked in a soothing voice.

Kapalin wanted to laugh out loud but restrained himself in the nick of time. The American Embassy, like all the other foreign embassies in Chandrapore City, leaked worse than sieves and colanders. Through WLCI's Tel Aviv- and Taiwan-developed eavesdropping electronic gadgets, the PSB could intercept, decipher and read every cipher message that went in and out of any embassy and every handphone call that invaded the cyberspace over Tiger Isle.

Haniff had a list of every bogus liaison officer and embassy third secretary in Tiger Isle who reported to the CIA, KGB, MI6, MSS China, SIS Australia, DGSE France, SS South Africa, IAS Japan, BIN Indonesia, RIC Malaysia, SID Singapore, NIA Thailand and more. WLCI claimed its list of Mossad agents and intelligence was genuine, but Haniff and Kapalin suspected they were being fed fake names and misinformation. But there was no way for PSB to verify that independently.

"Sure, sure, John, you are absolutely right. Everyone knows Uncle Sam has the best system in the world," Kapalin said. That was true, but theirs and everyone else's system had been compromised by twelve-year-old boy hackers in Russia, Romania and China. "But I also had in mind that I might accompany you to Washington so there'll be no doubt the offer is genuine. I can answer any awkward questions, from the horse's mouth as it were," Kapalin expanded.

Bell was suitably flattered by Kapalin's obsequious pretence and appeared mollified. "Oh, I see, Mr. President. I thought you might be too busy, what with elections and all in the offing soon. Yes, I can see where you are coming from. As you suggest, a personal appearance by you will be worth a thousand words by phone. Yes, I might even be able to get you an audience with President Obama. Would that fit in with your plans?"

Bell had almost given the game away. Only Kapalin, Haniff and WLCI's head knew about the surprise early election he had in mind. Kapalin seethed inside and for a brief second or two flirted with terminating the contracting with WLCI and taking up that KGB offer.

"That'll have to wait a little," Kapalin thought to himself. Aloud he replied, "Certainly, John. If you can swing President Obama and a guided trip on board one of your nuclear submarines like the Ohio Class SLBM or a nuclear-powered warship like the USS Nimitz, I'm your slave for life."

"Ha! Ha!" boomed Bell. "We'll see about that. Sure, why not? I'm sure I can get both the submarine and warship tours arranged. I need a full day to make all the arrangements. We leave day after tomorrow, Mr. President?"

"Yes, that would suit me fine, John. I too need a day to clear a few things. It'll only be me going, but Haniff will liaise with you on the agenda, security, etcetera, ok? And John, please keep it all under your hat. Not even my Vice President or Minister for Foreign Affairs knows about my proposal."

As John Bell IV took leave, Kapalin crossed item number one off the Project X checklist in his head. He buzzed Shanita on the intercom.

"Get me General Vladimir Vissarionovich Lavrenty Trotsky on the secure line straightaway," he ordered. "After that make reservations at Aman Kila Bali for the last Friday, Saturday and Sunday of the month and give the schedule to Haniff. I want the whole Thursday before that Friday with Haniff here. Block all that off in my diary. No specifics. Just write it in as vacation. Got all that?" Kapalin barked.

After he finished with General Trotsky, he fished out his PSB handphone and dialed +62 21 for Jakarta, followed by the number for General (Retd.) Rudy Suknohartono.

"Salaam Aalikum, General. Good afternoon. I'll be in Bali as scheduled. You'll be contacted by Haniff, who will brief you on the funds. But don't wait. You should start doing the groundwork now to reach your president. Do you have any questions? No? Bye."

He flipped the lid closed and tossed the handphone into his in-tray. Only after that did he put his feet up on his desk. Just as he lit up a Cohiba to blow rings into the ceiling and dream his dreams, the handphone alerted him with the ringtone of The Sting. He sighed, shook his head in disgust, picked it up and flipped it open.

"Thakshin," it spoke.

It was going to be one hell of a busy month shuttling between Washington DC, Moscow, Kuala Lumpur, Phuket, Tokyo, Taipeh, Bali and now, Dubai and Bangkok.

Project X

Project X, or PX, classified "top, top, top secret," was actually four projects in one, with a possible fifth on standby. Kapalin had shelved a sixth in fear of superstition, and left that to Thakshin from Thailand and General (Retd) Rudy Suknohartono from Indonesia to attend to.

"Run that by me again," croaked an ashen-faced Haniff Hassan.

"Ho, Ho! I never thought I'd live to see the day your face registered a shock. Ooh, a little fear too, I think. All right, it's quite simple," teased Kapalin.

"The 2010 economic statistics on performances in this region show Singapore with 14 percent seasonally and annually adjusted Y-on-Y growth. They are the top cats. Can you believe that? We are ten times their size and had every advantage they had and more. By comparison with China, India, Korea, Taiwan, Hong Kong, Tokyo, Thailand, Vietnam, Malaysia, Indonesia and the Philippines today, we are just above Bangladesh, Zimbabwe, Botswana, Ethiopia and Somalia. Ditto for FDIs.

At this rate, if we take no precipitate action, Somasundram White Cheetah Chandran's predictions that we will become a bankrupt nation will really materialize, sooner rather than later. But it's too late. Our only way out will be to literally print money, trillions of dollars. Even then we'll only be kidding ourselves, postponing the inevitable for perhaps another two years at most, when our dollar will be worth less than the paper it's printed on.

Almost all our decline has its roots in 'Father of Modern Pulipore' Bhairav's NEA and mega white-elephant cost-inflated projects. It may surprise you, but the social-engineering policies were more devastating in wrecking us than the economic ones. Most of our money is today sitting in offshore tax-haven bank accounts in Jersey, Guernsey, British Virgin Island, Singapore, Geneva, Zurich, Luxembourg, Panama, Cayman Island, Bahamas, Liechtenstein and elsewhere. So, what would you do?

Once before, we took a leaf out of Singapore's book and invested in those life-giving oil refineries and chemical plants. So I am going to take another leaf out of Singapore's book. Do you realize what they have done? No? Let me tell you.

Thirty years ago they started investing heavily in China, gave them a lot of free, sensible advice and became their only real buddies in the world. They did not lecture them on human rights abuses, not in public or in their media anyway. Oh, they lost a few billion dollars initially, but today they are reaping the rewards of foresight.

But you see, the Singaporeans don't trust China any more than they trust the Japanese or the West and certainly less than their immediate neighbors, Malaysia and Indonesia, both Islam-dominated countries.

So, they hedged their investments and bets. They invested billions more dollars in transforming their ports, airports and infrastructure into world-class facilities. Then they invited the USA. Today the U.S. Seventh Fleet and USAF regularly use Singapore's facilities. Others like the Philippines, through misplaced patriotism, drove them away. All I propose to do is take that Singapore strategy to a new level.

We need to counter China internationally and Singapore regionally. I've invited the Americans to set up naval, air force and submarine bases, including those death machines fitted with nuclear-powered engines, ICBM arsenals and hydrogen bombs, in northwest Sivapore. I'm prepared to grant them a 999-year lease for that. They now have Diego Garcia, which is mainly for their Afghan and Middle East forays. Once they establish themselves on Tiger Isle, they will have easy and quick reach of the whole of Asia. The Indian Ocean will truly be theirs.

The Singaporeans are caught between the devil and the deep blue sea. They can't be seen being too chummy with Uncle Sam for fear of riling China and vice versa. I am not bound by those considerations by which they have painted themselves into a corner. All their free-trade agreements with Australia and New Zealand mean nothing. They will be broken the day cheaper alternatives surface from Bangladesh and Pakistan.

But I don't trust the Americans that much either.

So I've invited the Russians to set up a 'research station, marine studies and monitoring base' with 'minimal' military and naval presence, in southwest Sakhthipore, with a 999-year land lease again. And that's two prongs of my hedge.

The third prong will be to form a confederation with Indonesia. Well, Malaya did that with Brunei, Singapore, Sarawak and Sabah in the 1960s to form Malaysia. Brunei and Singapore dropped out early, but Malaysia still lives on, though they don't seem to realize that their real goldmines lie in Sarawak and Sabah.

Why Indonesia, you ask?

They are finally emerging from a long rut, can accommodate Tigerism and absorb us while we can offer them our strategic location. More than that, they can befriend Russia. What's the icing on the cake? They can approach the USA through us without seemingly bootlicking Satan and Communism at the same time.

I've suggested to their president we call the new confederation, Indopore.

Indonesia's official religion, although 85 percent of Indonesians are Muslims, is governed by the Pancasila, which gives us lebensraum. We have four hundred million Indonesians as our godfather in South East Asia, the Americans to neutralize China and the Russians to keep Uncle Sam in check. We don't have to worry about that other emerging giant, India. They haven't invaded anyone in five thousand years and they won't be for another five thousand to come. Isn't that just beyootiful?" Kapalin waxed as he got up excitedly and executed a Michael Jackson kick and judo punch in the air.

"Okay, I get it. But how do we neutralize Singapore? Explain that. After all, as you say, there's the small matter of the Bald Eagle and the Red Dragon of the East to fret about?" Haniff slyly provoked him.

"Oh, try something really difficult, man. It's game over. Tell me, what is the one thing that keeps Singapore afloat?" Kapalin asked.

"Could it be Chicken rice? Or, Old Chung Kee Curry Puff snack food? Sarong Party Girls? Roti John buns? Casinoresortopolis? Geylang china-doll prostitutes? Night Safari? Mentor Minister Lee's memoirs? Talkingcock.com?" Haniff shot back, attempting to inject some humour to the dark atmosphere.

"Nonsense. With one stroke of the pen, Malaysia, Thailand and every country in South East Asia can mimic Singapore's success if they come to their senses," Kapalin spat in dismissive retort.

"It's their strategic location and port, of course," Haniff answered.

"Yes, absolutely. So, how do you make the port disappear?" Kapalin posed.

"Impossible," was Haniff's reply.

"Really? Have you heard of the Isthmus of Kra in Thailand? They have been trying for four hundred years to develop a water throughway to the Far East at the narrowest part of that land link with Peninsular Malaya. The only reason they haven't done it is because the generals there have been plotting against one another to take control and failed. I will not. I have contacted Thakshin in Dubai and he's game. I spoke to the generals and those with extremely close links to the royals. I have the perfect solution.

We'll need $50 billion to excavate and build that forty-four-kilometer canal that peaks at seventy-five meters above sea level at its highest point. It will take five years to complete the Isthmus of Kra Canal, a new route from west to east that saves ships twenty-four hours going around Singapore to get to China and Japan.

It will be like the 1859 Suez or 1904 Panama Canal projects. Thakshin will put together an international consortium to undertake a world-class project. You and I will share in the 10 percent free "sweat equity" allocated to Natasha's maid's Thai husband. The yellow shirts, red shirts and royals in Bangkok are agreeable. The Isthmus of Kra Canal will cut off and isolate that part of southern Thailand in Pattani, Narathiwat and Yala infested with Malay Muslim militant separatists. Everyone will be happy," Kapalin explained.

"That's not going to make Singapore or Malaysia very happy, is it?" Haniff lamented.

"Look, the equity in the project will be allotted 51 percent to Thailand, 15 percent to Malaysia and 34 percent to Singapore, if they want it. They would be foolish to reject that offer. Thakshin will know how to cost in his margin and our 10 percent cut. That's $5 billion for our troubles. A Singapore GLC will also be unconditionally awarded the post-construction operations and maintenance contract. They are the most honest and efficient managers in the world who will make it the most viable and profitable world-class going concern ever. But they can take it, or leave it and perish. I don't care either way.

As for the Malaysians, the sudden influx of two million Malay Muslims is exactly the windfall they have been planning for, I believe. Never mind that it includes not a small lethal group with suicide bombs strapped to its chest and C4 plastic explosives lining its pockets. As for our own ports, they are all hemorrhaging severely. I am going to offer the same terms as the Isthmus of Kra Canal to the Keppel Group in Singapore. That's slam dunk, I believe, Haniff," boasted Kapalin as he slid on his knees along the carpet and posed with a huge smile and chin on fist like a footballer after scoring a spectacular goal.

Kapalin spoke as though he had not been part of the government of thieves since Bhairav's days. He was guilty by association as well as by commission.

"Oh, it slipped my mind. That's four prongs—the USA, Russia, Indonesia and Thailand. You spoke of a possible fifth tine. What's that, Sri?" Haniff reminded him.

"A consortium of Taiwanese and Japanese investors has submitted a very detailed proposal for the direct nego privatization of Mt. Kailas in Sivapore, to make way for the highest golf and country club resort in the world.

Besides a seventy-two-hole PGA-standard golf course, it will include Disney-style theme park, sumo wrestling, sports and athletics stadium, karate, judo and kenjitsu domos, horse riding and hiking trails, shiatsu spas, as well as an ayurvedic university and treatment center, 'Cosmos of Feng Shui Mega Mall' and a sushi and tempura restaurant with pachinko parlor. The Taiwanese have appealed for exemption from dog-meat restrictions, but I've put that on hold until I figure out how I'm going to neutralize the international animal-cruelty movement," Kapalin outlined.

"One heck of a 'countryside-feel' project, don't you think?" Haniff interjected.

Kapalin ignored that remark. "Also, apparently a Japanese boffin has come up with a prototype solar- and/or wind-powered gigantic snow machine that will keep the temperature at Mt. Kailas equable throughout the year. They have offered $120 billion over ninety-nine years on staggered terms with interest thrown in, but I think I can squeeze them for more," Kapalin continued to enlightened Haniff.

Haniff got up to bid good night. But Kapalin was not through with it yet. He was on song.

"Then there's the coup de grace, the sixth prong I've left to Rudy and Thakshin, if Singapore won't negotiate," he announced quietly, pronouncing it "coop de grass."

Haniff slowly sank back into his chair and said, "There's more?"

"Yes, the three sea bridges," Kapalin whispered.

"Three, not one?" Haniff asked.

"You know what your problem is, Haniff? You think too small. About two thousand years ago, the aborigines used to walk over from Sumatra to Melaka on the west coast of Peninsular Malaysia. There was another isthmus there that explains why before that, there was little mention of Malaya in old historical records. Boats and larger ships could not get through that impasse. So they took the land route through Burma and Thailand to get to China, as superstition forbade them from going around the unchartered waters of west and south Sumatra. When it disappeared due to rising sea levels, it opened up the Straits of Melaka.

Now if we build a toll bridge linking Melaka with Sumatra, guess who will no longer drive to Singapore via the old causeway or the new second link after it's reduced to a secondary port when the Isthmus of Kra Canal is completed? Thais and Malaysians will be able to drive to Sumatra and stretch their ringgit more, shopping and holidaying there.

"Why, I've been talking to one or two of Malaysia's former Prime Ministers in Kuala Lumpur and they seemed very, very excited and enthusiastic about it," Kapalin let on.

"No. No way. Not the crooked-bridge specialist Prime Minister. You wouldn't, would you?" cried out Haniff in horror.

Kapalin laughed loudly. "No. Not a crooked bridge. We need one that goes all the way to the other end, unlike one they planned to end in the middle of the Straits of Johor. I have in mind first a toll bridge linking Sivapore to the Isthmus of Kra. A second one will link Shakthipore with Aceh. Together with the Melaka-Sumatra bridge that will be three. The full damage will be $100 billion over five years.

Thakshin, General Rudy Suknohartono and the Malaysians will put together another international consortium funded by sovereign guarantees from Thailand, Malaysia and Indonesia to get it off the ground.

Rudy is already talking about a fourth sea bridge over the Sunda Straits linking Sumatra and Java. That I think will be the final nail in Singapore's coffin, unless, of course, they cooperate with us.

Oh, there will be billions of dollars worth of consultancy contracts for wind, sea and wave action and salt-water corrosion and erosion studies, environmental-impact assessments and the works. We'll have a beauty contest of all the world-class architects and get them to draw up the RFPs for bridge-engineering and construction companies, excluding anyone from China or Singapore. There's another $10 billion for us. And that's it Haniff, I've actually finished," Kapalin concluded and then danced a jig around his desk.

Haniff dreamed of his one-third share and possibly billions more from the privatization of Mt. Kailas and the three if not four sea bridges as well. Kapalin fantasized about saving Tiger Isle from descending to fourth-world status and of himself becoming the world's first trillionaire.

The reality was it revealed the stark paucity of intellectual depth and sensitivity of the barren soul in these two men. Their plans were more bent than any crooked bridge in Johor Bahru in southern Peninsular Malaysia. Drunk with power and blinkered by years of abuse they had gotten away with, neither of them realized what Kapalin was actually proposing.

It was the greatest sellout of any nation and its people in the history of the world.

More than all that, it was surely the harbinger of global doom, the match that would light the fuse for the shattering explosion of World War III, the war of all wars to end civilization forever.

Three Desires/Vices

If religion is the opiate of the masses, as it pretty much is in most of Asia and the Middle East, then Tiger Isle was the drug capital of the world.

It did not help that most Tigerists lived in a state of denial, in particular about their religion. It was obvious to the most learned of neutral scholars that the Tiger Puranam was written and revised by men several times, long after 200 CE. A few would even place the advent of the Puranam and Tigerism after the arrival of Islam in 632 CE.

It was a clever and cunning child of its time, as it drew extensively with a clear touch of genius from earlier religions and fused them into Tigerism with great scholastic skill. "WE are and WE shall be for all time your ONLY God for there are or were none others…. All other gods and prophets who claimed to be so before, now and those who may lay claim otherwise in the future shall all be false gods and prophets" seemed a little too prophetic even in a world that hung on every quatrain of Nostradamus.

But then, could not the same be said of another popular religion or even three or four?

The Tigerists had to dig in, as their creed held no currency in a greater part of the world where the new religion was money. In a nation where a purportedly free-market economic and democratic model, in reality "some will forever be more equal than others," was as skewed as was its bent religion and religious bent, equilibrium could only be maintained by leaders through a system that perpetuated iron-fisted rule and blind hero-worship.

Adhi Gurunadha and his cult were thus firmly entrenched as the fifth force. Anyone who contemplated a long-term career in politics or high office, or a senior high position in government, would not dare embark upon such a path without the blessings and patronage of the incumbent Adhi Gurunadha.

The present Gurunadha was said to be the thirteenth in his line. The first five, though not documented anywhere, were said to have each held office for over two hundred years. Opinions were divided as to whether thirteen in this context signified good or bad.

A small band of defrocked clerics, branded as heretics, claimed to have copies of a version of the Puranam referred to as the Satanic Pelt. It foretold the cessation of the line of the Adhi Gurunadhas after the thirteenth, and it made vague references to its revival much later in "a golden land." The Satanic Peltists held that theirs was the original Puranam written on the rarest of white tiger skin.

Shortly after Kapalin took office in 2004, and before his one-hundred-days performance review was due, secret opinion polls showed the president's popularity at a shockingly low 25 percent. It was a "never before" in Tiger Isle history. However, pro-government and pro-Kapalin bloggers, fed by the Independent Opinion Station, both part of UNTA's secretly funded spin-doctoring apparatus, saturated blogosphere with the news that the new president had garnered 70 percent favorable public approval. It was yet another "never before" in Tiger Isle's history.

Kapalin, of course, did not swallow his own excreta and realized something had to be done quickly, or he would go down in the Guinness Book of Records as having enjoyed the shortest tenure of any president, yet another "never before." Fortune appeared to come to his rescue in the form of a highly incendiary and explicit DVD that landed on his desk courtesy of Haniff Hassan and his Special Branch.

It contained an hour-and-a-half-long footage of Adhi Gurunadha in a no-holds-barred ménage à trois sex romp with two young voluptuous actresses who had not quite attained star status yet. It was entrapment pure and simple. Gurunadha's sexual escapades and indiscretions were well known to the PSB. Bhairav had been briefed about it during his time.

The Bhairav years had seen an explosion of wealth and elite Pulirajaputrans were raking it in by the billions. With easy and tainted money came bulging guilty consciences. Temple collections swelled and flowed in rivers from all over Tiger Isle to the bank accounts of Gurunadhapore's Tiger Sangam, operated and controlled absolutely by Gurunadha.

The thirteenth Gurunadha had succumbed to the three vices: wine, women and cash. But with one eye on massive modernization and the other on simultaneously lining his children's pockets, Bhairav let sleeping dogs lie. He saw no percentage in getting on the wrong side of a man worshiped as a living god.

Kapalin had no such qualms. If Bhairav was a control freak, Kapalin was in the super class of it. He did not have the same level of grassroots political support as Bhairav once had. He wanted Gurunadha under his thumb to improve his PR via "God who walks on Earth." More than that, the cunning man with Stalin's face needed Gurunadha's wholehearted, if not public than certainly tacit, involvement and support in wrecking permanently the career of the one man in Tiger Isle he and Bhairav too, feared more than any other, i.e Maitreya Blue Dolphin Suryan.

Kapalin, a stickler for protocol, made a personal trip to Gurunadhapore with incriminating evidence in hand to confront His Holiness and cement further his assured place in hell. At their one-to-one private meeting, the extraordinarily youthful-looking sixty-year-old Gurunadha seemed bored and unfazed by it all. He was no mere prayer-bead-twirling and holy Tigerist, Sanskrit- and Pulish-verse-spouting village priest.

He had a first-class degree in theology and comparative religion from Oxford, spoke five European languages fluently, and Japanese, Mandarin, Hindi and Tamil as well. He could hold his own with Oxford, Harvard and Benares dons. Here was a man whom the pope consulted and who had more gravitas in public and private than Kapalin and Bhairav put together.

He saw through Kapalin in an instant and scoffed inwardly when Kapalin waffled on about how he had personally intervened in ensuring the DVD did not get posted on YouTube. He snorted loudly, which Kapalin misunderstood, when he let on that Maitreya and DJP were behind a huge conspiracy to topple His Holiness and undermine Tigerism and UNTA to gain political support from weak Tigerists, Hindus, Christians, Buddhists and Muslims. As Kapalin was about to launch into a ringing prepared speech about the dastardly Maitreya and his "terrorists in sheep's clothing" supporters, Gurunadha held up his hands for silence.

"I have no illusions about myself, Sri President. Power has corrupted, and absolute power absolutely corrupted me. I believe that's emblematic of the times across the world. I am guilty as charged," he spoke with remarkable sangfroid in a cultured, soft, but firm voice.

"Let's skip the games. Haniff has already hinted to me the conspiracy you'd like to hatch to get rid of Maitreya. It's a simple enough matter.

You will be contacted with the name of a girl you can employ for your charade. Make sure you take care of her financially and that she's not harmed. The rest, I will leave to you and your mafia. I don't want to know the details now or ever. I don't care either way what the actual end outcome is. You will make sure nothing bounces back on me. My father before me, and I, have always enjoyed very mutually beneficial relations with past presidents and when dealing with UNTA. Whatever you do, don't upset the status quo.

Two things before you leave. First, you will return all copies of the incriminating DVDs to me by tomorrow. You and Haniff will sign a letter for my retention confirming that's the case. Second, and this is more important than anything else we've talked about today, if the slightest harm befalls Aminah, I'll have your carcass and entrails hanging from the top of the Tiger Thoon in Mt. Kailas. I trust I have made myself clear." So, saying, Gurunadha dismissed

Kapalin, who slunk out feeling very ill and as though he had been savagely raped on all fronts and had paid for it from his own back pocket, without any resistance or protest.

Arrest and Trial

It was a trial that played right into Maitreya and DJP's hands. It split Tiger Isle right down the middle. Maitreya could not have dreamed of an earlier Christmas gift than the one that Kapalin, with Gurunadha's tacit but culpable complicity and Bhairav's public approval too, contrived to hand over to him on a silver platter.

The Chief Justice and his bewigged dishonorable brethren at the High Court, Court of Appeal and Federal Court, the director of public prosecution, Haniff Hassan and his Keystone Cops, medical experts and the full machinery of the UNTA-controlled MSM stumbled over themselves as they swung into mass action to ingratiate themselves with Kapalin and UNTA for rewards of unbelievable fortunes.

It appeared to the world that it was only a question of when Maitreya would have to start serving time, a long time, in Bay of Pigs in company with his bosom pal and comrade-in-arms Kirpal Singh.

The charge was simple and straightforward enough:

"That you, Maitreya Blue Dolphin Suryan of...born on...and holder of Pulipore local passport number...did so willfully at the time of...on the day and month of the year...engage in non-consensual violent sex against Ms...of...born on...and holder of... Pulipore local passport number...at the premises at...in violation of Section...of the penal code...punishable by imprisonment for a duration of not less than ten years and not more than twenty years...and six strokes of the cane as specified.

"That further to the foregoing and aforementioned you did on the day of...willfully insert your...into...and...into...Ms...thereby having non-consensual violent carnal knowledge of Ms...against the order of nature in violation of Section...of the penal code...

punishable by imprisonment for a duration of not less than ten years and not more than twenty years…and six strokes of the cane as specified."

"Opposition leader charged with multiple counts of violent rape…unnatural non-consensual sex…Tigerist lady forced into sex slavery," the headlines screamed. The NPST, fed by all sorts of information and documents leaked by the DPP, had next tried Maitreya in print and demanded the law be changed with retrospective effect so that Maitreya could be legally castrated for his "heinous crimes against humanity."

By law, the identity of a rape victim could not be disclosed in any form of media until the trial commenced. But details were exposed in various blogs like TJ4KWLC or Truth and Justice for Kamala Willow Leaf Chandran replete with scanned copies of charge sheets, photos, medical reports etcetera. It clearly served to incriminate rogue elements within the police force and DPP's office.

Maitreya and his lawyers remained cool throughout the six months it took for the trial to commence after declaring, "Not guilty" at the plea-motion stage. They maintained calm even when they discovered the CJ had manipulated the rosters to ensure that the Right Dishonorable Octavius Sextus Saul, popularly referred to among the legal fraternity as the "Hanging Judge" and "Whiskey-Water Saul" would preside over the hearing.

While Maitreya's lawyers and investigators worked on the conspiracy theory, they submitted affidavits specifying a defense of "innocent by irrefutable alibi" based on Maitreya's office and personal diaries and supporting documents and proof that indicated he had been in Washington DC on the date of the alleged crime.

In turn, DPP Ganesh Patel immediately amended the charge from "on the day of" to "on or about the month of" in the face of local and international condemnation. Nevertheless, Saul who was as compliant as a fresh rubber band accepted the amendment.

Maitreya next submitted a fresh affidavit backed up again by his diaries, statutory declarations by his personal secretary, office staff and several MPs and supported further by his international passport, air tickets, hotel bills, TV footages and MSM articles. The SD stated that for a period of three months, spanning either side of the new date for the alleged rape incident, he had not set foot in Chandrapore.

The police and PSB swung into action with joint raids of Maitreya's and his lawyers' offices and residences. They confiscated all their diaries. Soon after, Patel submitted yet another amended charge sheet stating the crime was committed "on or about the month of January 1999," for which period Maitreya had a gap in his diaries. The delightfully resilient rubber band stretched itself nicely for the DPP again.

The next crack in the prosecution's case was riven when a pro-DJP blog revealed a scanned statement that the police had suppressed. Ms. Willow Leaf, an incredibly sexy and pectorally well-endowed part-time model and PNTVS4 soap-opera actress, had originally "confessed" to an "incident" with Maitreya that she claimed had occurred in 1997 when she was nineteen.

She professed to be a born-again Tigerist and claimed higher moral ground for her belated accusation. All efforts by the PSB to trace the identity of the bloggers behind TJ4MBDS or Truth and Justice for Maitreya Blue Dolphin Suryan failed as the account was registered in London.

The news quickly surfaced in other pro-DJP blogs. Bar the alleged rape at her upmarket condo in downtown Chandrapore City, as detailed in her signed statement and SD, Willow Leaf could not recollect the venues of even one of seven other horrendous rapes also allegedly committed on her by Maitreya.

The bloodhounds sniffed everywhere and discovered Willow Leaf had married and divorced in 2002. She had not contested the award of custody of her baby son to her ex-husband. While the NPST and UNTA-controlled MSM suddenly went to earth, pro-Maitreya and DJP bloggers went to town. They demanded the DPP withdraw the case, which now boiled down to one woman's word against one man. There was no credible forensic evidence to authenticate or substantiate rape, oral and anal sex, or a single witness' corroborative SD to reinforce it.

On the opening day of the trial it was a supremely confident defense legal team of five that entered the courtroom, exchanging high fives and chest clashes like American NFL players. Judge Octavius Sextus Saul, suitably fortified by earlier downing two swift shots of Black Label whiskey, banged his gavel and called the court to order. But it was Maitreya's lead counsel, Christopher Raja Nair, who surprisingly stood up first.

"My Lord, we humbly move that the charges against our client, Maitreya Blue Dolphin Suryan, be dismissed forthwith."

"Order! Order!" bellowed Saul as pandemonium broke out. Saul banged the gavel down hard on a wooden block several times. "For God's sake counsel, the DPP has not even called his first witness. This had better be good, or I will not hesitate to charge you with contempt of court and let you cool your heels for a week in the court lockup."

"My Lord, this is preposterous. It's a puerile attempt by defense counsel to disrupt and delay proceedings. This is grandstanding and an attempt to bring into disrepute this court, the CJ, our nonpareil legal system and our great leader, President Kapalin. I shall be filing misconduct charges with the Bar Council later. I demand you cite all of them for contempt of court immediately," a furious and red-faced DPP Ganesh Patel howled.

"Sit down counsel, sit down. This is my courtroom and not a forum for election speeches. Let our learned counsel Nair proceed," ruled Saul and motioned Patel to get back to his chair.

"My Lord, the charge reads that the alleged rape and unnatural sexual acts were allegedly committed at the alleged victim's condominium at Iguana Villa in January 1999. We now have proof, delivered to us only yesterday evening, that the construction of the Iguana Villa building in question did not commence until March 1999 and was certified fit for occupation in December 2001," smirked Nair. After walking over to Saul and handing him a thick file of documents, he exchanged more high fives with Maitreya and co-counsel on the way back to his chair.

Saul and Patel pored over certified copies of condominium-construction and project-management contracts. They sifted through design blueprints signed off by Chandrapore's leading architects, Cubist Tiger Design. They stared again and again at the city hall certificate of fitness.

The "public" comprised some twenty mostly pro-UNTA journalists, fifty police and PSB officers, a few observers from the International Law Society, a couple of U.S. senators, top aides from the USA, the UK, Australia and European embassies and fifteen Puliporeans who had queued up at 5:00 a.m. for PSB screening. It held its breath. All looked around at each other and smiled at what was clearly turning out to be a farce and egg on the face of the DPP, police and PSB.

Foreign journalists and press agencies that had failed to apply to the police for accreditation were barred entry to the hearing. Haniff Hassan, who was sitting right at the back in the courtroom, could be seen holding his head in his hands and studiously gazing down at the mosaic tiles on the floor as if he'd discovered a new Renoir there.

"In your learned and honest opinion, counsel, are these documents not irrelevant to your case?" Saul asked Patel in a half-strangled voice.

The audience broke up in stitches.

"Silence! Silence! I will not hesitate to clear the courtroom if more such hooliganistic behavior persists. Bailiffs, take note," roared Saul.

They burst out in uncontrollable laughter again as they knew they would be leaving the courtroom in a matter of five minutes anyway. A black-faced Saul pretended to not notice that eruption.

DPP Ganesh Patel realized he was being thrown a life-line. "My Lord, we need time to study these new documents. We request a discontinuance. We will not be held hostage to ambush tactics and an utter lack of professionalism by the defense."

"Ambush tactics? Ambush tactics? Trial by ambush? Lack of professionalism or integrity?" growled Nair, as he stood up to his full six-foot-two height and walked over to Ganesh Patel. With his dark and African-like features he looked like a black panther cornering a plump baby wild boar. Patel involuntarily cowered in his seat.

"Till today we have not received a single scrap of statement, evidence, medical report, materials, or witness list from you, due us legally under mandatory legal discovery laws. This has been systematically denied us by this court, the Court of Appeal and the Federal Court with the peculiar ruling that our lordship has not denied us our rights in finality.

When we ask our lordship here, he says if we are not happy with his ruling, we can appeal to the higher courts. If ever there was a conspiracy, we are seeing it here today. The whole world is witness to it. We will not, I repeat, we will not put up with this ping-pong game for one second longer, you hear me?" Nair argued.

"Will a month…" began Saul and paused as he was cut short by Nair.

"We object!" Nair protested.

"On what grounds?" Saul demanded.

"My Lord, the documents have been authenticated by the director general of public works, senior registrar of courts and the senior most sitting judge of the Federal Court, the highest court in the land. So, the DPP will really be wasting everybody's time investigating further" Nair submitted.

"Nonsense!" objected Patel. "We have to look at the case in its holistic sense. We have other evidence, DNA and medical reports."

"Ah yes, medical reports that will prove she was not a virgin before her marriage in 2002? The rest of the world doesn't have one, but I presume you have an expert Tigerist doctor who will testify as to scars in her anal tract and mouth that prove she could only have had anal and oral sex before her marriage in 2002? Or of injuries on her body that could only have been inflicted in 1999? Do tell us, my learned friend," Nair invited in the slyest of tones.

"We have lots more incriminating evidence you don't know about, like bed sheets, mattresses and semen stains that match the accused's DNA profile to perfection," Patel divulged in panic.

"Ah, but we do know about it. You mean your star witness kept souvenirs of semen-stained bed sheets and mattresses for the past five years, even though no sexual contretemps with my client could have taken place in her condo, which was under construction at the time as originally claimed by the accused?

And what about that statement of rape made in 1997? As far as he or we are aware, my client has never provided DNA samples to anyone in his life. Then again how will you prove it was violent rape and not consensual sex? You don't have a single eyewitness to a crime you say took place five years ago," Nair shot back.

"Enough, enough. We have not heard from a single witness and the two of you are already debating about the quality of the evidence. I'm granting the prosecution a discontinuance. We'll meet again in one week's time," ruled Saul, banged his gavel and vanished before anyone else had a chance to move or object.

When the trial resumed a week later, two groups of sullen lawyers appeared in Saul's court. One was the defense, subjected to tension although they were, by any account, in an unassailable position. The other, the prosecution, suffered a horrible sleepless week of brainstorming on how to snatch victory from the jaws of defeat.

They were seemingly saved by none other than Bhairav's son, Duryodhana, now a junior Minister in Kapalin's cabinet. In 2002, Bhairav, planning ahead for postretirement insurance against any witch-hunting and backstabbing moves by his future successor, had pushed through Duryodhana's candidacy for a Parliament safe-seat by-election. Following that, he threatened and bribed UNTA's members into voting in Duryodhana as one of five Youth Wing Vice Presidents at UNTA party elections. Duryodhana, in consultation with Haniff, came up with Plan B.

Saul had deliberately forsaken his Black Label that morning. Alone in his chambers, he had gotten down to the serious business of begging God for a smooth passage before heading out to open court.

He looked down at DPP Ganesh Patel. He secretly wished Patel and everyone else would disappear. Then he could return to his chambers and reach for the bottle he so ached for. "Proceed," he ordered.

"My Lord, may I approach the bench with learned counsel for the defense?" requested Patel in his most engaging manner.

Outwardly, Saul smiled; inwardly he groaned and then screamed silently in rage. His instincts told him Patel's request was going to be bad for him. He would have dismissed the charges a week ago, were it not for the shotgun the CJ and PSB held over his head. He was in serious debt from a compulsive gambling habit and the casinos were threatening to expose him. The $20 million Haniff promised him would enable him to not only get a fresh start, but mend fences as well with his wife, who was struggling in Sydney to make ends meet putting their three children through high school and university.

"Proceed," Saul motioned.

"My Lord, we propose one final amendment to the charges against the accused," Patel whispered.

Saul held his hand up to silence Nair. "What's it going to be this time? No, let me guess. You have a Google Earth satellite picture of the accused raping the victim and engaging her in sodomy, not in her condo, but on the rooftop of Pulipetro Tower. Am I right?"

"Very droll, my Lord. Very witty. But no. We have firm evidence the accused bribed a very senior PSB officer to try to intimidate the victim into retracting her accusation. That's attempted perversion of justice and abuse of power. We have here the new charge," beamed Patel, as he dug into his briefcase.

Saul stared at Patel, then at Nair and then at Patel again.

"Let's adjourn to my chambers where we can talk informally," Saul ordered.

As they entered his lordship's lair, Saul snapped and let fly with, "Motherfucker! Are you seriously telling me that after all the previous amendments and painting a picture of violent rape and dirty and illegal sex, you now want to drop it all? And substitute it with a poncy charge of one man's word against another. I'm sure you have no damning tape recordings or DVDs, do you?"

"No, my Lord, we don't. But our witness is the number three in the PSB, so his integrity is unimpeachable. He's served the government loyally for thirty-five years and will be retiring next year. It's all true. As leader of the opposition with an openly stated ambition of toppling the government, Maitreya is capable of indulging in any crime to ensure his march to Pulijayam will not be interrupted," Patel expanded.

"Oh ho ho! That's the very reason this PSB officer's silly testimony will be very peachable. I'm sure he will get a humongous golden handshake for saving the Government's behind. It's a little too convenient a little too late, your Lordship. Patel will make you look a fool in your own court if you accede to his amendment and then we tear the PSB officer's credibility to shreds on the stand in open court. The whole world is watching you know. Think carefully my Lord," warned Nair, who held his fury in check, only just.

"This is ridiculous," moaned Saul. "I too am due to retire soon after forty years on the bench and this trial is going to be what they will remember me for? I can put up with "Hanging Judge," but what you are asking me, Patel, is to stab myself to death. Shit! Damned if I do, damned if I don't. Anyway, let's take a break and reconvene after lunch at 2:00 p.m." Never had any rubber band looked more flaccid and beyond resurrection than now.

But that instinctive move by Saul is what really saved him in the end.

Shortly before noon, Nair received a brown package by Tigerex courier while having lunch with his team and Maitreya in his room at the court complex. It contained a shiny DVD. When he slipped it into the player in his laptop, they were all entertained by an hour-and-a-half-long footage of Adhi Gurunadha in a no-holds-barred ménage à trois sex romp with two young voluptuous actresses, one of whom who had now attained star status.

One of those voluptuous actresses bore an uncanny resemblance to Kamala Willow Leaf Chandran. The high fives and chest clashes flowed once more amid breakdancing and Native American whoops. They sent a carefully worded, bootlicking request to Saul and Patel to reconvene first in the judge's chambers at 2:00 p.m.

When they had completed viewing the pornographic DVD, a deathly silence descended on the chambers.

Patel broke it when he exclaimed, "Bloody hell! They can't now ask me to charge Gurunadha as well, can they?"

Saul sprang from his leather chair and smacked Patel across his lips. "Shut up! If I were you, I would be drafting my resignation letter and thinking of a new career in private practice. Don't speak again unless spoken to. There's obviously a deeper game being played here than even the CJ or Haniff and PSB are aware of, probably even the president." He looked up at Nair and Maitreya. "Any suggestion what course we should take?" Saul begged.

Later that afternoon, Saul announced his decision in open court to grant the prosecution a discontinuation of proceedings for a week to enable them to provide all legal discovery documents to the defense before they called Willow Leaf to the stand.

A week later Saul announced, in very sad demeanor and voice to a stunned overflowing courtroom, that the prosecution's key witness, Willow Leaf, had been admitted in a deep coma to the intensive care unit (ICU) of Chandrapore's most modern of private hospitals, the Gurunadha Specialist Medical Center. Apparently, she had suffered a serious stroke from a burst brain aneurysm and collapsed in her condo.

The case was adjourned sine die until Willow Leaf recovered and was able to testify in court. Thousands of anti-Maitreya and UNTA supporters visited Willow Leaf in the hospital and prayed she would recover whole soon. DJP supporters did so to satisfy themselves it was not all a hoax to save the government from conspiracy charges. Many in Tiger Isle and abroad were already calling for Kapalin's resignation.

Almost a year later, breaking news revealed Willow Leaf had contracted lung cancer while comatose in ICU. Willow Leaf breathed her last in late December 2005, succumbing to a most virulent form of cancer.

A most peculiar event took place in mid-2006.

None of the newspapers published it, nor was it announced by any TV station. Included in that year's President's Honors List was an award of the title of "Sri" to one Christopher Raja Nair. Never before, or since, had any known opposition supporter been honored so.

Judge Octavius Sextus Saul's receipt of a "Sri" title that year was of course expected and became common knowledge. Soon after receiving it and a huge ex-gratia payment of $10 million for a half-completed job that the public knew nothing about, he departed to Australia, never to return.

Patel quit law and opened a sandwich-and-soup deli shop.

The truth, however, was that Maitreya did have glorious and rough sex with Willow Leaf in 1997 and 1999. It was totally consensual. There was hardly any Tiger Isle politician who did not have premarital and extramarital sex or multiple-partner sex. The higher the office, the more they attracted admirers like bees to the honey pot. Many came purely to enjoy, and others to, milk the cows of plenty.

Willow Leaf had been indiscreet about Maitreya to Gurunadha and when the PSB entrapped him, he decided to have some fun and games. He decided to pit Maitreya against the might of the establishment. In his own way Gurunadha realized that the excesses of UNTA and its presidents of late were pushing Tiger Isle dangerously to the edge of the precipice. It was more a test of Maitreya's mettle than that of Kapalin.

When Haniff's and Patel's lack of thoroughness and their abject, absolute ineptness, threatened to make Tiger Isle the laughingstock of the world, Gurunadha decided the game had gone too far and had the DVD couriered to Nair. Nair's reward was earned by his genius in concluding the charade without any of the big figures being directly implicated, publicly embarrassed, or hurt.

It was Nair who instructed Haniff to find a Willow Leaf lookalike terminal cancer patient, who, with a little makeup, could pass for the real one when viewed through the thick viewing window glass at the hospital ICU. They found one easily enough who readily agreed to it when promised the government would spare no expense in providing her with the best cancer treatment money could buy and if she recovered they would find another substitute. Nair left it to Haniff and the PSB to manage the doctors and that was a cinch as the center was owned by Gurunadha.

Nair, through Maitreya's briefings to him over many years, also realized that Willow Leaf's life was in jeopardy. She would be a constant source of danger to Gurunadha, who was not beyond terminating her life like he might casually step on an ant. So he also instructed Haniff to spirit Willow Leaf away to California. There, she was provided with sufficient funds for a face lift and a comfortable lifestyle for the rest of her remaining days.

Gurunadha admired that strategic thinking brain of Nair's and agreed to all his "suggestions." He made it clear to Haniff, though, that he would have to get the money from Kapalin for "this black op," as he put it.

Yet, Gurunadha made an elementary error, as most with overblown egos sometimes do. Nair and Maitreya burned several copies of the DVD, which they stashed away in their safe deposit boxes in Tiger Isle and in Geneva.

Yet another outcome of the Willow Leaf affair was the creeping into Tiger Isle legal circles of the expression "to do a Saul," meaning, "to idiotically attempt to or actually classify something irrefutably incriminating as irrelevant."

Allies Without Borders

During the trial and before that at candlelight vigils, DJP gatherings, debates, panels and public protests against the Maitreya conspiracy, many had noticed the unfailing appearance of a thirtyish, attractive lady in black sporting huge, dark sunglasses and a hairstyle that hid much of her face. In court, when challenged by the bailiffs, she produced a fake medical certificate confirming her sunglasses were for correcting an eye condition and not a vanity or fashion statement.

The lady in black mingled freely with members of the foreign press, news agencies, embassies, United Nations and human rights NGOs. She could be seen requesting their calling cards but not offering hers. She talked to the twentysomething doctorate-holding Frenchwoman Sophie from Advocates Without Borders and the equally twentysomething doctorate-holding human rights activist and Spanish woman Julia from Allies Without Borders and a dozen other twentysomething doctorate-holding girls from NGOs based in London, Glasgow, Brussels, Geneva, California, Toronto, Sydney and from all over the West.

She told them all she was past fifty (and they all protested and said, "No, you are joking.") and how much she was impressed and inspired by the work they did. She shed genuine tears as she congratulated them for their courage in leaving the comfort of their first-world status countries to travel to the backwaters of places like Tiger Isle to walk the talk for freedom and democracy. She confessed to them she was nowhere near as well educated as them and wished she could start her life all over again because no one had told her or shown her that the so-called weaker sex could actually compete on equal footing with men and in their cases achieve more.

Only now, regretfully, was she beginning to realize the true extent of the cloistered and irresponsible existence she had led. She wanted to talk to them day and night to know and learn more. They took her into their hearts not because she was like them, a woman, but because they recognized a kindred soul when they saw one.

The lady in black marveled at the intensity of their commitment to their cause, their fearlessness and their sincerity. They in turn told her that if Tiger Isle had just five more women like her, that was all it would take to create a bright, brave new dawn. She asked for help and they did not just promise her and go away. When she contacted them by secure email from Singapore, they responded not with homilies or mere platitudes and rhetoric. They wrote back, asking when she could visit them and in whose name they should send the fully paid air tickets to.

With the clandestine support of Kirpal, Maitreya and DJP, and now her foreign friends who guided her on how peaceful revolutions are achieved step by step, Rekha Krishnasamy Roshan prepared herself late in life for a complete makeover and change in lifestyle, life goals and legacy. She had not forgotten about the pursuit of happiness, for that was an integral part of her new direction. But of late she had reached beyond her grasp and sensed a tantalizing heaven beyond that she could no more ignore than if Mandela or Cheah Thye Poh were to step across the threshold into her house.

She was responding to an ancient part of her soul, for she sensed impending danger all around her. By the end of the Maitreya trial saga she realized, as did many, many others, that thugs controlled every facet of life on Tiger Isle, from religion to government to the generals, the CJ, the courts, the judges, the prosecutors, the police and even the taxi drivers. One might think that the doctors were the last bastion against corruption and untimely death and one would be palpably wrong.

Slowly, but surely, the tide was beginning to turn. Kapalin paid a huge price for his miscalculation. As cunning and Machiavellian as he was, he had underestimated Gurunadha's intelligence, born of eighteen centuries of manipulating kings and princes and lulling them into a false sense of security.

Kapalin compounded his mistake further by calling for early general elections in November 2006. The backlash from the failed persecution of Maitreya came home to roost. UNTA barely won half the votes. For the first time since independence, UNTA lost its two-thirds majority control of Parliament. With it went the Tigerists' power to amend the constitution as they pleased. Maitreya and DJP made huge gains.

The writing was clearly on the wall and Kapalin had to muster every ounce of support to keep hold on the presidency. He needed to pull a rabbit out of the hat before the next general elections or be satisfied with being a mere footnote in history. The sharks scented blood from afar and were heading for the kill, as yet some distance away.

The biggest and most dangerous of the super order of these Selachimorpha was the shark which swam on land and was a half, if not a full, Indian Constitutional Tigerist Puliporean who went by the name of Adhi Sri Dr. Bhairav Oak Broad Leaf Sivan.

Dawn's Dusk

She had known of her husband's infidelities even before she snared and married him. She was money ambitious and realized she had the looks but not quite the talent to make it as an actress in even the $1 million per-movie bracket. Natasha was therefore prepared to overlook Kapalin's flirtations and premarital and extramarital affairs as long as he kept feeding her the overinflated billion-dollar contracts.

Nevertheless, she kept close watch on him. Natasha, as Kapalin's third wife, knew the tenuous links by which marriages such as her hung by. Now that she had the money, it dawned on her that there was no real love with Kapalin. Had she not wormed into his money-churning empire and knew and held the strings to all his numerous off-shore nominee bank accounts, she might well have been consigned to the scrap heap a long time ago.

Still, the sight of those photographs and DVDs shocked and induced nausea in her. She was paralyzed and bedridden for two days. She cancelled her usual engagements to visit orphanages and old folk's homes, with the press right behind. She even ran up a temperature from all the throwing up and headaches and the sleeping pills she took. Nothing worked to get rid of that nagging pain and that sinking, queasy feeling in the pit of her stomach.

It had cost her a cool $250,000. But it was worth it. It confirmed her suspicious that not only was Kapalin's affair with Dawn more than a casual fling but that it was a serious threat to her marriage and survival. Deputy National Director of Police and Security Sri Abu Bakar Greyhound Suryan, number two to Haniff Hassan Foxwolf, had personally delivered the incriminating evidence to her.

She had made a pact with him when he had first been assigned to take charge of her security details. Natasha had promised him that she would block any attempt by anyone to leapfrog him to the number-one position should Haniff be cashiered, retire prematurely, or retire when his term was up, in return for his absolute loyalty to her. It was the norm on Tiger Isle that party loyalists and apple polishers, men and women, were promoted over the heads of their seniors and more qualified and experienced peers.

It had occurred with the appointment of the Chief Justice, UNTA's legal advisor and party strategist who had previously not put in a single day's appearance in any of the higher courts in his career. Maitreya and DJP had demanded an explanation in Parliament. Bhairav had stumped them with, "Why, that's exactly what meritocracy is all about. We should not be slaves to tradition and conventions."

Natasha had also promised to "take care" of Bakar and somewhat lit his hopes when she playfully added, "Why, if Kapalin had not swept me off my feet, I might have fallen for a handsome bachelor like you." Her cunning mind also knew that mere promises and hints would get her nowhere. Soon she tossed Bakar's father and brother a few bread crumbs, $10 million worth and other easy flip-over contracts to Bakar's nominees. That kept his loyalty secure.

Bakar had organized it perfectly. While Haniff always travelled with Kapalin, he left the security arrangements entirely to Bakar, whose agent snapped Dawn and Kapalin on board PAF One. The compromising DVD was shot from the attic window of the villa opposite the one occupied by Kapalin and Dawn. The cameraman had been recruited from the Philippines and his assistant, from Vietnam. Both were perfect strangers to each other.

Before and after they completed their assignment they were strip searched and their equipment tested to ensure they had not made copies for blackmail or that might soon find their way to

YouTube. The sound recording was the work of a master and his state-of-the-art listening and recording equipment. Bakar had the miniature equipment hidden outside the bedroom windows. Its powerful microphones could pick up a whisper a mile away through two-foot-thick walls.

She played the recording again and made a dash for the bathroom as "Oh, Aminah, my soul mate, I want to marry you" and the nausea hit her at the same time.

Natasha waited patiently, plotted and planned until the timing was right. The opportunity came three months later when Kapalin, Haniff and a whole plane load of UNTA's senior politicians headed to the Balendrapore district in Sivapore for a crucial by-election. Surprisingly, the incumbent UNTA MP for Balendrapore had been jailed for corruption.

It turned out the MP had been betrayed by his own party members for obstinately refusing, despite receiving good advice from Kapalin's aides, to share the spoils, $50 million, with suitable donations to UNTA.

Bakar had the security cameras disabled and gave Natasha the duplicate keys, with which she entered Dawn's penthouse condominium and waited patiently. When Dawn returned home at 9:00 p.m., the news was already out that UNTA had lost the by-election. As soon as Dawn locked her door, Natasha smashed her head with a champagne bottle and knocked her out cold. She dragged her bleeding all the way to the sofa and secured her hands and legs with handcuffs and leg chains.

When she regained consciousness and moaned, Natasha landed two solid blows to her nose and lips that knocked her out again. She came around when Natasha sprinkled ice-cold water from a jug in the refrigerator.

"Listen, bitch," Natasha screamed at her. "It won't take much for me to have you slaughtered and have your carcass fed to the crocodiles in the Ganga River. I can make you disappear with a snap of my fingers and the world won't be wiser to it. Understand?"

Dawn nodded. Her head and face ached. She could not speak clearly. The smash to her lips had taken care of that. But she knew instantly who was speaking to her and the reason for it.

"Here's what you'll do as soon as I leave. You will patch up your face and head, pack up your suitcases and take the first flight out of Chandrapore. I don't care where to. Paris, Washington, Mongolia, I don't give a damn. As long as you live, you will never return to Tiger Isle. If you are spotted on so much as a transit stop-over in PRIA or any port here, I will have you delivered in a body bag to your mother in Ulaanbaatar. And don't ever try to contact Kapalin, either here or when he's overseas. I'll hunt you down and finish you off myself if I have to. Nod if you agree," Natasha shouted.

Dawn gripped her head and moaned, "Some water please." She begged.

Natasha obliged her as she sat her up and held the jug to her lips. Even with the blood dripping down her back, face, lips and mouth, even with all the swelling, Dawn's extraordinary beauty shone through. Something snapped in Natasha and she smashed the jug in Dawn's face and threw her off the sofa to its foot. As Dawn collapsed there screaming, panting, heaving and moaning, Natasha pulled her leg back and kicked her hard in the belly.

"Please, please, not there…the baby," Dawn gasped.

"What? What are you saying, you whore? Are you carrying Kapalin's child? Answer, you prostitute!" Natasha shouted. She did not wait for an answer and went berserk, kicking and punching her wherever she could land a blow, as Dawn tried to evade her.

"Oh God, yes, I'm pregnant with Kap's child. He doesn't know about it. Don't, please, please stop it…don't," Dawn rasped through swollen and bleeding lips and mouth.

Natasha paused to rethink. She had only planned on giving Dawn a severe beating to ensure she would not have second thoughts about staying on or contacting Kapalin ever again. She wanted Dawn out of her sight and out of Tiger Isle, fast.

The baby changed the equation. It would be fairly easy to arrange an abortion, but their enemies were everywhere and if they got wind of it, the bloggers and DJP-friendly press would go to town with it. They could ride that storm, but the insults she would have to suffer, the embarrassment and loss of face, would make life unbearable for her. She hated the "Big Porka" moniker they had slung round her neck. But this would be infinitely worse. She walked over to the bedroom, shut the door closed and rang Bakar. She gave him very detailed instructions.

All Bakar asked was, "How much?"

She gritted her teeth and replied, "One mil."

"Five," Bakar demanded.

She had no choice. She assented.

Then she returned to the sofa and found Dawn on her knees trying to crawl away. In her pain and disorientation she was trying to crawl under the sofa, where her hands had already disappeared. Something in the way she had said, "Kap" infuriated Natasha. She dragged her out, reached for the champagne bottle and finished the job she started.

An hour after Natasha cleaned up and was whisked away in an unmarked security car sent by Bakar, the Cleaners arrived. They donned rubber gloves and carefully slipped Dawn into a black body bag that, in turn, was packed into a large suitcase they had brought for that purpose. Then they used chemicals to remove all the blood stains and spatters and had the carpet shampooed and vacuumed till it looked pristine. Next they went about carefully dusting and removing all fingerprints. They inspected and searched the entire apartment with a fine tooth comb.

When they finished dusting and removing all fingerprints, they carried out another round of inspection. The Cleaners' thoroughness was legendary. Yet when they found the secure handphone under the sofa, they didn't give it a second thought and placed it back on its charger. Yet again they thought nothing of the babycare and mothering magazines in the newspaper rack or of the bottle of morning-sickness pills in the bathroom medicine cabinet.

They were oversights that would cost many in the police and security forces their jobs and lives.

Dynamite

"Where did they find the body?" a pale, shaken and distraught Kapalin asked Haniff.

"In the jungle. About a hundred kilometers in the boondocks," replied Haniff.

"I'd like to see her," Kapalin whispered.

"Not advisable," Haniff replied.

"Oh, why not?" Kapalin queried.

"We only found bits and pieces of her in the bushes and trees, not even her head. We identified her from fragments of bones and teeth and from matching them with her dental records and from extensive DNA testing," Haniff explained.

"How did that happen?" Kapalin asked.

"They blew her up with dynamite!" Haniff answered, then gazed down at the floor.

Kapalin's grief was inconsolable. Haniff sat shaken at the sight of his Chief Executive crying and sobbing like a child. Haniff poured him a double Black Label whisky, neat, which he gulped down in one go and asked for a refill.

When he'd finished that and sat back, Kapalin asked, "Any leads?"

Kapalin had reached the pinnacle of his career by being ruthless and when necessary, blanking out all other thoughts to focus his complete attention on the problem at hand.

"No, none," replied Haniff.

"Run everything by me, who found the body, where and what they found in her apartment and anywhere else," Kapalin demanded.

"The police had been notified of the unusual sound of an explosion in the jungle by a couple of Aborigines out wild boar hunting at night. The disposers had not counted on that. They thought they had been extremely circumspect. Otherwise, all indications are they were thorough professional killers. There must have been at least three of them; one, a car or van driver, and two others to carry the body. There may have been a fourth man, an explosives expert. They must have parked their car on the tarmac to ensure tire treadmarks would not be detected and they donned light rubber shoes and trod on the grass, avoiding the dirt-track path or muddy and damp edges and they carried the suitcase balanced carefully overhead so it would not fall.

They obviously moved cautiously and yet were rapid in executing their task. They would have placed the dynamite all over the body and under, especially over the head and belly as obviously instructed, lit a long fuse and headed back to the car, again avoiding stepping on the dirt track or wet patches," Haniff droned.

"And her apartment?" Kapalin questioned.

Haniff passed over to Kapalin the detailed inventory list the police had compiled.

Kapalin went through it three or four times. He got up, walked over to the window, opened it, took in several chestfuls of air and breathed in and out loudly.

"Isn't it unusual they dynamited her? I mean, what kind of animals would do that, Haniff?"

"Oh, we have all sorts of loonies and serial killers these days you know. They watch CSI on TV and then life imitates art. Then there are all these "Kill" computer games. It's becoming a crazy world out there," Haniff opined.

Kapalin held back his anger. "Yes, it could be a crazy killing. But then, your security detail would have picked up any stalkers. Neither Dawn nor you reported anything of that nature, not even a single crank or dirty phone call. So there's a clue. Had they wanted to torture, rape and kill, they would have done it in her soundproof apartment or in some other apartment, house, warehouse, wherever and left the body there. But in the forest with the body blown to bits can only mean two things. Either they wanted to make sure the body was never found, or there was something in or on her body the killers didn't want anyone to see, or both. What do you reckon?"

"Well, they were pros. There's not a single car track or shoe imprint. Nothing," Haniff explained.

"Go through that inventory list again. You didn't see anything unusual there? What about the babycare and mothering magazines, or the morning-sickness pills?" Kapalin probed.

Haniff began to squirm and didn't volunteer a reply.

"This is the sms I received from Dawn at exactly 11:03 p.m. the night of the Balendrapore by-election. It reads "BP, poor baby." I thought she was consoling me for our election loss. You think there could be a link?" Kapalin asked.

"Who to? I mean we don't know whose magazines and morning-sickness pills they were. She had lots of actress and lady friends who stayed over now and then. And BP, sounds like Balendrapore to me," Haniff reasoned.

"Put your fucking thinking cap on, motherfucker!" Kapalin screamed at him, finally letting his frustration explode. "You call yourself the national director of police and security and can't add two and two? Think man! She's never been interested in my politics. She didn't have any enemies. She's the most famous and popular woman on all of Tiger Isle. Can't you see? She died because of me. Someone found out about us. What else do the initials BP stand for in this country? Don't tell me you never read the fucking gossip magazines or blogs?" Kapalin ripped into Haniff.

"My God! You don't think…you are not suggesting Big Porka? There's no way Natasha could have found out about it. Our security is impregnable. I'll swear to that," Haniff defended himself.

"Impregnable my ass! Fool, you are not paid to guess or assume. They were smart enough to use untraceable dynamite available at any road, bridge, or tunneling construction site. They could have used C4 plastic explosives or hand grenades. Why didn't they? Who is smart enough to plan it that meticulously? Get out of here now. Find out who Dawn's doctor was and then come back and tell me what you guess or assume. Get her handphone back and get out of my sight," Kapalin shouted. He pulled out his revolver from his desk drawer, ready to fire if Haniff uttered another word.

Poor Haniff Hassan. He had joined the police force as a private, a beat cop. He had worked his way up by "know who" and not "know how." He had even faked his London law diploma certificate and claimed on Facebook he had a law degree, though he was careful not to state where from. As Haniff scooted his burnt tail out, for a moment there he could see his life flash past him.

Kapalin sat back, poured himself another liberal glass of whiskey, neat and contemplated who the next national director of police and security should be. He searched for the words that were flitting in bits and pieces at the back of his mind and found it:

Hell hath no fury like a woman scorned.

The Bargain

When she got home from Tigers, it was well past 2:00 a.m. She checked on the children in their bedrooms on the way to hers. Lakshmi and Karthik were sound asleep. So was Roshan. She took a long hot shower, dried up, put on her snow-white bath robe, made herself a hot cup of Milo, lay down on her favorite comfy sofa and switched on Astral TV to the History Channel.

A Battles BC repeat was on about Alexander's invasion of the Punjab, his epic battle with Porus and his elephant phalanx. There was too much to think about now and mull over for her to concentrate on Alexander, Hydaspes/Jhelum River and 326 BC. She was thinking how useful it would be to have a thinking mind like Alexander's to help her prepare for the war that lay ahead.

She got up, switched the TV off and dropped a CD, Best of James Taylor, into the player and forwarded the track to her favorite You Got a Friend. She relaxed to the strains of "winter, spring, summer or fall." She wondered why some remakes, like George Benson's brilliant Greatest Love by Whitney Houston and Billy Joel's Just the Way You Are by Barry White outperformed the original, when she dozed off.

She was floating somewhere, and it wasn't like astral travelling or a floating-body experience at operating theaters she'd read about in Reader's Digest. There was no shining cord linking her back to her physical self lying on her sofa or "the kindest voice ever imaginable" to welcome her. She looked down and there was nothing. She could not see herself below, nor was there anything else up or sideways or anywhere. There weren't any green falling numbers and symbols, or a matrix or doorway, dimensional door, plunging and twisting wormhole, or black hole waiting to rip her down to her atoms. She realized it wasn't cold or hot. It was, well…nice.

But she also sensed the presence of something, someone, and yet there was nothing. There was some kind of fabric, nothing she could identify from any of her life's experiences. When she reached out with her hands, there was no sensation of "touching" anything. But there was energy and power. There was life.

She risked it and asked, "Where am I?"

"You are here."

The voice was neutral. She could not tell if it was male or female.

"Who are you?"

"I am."

"Are you God?"

"Do you know God? Have you met God before? How would you know it's God?"

"I guess I can't answer that. But I have faith."

"That's a good start."

"Is that all I need, faith?"

"No, that alone won't do. But it's a good start."

"Am I dead?"

"Do you want to be dead?"

"No. Not yet, not now."

"Then why are you here?"

"I don't know."

"If you are seeking death, why would you be somewhere you don't know of? There are easier ways."

"I don't remember asking to be here."

"Yes, you did."

"When?"

"Think back."

"Oh, I wanted answers, directions."

"That's right. Now you know why you are here."

"But how did I get here?"

"Is that important?"

"I don't know. Perhaps."

"Do you feel unsafe, threatened? Hurt or harmed?"

"No, I guess not."

She had never felt safer in her life.

"Then how you got here is not so important, is it?"

"I guess so."

"Your question?"

"Why can't we win?"

"Who says you can't?"

"It's been so difficult. Impossible."

"That doesn't mean you can't win. It's not impossible."

"How do we win?"

"You already have the means."

"I have?"

"Yes."

"Could you give me a clue?"

"No."

"Oh?"

"The thinking and effort must come from you. Then I can confirm or deny."

"Why?"

For the first time there was laughter.

"No pain, no gain."

"Are you making fun of me?"

"Absolutely not."

"Where do I start? There's Bhairav, and there's Kapalin. Then there's Adhi Gurunadha. They are all so powerful, invincible. They have the PSB, the police, the judges, the courts, the laws, the executioners, the PSA, Bay of Pigs, and the guns and swords. How do I start?"

"They are not invincible. They are made of the same stuff as you. What is it that you have that they don't?"

"I don't know."

"If you keep saying, 'I don't know,' we'll get nowhere. Start with what you know you have."

"I only have seven good friends, a good loving husband and two children, all of whom I think the world of. Then there's my father, brother and sister."

"They don't have that, do they?"

"Friends? Fathers? Children?"

"Seven good friends and six others who worship them. Do any of them have even one good friend?"

"Don't they?"

"If any of them were on your side, would you call them friends? Good friends?"

"I guess not."

"Any worshippers?"

"I guess not."

"Guess what else you have?"

"I love my friends and family."

"There you are. You have love."

"They don't?"

"Do you steal, loot, plunder, rape, kill and murder if you have love?"

"No."

"Good."

"But there are only seven of us. They have thousands."

"No, you have more. You may not be able to see all of them. But evil can't keep silent, be still, or not announce itself. Love doesn't have to do any of that, yet it can conquer all."

"I never thought of it that way."

"Good, you are learning. That's a sign of love."

"Am I a good person?"

"Don't fish for flattery. Just do it."

"If you know so much, you must be God."

"I don't know what you mean by God, so I can't answer your question."

"You can read my mind."

"No, I can't, or else why would I be having a conversation with you?"

"But God can read human minds!"

"How would you know? Did God tell you that?"

"No."

"So you are wasting precious time talking about things you know you don't know."

"Ok. I want to defeat them. I want to save the good people."

"Who are the good people?"

"The ones who stand against the evil Tigerists."

"What about the poor, the sick, the old and the incapacitated? What happens to those who can't make a stand?"

"They have to be saved."

"What about the Tigerists who don't agree with Bhairav, Kapalin and Adhi Gurunadha? Those who are too weak or afraid to make a stand? Save them or destroy them?"

"Of course, we have to save them."

"How will you know who they are?"

"What are you saying? You can't save the good Tigerists? There are millions of them."

"Did I say anything about me saving anyone or is this about you?"

"I don't know!"

"But you do. You didn't come here to die. So you must have come here to live."

"But it's so dangerous. I could die."

"That's possible. But you'll have to go someday anyway."

"So it's all a question of time?"

"Now we are getting somewhere. How much time do you want?"

"Who do I save?"

"It's up to you."

"Myself?"

"It's up to you."

"Myself, family and friends?"

"If you want."

"Tiger Isle?"

"If you want."

"Who in Tiger Isle?"

"We've been through that. You can't know. You can make a guess and take the risk. There's always collateral damage."

"The world?"

"If you want."

"All four?"

"Do you have the time or means?"

"Why not?"

"You are the person who best knows your own limitations."

"Why not all four? You know it's possible, but you won't help."

"You are making that assumption and mistake again that I am God who has unlimited powers."

"Doesn't God?"

"I've already answered that question. Do you know God? Have you met God? How would you know if it's God or what God's range and limits of powers are?"

"You are being deliberately difficult."

"No, I'm not. Ask the question."

"I want to save all four. Tell me how to do that."

There was a sigh.

"That's not possible. It's too far gone."

"So you are God."

"No, no. I did not say or mean that."

"What's too far gone?"

"The equilibrium."

"Who decides?"

"Humans do."

"They can't fix it? I can't fix it?"

"Not all by yourself. It's too far gone."

"What does it depend on?"

"The First Law of Thermodynamics."

"The what?"

"Energy can neither be created nor destroyed. It must be conserved."

"Not all by myself. That's interesting. I get help?"

"Yes."

"So I can save myself, or myself, family and friends, or Tiger Isle, or the world. That's my decision matrix?"

"You have reasoned it out."

"Then, if I save myself only, or myself, family and friends only, or Tiger Isle only, the world is in danger?"

"You have reasoned it out."

"And if I do nothing? Then the world is not safe?"

"You have reasoned it out."

"If my family and friends and I live and Tiger Isle ceases to exist, where's the purpose or meaning? Where's our quality of life? We start all over again in a foreign land?"

"You have reasoned it out."

"And if my family, friends and I perish, who will deliver justice to Tiger Isle?"

"What does it matter to you, then, if you are not there? Revenge?"

"It's not fair. Who will deliver justice? I have to know. I demand an answer."

"What does it matter to you either way if it's not revenge or vengeance?"

"It matters that the good must not be totally destroyed with the bad."

"It's not possible to guarantee that."

"What can you guarantee?"

"I cannot guarantee anything."

"Not even one or two? Five? Ten? Thirteen?"

"They are only numbers. Who decides?"

"Aah, aah, now we are getting somewhere. Are you saying I can bargain?"

"What is your offer?"

"No more questions. I will decide!"

"Ah! The power of one. As long as there is no disequilibrium and violation of the First Law of Thermodynamics."

"Yes, yes, conservation in total. I understand that completely now. The world is safe."

"So you will save five. Tiger Isle started with five and we will end with a minimum of five. I will leave Tiger Isle to you."

"No, YOU will save five. Are we are finished?"

"I want my friends as well."

"That's seven more lives. There will be more disequilibrium."

"You have me, then, don't you?"

"Well done. That's all I needed to know."

"And you still maintain the fiction you are not God?"

"There is no fiction. I am not God."

"Who are you then?"

"You may come to know in time. It depends."

"On what, the First Law of Thermodynamics? Who invented that?"

"The First Law of Thermodynamics IS God."

"That's all there is to God?"

"No, you know better than that."

"And while we are at it, was it really God who gives us Tigerism?"

"Do you think any God worth his salt and who bothered to create us would really ask his followers to refer to unbelievers as pariahs or kaffirs and encourage the extermination of Christians, Hindus, Muslims, or Jews? Hate and revenge do not exist in divine thinking or action."

"So the first Adhi Gurunadha invented it all? And all that call for annual pilgrimages, the Tiger Cub ceremony, temple construction everywhere and reciting from the Tiger Puranam?"

"A great marketing tool copied by many others in human history. Sounds very familiar, does it not? After all, even Gurunadha has to eat and is not, despite all his homilies about self-sacrifice and selflessness, above seeking a kind of immortality, is he?"

"You again answered a question with another question."

"We'll talk about all that another time. I must go. The clock is ticking."

"Oh, I'll be meeting you again? Next time you'd better have a hell of a lot more answers than questions!"

She could have sworn she heard deep and continuous laughter.

Farewell, My Loves

When she woke up she knew she was ready. Roshan had left for work and the kids had gone to school. Later, she went to see her doctor. She feigned sore throat, headache, fatigue and tiredness. Her GP, whom she had been consulting for over twenty years, murmured something about late menopause and wrote out a medical certificate, no questions asked, for the rest of the week off, which is what Rekha had really come for and which the GP had figured out. She paid thirty dollars, collected her Panadol and throat gargle and rushed home. She called her office, faxed the MC and receipt to the receptionist and lay down on the sofa to do some more thinking.

She sent out a whole load of email to her close friends and relatives and even to not so close friends and relatives, inquiring about their health and the status of their nearest and dearest ones, something she had neglected for years. She called her brother and sister, Shivaji and Sharmilla, in Melbourne to hear their voices and those of her nieces and nephews. The siblings had always been close and the memories of how they all had struggled to rise from humble beginnings flooded her.

She and Roshan had never been able to afford the luxury of a holiday there, though her brother and sister had returned a couple of times to Chandrapore and stayed with them after they had emigrated. She dug up old wedding and family photo albums, dusted them and inserted in them neatly other photographs she had stored away in envelopes and folders over the years but never had time to update.

There were fading pictures of when she was a baby and of her mother she could not bear to look at, for fear she would fall apart. She drifted back to the glorious VA days of form-six trips in battered school buses with her classmates while still in plaited hair and ribbons. They'd gone to Sati Coral Reef and Gurunadha Diving Spot Beach and to picnics at waterfalls while singing, "Over hill, over dale, as we hit the mountain trail..." and laughed and giggled hysterically like little girls.

She removed the rubber band from a bundle of Roshan's love letters to her of old, read and reread them. She laughed at how silly they sounded now and she retied them with pink ribbons and stored them in a new red box she'd bought at the stationer's on the way home. From two other orange folders she removed crayon and colored-pencil drawings by Lakshmi and Karthik of strange whales, dolphins, hens, ducks, seals and a whole zoo of animals shaded pink, green, yellow and orange from their kindergarten days. She loved the one by Lakshmi of a whale that had two curved fins longer than its body and said, "I luv my mama and dada so big." She never failed to smile at Karthik's pink-striped tiger with butterfly wings.

She had stopped adding to the mini photo albums of their birthdays, first day at school, school concerts and prize-winners' days. There were several of Karthik, regarded a "maths king," claiming his medals and of Lakshmi for English language and literature.

She went through her teenage years' Song Book and laughed at the newspaper cutting of Bob Marley and his "rasta" hair, on which she had scribbled, "No Woman No Cry." Pressed between the pages of her Poetry Book were rose petals, jasmine flowers and pledges of "friends forever," signed by Chandrika, Simran, Mastura, Kim and the others. When she could stand it no longer, she wiped away the tears, curled up on the sofa thoroughly but satisfactorily depressed and slept till the children came home.

She decided she would brief them Saturday of her dream, mission and plans after a special surprise lunch. On Friday night she skinned chicken quarters and marinated them overnight with yogurt and Dawood's tandoori sauce, mixed in a huge Pyrex dish for her tandoori chicken special, which was their favorite. She sealed the Pyrex with plastic cling wrap and stored it in the refrigerator.

The secret to Rekha's mouthwatering tandoori chicken lay in the overnight marinade and baking the chicken for no more than twenty-five minutes per pound of chicken with the marinade. After that came the special treatment: removing and brushing each piece on all sides with melted salted butter and grilling it for another five to ten minutes on both sides and serving it straight from the grill onto a bed of saffron-laced Briyani rice on a plate. That gave the chicken a reddish hue, as opposed to an orange one, and brought out all the taste of the tandoori mixed spices to the palate. The tiniest of them, Karthik, would not stop at three pieces.

Briyani rice and lamb, she always had stock. Briyani rice went very well with lamb curry and cool, crunchy salad of her own invention. She would line the insides and bottom of the salad bowl with fresh lettuce and then toss in fresh bean sprouts with the brown tails snipped off, thinly sliced white Japanese mushrooms, onion rings, cucumber and vinaigrette dressing.

It was important that the round ends of the cucumber be first sliced off and then used to rub the two ends of the large piece until a milky white foam emerged. The foam would have to be washed off, the cucumber skinned to expose the lighter shade of green flesh inside and the pieces sliced a little thick and round. For dessert, she'd already shopped for Walls Vanilla Ripple ice cream and Tinned Lychees at the mini-mart in Sherwood Villas. The lychee and its sweet, colorless, syrupy sauce had to be served ice cold with the ice cream.

She began after they staggered from the dining table and collapsed into their favorite leather sofa and arm chairs, each hugging a cushion, and Karthik, his comforter. She made for herself a hot masala tea brewed from leaves and an instant Eight O'clock Hanjian Italian Cappuccino three-in-one coffee for Roshan. It was infinitely better than the stuff they served in Tigers for fifteen dollars a cup with that silly biscuit just because they imported that steel-and-glass jet steam and milk machine from Palermo. The kids wanted nothing. It they ate out, inevitably they would shoot for the ice-cold latte and mocha; at home they stuck to mineral water.

"Stuffed!" exclaimed Roshan as he loosened his leather belt and top trouser button. Rekha was pleased at her groaning family. They had, as usual, done justice to her culinary skills.

"Okay, listen closely Roshan. I have something very important to discuss that will change our lives and turn it around completely," Rekha began.

"Yes, Roshan, please listen attentively. You always switch off when I start talking," Karthik squeaked in perfect mimicry of his mother, as he slipped one leg over the arm of his chair, leaned back and yawned. He was ready to slip into power-nap mode. Karthik had noted well that universal accusation by married women everywhere who gushed to their mothers and girlfriends, "He respects me and hangs on my every word," and changed their minds the day after they tied the knot.

They burst into laughter simultaneously as Karthik closed his eyes and began to snore.

"Oh really, young man, why don't you come sit next to me and I'll educate you all about paying attention," Roshan said.

"No thank you, Roshan. I'm doing perfectly well where I am. Don't forget Rekha knows best," replied Karthik with his eyes closed.

They laughed some more. Every now and then Karthik, with whom, like most fourteen-year-old boys, his parents could only engage in monosyllabic conversations, punched with "Okay," "I guess so," and "I don't know," would pull out one of his zingers and surprise them all.

He had wit, which at that age was more important than genius.

"Kar, come over and lie down next to me, darling," invited Rekha as Karthik's humor had relaxed them all. He bounced over in a jiffy and made himself comfortable on his back with his head on her lap. She cupped his chin and planted an affectionate kiss on his lips. He turned around and hugged her like a bear. Had one of his classmates been around, he would have blushed and cried out, "Aw, mom, cut that girly stuff out already. I'm not a baby!" But here, in the warm cocoon of home and family only, he hammed it up and showed traces of the fast-vanishing child in him.

"That's right, my little baby cooby, come lie next to momma. Shall I fetch your feeding bottle and diapers kootchiecatchiegootchie? Here let me snap one and post it on Facebook," threatened a disgusted Lakshmi.

"Don't you dare!" snapped Karthik as he hid his face behind his huge comforter. "Mom, tell her she's grounded and send her off to her room." He took out a football referee's whistle from his pant pocket and blew on it. Preet! Preet! "Foul. Red card!" he bellowed.

"Ok. Enough, enough," Rekha ordered gently as she restored peace. She ran her fingers through Karthik's hair and continued. "Roshan, honey, we've discussed this before. I told you the stakes were high, and the time has arrived. We have to act fast."

"Beef steak?" inquired Karthik as he pulled out his PSP and switched it to silent mode as it revved up to the FIFA 10 football game. He was with Pele and Brazil, playing their arch enemy, Argentina.

"Ssh! Silence. Let your mother talk. This is serious," warned Roshan. "And we don't eat beef."

"I've spoken to Jess, and she's made all the arrangements through Maitreya's people and connections. We'll be emigrating to Australia soon. I telephoned Shivaji and Sharmilla and let them in on the good news."

"We going to Melbourne mom? That's cool," enthused Karthik as he couldn't wait to link up with his cousins Avnesh and Ashwin, who were also 14.

"Mom, are we all going? What about school and my PCE next year? And who's Jess?" inquired a worried Lakshmi.

"Yes, we are all emigrating to Melbourne. But you two and Dad will go first, and I'll join you later. Oh, don't worry about PCE. You can do the Oz matriculation. They have some really good schools in Melbourne and of course it will all be in English. Your English here is above average so you shouldn't have any problems. But remember above average here may be just average in Melbourne. So you'll have to buck up on that, won't you, sweetie?" Rekha engaged her. "Oh, Jess is our local immigration agent who helped me sort out the papers, application and submission to the Oz embassy here," she lied soothingly.

"Why can't you come along with us at the same time, Mom?" Lakshmi sulked.

"Oh, it's to do with my work. I'm in the middle of a major audit investigation and can't just up and leave. I have to tender my resignation, giving three months notice in writing. Then there's the pension-fund money I have to withdraw and a thousand and one other little things to attend to," Rekha continued fibbing.

"Oh, Dad's in government too, isn't he? Why is it different for him?" Lakshmi shot back. She was growing up fast and sensed that all was not right.

"I've just been transferred to Suryapore, and that's another reason we've brought forward our emigration plans. I don't think I can manage that situation and being separated from you guys. I'm not bogged down by any outstanding work and can leave soon. I have lots of unused vacation leave, which I can offset against the resignation-notice period. Besides I'm the one who has to first find a job in Melbourne to pay for a new house and car and perhaps a smaller auto for you to get around. Cars there are half the price here. Did you know that, darling?" Roshan chipped in with more fibs and knew exactly how to misdirect Lakshmi.

"What, a new car for me? I want one of those new beetles. You heard that, Kar? Eat your heart out, baby!" screamed Lakshmi.

"Bully for you, Laksh, but didn't Dad tell you you'll have to drop me off and pick me up from school every day, uh, Dad?" jumped in Karthik with a spoiler.

"Mom, why do we have to leave? I mean, what's so great about Melbourne? Why not New York or London? This is our home. We have Grandad too. I don't understand," Lakshmi still protested.

"Listen dear, it's a little complicated and difficult to explain. Your dad and I have been discussing it for over two years. Try to understand. Things are getting difficult for us here and we may even be in danger, your father and I. Your father and I have travelled all over this beautiful country and we love it just as much as you do. We have more friends than you or Karthik. You think I won't regret leaving my father? And we'll miss Sherwood Villas, Chandrapore and Tiger Isle. I mean, when we bought this expensive house here, we thought this was going to be our permanent home. Now, things have changed. We have to sell this lovely place."

"Why, what danger are you and Dad in, Mom? Can't we go to the police and ask for help?" Lakshmi said.

Roshan laughed lightly. "That's where the problem really is, Lakshmi, the police. We love our country, but our country doesn't seem to love us. And it's not just us. There are many others like us, millions. They can't leave because they don't have the money or qualify with the immigration requirements of foreign countries. We are lucky. We have your uncle and aunty in Australia to sponsor us. That's why we chose Melbourne. If we stay here too long, your and Karthik's future will be affected badly, and we don't want to risk that. Understand?"

"No, I really don't," Lakshmi answered.

"Trust us, my darling. We know what we are doing. And don't forget, if we stay here, you'll be commuting by bus to university in two year's time, not with your own car," Roshan said.

"Of course, I trust you and Mom, Dad, but what about my friends and Karthik's friends?" Lakshmi asked.

"Oh, you keep in touch with your friends more through Facebook, sms and email than by actually meeting them face to face. That's true even for Karthik. You can do the same from Melbourne. Besides, it's not the end of the world. Mom and I will be earning a lot more in Melbourne and we'll visit Chandrapore every year."

"Really? Oh, ok then. That's cool," Lakshmi said.

They talked about it over and over until Rekha and Roshan were near exhaustion. But it was crucial the children were not so much convinced they were emigrating as that they would soon be leaving for Melbourne and Australia. They needed them to trumpet that and inform their friends and their parents and teachers in school. It would take a few more days of brainwashing, but they knew the children would come around. Their cousins, uncles and aunties would be telephoning them from Melbourne to give their assurances.

Husband and wife glanced at each other and realized they were getting there, and they talked to them about the great Oz outback, the Sydney Opera House and the beautiful weather all year round there, the Great Barrier Reef and the marsupials. It was near 8:00 p.m. when they called a halt to the family discussion and decided to continue with the psyching exercise Sunday.

Rekha mentioned nothing about her dream and mission to the children. It was obvious they were too immature to understand any of that. She spoke to Roshan about it when they were in bed that night. Even he had difficulty in quite grasping what it all meant and wondered if it was not due to her anxiety and her subconscious playing mind games. He wasn't sure and neither was Rekha, about what "You have me, don't you? Well done. That's all I needed to know," meant.

But Roshan was a practical man. He knew the actual plan was for them all to reunite in America and not Australia and what his part was in all that. As for Rekha's dream, he would leave that to unravel as it may. Before she went to bed that night, Rekha made a conference call to her seven friends.

"Listen up guys, I'd like to meet up with you all Monday evening, 7:00 p.m. at Tigers," Rekha said.

"Oh, that'd be full price, you know?" Fahrizat exclaimed.

Rekha laughed. "That's okay, I'll be buying."

"Why, you struck the lottery first prize or you got an incentive bonus from the comptroller of GAD or what? Wait, I know. They finally promoted you to auditor, didn't they?" Suryani demanded to know.

Rekha laughed some more and replied, "Fat chance of an ad hoc government incentive bonus or promotion for me. Wrong religion. No, I have something important to discuss, but can't talk on the phone about it. All in?"

"Confirmed, Captain Demon Auditor," they all chimed back.

Roshan and Rekha went to tuck Karthik into bed that night, just so he wouldn't stay awake too late from all of that day's confusing proceedings. As they got up to leave and he separated from another mauling bear hug of his mother, Karthik pocketed his PSP, looked up a little puzzled, and asked, "Oh Dad, what's emigrate mean?"

Dirty Cocktails and Tequila Shots

As was normal for rainy days and Mondays, Tigers was virtually deserted. They had the back garden all to themselves. It was also "Cocktail Night" at Tigers, and that was half-price.

"Listen men, first the bad news and then the worse," began Rekha and briefed them about Melbourne.

"What the fuck?" Mastura asked. "Australia? Shit!" she swore as she drained her glass in one gulp and signaled to Farid and Jaimie for another Bosom Caresser of brandy, curacao, grenadine, egg yolk and ice with a delicious plate of fried anchovy-onion-red-chili-lime-squeezed finger-food snack.

"Yeah Rek, why now?" asked Fahrizat as she ran her fingers round the rim of her fast-depleting cocktail glass of Slippery Nipple and tossed the tiny umbrella into the gutter.

"Goodness!" exclaimed Rekha. "The papers just came in Friday, or else I would have informed her majesties earlier," she protested.

"And how are the little ones taking it? Must be a wee bit traumatic, don't you think? They probably can't stand being separated from their school friends more than anything else. They can't live with them and can't live without them," joined in Shanita.

"Yeah, too right," Rekha agreed. "Why don't you come over and talk to them, Shan. You know, I think, Karthik has a crush on you all? You should drop by and give them assurances, except maybe you Simran. Kar think his Aunty Simran is James Bond's sidekick and that if he annoys you, you will land a karate kick and chop on him."

"Hey, your son's been brought up the right way. He knows how to respect a real lady. Chop, chop," signaled Simran with her hands, and they burst out laughing.

"I bet the girl's taking it badly though," chipped in Kim, "and knows what's what. She's sixteen and don't be fooled by her demure looks. She probably knows more about the birds and the bees than my old man and I put together. Nowadays they learn everything online. You think you are being smart with parental security lock and all that, but they'll go to the cybercafés after school or to one of their rich friend's house, and poof, next they'll be writing a thesis on it."

"Jeeze, when I think of my wedding night and there I was trying to figure out what goes into where, you could have knocked me over with a feather how I had to guide my shaking husband to enter my holy temple. Then last week my fifteen-year old girl asks me about fetus and baby dumping, mainly by Tigerists under twenty years old and why can't they just use condoms. I mean a chill ran through my body, I had to put on my woolen sweater," lamented Kim as they screamed at the risible story.

"If I tell you what happened on my first night, Kim's husband would have proclaimed her sex queen on hers," volunteered Chandrika.

"What? What? Tell! Tell, slut! You can't hide it from us. You should have told us years ago. It's not fair you keeping a Penthouse expose like that from us. Confession is good for the soul," scolded Suryani.

"Oh, all right, all right. My father-in-law booked and paid for our honeymoon in a floating gondola at a riverside resort near Mt. Kailas, you know like the India Kashmiri Shikara? I was thinking how romantic it was going to be until it was time to leave for the train station and there were my fil and mil AND my two unmarried bils and two sils as well, all packed up to board the same train with us. Apparently, they thought there was nothing wrong with them joining us and the bookings included them. I think it was more Rakesh's mother who could not bear to be separated from him. If only that was all of it.

When we got there the old man had made a balls-up with the bookings, so the eight of us had one gondola to share. Thank God they didn't fuss about Rakesh and I taking the Honeymoon Suite, which had the only shower and toilet attached to it. The rest had to manage as best as they could with sleeping bags on the floor and sofas. Then after the most delicious dinner cooked by our ancient Shikara driver, we of course yawned and adjourned to our boudoir, as the driver started a slow float down the river. We were a bit apprehensive with the flimsy door, but hell, it was our night and we weren't going to chicken out just because there was a cheering team parked outside our door.

Just as we were getting down to serious business, my mil knocked on the door. She apologized profusely, but it was an urgent call of nature and she couldn't bring herself to do it over the side of the moving boat standing up, as suggested by the Shikarist. My sils followed soon after, as did my fil and bils to brush teeth and wash up before retiring for the night.

And with all the tension and interruptions, Rakesh couldn't get it up. I wasn't worried. We hadn't had premarital sex, but we'd engaged in some fairly heavy petting and kissing during our courting time and I knew he was alright in the family jewels department. But would you believe we spent our first night drinking tea and chatting all night and pretending it was better than rutting like stags? I swear next morning, as Rakesh and I returned from an early morning walk, my mil was inspecting the bed sheets like some Kunta Kinte in Roots?" Chandrika howled.

After they recovered from that some ten minutes later, it was Mastura who said, "Yo, as I recall, you delivered your first son exactly nine months later. So how did that happen?"

"Christ, there's more. You see, Rakesh couldn't get it up for a whole week in Mt. Kailas. So when we returned home, we didn't let on to anyone, but booked a deluxe room at the Chandrapore Hilton the day after. I didn't want to start a family so soon, and so Rakesh tipped the bellboy to get a packet of Durex. You know, we were married and all, but the snoop squads were everywhere and we didn't have our marriage certificate with us.

The idiot bellboy buys a loose single from 7-Eleven and sure enough Rakesh slips it on the wrong way and couldn't get traction. He gets the same bellboy to get another condom. This time he gets it on the right way, but he's oiled both sides and after we finished we found the rubber had slipped out in our frenzy. That explains why my son came earlier than we planned and why my second, a girl, came only four years later. I had to house train Rakesh on the intricacies of the condom," Chandrika completed her misadventure.

As they split their sides from that one, Simran ordered a round of the award-winning Australian Wetspot cocktail for all. Farid served it and tossed the menu over to Simran.

"Looks like you are all on a bender tonight. Be adventurous," he invited.

The drink names that caught their eye from a long list were the following:

The Leg Spreader

Bend Over Shirley

Sex On The Beach

Long Slow Comfortable Screw Against The Wall

C**k Sucking Cowboy

Blowjob

Screaming Orgasm

"Wow, and I thought 'Screwdriver' was pushing it," remarked Mastura Jalil as she downed her Wetspot and said, "C'mon guys, Sex on the Beach is on me. Brings back fond memories, it does."

"Well, I never! You? On the beach? Ooh, still waters do run deep," Rekha encouraged her.

And when Mastura had finished relating that hilarious episode about the entanglement with tiny crabs and sand in the crack, it was Farizhat Hamid who excused herself with "I need a slash," and on her way back from the ladies' room staggered to the bar and ordered a round of LSCSATW.

As the night wore on the swearing came easier and faster, the stories more risqué, and the cocktails, dirtier.

It was close to midnight, when Rekha shushed them.

"Listen guys, I have to leave soon. Now for the worse news. There's big danger approaching. I don't really know what it is and can't explain it in a sensible or logical way. But I'd advise you and your families to put some distance between you and Tiger Isle for a month or two, the farther away the better. You can come back after it's all over. I know exactly what you are going to say. You can't just up and leave, there's office, husband, children, mother, father etcetera, etcetera, etcetera blah, blah, blah. But if you want to save yourselves and those you love, do exactly what I say. Capisce?" warned Rekha.

There was absolute quiet. You could have heard a pin drop. It sobered them up fast.

"Listen Rek," Kim answered, "we understand about your involvement with Maitreya and DJP and all that, but are you sure you are in full possession of your senses? If I go back and tell my husband what you just said, he'd ask me to go see the psychiatrist. I'm not suggesting you've lost it or something, but perhaps it's the stress of it all. Maybe you should take some time off and go relax in the mountains or spa."

"Oh, Kim, believe me, it's not the stress. I've received a warning and if something catastrophic should occur, I can't think of seven other people I'd want with me safe, sound and alive more than this bunch right here. Can you understand that? Put aside all your sensible, normal way of thinking and trust my instincts. Don't ask me for proof or evidence or insurance. I can't offer you any. I beg of you," Rekha pleaded.

"What is it sweetie? Is the PSB on your back? Anyone threatened you with Bay of Pigs? What? Or have you had some visions like Nostradamus? Is that it?" Mastura chipped in, as she took Rekha's palm in hers and gave her a reassuring squeeze.

"No," Rekha lied. "No visions or dreams or Nostradamus. The PSB has been on my and Roshan's back for some time now. We are not afraid. It's all cat-and-mouse games, but I know how to maneuver and move my pieces on the chessboard. But this is something different that's going to affect us all, Tigerists and non-

Tigerists. You can't stay and fight. You have to run to live and fight another day," she moaned.

They talked about it for another half an hour when Rekha realized she wasn't going to convince them just then. The impossibility of it dawned on her. If she couldn't convince her best friends of thirty-two years standing, how on Earth were they going to persuade their families?

"Okay, at least promise me you'll think about what I said over the next few days. I'll be on your backs every hour of the day," she warned them. "So let's part on that positive note. But before we leave, I have something for each of you," she announced cheerfully. She pulled out seven reddish-orange, small, gift-wrapped boxes from a huge carrier bag and handed them over to her friends.

They tore open the wrappings, and when they lined the contents up on the table, there were seven identical origami-like paper things that looked like four propellers, under which you could slip fingers and manipulate them. When pressed they flattened into four panels that had been shaded brown, yellow, black, red, orange, purple, or blue with colored pencils.

It was paper game called What Color Do You Want, which little kids played while waiting in the shade by the school gates for their school bus or parents' cars to appear. Your friend picked a color, say, yellow, and the paper holder would say, "Yellow" and move the propellers up and down spelling, "Y-E-L-L-O-W," and then stop and lift the panel, under which there would be a neatly penciled question like, "Spell banana." The friend would have to spell it out and if they got it right, it would next be their turn to manipulate the propellers. If they got it wrong, they'd have to try another color. It was one way for beginners to grapple with spelling difficult words.

"You want to elaborate, Rek?" asked Kim gently, as she reached into her handbag under the table and fished around for her tissue pack.

"Oh, it was all a long time ago," began Rekha. "Roshan and I were transferred to Sivapore for our outstation stint of government service. They called it rural service. Lakshmi was eight and Karthik five and just enrolled at kindergarten. Sivapore was totally new to us, we had no friends and we were just getting acquainted with our new environment.

One Sunday afternoon we took a drive at 4:00 p.m. to the local lake gardens in Nilagiri, where on normal days the mist doesn't clear up till mid-afternoon. But that day, it was truly a beautiful summer's day. The sun was out and it remained at about eighteen degrees right up to 7:00 p.m. in the evening with just a light pleasant breeze. You wouldn't believe how heavenly that park looks.

We had our picnic hamper and spread our mat under the shade of a large pine tree, and there were hundreds of them by the lakeside. Nearby was a huge playground with swings, seesaws, trapeze bars, slides and a five-station climbing maze. The crowd was slowly trickling in. At first Laksh and Kar kept pretty much to themselves, scoffing the food and Coke and tossing bread crumbs to fish in the lake.

But soon, the sound of older kids having a smashing time on the swings, slides and seesaws caught their attention, and we wandered over there with them. All sorts of families started arriving - Puliporean, Chinese, Indian, Malay, Portuguese and even an Aborigine or two. There were harried mothers chasing after their little boys, little toddlers hanging on to their grandpas' pants, fathers sliding down with their daughters in their laps and grandmas pushing the swings gently and some in fury, for their little girls.

Wild horses could not have stopped Laksh and Kar. We were there until it was really dark and only then could we pull them back to the car. Perfect strangers sidled up to each other and expressed welcome wholeheartedly and chatted about the weather and kindergarten and school and offered their fizzy drinks and mineral water. Previously shy and withdrawn babies and children mingled, talked, laughed, chased one other, fought, cried and made up. They hugged with unmitigated joy and pleasure and refused to go home. Oh, it was a miraculous day.

You know, my kids never said much that night. For sure they were truly exhausted and slept in the car all the way home. But they did not bring it up the next day either, though on the following Friday, Kar asked about going to Leggaden. When I was clearing up their playroom at home the day after we returned from Nilagiri, there were about two dozen of these multicolored What Color Do You Want things all over the floor. I thought it cute. Even Kar had made a few. I never gave it much thought, but instinctively swept it all into a box and stored it.

Then one day when Laksh was twelve, we were spring cleaning and I came across that box. I opened it and Laksh and Kar screamed, "Our happy people paper!" It struck me at once what they were saying. When I prodded them, Lakshmi said, "Oh, we were so happy that day in Nilagiri, Mum. We wanted all the colors to become one. So I taught Kar how to make the origami and color the panels. You see the panels appear to be separate, but they are all actually joined together. The colors don't matter. You can rub it out and reshade them any color you want them to be."

Out of the mouths of little babes, you can say that again. It flashed across my mind that we humans are all really from the same mold. Look at us. Has it, or even religion, ever come between us?" Rekha asked and paused as her voice faltered and broke.

Mastura, Fahrizat and Kim sobbed uncontrollably while Suryani dabbed at her running mascara. Simran and Chandrika each took one of Rekha's palms and squeezed gently and lovingly as the tears streamed down their faces. Shanita fared no better with her emotions. They formed a tight circle, hugged each other for long minutes and told each other how much they loved one another and how great God was. They broke up as Rekha disentangled arms and went with all seven in tow to the bar to settle the bill.

There, lined up on the bar top were eight tequila shots with salt around each glass rim wedged with a slice of fresh lime.

"One for the road, mothers," Simran/Jess announced as she goosestepped up to the bar like a German paratrooper, clicked her stiletto high heels, siege heiled and educated them. "You vill first lick ze salt round the rim, Ja? Zen you vill at vunce throw ze tequila straight to ze back of your throat and svallow it. Got it, Ja? Zen, you vill immediately bite ze lime peel. You will next fling ze lime peel on ze floor and grind it mit your high heels. Lastly, you vill do vat I vill do, or I vill hav you shot and bayoneted. Schnell! Schnell!"

"Ja wohl, mein fuehrer!" they responded as vun.

In one fluid motion Simran/Jess tongued the rim, knocked back her tequila shot, bit on the lime, crushed it underfoot and then unleashed her glass into the grand, shiny Balinese framed mirror. She watched in fascination as it developed spidery cobweb lines, then huge cracks and shattered. Seven more glasses followed in a nanosecond as Farid and Jaimie hugged each other for dear life underneath the bar counter.

In their drunken stupor the girls had not taken notice of the funny wires in the wall or a tiny, little red dot of light. If they had looked closer they might have spied the hairs-breadth thin lens of a video camera and more sophisticated snooping and listening devices, some cables of which ran along the roof's gutter and behind the mist sprayer in the garden. Farid and Jaimie rushed to cover it all up with a thick white tablecloth secured by thumbtacks pressed into the wooden frame.

"SS Eva Braun Rekha Cherman Gestapo Kraut Jerry Fritz Nazi, you vanted to pay for it all? Chus add anozzer $250 to the tab and we'll sort it out tomoghow," Simran/Jess continued. "And now ladies and chentlemen, spraken ze deutsche and we'll all fricken fricking frigging fuck Kapalin off to glory!" she wailed in a high-pitched voice as she toppled forward and passed out. Suryani caught her in the nick of time and prevented a serious injury.

Rekha volunteered to send Simran home after she settled the tab, which included the broken mirror and a huge tip. Farid and Jaimie helped carry their favorite customer to the car, not for the first time. The girls followed behind in a group and bonded once more in a last round of hugs.

Fahrizat, clearly floating in the vapors of an alcoholic cloud, blurted out of the blue, "Did I tell ever you about the time my first boyfriend and I experimented with that other kind of sex and I told him it tasted like there was salt round the rim?"

"Good lord, Farz. Have you no shame, you hussy! You kept that from me all these years, your best of best friends? Was it that tall cricketer Kapil Dev? I suspected you had a thing for him, but I never thought you'd go that far. Ya Allah!" Mastura Jalil swore before she got the giggles.

Rekha made sure Simran was safe on her back on the rear seat. She rummaged around in her car boot and found a recycled cloth carrier bag containing a thin cotton blanket which she used to cover Simran from under her chin to her toes. Satisfied, she climbed into the driver's seat, closed the car door and pressed the 'lock' button.

She pressed the automatic button to wind her car window down. For no reason, she burst into a fresh long bout of giggling. When she'd finished, she looked at her friends fondly. She wiped away her tears with a Kleenex, waved and said, "I'll see you alkies Wednesday at Tigers. I gotta go before Simran throws up at the back and I have to explain it all to Rosh. Drive safely and drive slowly. And if the cops stop and breathalyze you, please, please, don't call me."

As she was about to autowind the window up, she could not help shouting out to the others, "Remember my dears, we are all of one race, the human race."

Best Friends

Simran's apartment outside the city was on Rekha's way home, so it was not too much trouble for her to drop Simran off. Rekha helped Simran all the way out of the car, into the elevator and onto the sofa of her living room, where she collapsed like a sack of potatoes. Rekha had been here many times and knew her way around the apartment.

She knotted a wet hand towel wrapped in ice cubes and placed it on Simran's forehead. She then made two cups of instant Nescafe, which she brought over to the coffee table by the sofa. By then, Simran had sat up and taken stock of where she was.

"You in a hurry?" she croaked to Rekha.

"No, I actually wanted to have a chat with you. Otherwise, I would have left it to Farid and Jaimie to sort you out."

They both laughed.

"Let me take a cold shower, and then we'll get started," said Simran as she excused herself.

She returned twenty minutes later in her night robe looking as fresh as a daisy. Rekha had long wondered why this woman had not taken up modeling or acting. She might have given Dawn a run for her money. Rekha made another two cups of Nescafe and they settled down with a cushion each on the sofa.

"Listen Sim, there's something big going on. I'm hearing strange things from Shan. There's a huge shakeup in Kapalin's security detail. I mean, who would have imagined the national director of police and security and his deputy would both kick the bucket at the same time? That's never happened before. There are also all these rumors about Dawn and dynamite and three security officers charged with her death who are linked to Natasha. What's the connection? Jesus, it's the president and his wife we are talking about!" said Rekha.

"Yeah, it's all over town. I heard Rambo and his cronies discussing it and even Jeff, Isa and their mates. Well, lean back and get yourself comfortable, honey. I'm going to tell you a story you won't believe if your own mother told you," Simran replied.

When Simran had finished with what Jeff had told her about Kapalin and Dawn, Rekha sat there with her hand covering her mouth for a long while.

"Bloody hell, woman, if we take this story to the Washington Post you and I could both retire tomorrow. It might blow the whole country apart, but what the hell, we've been paying more taxes than all these bloody Tigerist Puliporeans put together. Look where I am after thirty years in government service. We deserve the money. Let's go for the money," Rekha pleaded.

"No, my dear, we can't. It might also result in a bullet in Jeff's and Isa's head, or worse, they might dynamite all four of us in some godforsaken place in the jungle. No way. You can't tell a soul about it. Besides, it still doesn't explain who killed Dawn and why, does it?" Simran quickly interjected before Rekha got carried away in her frustration.

"Okay, okay. Shit, I understand. But that's not all. Forget the Washington Post and ten million bucks. I was born to be a slave and wallow in poverty. Anyway, Chand reports that Bhairav and Quasi have arranged to meet up with Kapalin in Langkawi Island in Malaysia. We know Kapalin hates Bhairav's guts, so what's he doing agreeing to meet him when he and Quasi have been doing everything they can to undermine him?" said Rekha.

"I heard the same stuff from Kim about them planning to meet at Langkawi, and from the other girls too. Quasi and Bhairav too are smitten by her high heels and miniskirt and have been indiscreet in her presence. Something's wrong!" Simran shot back. "That can only mean Jeff and Isa will be flying off soon in PAF One. They'll have to land in Kuala Lumpur International Airport and then charter a local flight to Langkawi, which certainly can't handle a plane the size of an A380. That's a strange choice of venue, Langkawi. Jeffie tells me Kapalin would have picked Bali nine times out of ten," Simran wondered aloud.

"Jeffie? Ooh, look who else is smitten. Look girl, I haven't thought this through. But if need be, and we may have to, to save Tiger Isle, can you find a way to get us on board the A380? We need to find out what these crooks and thieves are up to. What do you say?" Rekha asked.

"Look, I just confirmed he's not gay and you want me to ask him to break national security and lose his job?" pleaded Simran.

"It's important, that's all. You know what we've been fighting for, and if we can find something to unhinge this racist and crooked regime, we have to take it," Rekha argued passionately. "Okay, just think about it. We'll discuss it next week at Tigers. But the real reason I wanted to talk to you is something else."

When Rekha had finished narrating her dreams, it was Simran who broke the long silence.

"Listen Rek, you are fighting for a cause. I know I should be, but I don't have the same drive anymore. I've left it to Kirpal and his friends. I just don't have the fight in me. I want to enjoy life a bit before I go. And I don't know what to make of your dream. But I believe in our friendship and I believe in you.

So I'll see how to get Jeff around to doing you and us a favor. I'll call if it's confirmed. Anyway, you should take up Kim's suggestion and go for a break in the mountains with your family. With all this talk of danger and cataclysmic destruction you are having dreams about, sms me if anything big happens. 'D' for death and 'V' for victory, okay?" Simran made Rekha promise.

Two old friends parted on that note, each caught up in their own thoughts about the uncertainties that lay ahead in their lives.

They kissed each other farewell, not knowing it would be the last time they would ever see each other.

The Pampas of Argentina

"Know anything about the Pampas?" Bhairav asked Mahamaya.

"Yes, of course, Adhi Sri. Of course I do. My youngest wears them. A bit pricey, being imported and all, but they're definitely more absorbent than the local brands. And they don't leak. That's what my wife says," Mahamaya quipped back chirpily.

"What?"

"What?"

"No, never mind. Please hand in your international passport to Chandrika on your way out so she can get your visa done. She'll email the agenda for the meeting in Argentina tomorrow and tell you where to collect your flight tickets. Make sure you follow her instructions to the T," Bhairav continued testily.

Try as he could, he could not hide his irritation at Mahamaya's lack of general knowledge. Bhairav had lately come to the sad conclusion that one could no more create a genuine entrepreneur than guarantee a cloned Einstein would bear the same genius traits as the original. The failed government-mooted and looted $20 billion entrepreneurship fund and the $40 billion higher-education loan scheme had created huge irreparable holes in the government's balance sheet. Giving away diplomas and degrees to any Puliporean Tigerist student who cared to register and turn up in the colleges and universities was costlier than Bhairav ever imagined.

Although it's known to the world as the Pampas of Argentina, or La Pampa, parts of it do stretch into Uruguay in the east. These low, flat plains extend for about three hundred thousand square miles from the Atlantic Ocean in the east to the foothills of the Andes to the west of Argentina. It was about as far away a place from Tiger Isle as any.

There was a time not so long ago when the average Tiger Islander, who had completed his form-five government public examination at age seventeen, would have known about the alfalfa grass found growing on the Pampas and how important it was as cattle food. It would not have surprised anyone to have found out the same islanders knew where Vladivostok, Ulan Bator and Wanganui were on the world map, all perhaps equally as far away and remote from Tiger Isle as the Pampas of Argentina.

These islanders knew too of the Eskimo, Native American (once called Red Indian), Australian Aborigine and New Zealand Maori, the Greeks, Alexander the Great, Julius Caesar, Socrates, Saladin the Turk and the events leading up the American War of Independence in 1776 and the American Civil War of 1861–1865. They had gobbled up pre-history and then 1066 and all that about the UK and European, Indian and Chinese history, World Wars I and II, the Cold War and modern history as well as that of Tiger Isle. Words such as Vandals, Goths, Visigoths and Huns were not strange to them.

The Tiger Isle education system had once been second to none. Those who did not possess a university degree were nevertheless well grounded in history and geography by their exposure to secular education.

For a reason the world quite does not comprehend yet, these South American countries once did, and perhaps still do, attract from across the globe fleeing criminals seeking a hideaway. Perhaps it was because most countries did not and still do not have extradition treaties with Argentina and Paraguay. More specifically, Argentina had drawn German Nazi war criminals like Adolf Eichmann, one of the masterminds and executioners of the Holocaust plan and Klaus Barbie, the Butcher of Lyon.

The vilest of them could have been Dr. Joseph Mengele, knighted the White Angel of Death in the concentration camps at Birkenau and Auschwitz. Mengele operated on many without anesthetics and performed genetics experiments, especially on identical twins, his pet subject. In one such experiment, he killed fourteen pairs of twins by injecting chloroform into their hearts and then coolly continued dissecting their organs and making notes. Some believe the unusually high incidence of the birth of twins in the town of Candido Godoi in Brazil was the result of Mengele's illegal work and further experimentations there while fleeing the Nazi hunters. The escape route of these sadists and mass murderers were carefully organized by ODESSA. It was an organization formed by ex-SS members who established "ratlines," or escape routes abroad to avoid prosecution at Nuremburg.

Bhairav and his inner circle comprised men who had benefited immensely from the education system devised by the very Caucasians they now openly professed to detest. So it was not unusual that Bhairav and his three closest cronies were in Buenos Aires, out horseback riding in his estancia, which had sprawling grounds that extended as far the eye could see and farther. Bhairav's cattle, sheep and horse ranch near the Andean foothills had been carefully chosen so that in an emergency, they could scoot off over the mountains in their six-seater Cessna and head for Chile, Peru, Ecuador, Columbia, or beyond. Why, he had even "persuaded" PRA to regularly fly the huge loss-making Chandrapore-Buenos Aires route to facilitate his thrice-a-year trips to the Pampas, not to mention those of his cronies.

They were completely at home in Buenos Aires. They were criminals in every sense of the word, hoarders of blood money squeezed from the arteries and veins of their fellow Tiger Islanders even as they twitched in epileptic fits from the enforced phlebotomy. The NPST carried an exposé that astounded its readers with news that the caring Bhairav spent a lot of time in Argentina, apparently studying the social habits of the blue whales and seals found in staggering numbers in the waters off its coastline. Bhairav had about as much affinity with the leviathans as the whales had to orcas and seals to polar bears.

There was Bhairav, his think-tank Sanat-Yoh and master money-launderer Peter Weller Brown Mole Suryan. They were all in full gaucho gear, including hat, poncho, the loose-fitting bombachas trouser, leather belt with silver coins, long-knife facon, leather whip, lariat and tan riding boots handmade with the most expensive and finest quality soft, full cow's leather imaginable. They had arrived there a week earlier and had already acquired darker tans. With all the gaucho accoutrements it made it impossible for anyone to recognize them as foreigners from a little distance.

Certainly, Quasi Mahamaya could not identify the quartet individually through the heavily tinted glass of the ranch windows. It was made more difficult by the cloud of dust across the Pampas, as they raced each other on their thoroughbred stallions imported from Ireland. Even their studs had been shipped in from the world-renowned Coolmore Stud Farm in South Tipperary, Ireland. Bhairav's three friends too owned huge estancias in adjacent properties.

These four men were of an age where they had been through several trophy wives and mistresses who could no longer provide the extra thrill they craved. Even Viagra had failed them. In their desperation they had even experimented with Malaysia's Tongkat Ali, literally meaning Ali's cane, in all three forms: as pills, mixed in instant coffee and put in instant tea sachets for brewing. A Tiger Isle fringe standup sopo comedian had brought the house down with, "Why, if the four of them were to drop their boxer shorts, the time would always be 6:30. They would be right twice every day without fail." So they settled for horse stud farms and horseback riding and racing.

For an altogether too-brief hour they exulted in the thrill of racing each other. Disturbing thoughts of their mortality, of which they were reminded each additional day they woke up alive in the morning, slipped from their minds as they whooped and cheered in excitement and cried out, "Hyah! Hyah!"

It was the fourth man who interested Mahamaya more than the others. He was the shortest among that group, shorter than even Mahamaya. That almost pitched him in the dwarf league. He had a full head of striking silver hair and a hawk's beak nose. With his John Lennon-type, titanium-silver rimmed, round spectacles he reminded everyone of the bird of prey after which he was named. Unlike Mahamaya however, Damien Bukhary Serpent White Eagle Chandran was thin to the point of emaciation.

Dami Bukhary Serpent White Eagle Chandran, The Quiet Billionaire

Dami, as Damien was called by even waiters and car jockeys, so easygoing and unassuming in public was he, was easily the richest Tigerist billionaire who never, ever tipped. He did not live on Tiger Isle anymore. He rarely set foot there nowadays, having divested all his businesses and assets and transferred most of his cash to a many-layered trust set up in Lichtenstein. Puliporeans were, however, fooled into thinking that Dami was an ultranationalist who kept all his money in the local bank accounts of his "non-profit" White Eagle Foundation. They were also misled into thinking Dami was already a millionaire property developer when he was appointed Bhairav's Chief Economic and Finance Minister. Income Tax records told the true story of Dami as a failed real estate bunko artist.

Word was out that Maitreya had been leaked documents incriminating Dami for some of the most blatant violations of the PSE in acquiring a spate of banks and financial institutions on the cheap. Dami was not about to put to the test whether that was fact or mere conjecture. He did not need to. So, he spent his time in voluntary self-exile in his favorite holiday spots across the world, chief among which was Bali. A very grateful crony had built a $15 million Balinese-style mansion for him in the Sanur district, in a secluded spot dubbed Pulipore Billionaire Robbers' Row.

"Mahamaya, I've heard only good things about you from Bhairav," Dami whispered (as was his nature), on entering Bhairav's cavernous ranch house.

Before Mahamaya could reply, the four collapsed into the hard wooden chairs surrounding a huge oak table in the breakfast lounge and ordered a round of whiskey from the Macallan Fine & Rare Collection, which at forty thousand dollars a bottle was as rare as a poor Tiger Isle government Minister. They knocked it back in the blink of an eye and ordered another round as they threw their whiskey glasses into the fireplace to the collective roar of "L'chaim!" in jest.

The collective greed around that table would have done in twenty Bernie Madhoffs, and without the emergence of a single embarrassing burp, they would have ordered ten more bottles of Macallan's.

"Thank you...Sri...Dami," Mahamaya finally voiced haltingly, cowed as he was by the presence of the greatest looters in Tiger Isle history.

"Would you like a glass of the finest whiskey, Maha?" Peter offered.

"Or, perhaps you'd prefer a bottle of your favorite Mateus Rosé?" Sanat-Yoh chipped in, hiding his smile superbly.

"No, thank you. These days, I'm totallytee. Just a cup of tea will do," Mahamaya replied.

Mahamaya then yawned loudly.

"Must be the jel tag. Adhi Sri and gentlemen, if you'll accuse me, tonight, I'll retire early. I want to be fresh for tomorrow morning's most important mating. The agenda's very long, I notice," Mahamaya said as he got up and headed for his bedroom on the second floor, without waiting for Bhairav's permission.

They laughed without restraint after Mahamaya closed the heavy soundproof door to the breakfast lounge.

"That's a stroke of luck," Bhairav announced. "Now, we can talk money. Dami, let's have your money report," he commanded.

"Briefly, UNTA's original $100 billion slush fund has grown to $200 billion in the last five years. Details of certified copies of income, bank balances, investments and relevant profit and loss accounts and master balance sheet are to be found in read-only attachments forwarded by me to our highly secure and twenty-six-digit-encrypted and alphanumeric password-protected email account. It's all boring stuff that you can check out via the laptops over there. If you have the slightest doubt about anything, we can depart immediately for Geneva, Channel Isles, wherever and carry out an audit as you please," Dami answered. "And if you find anything amiss, the gun's over there," Dami offered.

"What has Kapalin been told?" Peter asked.

"He's got the first set of books. It says $50 billion," Dami replied.

And that was that, because Dami was a known master of the "two-book" system of accounting. Of course, he had lied and kept a third set of ledgers that had Bhairav and the other two really understood accounting, would have shown the true extent of Dami's treachery. But even by today's standard of trillion-dollar government bailouts, $200 billion was a staggering sum, sufficient to please and silence the greedfathers of Tiger Isle.

"Yes Bhairav, to answer your question. Yes, we have enough cabbage to bury Kapalin alive tomorrow, if need be. Well, you can all study the figures at your own leisure. We have a full week here. I don't know about you, but I hear the meows of the best from the cat houses of Macao, Bangkok and Shanghai coming from the next room. Let's partay!" Damien roared.

There is an old saying from Chennai that you may have occasion to trust a thief. But a short arse? Never!

But the following week-long unrestrained rejoicing and pulsating excitement proved to be Dami's eventual undoing. He succumbed to a massive coronary attack. His body was cremated and half the ashes buried within the grounds of his own estancia, with the balance in Bali, as specified in his will. Dami's quickly flown in replacement, Zara, went through the books and totted up all the little holes in the balance sheet. When she reported the Three Gorges Dam-sized embezzlement schemes by Dami, Bhairav was aghast and close to his own heart attack. He looked desperately at Sanat-Yoh.

"Wake up, Stanley. There's enough alcohol in you to function as a thermometer. Dry out. Get the motor into fifth gear," Bhairav coaxed Sanat-Yoh. He did not waste time asking Peter to put on the thinking cap. He knew only too well Peter's limitations when it came to lateral thinking on any matter other than moving money across the globe at warp speed.

"You know, we never got around to capitalizing fully on that MRT line to the new Botanical Gardens. But off the cuff, if we extend it into a fully integrated transport system, including buses, taxis, and even trams covering the whole of Chandrapore City, we could do it at a base cost of about $50 billion," Sanat-Yoh articulated smoothly.

"That's $100 billion then?" Bhairav asked.

"Oh yes, of course. But excluding annual maintenance cost," Sanat-Yoh replied slyly. "But we could also look at replacing PRA's old Boeing fleet with A380s and the air force's Russian MiGs with Eurofighter Typhoon multirole combat aircrafts. There's another $5 billion to $10 billion there, to start with," Sanat-Yoh continued.

"Wouldn't that be dipping into Big Porka's pretty Birkin handbags?" Bhairav queried, eyebrows arched.

"Yes, but we'll offer her that dodgy patrol-boat contract for the navy. Worth a couple of B's. If that's not enough, there's always that contract for three hundred armored vehicles for the UN's Afghan Taliban Watch Program. A few more B's," Sanat-Yoh replied.

"Those navy boats, that's been done before. They'll never be able to deliver a paper boat that floats on water, you know," Bhairav mused.

"Oh sure. But that's the whole idea isn't it?" quipped Sanat-Yoh, fully aware that Bhairav's crony for that earlier contract, Zamani Shah Rukkh Omani, had fled to Jeddah with the navy's billions after delivering a couple of expensive tin cans, sans lids.

And so they continued for the rest of the day and week, as the cut-and-thrust and smell of exciting multibillion-dollar highway robbery hung in the air, and Peter Weller Brown Mole Suryan made notes for his Economic Plundering Unit to swing into action soon.

Sherwood Villas

They came for her at 7:00 p.m. It had gone pitch dark by 5:00 p.m. Weather patterns all over the world were going haywire. Rekha was prepared for it. She wondered where she had made a mistake and who had managed to penetrate her secrets. But it didn't matter. The die was cast.

Her house in Sherwood Villas was one of sixty single-story brick bungalow houses built on sixty-by-eighty-foot freehold land carved out from farmland subdivided and converted for residential homes. It was some fifty kilometers from Chandrapore City's center, heading north.

All these modern housing estates had evocative English, European and American names. On the other side of the connecting highway lay Valencia Villas. Farther east was Florence Villas. Westward, Bordeaux Villas was a mile away. The more exclusive ten-thousand-square-foot double-story bungalow houses, with a view of the sea or valleys or both, were located on a hilltop in the southwest at Champagne Estates.

Another housing development to the south was called California Dreaming, with individual estates like Sacramento Lodge, San Diego Heights, San Francisco Village, Los Angeles Park, Santa Barbara Hills and Santa Monica Drive. The $5 million-per-piece hilltop bungalows were aptly named Hollywood Villas, with the same font and huge white spotlight-lit letters on a billboard surrounded by palm fronds to announce it from a mile away. The advertising billboards, posters and banners all had the tagline "You can check out anytime you like, but you can never leave," oft quoted on Tiger Isle.

At the launch of California Dreaming, they had fifty or so stunning, leggy and amply endowed local models in blonde wigs, dressed in black leather cowgirl attire with plunging necklines and miniskirts. California wines flowed while they endlessly played Hotel California and Life in the Fast Lane by the Eagles.

There was not a single vineyard or winery anywhere on Tiger Isle, though they did sell in the local supermarkets, for twenty-four dollars per kilo, organic seedless grapes purportedly imported from South Africa. "Organic" being all the rage actually meant most of it was grown using standard fertilizers and DDT insect-spray in places like the hills of Chiang Mai in northern Thailand, or Bandung in East Java in Indonesia, where workers were paid less than one U.S. dollar a day. The same applied to organic banana, French beans, cauliflower, soy beans, spinach, carrots, potatoes, snow peas and eggs.

Original import labels and documents were switched and replaced with cleverly forged ones. And if the spot-checking Agriculture Ministry enforcement officers, gentlemen and ladies, turned out to be too nosey or clever, there were always the ready and waiting generously stuffed brown envelopes. Hell, at twenty-four dollars a kilo, they could afford generously stuffed gunnysackfuls.

Few knew the difference between red and white, Claret and Rosé, Vin de Pays and Vin de Plonk, or of the gulf between dry and sweet. Nevertheless, house buyers paid a staggering $888,888 for houses in Bordeaux Villas and $1,288,888 for those in Champagne Estates to Chinese developer Euramerica Realty Ltd. Plc., quoted on the PSE. Equally, house owners, occupiers and speculators in "Bordeaux" and "Champagne" expected an even larger capital gain of not less than 50 percent within three years of their purchase.

What really raked in the sales at the launch, more than the Eagles and leathered-down cowgirls' thighs, was that wedding dance of Marlon Brando, Godfather Don Corleone, with his daughter Connie to the strains of "Speak softly love...wine-colored days, kissed by the sun." The whole clip was projected onto a huge screen set up by the event managers appointed for the day. They had cleverly edited the original movie clip so that instead of just the orchestral music, they had Hong Kong's superstar pop singer Andy Walliau's voice beautifully crooning the lyrics in perfect sync.

The masterstroke was the editing of the clip to complete black and white and the original lyrics "...wine-colored days, warmed by the sun..." replaced with "wine-colored days, kissed by the sun," which warmed the cockles of everyone's heart. That projection of a tightly knit family and home, protected, "gated and guarded" from rampant, thieving and corrupt law enforcement officers, rogue police captains and senators captured perfectly the sentiments of Puliporeans who were fed up to their eyeteeth with soaring crime, committed mostly by their own government.

And when they slotted in that anguish-struck tirade from a choking Amerigo Bonasera about how gangsters brutally beat up and raped his daughter, and he did not get true justice from the police or the courts and how now he needed Don Corleone, the Godfather, to dispense the unique Sicilian brand of an eye-for-an-eye redress, it struck the deepest of chords in the hearts and minds of buyers. It seemed to etch itself in the innermost recesses of their psyches as though to say, "What happened to poor, law-abiding Bonasera and his innocent and beautiful daughter could happen to your women and virgin children if you don't own an Euramerica gated-and-guarded (overpriced) HOME."

Both were the work of pure geniuses. They had toyed with clips of Charles Bronson in Death Wish and Clint Eastwood as Harry Callahan in 1983's Sudden Impact and his infamous "Go ahead, make my day" with "punk" edited in. After intense debate, they shelved it for another day, as they feared the Ministry of Housing and Development (MOHD) would have probably banned it as promoting vigilantism. The MOHD would probably not have been too happy either with .44 Remington Magnum revolvers loaded with dum-dum bullets being waved about, which when fired would leave a tiny pinpoint puncture at its entry into the forehead and blow the brains and entire skull out at the back of the head.

Euramerica's main controlling shareholder was Charlie Chan Chin Chai. His father was an immigrant from Fujian Province in South China who had never stepped outside Chandrapore once in his entire life after he'd settled down there. He had started twenty-five years earlier as a pipe-laying coolie, and by dint of sheer hard work, endeavor and a keen sense of opportunism, had built his real estate empire.

There was only one system of entrepreneurship these developers operated by and that was the two-book-cum-pay-undertable capitalism-driven model. Often, there were three books. Charlie's success was shared with his righthand man, Ms. Man Siew Pau, whose marketing strategy never wavered once in twenty years.

All pricing ended with the numbers 888. Early birds were given an 8 percent discount. All land lots and house numbers ended with the number eight and new launches always commenced on the eight of the month. If the soft launch was just before or after Chinese New Year or on the eighth day of the eighth month, roast pork and eight-spices-sauce-marinated roast duck were served with rice, pork knuckle and cabbage soup and, as Charlie was fond of saying, "Washed down with barbecued pork buns and Chinese wine."

Feng Shui consultations were thrown in free as well for very basic advice on whether the buyer's name and house number were "ngam ngam" or matched astrologically. For more serious advice on the suitability of the house for a mistress, they charged at the rate of one thousand dollars an hour. Of course every visitor was presented an eight-dollar red packet "ang pow' by a Chinese model sexily molded into sprayed-on, hip-to-ankle-length, slit, red "cheong sam" attire. You think eight and red were her's and Charlie's lucky number and color and they knew it?

The houses were set in six blocks of two rows of five each, ending in cul-de-sacs so that while everyone had a neighbor in front, they were separated from the neighbor at the back by buffer zones of copses. The exception were of course the two end rows, one of which had the highway a hundred meters away, while the other had a low hill behind which lay fenced-off farmland.

Children's playgrounds with swings and seesaws and bicycle and jogging tracks were all woven into the design layout. It was an hour's drive to the city from Sherwood Villas. But Rekha and her husband did not mind that. They had so much greenery and fresh air for the bargain while the kids had space and enjoyed the company of neighbors and animals in farms, especially the horses. Not for them the cooped-up lifestyle of overbuilt and congested "gated and guarded condos" with their smelly rubbish chutes, elevators that jammed every other month and extortionate service charges.

She had copied and pasted all her files from the hard disc of her $2,600 Dell laptop to two non-branded thumbdrives and a 500-gig Fuji external hard-disc storage gadget. She made another backup on a Buffalo 250-gig hard-disc storage gizmo. These she had handed to Harris N. Bhupalan, Haroon Rashid and Bernard Chong the previous week. They would carry them to Wikirat Leaks, Allies Without Borders and Advocates Without Borders in America and Europe.

Being of typical kiasu (overkill) mentality, she had made a two-day trip to Singapore by air. From her hotel room in Traders Inn in Orchard Spring near Tanglin Mall, Orchard Boulevard and Orchard Road, she attached more thumbdrive backups of the same files to her laptop. She emailed these to new accounts she had opened with Yahoo, Gmail and Hotmail. Details of the account names and passwords were emailed to her lawyer and blogger friends, ten of them in Tiger Isle, London, Washington and Paris.

When she'd finished with all that, she erased all the data and files from her Dell hard disc completely, emptied the recycle bin and had it disc cleaned and disc fragmented twice before removing the hard disc from its internal casing. She packed it all in a XL-size black plastic carrier bag and knotted it tight with raffia before flinging it into the depths of the Singapore River.

When she returned home, she retrieved her damaged, old and clunky $7,500 Fuji laptop from storage, placed it prominently on her desktop in the living room corner and attached to it a host of thumbdrives and external hard-disc drives loaded up with cooking recipes, Sudoku, poems and inspirational quotes. She stuffed the USB end of the printer cable into the printer port of the Fuji to give it an air of authenticity.

Later she would claim a power surge during a late afternoon flash thunderstorm had burnt out the motherboard of her Fuji laptop, wiping out all her systems, working applications and backup files. She engineered a circuit burnout so the acrid smell of fire, smoke, chips, plastic and wires still hung in a pall in her study corner and scorch marks scarred her desktop.

She packed her husband and kids off to Melbourne for a month. She made sure they took their precious laptops while their PCs remained on the computer tables in their bedrooms, switched on and logged in. Then she sat down at her desk and peered at the images beamed to her TV from the pinhole lens of the special camouflaged micro CCTV spy camera she had secretly installed in the roof of her neighbor's house directly across the street. She was ready. She waited patiently for all hell to break loose.

Chief Inspector (CI) Kevin Little Deer Pereira, Chief Investigating Officer (CIO) Jude Yellow Python Moraes and Senior Inspector (SI) Mohamad White Rabbit Saiful from PSB crouched safely behind the rear of their squad cars as the experts blew the solid teak front door off its hinges with C4 plastic explosives. Then eleven ninja-like Elite Anti-Terrorism Stormtrooper Squad (EATSS) men in black, decked out in protective bulletproof vests and reinforced plastic helmets over menacing black balaclava masks, led by Black Ops Commander Rahim Nor Black Bull, rushed through the smoke, debris and collapsing ceiling with handheld protective plastic shields close to their bodies.

They advanced swiftly in trained phalanx formation, ready to toss stun grenades or open fire with short-range Remington 870 pump-action shotguns favored by the Special Air Services (SAS) UK in counter-terrorist offensives. They came after her in intimidating killer fashion, even though they had agreed with her lawyers she would voluntarily come forward to be interviewed by CIO Jude Moraes the following Monday morning at PSB HQ.

It was 7.00 p.m., Friday, August 31, 2012. The numerology was a horror. All the numbers added up together with the time produced 6.

Hovering high above the house was a medium-weight Asiacopter Tigre HCP, or French Helicoptere de Combat Polyvalent or Multipurpose Combat Helicopter, armed with machine guns and Mistral infrared homing AAM, air to air as well as SAM, surface-to-air missiles. The body of the Tigre was reinforced with carbon fiber, polymer, Kevlar, fine copper and bronze sheets, and circuitry to withstand combat and bird strikes.

Originally, the Ministry of Defense had only approved a budget of $1 billion for thirteen Pulipore Asiacopters for search-and-rescue operations and missions. But as in so many previous dealings with the French, they discovered the sting in the tail later than sooner. All the instruction manuals, signage and spare parts were labeled in French and had to be replaced. The costs of a flight simulator or maintenance contract options past the standard warranty period of two years were not included. All prices were subject to change without notice.

The MoD received verbal instructions from the Economic Planning Directorate that the president had personally recommended a local "approved agent" be engaged to finalize the negotiations with the French. The president had also mentioned "not a commission, but facilitation, support and administration fee," ballpark figure of 10 percent to 15 percent of the contract sum, for the agent.

Someone pointed out that for that price, the copters, marketed as "Sudamericopter" in Chile, included onboard computer and laser-guided state-of-the-art missiles for search-and rescue missions against Shining Path rebels. Eventually the Asiacopter price escalated to $2.4 billion and the supplementary bill was patriotically approved by Parliament when told Tiger Isle would have the best and most advanced search, rescue and destroy copters in the world.

CI Kevin had earlier claimed he had "information from highly reliable anonymous sources" that the entire neighborhood of Rekha's house was a haven and hideout for dangerous separatists and terrorists hell-bent on starting an armed insurrection to overthrow their freely and fairly elected government. He had requested the PSB to sound out the Defense Minister if the air force could deploy BLU-118/B thermobaric bombs, of the kind dropped recently by United States forces in the Shahi-Kot Valley, ninety miles south of Kabul in Afghanistan, as standby.

The thermobaric bomb sucks all the oxygen out of the air, literally causing it to burn, while bomblets shred bodies to bits and flatten whole valleys and underground bunkers in nanoseconds. Its other version is the six-hundred-pound Daisy Cutter BLU-82 B/C-130, or the MOAB—Mother of All Bombs—used in Operation Enduring Freedom in Afghanistan by U.S. and European forces. Its father had been filled with napalm and dropped in Vietnam.

This request by Kevin was immediately and summarily turned down by the chairman of the Joint Chiefs of Staff, five-star General Sri Arjuna Black Falcon Suryan, who summoned his director of the JCS, three-star General Drona Red Hawk Sivan.

"Shit, go find out what the hell is happening out there. Have the idiots declared war on Indonesia or Malaysia? Is Al Qaeda operating here or what? And who the hell does this bozo think we are, Uncle Sam? Motherofthermobaricfucking and Daisy Cutter bombs indeed! We haven't got past tossing hand grenades out plywood planes yet, don't they know?"

Waiting patiently in a copse in the park directly behind Rekha's house, ready to spring into instant action if required, was another unit of eleven EATSS men armed with shoulder-fired air missile grenades, tear gas launchers and pepper water-spray canisters. They were packed to their eyeteeth with automatic firearms of all kinds. The air all around them buzzed with the hum of sotto voce whispered commands and "Do you copy?" "Yes sir, we copy, sir!" and "Ten four, over and out, sir!" short-wave transmissions and the "click, clack" metallic crackle from their U.S. Special Forces earpiece and throat swivel mikes.

Rekha positioned herself on the floor with arms and legs akimbo at the foot of her chair and writing desk, as though she'd been flung and rendered unconscious from the blast of the exploding door. She had already prepared herself for the assault by inflicting small bleeding cuts on her face, arms, legs and thighs and making a couple of minor tears on her shirt, blouse and jeans. She padded a glass milk bottle with a hand towel and knocked herself over the forehead until a bump appeared over her left eyebrow. She made sure the Fuji laptop and printer were dashed on the floor with the cord and plugs ripped off from their wall sockets.

"Don't move! Don't move, bitch!" EATSS team leader Rahim Nor Black Bull screamed at Rekha as she moaned in pretence and started fluttering her eyelids. "Two, three and four, check out the front rooms. Watch out for trip-wire bombs and traps. Five, six and seven to the back rooms! Eight and nine, outside, back."

The earlier infrared thermal scans from their stealth mobile-ops van parked in the copse at the back of the house had not shown signs of other live human bodies within. But you could never be too certain. They might have been hiding in underground bunkers, basements and under trapdoors.

"Ten and eleven, get the bitch. Make sure she's got no weapons or suicide bombs strapped to her chest. Move!" screamed Rahim as he positioned himself behind the generous couch in the living room now littered with pieces of wood, metal, door frame, ceiling plaster, books, newspapers, curios and glass from exploded mirrors, patio doors, windows, display cabinets and television sets.

Rekha sniggered inwardly. Suicide bomb? Hell, suicide was the last thing on her mind. And it was a wee bit ticklish being poked and prodded by gun snouts. But she controlled herself and moaned even louder and tried to sit up.

"Shut the fuck up, terrorist bitch scum. Stay still!" barked number ten as number eleven grabbed and snapped her hands behind her back, cuffed her forcefully and slipped a thick black hood with no breathing holes over her head. The hood reached the base of her neck, where they cinched a knot to keep it tight.

Rekha now moaned for real as they had jerked her hands and arms roughly and painfully.

They lifted and flung her on her back on the couch in one swift, effortless motion as if she were a feather. Rekha screamed as the handcuffs bit into her spine and gunshots rang out from the bedrooms, kitchen, bathrooms, utility room and the backyard.

"Shut up, lesbian mongrel whore! Where are they? Where are they? Quick or I'll blow your fucking brains out!" threatened number one.

"No! No! I'm all alone. Who are you? What do you want?" Rekha screamed, now letting the panic show a little in her voice.

"There's nobody else here, boss. No trip bombs, no basement, no guns, bullets, knives. No nothing," informed forlorn and disappointed numbers eight and nine, known sadists in uniform who were trained to shoot first and ask questions later.

"What the fuck! What the fuck!" Rahim bellowed as number two to seven also trudged back into the living room, looking thoroughly downcast. They too reported finding nothing that warranted an EATSS invasion. "Get me that poofter Kevin on the line, now!" he shouted into his throat mike back to command base. "That you, Kev?" he barked.

"No, it's your fairy godmother, who do you think? Wazzup?" asked Kevin.

"Why the fuck don't you come in here and take a look?" Rahim invited him. "There's a lone lesbian bitch and not a single separatist or frigging Al Qaeda terrorist in here, cocksucker!"

The three cops from PSB, five of their minions and the eleven EATSS men stood in a circle in Rekha's living room as she writhed and struggled on the couch. To be truthful, Rekha had not expected this over-the-top assault. They had just blown away $2 million on an operation to get incriminating evidence and all they had was her and wood and plastic chips.

Kevin swore like a trooper as he looked at the damage around him. "Okay men, tag all the laptops, handphones and PCs and get them over to HQ. I want the techies to have a crack at it straight away. Get the CSI guys and gals started now. And you ninja flatfoots, don't touch anything. Leave. Now!" he ordered.

Commander Rahim Nor would have strangled Kevin then and there with his bare hands. But years of army training had forged into his soul the rules of hierarchy, rank and authority. He and his men had been instructed by higher ups that CI Kevin Little Deer Pereira from PSB was in charge today, to obey his orders implicitly and not ask any questions. They left quietly, merging with the other unit aboard the Eurocopter, which headed back to the special-ops base in a secret location in Chandrapore Hills.

Kevin personally escorted Rekha and shoved her into the backseat of his unmarked Mercedes 350S car. He did not bother to duck her head as was the custom. That got her another small bump on her forehead. They whisked her off to PSB HQ as stunned neighbors milled about in the streets, talking to each other and the hundred or so cops and men from the Volunteers Auxiliary Reserve Service. They assured the good people that it was all right, not to worry, and persuaded them to get back to their homes and beds.

All internet, landline telephone, handphone, radio and television signals in the Sherwood Villas vicinity were jammed or switched off by the authorities for seventy-two hours as the PSB got cracking. They talked to each other with walkie talkies. Teams of three each, led by a senior inspector, went from house to house to warn their occupants of suspected Al Qaeda terrorists and/or separatists who were using these remote farms to plan a 9/11-style attack on Chandrapore and eventually overthrow their freely and fairly elected government.

They were warned never to speak to anyone about it—"national security you understand"—sms their friends, post anything on their blogs, comment on other blogs, or contact the online news portals or mainstream media "unless of course you are part of it or wish to be hauled up to PSB HQ to pay a visit to our esteemed interrogators, do you?"

"But I've known Rekha, her nice husband and children for over three years. I mean, we carpool and my girl sleeps over there on weekends. We go shopping and marketing together, the guys are golfing buddies and the two boys are in the same Boy Scout troop in school," a neighbor remarked.

"Yeah, that's what they said about Mohamad Atta and Amrozi too."

"Mohamad and Amrozi who?"

"The New York World Trade Center bombers' ringleader and that smiling Bali bomber."

"Oh."

It was a walk in the park for the PSB pros, as fifty-nine households in Sherwood Villas slunk back to bed, cowed by the spin doctoring and misinformation they had just been force fed. Most of all, the neighbors didn't fancy being dragged to SBHQ or God forbid, to Shakthipore's National Detention Center for indefinite incarceration without charge or trial under the dreaded PSA. The PSB had performed superbly in crisis management.

But they did not have an inkling of the tiny concealed CCTV camera across the road from Rekha's house, did they?

The IR

Senior Inspector Ahmad White Rabbit Saiful pointed Chief Inspector Kevin Little Deer Pereira's infrared remote control to ping the barrier up. He brought the unmarked Merc police car to a screeching halt in the secured basement car park reserved for inspectors at PSB HQ on Peace Hill. Jude bundled a totally lost and still-hooded Rekha out of the backseat of the Merc and guided her toward the elevator.

One by one they positioned their faces on the chinrest of the Biometric Access System's (BAS) laser scanners to gain access into the Otis.

Kevin used his special remote to override the controls for Rekha, also making sure the system did not log her into the permanent database after erasing the temporary record.

Yes, the government spent a small fortune, a couple of billion dollars, installing this state-of-the-art security system in PSB, police HQs and stations throughout the country in the face of teething protests from the opposition. They did not employ the usual "if the White House, CIA, MI5 and especially Mossad have it, then so must we" spiel. Or the "if we must have it, we must have the best" recognized internationally as the Rolls Royce argument to steamroll the extravagance through Parliament.

The president did not say it publicly. The real reason was he and his cabinet had seen it at a private screening of Charlie's Angels: Full Throttle at the home movie theater of his palatial $65 million mansion, Xanadu. He had been convinced because Big Porka had gotten excited and bubbled, "Darling, now that's what cooool is. Can we get one?" Well, that and the sexy and chirpy platinum blonde Cameron Diaz/Natalie Cook's pouty derriere had won Kapalin over.

BAS was also installed in Parliament House and Government HQ at Pulijayam as well as the president's office. Of course it goes without saying that the direct nego contract had been awarded to a Tigerist crony at twice the actual cost with the usual quid pro quo "donation" to UNTA paid into its bank account in Zurich.

The jet-speed silent elevator zoomed them up to the fourteenth floor of Plaza M, where the soundproof interrogation rooms (IR) were located. Above were six more floors. Kevin did not bother stopping at the ground floor to officially log her in. He wanted to precisely avoid that. He was not a great respecter of Miranda caution rules or constitutional rights to prompt legal representation.

No one other than his two men knew Rekha was there with them, or so he thought. He sent her sprawling across the carpeted floor of IR Number Nine at the far end of the corridor to the left of the elevator lobby, and then locked the solid wooden door behind him. To the right of the elevator lobby there was a small "visitors" area with a set of cane sofas and two single seaters with side tables. There was also an "inquiry" counter with a door farther back, leading to administration cubicles and offices.

Directly opposite the door, in the center of the wall at the other end of the IR, was a glass window secured by a grill with a sliding bolt, which rested in a bolt holder and was padlocked at its latch hole that slotted into a holder screwed into the room wall. A black curtain covered the entire window.

Through that window, when the curtains were drawn, you could see across the street and beyond that the gigantic dome of the magnificent Chandrapore Al Aqsa Mosque about a half mile away. It was made from pure marble imported from Langkawi in Malaysia.

The dome alone cost some $100 million. The entire mosque cost $800 million, funded by devout Muslims and the government on a dollar-for-dollar contribution. The actual money collected from the public was no more than $50 million, but the accounts were creatively "massaged" and costs inflated to reach the $800 million payout. The matter had yet to be tabled before the PARC, but it was rumored that the contractor and consultant involved had vanished to Yemen.

Nine floors directly below the window was the concrete roof of an annex shopping mall.

The walls, floor and ceiling were all well padded with soft material and lined with jet black fabric. IR design and sound consultants from Israel and South Africa had been handsomely paid to keep the acoustics in and to accommodate the tossing about of suspects without cracking their skulls and bones. In the middle of the IR stood a specially assembled white PVC table, bolted to the floor of the twenty-four-by-sixteen-foot room. Positioned around it were four PVC armchairs, also bolted to the floor.

A single, clear one-hundred-watt non-energy-saving bulb burned brightly in its socket, screwed into the plaster of the fifteen-foot-high ceiling, protected by a small steel mesh cage. The bulb's luminosity could be increased or decreased by means of an adjustable rheostat switch located in a panel on the side of the table.

Laid out neatly in the left-hand corner of the IR, on a silver tray resting on a small table bolted to the floor, as though awaiting a catalogue photo shoot, was a complete dental-extraction kit with several drills and pliers. On a similar adjacent tray and table were a surgical kit with scalpels, two hacksaws, which could be used for a major amputation operation, a couple of twelve-inch-long hypodermic syringes and a half dozen Malayan bamboo canes or rotans. In one corner of the table rested a plastic jug of tap water and a stack of Styrofoam cups.

They picked Rekha up from the floor and tossed her carelessly into the chair at the PVC table. In a way it was fortunate she was still hooded. Had she seen the stark room, which was designed to strike abject terror into any suspect's heart and soul, she might have spilled everything out at once and given it all away. Kevin had read somewhere that it was imperative to disorientate a suspect as much as possible to secure quick and best results, so the hood stayed where it was.

Most of the office staff would have left early Friday evening for their long weekend. Few officers would be reporting to PSB HQ on Saturday unless some emergency cropped up. No one, including security, would come up or down to the IR floor without special clearance. He had taken care of that. It was now 1:00 a.m. Saturday. He had till 6:00 a.m., Monday, September 3, to break Rekha.

He lit up a Marlboro as did the other two. The nicotine stains on their fingers were dead giveaways. They easily did sixty sticks a day each. It was the stress of the job, they would aver. However, it was their addiction that caused the stress and made them hover on the edge whenever they missed a fix. There were no ashtrays in the IR, so they tipped ash onto the carpet wherever they sat or stood and tossed the stubs into their Styrofoam coffee cups. Sloppiness of that kind was much admired in these hallowed circles.

"May I have a glass of water, please?" Rekha asked in a voice choked with fear.

Before she could utter another word, Ahmad got up and smacked her four times rapidly across her face, drawing blood from inside her cheeks and nostrils. "Rule number one is to speak only when you are asked to. Otherwise keep your trap shut, stupid. Understand?" he warned her calmly and smiled. She could not see the smile, but the manner of his addressing her enhanced the menacing atmosphere.

She nodded her head. Her face had turned white. Blood and spit began seeping from the corner of her lips, encrusting on the hood, where it touched her lips and neck and dripped on to the floor from under the hood. She wanted to throw up from the acrid taste of iron, but somehow maintained her composure. Her cheeks had started puffing up.

"Now," started Kevin in a low and controlled voice, "we know everything about your intention to bring the government down. We know you want to start a revolution and overthrow the government. Don't deny it. We have been monitoring you for the past year, ever since you wrote that memo to the comptroller of GAD about your investigations into remittances by the Central Bank to offshore accounts in Zurich, Guernsey, Panama and the British Virgin Islands. We want the names and identities of all your accomplices. Are you ready to confess?"

"Let the games begin," she thought to herself.

"I don't know what you are talking about. I am a happily married woman with two kids. I work in the comptroller of GAD's office. I have done nothing wrong. I demand to see my lawyer. Why have I been arrested? What's the charge? I have my constitutional rights. I demand it!" she answered back confidently, but in a neutral tone without showing traces of anger or fear this time.

Jude Moraes, who had been standing behind her chair, pulled her up and landed a shock rabbit punch delivered kung fu style on her right kidney. It caused a small internal renal rupture and sent her sprawling forward. She could not grab the table's edge for support, so she collapsed forward, first banging her head on the table and then the padded floor. The plastic, thick carpet and floor padding saved her. But the shooting pains in her back made her head spin. She felt nauseated as she lay on the floor. Her breath came in short spurts.

"Bitch, rule number two is you have no rights here. You don't demand anything. Start answering or you may never see anyone again," Jude too uttered in that neutral, almost robotic and grim menacing tone. They had been trained well.

Kevin got up and started pacing the floor. They made no attempt at the "good cop, bad cop" routine; it was bad cop all the way. "Listen Rekha, there's no need for violence and pain. You can make it easy for yourself. How much money do you want, one million dollars, two million, three million? We can arrange that. Then you can go back to your lovely retreat in Sherwood Villas.

Hubby wubby Roshan and your darlings, Karthik and Lakshmi, can return from Melbourne. You'd like that wouldn't you? Oh, you thought we didn't know about Melbourne, did you? All we want are a few names, files and your signature. See, we've already prepared your confession. And let me tell you nicely. We always get our way," coaxed Kevin, sounding like he was her father, yet all the words were wrong.

Ahmad pulled her up roughly on to her wobbly knees. "Sit!" he ordered with no sympathy whatsoever.

She sank in the chair like stone in water. Her head swam and her face and back ached. The sweat poured from her face and back. She could feel her insides were damaged. She knew he was bluffing, as she had made no attempt to hide the departure of her husband and children. Rekha had trouble focusing and stringing her words, but she was not ready to give up yet. She spoke in short gasps, "I want a doctor, I want my lawyer and some water," she demanded quietly.

Kevin Pereira could not contain himself any longer, as he launched himself at her chest with a flying kick which broke two of her right ribs. He quickly extricated himself from Rekha and the chair whose bolts had held true. Rekha screamed with shock and pain and passed out. They revived her with cold water and smelling salts. She could hardly sit, and every breath she took caused nausea as the nerves pinched at the cracked ribs. Her left arm went numb.

They were just warming up to their tasks. All three removed their jackets and slung them over the chair. They unbuttoned their collar buttons, loosened their ties and rolled up their long sleeves.

These were sadistic beasts who enjoyed inflicting pain and torture on their fellow humans. They forced her to strip to her brassiere and panties and stand with her back to the full blast of the two-horsepower air conditioner with the temperature setting on maximum cold. She began to shiver and shake all over, but could not hold or rub herself. She collapsed in a heap again.

They took turns burning a tattoo of marks on the back of her hands. As she screamed and struggled, her half naked body came into contact with their thighs. Her deathly screams got them even more excited, but they reckoned there would be time for that later.

If she attempted to bend her knees or sit on the floor, one of them would whip her with the rotan across the buttocks, which were soon marked with a criss-cross of cane marks and red welts. While she lay there on her sides panting and screaming, they rained strokes on the soles of her feet. They took turns to beat her all over her body with a thin, hollow rubber tube that left no marks but damaged her kidneys and liver.

They inserted sharp needles between her fingernails and used the pliers to rip off a few. Her hands were a bleeding mess when they started hitting her with a rubber tube filled with sawdust. Her body was covered with a uniform layer of purple bruises and welts.

"You ready to sing yet?" Kevin taunted her, whispered in her ears and laughed a low psychopathic laugh.

She came in and out of stupor, but still found strength to say, "Water."

This infuriated Kevin even more. He grabbed her arms from behind, while Ahmad and Jude held her by the waist and stretched it upwards until it looked like the humerus would pop out of its ball-and-socket joint attachment to the scapula.

As she was blacking out and trying to slide to the floor, Kevin suddenly released her arms, took ten paces back, bunched up his rock-hard right fist, rushed forward and delivered a neat and brutal martial arts punch to her left upper forearm, cracking the bone neatly into two pieces dead center.

Before she hit the floor, he completed his forward momentum with a high flying kick in the air and landed with a fancy, almost graceful, pirouette as though he was Nijinsky in Swan Lake.

When she came to, it was 4:00 a.m., Monday. Her left upper arm had swollen to the size of a football and was completely useless. She had expected some pain and torture, but this, she had not gambled for. There was pain and more murderous pain. The throbbing from head to toe was unbelievable. She had to think fast, restrategize. She was completely dehydrated. She now begged for the handcuffs and hood to be removed and water to quench her parched throat.

They had been at it now for fifty-one hours straight. Suddenly Kevin relented and signaled to Ahmad and Jude to attend to her. But first he dimmed the light, not so much to make it easy for Rekha's eyes to slowly adjust to a little brightness, but so as to gain a psychological advantage with a macabre atmosphere. The combined threat posed by the dental drills and pliers, hacksaws and hypodermic syringes, which while not used, frequently never failed to reduce the most stubborn of men and women to a mass of quivering compliant jelly. Oh, the Marquis de Sade could have taken lessons from this PSB trio.

Rekha scanned the faces of her torturers through the haze of pain for the second time since Friday night as she gulped water from a Styrofoam cup and asked for more. She studied and memorized the room and its layout in seconds. She shivered involuntarily when she spotted the dental pliers and drills, hypodermics and hacksaws.

She was a quick thinker and realized the situation was hopeless. She closed her eyes and the images of her children and husband floated by. She remembered baby Karthik sliding his little cheeks against hers and habitually falling asleep there and little Lakshmi, who promised to marry her and look after her forever when she was four.

Memories of her courting days with Roshan flashed by in her mind. She thought of her beloved mother, who had passed away five years ago, and of her wise and kind ninety-six-year-old father, who lived alone in Chandrapore and whom she'd not had the time to visit on Thursday.

She was glad she had telephoned her only brother and sister in Melbourne the previous month. She fought the panic and tears back. She said a silent prayer to them all and shut them out of her mind. "Focus, focus," she said to herself. But how could she? Her body and head were broken, inside and out. She didn't know where the pain began and where it ended. She willed herself to shut the pain out, knowing that it would not do to weaken mentally now. She visualized Gandhi and meditated on steel magnolias.

"You ready to sign? We'll start with the confession first, shall we and then move on to tape recordings?" quipped Kevin, all polish and charm now. She nodded her head in agreement and asked for assistance to be propped up with any cushions they could find. While Jude was sent off on this errand, Kevin fished out from the desk drawers voluminous documents all stamped on the top-righthand corner of every page with "P&C," "For Eyes Only" and "Government Secrets Act." He sorted them all out carefully and stacked them in neat piles with Ahmad's aid.

Jude returned soon enough with the cheap Styrofoam-filled cushions from the sofa in the "visitors" area.

Kevin was finally ready and turned the four sets of "confession papers" to the signing pages. He leaned forward to pass the black Cross ballpoint pen to her and said, "Well, there's no need to read all the legalese, mumbo jumbo and gobbledygook clauses, is there? You can read it later of course, but the sooner you sign, the sooner you can go off." He was careful to not to say "home" to her. "Don't you think so my dear?" oozed Kevin. "Oh and be sure to initial all pages in the bottom-right corner, even the ones left intentionally blank, please, except of course the signing pages, thank you," Kevin reminded her, now all smiles and chummy.

She reached for the pen. As her fingertips began to wrap around it and Kevin let go, she let the pen slip and roll under the table. As Jude dived to pick it up, she broke into a raucous coughing fit. She collapsed against the cushions in a half faint as her eyeballs rolled upwards. In between the wheezing and coughing she pointed to the windows and gasped for some fresh air. Kevin, sensing total victory, was only too happy to oblige. He pulled out a Yale key from another drawer in the desk and passed it to Ahmad.

Ahmad slid the black curtain to the end of its railing, unlocked and slid the squeaking and creaking bolt and grill all the way back till it rested against the room wall. He pushed open the glass window to its maximum. It was flush against the wall outside, secured by the last hole in its protruding arm, slotted in the metal peg on the interior sill of the window frame. Cool, invigorating fresh air rushed in as stale, musty cigarette-smoke-filled pollution flowed out. Ahmad tossed his cigarette stub out and leaned forward, taking in lung loads of fresh air. Rekha saw her chance. It was now or never.

Flutter of Wings

She leaped out of the chair before Kevin or Jude realized it or could react to her sudden movement. Though she moved like greased lightning, it all appeared as though it was being enacted in slow stroboscopic motion. An unknown part of the human brain took over to deaden Rekha from debilitating pain, nausea and agony that would have felled a leviathan. She grabbed a scalpel with her functioning right hand, scattering the contents of the trays across the floor. She spun around and flung herself at Ahmad, burying the scalpel to its hilt into his right kidney. Even as he tried to turn around, she lunged at him with her full body weight and sent him sailing out the window.

His trouser back pocket snagged on the dislodged window latch and he hung there briefly, fourteen stories up in the air, looking down at the roof of the fifth-floor annex staring up at him. He managed to get a right-hand grip on the window ledge and tried to get another with his left to haul himself back to safety. He twisted and turned like a panicked eel.

Rekha leaned forward and sank her teeth into Ahmad's right hand, through flesh, blood, phalange, metacarpals, bone and cartilage. He screamed and let go of the ledge. As a last-gasp effort, he tried to grab the latch. It snapped in the middle and he landed on his head, plunging 180 feet below onto the roof of the fifth-floor annex shopping mall. His body bounced on the concrete roof top and came to rest thirteen feet from the vertical wall of the PSB HQ building, the latch coming to rest next to his body.

Death had not been instantaneous, although the skull shattered into a thousand pieces and blood splattered in all directions. The body electrics caused it to twitch for two minutes. He had screamed all the way down and she took satisfaction in that. She took more satisfaction from seeing his body jerking left and right like a marionette. She exulted that in his dying moments, Ahmad had been engulfed in unbearable, terrifying pain.

She turned around and faced the remaining two killers. She bared her teeth in a rictus of terror and screamed in triumph. Kevin and Jude froze in their tracks. The odds were hopelessly impossible. Two highly trained and experienced bull professionals with a thousand kills between them, against a broken fifty-three-year-old mother of two kids? Even one of them against her would have been too many.

Kevin approached from her right and Jude from the left. Kevin paused to grab a scalpel and an oversized hypodermic from the floor. He tossed a rechargeable drill to Jude, who switched it on. The high-pitched whirr of the drill filled the room. They paused about five feet from her and made eye contact to time their twin assault. Then it happened.

Who's to say what really transpired? There were no witnesses. But to Kevin and Jude it appeared the IR and its ceiling had disappeared and they had been magically whisked away to a place they had never been before. Nothing appeared real, least of all Rekha, who stood tall like an Amazon in full battle armor and gear. They were on a mountain peak in the shadows of the seventy-foot-tall Tiger Thoon and Siva Lingam. They were on Mt. Kailas.

The duo too, in armor and helmets, armed only with sword and shield, rushed her. But this was no frail, battered, bruised and weakened woman they locked horns with. She was possessed and guided by forces beyond Kevin's and Jude's comprehension. The sparks flew as the clang of metal against metal echoed throughout the mountains, hills and valleys. She was more than a match for them. She toyed with them until they were run ragged and dropped their swords. She ran her sword through their hearts before lopping their heads off!

As she collapsed at the foot of the Tiger Thoon, exhausted and gasping for air, she discerned the four of them at the edge of the clearing, from the corner of her eyes. Sivan, Suryan, Chandran and Krishnan looked at her, smiled and gave her the sign of five. From their shadows, out stepped Gurunadha with his Kamandalu and released once again the waters of life.

The Malays have a word for it: amok. Sometimes when provoked beyond reason, a person can be given to violent rages of uncontrollable fury while in a trance.

Rekha took in lungfuls as she swooned onto the carpet at the foot of the IR window. Heaving and panting, totally spent, she looked across the floor at the gory sight of Kevin with a scalpel in his chest and Jude with a dental drill buried in his windpipe, with a pink bubble cluster around it. Jude's intestines were sliding out from a long cut in his belly. Kevin had several fingers missing and his leg appeared to have been nearly severed at the left knee. The hypodermic was jammed into Kevin's crotch. There was an ocean of blood on the carpet.

The dying Kevin pulled out his secure handphone from his trouser pocket and pressed '1' on rapid dial. The voice at the other end was that of the new national director of police and security, Sri Omar Bakri Din Grey Field Mouse Chandran. He had been plucked and promoted from obscurity by Kapalin to replace the recently terminated without prejudice Haniff Hassan and his deputy Abu Bakar. It said, "You got it?"

"Yes," he lied, unfamiliar with the voice at the other end of the secure phone.

"Good, excellent! What about the asset?"

"She's fine," he lied again.

"So?"

"We need a special team. Out-of-town cleaners," he requested, steeling himself to keep his voice steady. He was a true professional to the last.

"When?"

"Now."

"Done. One hour. Oops, almost forgot. Kev, you, Jude and Ahmad take a few days off. Then you come alone and look me up at the Mirage Resort and Casino in Suryapore. I'll have the penthouse suite booked for you and your pretty boys from Tigers. Hope they'll like your usual ménage à trois. Ciao!"

The line went dead.

"Bastard, he knows about Farid and Jaimie!" screamed a finally broken Kevin as he lay there dying.

Rekha dragged herself over to Kevin, grabbed his phone and dashed off her last sms, which simply said, "D." At the receiving end, Simran had just enough strength and resolve to forward it to six others before she collapsed in absolute devastation, despair and tears.

Rekha thought she was hallucinating when she heard the flutter of wings behind her from outside the windows. But Kevin and Jude heard it too and cocked their ears. It was too early for the pigeons, thought Kevin, though he could see the first rays of the morning sun emerging from behind Al Aqsa's dome.

"It's not fair," were the last thoughts of self-delusionists Kevin Little Deer Pereira and Jude Yellow Python Moraes, as they lay there choking and drowning in their own blood. They stared at what was approaching Rekha.

They slowly descended from above and enfolded Rekha in the warm embrace of their wings. They smiled at her, touched her with their divine hands and made her whole, complete and strong again.

They hugged her, kissed her, stroked her face, wiped away her tears and fears and rode the ether to deliver Rekha to a far, far better place.

It was the 3rd of September, that day I'll always remember. Yes, I will.

Poker in the Sky

It was strange indeed that Bhairav, Kapalin, Quasi Mahamaya and the new national director of police and security, Omar Bakri Din Grey Field Mouse Chandran were all trussed up like turkeys. Stranger still was that they were all handcuffed to the arms of their wide leather seats and bound further in leg chains in the special luxurious presidential suite of PAF One, on which no expense had been spared to provide luxury and comfort and that had, for its sheer opulence, put to shame Obama and U.S. Air Force One.

Adhi Gurunadha had pulled out of this gathering of super thieves on PAF One at the last minute. For once, and much to his regret, no amount of money could persuade him to desert the millions who had arrived in Gurunadhapore and saw in him their last hope for salvation. In hindsight, it did not matter either way. It was yet a strange confluence of events and circumstances that brought Bhairav, Kapalin and Omar face to face with Simran, Shanita, Suryani, Chandrika, Fahrizat, Mastura and Kim.

Bhairav and Kapalin had pooh poohed the doomsday predictors and Armageddonists as incessant rains and storms raged over Tiger Isle. They had each respectively perfected and finalized on paper Project Tigerism and Project X. Bhairav had of course fired the first shots by manipulating Quasi into swift action and unleashing demagoguery on an unprecedented scale. Now they briefed each other, compared notes and ensured one did not inadvertently sabotage the other in the execution of the mother of all stings.

The official flight time from Chandrapore to Kuala Lumpur was only forty-five minutes. Kapalin, however, had given strict instructions to Jeff not to land in Kuala Lumpur until he gave the green light. He knew it would be to his advantage to keep Bhairav in the air as long as possible, as old men like him had short attention spans and tired easily. That was why he chose Langkawi as their final destination, as the transit and connecting flight from Kuala Lumpur would further disorientate Bhairav.

Kapalin wanted that edge in the negotiations. He wanted to wear Bhairav out as much as possible so that when they met Suknohartono, ex-Malaysian PMs, Thakshin, Thai Red and Yellow Shirt leaders, John Bell IV and General Vladimir Vissarionovich Lavrenty Trotsky in Langkawi he could take center stage and call the shots. He did not want a well-rested Bhairav to upstage him in his hour of glory. Besides, he wanted to study Quasi at close quarters. If all went according to his plan, they would land in Langkawi at 2:00 a.m., Friday.

Kapalin had quickly realized that while Bhairav and Quasi had not quite checkmated him, it would be plain suicide to try to eliminate Bhairav or go it alone. Kapalin clearly saw through Bhairav's plans and that Quasi was being used and was inconsequential to the game. Any compliant dolt would have done as the patsy and Bhairav had cast the role to perfection.

He could also see that for Bhairav it was not merely a question of money; he had more than he could spend or needed for another hundred lifetimes. At eighty-three he worried more about his legacy. It did not matter if, in their hearts, Tiger Islanders or the liberals in Washington thought he was a vile, corrupt swindler or the worst kind of racist, dictator, or all of it.

He was willing to stake his bottom dollar that if the press and PR machinery stayed on his side, his honored and hallowed place in the history books would be assured. That really was the crux of the matter.

Bhairav would take anybody on, waste any human life and even squander his entire ill-begotten billions if that's what it took to ensure that after he'd gone to his maker, he would not be maligned permanently in print for his children, grandchildren and descendants to read about. The perception of him being the pristine Father of Modern Pulipore, a superpatriot, a defender of the Pulirajaputran Tigerists come what may, that he had bravely challenged the British colonials and fiercely fought for independence when he had done nothing of that kind, that he had stood up to Bush, Blair, Howard and the Israelis when the reality was that he was not even remotely on their radar screen—these were the things Bhairav wanted to be remembered for.

To save time and a lot of headache, Kapalin simply gave Bhairav what he wanted. He agreed to rein in his overexuberant nephew Kethu Desert Fox Suryan and his dogs, get the press and blogosphere to give him more space and coverage and be totally uncritical of his past misdeeds in the MSM, which UNTA controlled.

Without Bhairav asking for it, Kapalin conceded to neutralizing the findings of various PPCI hearings on bribery allegations against the judiciary, police, PACC and Adhi Gurunadha during Bhairav's presidency. Kapalin "caved" in because he was a realist. He could only protect Bhairav as long as he was alive and he did not care a toss whatever transpired once he was dead. Unlike many Tigerists, he had no fascination with the afterlife. He would take his chances and enjoy life to the maximum while he could and was assured of it.

Bhairav and Quasi too, conceded things had rapidly gone swimmingly well for them. They had arrived prepared for all-out war, ready to threaten exposing Kapalin and Big Porka, his weakest link, in senate hearings in the USA and court hearings in Paris and Moscow over kickbacks and inflated government defense and other procurement contracts.

Quasi worried a little that Kapalin had folded over in such supine fashion. Not Bhairav, though. For many years when Kapalin had been his deputy, he had observed the steely and cunning interior behind the seemingly soft and portly exterior. But Bhairav's confidence was not based on trust. He knew he held as many trump cards as Kapalin, but would still have settled for the same compromise had the shoe been on the other foot. Bhairav had no illusions that real power always lay in the hands of the incumbent president and besides, what each wanted from the other was not in conflict.

So they broke open a chilled bottle of Dom Perignon Rosé Vintage 1959, two of which had been auctioned off a couple of years earlier in New York for eighty-five thousand dollars. The night was still young and the bar well stocked with wines and champagnes of the rarest vintage costing thousands of dollars per bottle—Château Mouton Rothschild, Château Pétrus, Cristal Brut, Pernod-Ricard Perrier-Jouet, Shipwrecked 1907 Heidsieck at $275,000 per and more—not to mention the smoothest of rare scotch whiskeys.

Kapalin passed around the hand-rolled Cohiba cigars and promised his guests a fantastic dinner precooked by France's only six-Michelin-star chef extraordinaire, Alain Ducasse, which had set PRA back a cool hundred thousand dollars. The menu included the rarest of caviar, salmon, truffles, lobster, shrimps, crabs, mushrooms, chicken and pork prepared with rare and exotic ingredients and brilliantly concocted original sauces, accompanied with appropriate superb wines, with the whole dreamy experience completed with to-die-for subtle desserts.

It was a meal none of them would enjoy, for the best-laid plans of men and mice are often undone by the tiniest of indiscretions of their minions.

A Little Indiscretion

Jeff and Isa had been served twenty-four-hour's notice by Kim from the president's office to get PAF One in tiptop condition for Kapalin's trip to Langkawi. They were only told that besides the new NDPS, there would be two other male guests onboard, but not their identities.

Under normal circumstances, this would have been fine. However, nonstop storms and deluges had seen the indefinite cancellation of all inbound and outbound flights from PRIA. All transit passengers caught in the debacle had been billeted in five-star hotels in Chandrapore City two days earlier.

Kapalin had declared a state of national emergency. The airport was virtually deserted except for a skeleton crew of maintenance engineers and air traffic controllers in their towers. Many ancillary staff had gone AWOL and run off to Gurunadhapore, spooked and panicked by the doomsday cultists and Satanic Peltists. With the exception of the armed national guards at the main approach road to PRIA and the airport doors, passport control and passenger, baggage and security screening were completely absent.

When warned by Jeff of the dangers of taking off in such abysmal ground and atmospheric conditions, Kapalin instantly dismissed it.

"The A380 is built precisely to fly in these conditions. Imagine Obama being intimidated by a mere shower. I have worlds to move, a universe to conquer. Get cracking and that's a direct order. Besides, it'll blow over by the time we return," he had barked at Kim, who conveyed the message verbatim to Jeff. Prophetic words indeed!

Before Jeff checked in after lunch at PRIA, where he had left it to Isa to run through the usual thorough A380-checking routine with the engineers and ground crew, he had a brainwave. He ached for Jess with whom he'd not physically connected for over a fortnight. He knew that she and her friends were still grieving over Rekha's sudden, sad, tragic and shocking death. In the days that followed, Simran/Jess spent most of her time in Krishnasamy's home, looking after him and waiting for a call from Roshan and the children. But there had been absolute silence. So, Jeff called his "wife" on her handphone.

"Listen darling, I have a brilliant idea that'll get you back on your feet and bring the smile back on your mug," Jeff said. "Remember that personal tour of PAF One you wanted? Well, there's no time like today. There's hardly anyone around. The security guys have all gone AWOL and the national guards here are not going to question me, the boss of PAF One. Tell you what, why don't you pick up all six of your girlfriends too on your way here? We'll have a small, exclusive PARTAY for eight on board PAF One before I leave."

There was a minutes' silence before Jess crackled back, "Any chance we'll get at least a mile high up on PAF One?"

Jeff picked them all up in a PRIA security SUV about a mile away from the airport. The girls parked the two cars they had arrived in by the roadside. They reckoned there was not a chance in a million that under the present circumstances they would return later to find a couple of parking tickets stuck under the windshield of their cars, or their cars clamped or towed away.

Jeff drove them straight through to the A380, which had the airbridge already attached to it and was parked safely in its special bay. He quickly ushered them into the plane and inside the cavernous cockpit, left them there and returned after depositing the SUV in its nearby hangar bay.

He spent the next hour personally escorting the gang on a grand guided tour of the double-decked superjumbo while they feasted on superb, freshly cut meat sandwiches that would have shamed a five-star gourmet deli. They washed their meal down with classy wine and whiskey culled from the kitchenette specially reserved for serving presidents.

Jess was of course familiar with some of the layout of this A380, although, since it was a done deal direct nego rip-off contract, she had only put in an appearance or two to add a veneer of authenticity during the $125 million refit. They returned to the cockpit, where Jeff activated one by one the snoop security cameras and listening devices, through which he kept track of all the activities onboard while in the air.

That's when fate intervened.

Isa called to warn him that Omar had arrived alone to personally carry out a security check of the presidential suite on PAF One, virtually the most expensive condo in the sky in the world. After ordering the permanent exsanguinations of the clueless Haniff and his number two, the traitorous Abu Bakar, Kapalin had handpicked Omar from Army Intelligence as his replacement. He had completely lost his faith in the police leadership.

As an army man, Omar had the requisite experience and service tenure, though not quite the intelligence, which suited Kapalin fine. All he wanted was an unambitious, clean "yes man" who would do his exact bidding.

Jeff warned the girls to tone it down in the cockpit as he rushed down to meet Omar. Jeff escorted him to the upper deck and the presidential suite. Once inside, Omar snapped open his leather briefcase, pulled out the most sophisticated of electronic sweeping devices and began his task. "Leave me alone. I'll call you when I've finished," he growled as he dismissed Jeff without looking back.

Jeff dutifully double-timed it back to his cockpit, where the girls were living it up. As Fahrizat recommended the "let's flip a switch" game, the picture zoomed in on Omar deeply immersed in his round of electronic sweeping in the presidential suite. Just as Jeff put a finger up to his lips to silence them, not that there was any chance of Omar hearing them, they all heard Omar's handphone ring to the shrill tones of Who Let the Dogs Out.

"Yes, Sri President. How can I help?" answered Omar, snapping to attention.

"What's the news on that traitor's husband and children?" Kapalin said.

"Sir, just this morning I received bad news from Down Under. Haniff's intelligence was shitty. News of Rekha's husband and children heading to Melbourne was a red herring. It was all a sham. The three who landed in Oz were impersonators travelling on the Roshans' original Pulipore international passports. They have all disappeared. The trail is cold. If only those idiots had kept her alive. Anyway, be warned, sir, there's grave danger everywhere. We'll have to restrategize as soon as we return from Langkawi Monday noon," Omar reported.

"Well, make sure you keep me posted daily on developments, understand? Don't make me call you," Kapalin barked.

"Yes, Sri President," Omar bellowed and snapped to attention again and clicked his heels as Kapalin switched off.

The girls were in tears and bit into the fleshy part of their palms to avoid screaming in hysteria. They had just heard each and every word of a frightening murder confirmation through the most sophisticated of electronic security systems devised by man. Jeff, whose face was ashen grey, again motioned them to keep calm and silent.

He switched off the cameras and then whispered for them all to sit down and wait quietly in the cockpit till Omar had completed his job. As expected, Omar called him half an hour later and gave Jeff the thumbs up for the secure presidential suite. Jeff escorted him out of the plane and left him in the PAF One passengers lounge to await the arrival of the president and his guests.

In all their remaining days, Jeff and the seven ladies never forgot the exact hour, minute, second and date in their lives when their belief in God was irrevocably reaffirmed. When Jeff returned, they all hugged each other and wept some more.

"I want Kapalin in a body bag," Jess hissed.

"You may well see that wish and more realized soon," Jeff said. "Omar just informed me who Kapalin's two guests on this flight will be. One of them is your sweetie, Bhairav, who's singularly responsible for Kirpal's last ten years in Bay of Pigs. The other is our McCarthy and puppet head of PRAKASH, Quasi Mahaslimeballmaya."

"How do we do it, Jeff? How? I've never so much as punched another human being all my life. Yet I can't wait to stick a knife in Kapalin, Bhairav and Quasi! How will we get away with it? Don't forget, Omar will be there as well," Jess said.

"To start with, we have that entire confession recorded by CCTV cameras. But we can't take it to any police or government law-enforcement agency on Tiger Isle. Once there, it will never ever see the light of day again. It we take it to Maitreya and DJP, the government will claim it's all a fake shot by Avatar's James Cameron.

We could take a shot at the U.S. ambassador or one of the U.S. MSM. But they'll have to face the same Avatar accusation and be accused of interfering in the internal politics of Tiger Isle. Kapalin will orchestrate massive UNTA street protests and claim Satan Uncle Sam is out to destabilize his "democratically elected" government, assassinate him and replace him with their puppet. Bhairav and Quasi will add fuel to fire by waving the "Zionist plot" red flag. It will all be too messy. I can't see how we'll get justice for Rekha, her family, you and us if we take that route. No, I guess we'll have to take the law into our own hands," Jeff concluded.

"Are you saying what I think you are saying, Jeff?" Jess asked, incredulous.

"I'm not sure what you think Jeff is saying, Sim. But I'll say what I think, out loud. Right now, I can't think of another way out. We'll have to fit four dead bodies in four body bags and get rid of them without anyone else knowing about it. I've no idea how we are going to achieve that. Like you, I'm not going to allow them to get off scot free for brutal murder. Rekha was our collective conscience. We should have stood side by side with her all the way. I can't sleep nights thinking that somehow I betrayed her and am responsible for her death. I don't know where God is in all this, but when she had a premonition, she came to warn us first, remember? It may not have been my Muslim God who appeared to forewarn us. I have no clue. But all the gods were certainly here in this cockpit when Fahrizat miraculously flipped that one switch for our benefit. We may even have to consider a fifth body bag. I don't know where Isa's loyalties lie. I don't know about you guys, but I'm with Jess and body bags," Mastura choked out, not quite believing she was ready to join a conspiracy to murder not one, but four and possibly five men.

Before Jeff could respond, all seven ladies who had not hurt a fly ever had readily agreed to premeditated quadruple homicide, or more if it came to that. They were not going to let Rekha's murderers escape or go unpunished or let anyone stop them from trying.

"Don't worry about Isa. We need two to tango with an A380. We go back a long way and were colleagues on the Boeing 747-400s before. Like Mastura and Fahrizat, he too would like this government of thieves to fall. They haven't been kind to the minority Muslims and Isa will never forgive them for their sneaky, underhanded mosque-razing program. Leave him to me. I'll take care of it. So that's four body bags. I have a plan."

Jeff whipped out his handphone and pressed speed dial four for Diane, the scheduled head stewardess for his flight and said, "Listen sweetheart, there's been a change of plans. Kapalin and NDPS Omar have ordered a new crew for today's flight. They're already onboard for early security vetting, body search, etcetera. Top secret, hush hush and all that stuff. So please inform Rose and Jasmine as well. I envy you guys now that you can have the rest of the weekend off and Monday too. I'll approve your transport and meal allowances for the last-minute changes. Bye."

"So we're the new stewardesses?"

"Spot on as usual, Jess," Jeff said. "First, I'll take you all to the lower deck where the stewardesses' quarters are and where you'll find PAF One uniforms including high-heeled shoes. They have S, M, L and XL sizes, so none of you should have any problem finding a set that fits. But Chand, Shanita, Mastura and Kim will have to lie low in the bedroom at the back since you are known to either Bhairav and Quasi or Kapalin. Don't worry, once Kapalin, Bhairav, Quasi and Omar get onboard, they will never leave the upper deck.

"Jess, Suryani and Fahrizat will follow me back to the living room and kitchenette in the presidential suite. Remember, it's a specially renovated superjumbo A380, not a commercial plane. It will be just like your kitchen at home, only more expensive, a hell of a lot more expensive. All the drinks and snacks they will ever need will be right there in that kitchenette. There's some fancy French food they've preordered, but it's not a long-haul flight. I doubt they'll ask for dinner soon. If past experience is anything to go buy, they'll drink themselves blind on the most expensive wine and whiskey in the world," Jeff briefed them.

"And how do you propose to overpower these four men, especially Omar who's likely to be a judo expert and armed?" Kim spoke up.

Jeff pulled open a hatch in the cockpit wall and sorted out four sets of handcuffs and leg chains. There was other stuff in there as well, Tasers, pepper-spray canisters, coils of ropes, masking tape and more.

"We PAF One pilots are not just pretty faces, you know. We're trained to handle difficult passengers and even terrorists if it comes to a pinch. My strategy is to first knock out Omar alone up here with the Taser and then you guys, all seven of you, will help me take out the three VIPs.

We probably won't need Tasers for them. Once we've got them where we want them, let me do the talking. We'll have to get them to release Kirpal and some of the key DJP people from Bay of Pigs and negotiate safe asylum, money and other terms for all. If they cooperate, we still have a problem of what to do with them.

"You all do realize there's no turning back or returning to Tiger Isle for us, don't you? Not until this entire regime vanishes and Maitreya and DJP come into power and take control. That could take years. We'll probably have to bide our time in London or Washington," explained Jeff.

He could see fear and worry cloud their faces, followed by panic. The reality of their proposed hijacking of the A380 and homicide pact had not fully dawned on them. They had families on Tiger Isle. They looked up enquiringly at Jeff when his sms prompt buzzed.

"Sorry," Jeff said. "I'm really sorry, girls. It's too late. There's no time for phone calls and farewells. Isa is already heading to the VIP lounge to fetch our enemies into the lion's den, as it were. We have fifteen minutes to get ready. We'll have to play it by ear from here onwards. When in doubt, wait for my cue."

Justice for All

Everything went exactly to plan, up to a point. Once they were above the clouds, Jeff authorized the CCTV to be switched on for Isa to spy in on Kapalin and Bhairav. When Isa got wind of what was exactly being discussed, it didn't take long for Jeff to convince him not to interfere in whatever Jeff was going to do or that unfolded.

Simran, Fahrizat and Kim magically reappeared after Kapalin and Bhairav had exhausted discussions. The women put on their sexiest walks as they encouraged them to down a few quick shots of top-class scotch whiskey to shouts of "Cheers." The girls matched them shot for shot and openly flirted with the VIPs while awaiting Jeff's next move. The Great Leaders next waded into the champagne, wine and caviar with glee and gusto. Jeff allowed them to feast until they were fairly tipsy and began dancing with the stewardesses. Then Jeff made his move.

He sauntered over to the presidential suite and invited Omar for a visit to the cockpit with a spiel about it being good luck for first-time passengers on PAF One. Omar bought it hook, line and sinker. Isa, who had taken over from Jeff soon after takeoff, had switched on to autopilot and zapped Omar with the Taser as soon as he stepped inside. They handcuffed him behind his back and slipped on the leg chains before taping his mouth.

Jeff buzzed through to Chandrika and the others to come up to the cockpit. While Isa stayed behind to mind the controls, the five of them dragged the comatose Omar to the door of the presidential suite, where Jess and the others who had been alerted were ready and waiting. It took them mere minutes to overpower Kapalin, Bhairav and Quasi, who were in no condition to put up the slightest resistance even against grandmothers in wheelchairs. They used the ropes to tie them to their seats.

The quick turn of events and the adrenaline rush sobered up Kapalin, Bhairav and Quasi, but Omar was still out stone cold. They were shocked to see Chandrika, Shanita, Mastura and Kim and could not quite figure out the play here. He spoke first who had the most to lose.

"It's a dangerous crime to hijack PAF One, Shanita. You could end up in Bay of Pigs for the rest of your life. That is, if the judges don't hang a death sentence on you first. So if Jeff takes us safely back to Chandrapore, I'll let you all go without any charges. Why, I'll even let you all leave with $1 million each so you can settle down overseas comfortably. Isn't that all want you want, money?"

Kapalin posed in what he thought was a very soothing and persuasive voice, unaware he sounded like a demented idiot.

Simran/Jess walked over and smashed a crystal wine glass in his face. She let the blood drip down his cheek onto his Armani shirt and jacket and offered no assistance, helpless as he was. Then she launched into him. "Now when you are on the real receiving end and can't lift a finger to save yourselves, perhaps you'll understand how sick the people feel at your and Bhairav's gangsterism posing as democratically and freely elected government.

Oh, do you think we can't see through your lies? Dictatorships work better than democracy, that practicing meritocracy is racist, monopolies given for a song to cronies are better than free-market economics, that a purely race-based political party will not promote open racism, that one-sided and cornered affirmative action is superior to meritocracy, that the rights of the Tigerists majority citizens as enshrined in the constitution, must be respected and never be questioned even if abused to the hilt, but not those of the minorities. I'm sure Bhairav knows the source of the quote 'War is peace, freedom is slavery and ignorance is strength.[5]

We are not all stupid and we have been waiting for an opening to put things right. My husband Kirpal's been in Bay of Pigs for ten years by order of Bhairav and you, for what? What physical harm did he ever inflict upon you or your families? And today we found out you were responsible for the horrific murder of my best friend Rekha.

Look around you. We are Puliporeans first—me, Punjabi Sikh; Chandrika and Suryani, Tigerists; Shanita and Kim, Chinese and Christian; Mastura and Fahrizat, Malay and Indian Muslim; Jeff, Portuguese and Sri Lankan Tigerist; and Isa in the cockpit, Indonesian Malay. We girls have been the best of loving friends for over thirty years.

If we and our families can come together in peace, harmony and love, it makes nonsense of your Tigerism and Pulirajaputranism, which is nothing more than thinly disguised religious bigotry and racial supremacist philosophy. You exploit all that to rob, loot,

5   1984 by George Orwell.

plunder, rape and steal while you mow down anyone who stands in your way.

All that changed today for you. You see, we've put up with your evil all our lives. So today we'll tell you what to do and you'll execute it, or the Indian Ocean will be your watery grave. Jeff, pass him your handphone. He'll give the orders now to get Kirpal out to Singapore ASAP by whatever means and with sufficient money," Simran instructed.

It was just past midnight. The fates are kind and the fates are unkind. Or perhaps they knew better. In the heat of the moment, Simran had not considered how she would resolve a love triangle involving her, Kirpal and Jeff. These are imponderables humans cannot fathom. Jeff slowly walked over to her, took her arm, pulled her aside and whispered to her he had to go to the cockpit, as Isa had spoken to him frantically over the wireless headphones about an emergency. He wanted her to accompany him, more than anything else to calm and cool her down.

As they left, Chandrika and Kim grabbed a whiskey glass each to rearrange Bhairav and Quasi's facial features somewhat. They could not understand why Kapalin alone should enjoy the honor. The others joined in as well to dish out a bit of the "some are more equal than others" treatment the Tigerist elite had enjoyed by constitutional right. As they left, the screams of terror behind them brought a beatific smile to Jess's face.

Their hearts sank when Isa informed Jeff and Jess that at exactly midnight he had lost all contact not only with PRIA control tower, but also with the whole of the country. He had tried all the airports in the states, handphone numbers and landlines. For some weird reason, no electronic signal could penetrate or leave Tiger Isle. He had contacted the international airports in Bangkok, Singapore, Kuala Lumpur, Chennai and Jakarta. Everyone reported the same mysterious phenomenon.

An electronic blanket had descended over Tiger Isle. Over the next hour, slowly, the news came filtering in to PAF One from Singapore and India through NASA sources. Images taken by satellites equipped with sophisticated infrared cameras and analyzed by supercomputers showed that Tiger Isle could not be located on the globe. No one yet knew what that really meant. This was a phenomenon for which no one knew of a precedence on which they could hang their question marks.

"We'll find out as soon as there's daylight. But what do we do for now, Jeff?" Jess asked with a trace of genuine fear and helplessness in her voice.

"We can't go back," Jeff said. "No way, not without radar, control tower and air traffic support. If what they are saying is true, we can't rescue Kirpal. I mean, he may not be there. I don't know what to make of it when they say Tiger Isle cannot be located on the Earth. What, did it sink into the ocean or vaporize? What? It's too weird.

"Look, we'll all go mad trying to figure this out. So let's discuss it with the others, and then I'll make a decision. Besides, PAF One left with less than half a tank for the short trip to Kuala Lumpur and back. We've been cruising over the Indian Ocean for six hours. It's not safe. We have to land somewhere soon," Jeff replied.

Their joint discussion over the next hour did not resolve the issue of how to move forward. Isa continued to update them that news trickling in from Beijing, Tokyo, Moscow, Taipei, Seoul, Canberra and Wellington only quoted the NASA source. Tiger Isle had ceased to exist.

"I can't afford to cruise at this altitude any longer. We definitely can't go back to Tiger Isle with that electronic blanket there. If we land anywhere else with Bhairav, Kapalin and Quasi alive, then the game's up. We may all end up in prison there or back home. If this talk of Tiger Isle disappearing isn't all pure nonsense, we can't get Kirpal out, period. If it's true, and I still think it's all poppycock, God help us all. I don't know how to deal with it," Jeff moaned.

Once again Chandrika analyzed it out for them clearly, as she had done many years ago for Bhairav and Pulirajaputran Tiger Motors. She had that kind of rare brain that could slice through Gordian knots.

"Jeff, what you just said really means there is only one course of safe action for us to take. We'll have to get rid of our four VIPs before we land somewhere. There's no official record anywhere in Tiger Isle of who left on PAF One. Shanita was instructed not to log in anything at the office by Kapalin, who had given similar instructions to Bhairav, Quasi and Omar.

No one would know why they left for PRIA. It's obvious they wanted no one to know they were leaving Tiger Isle. No one knows we seven girls are on board, that was a last-minute thing. No flight plan or names have been filed with PRIA. So we'll just have to get our story right wherever we land. We'll cook up something up about having won a special prize for a free ride on PAF One and getting lost because of this electronic blanket thingamajig. In the worst-case scenario, we'll ask for asylum at the U.S. Embassy and show them all the CCTV recordings up to just before we trussed them up."

There was absolute silence. Then they all agreed that Chandrika was right and pieced together the story they wanted to tell when the time came. When they'd done that, the ladies headed to the linen cupboard for wads of dark towels and blankets and then to the galley where they had spotted the reinforced thick black bin bags and gleaming sets of steel-bladed and razor-sharp steak knives. When they were ready, they headed for the presidential suite, where as they entered, Simran/Jess screamed, "Mothers, let's rock!"

Bhairav, Kapalin, Quasi and Omar had not "gone gently into the good night." They had begged for mercy when they had never granted any. They had not even in their last hour understood the enormity of their crimes. They had offered all their wealth, which was not theirs by right. They had raged against the injustice of it all when they had sent others to their deaths at their whims and fancies, not caring about their infant babies and children who grew up without a memory of their fathers and mothers.

They went kicking, screaming and howling till finally insanity set in and mercifully, their hearts gave away. Most pathetic of the trio was Quasi Mahamaya Lion's Mane Jellyfish, who even as he succumbed, screeched grotesquely, "Shit! Shit! Shit!" and repeated it. Fortunately too for them, the ladies had steely resolve but not the heart for prolonged torture.

When they had completed their gory task, the ladies headed for the showers and a change of clothes, as Jeff and Isa wheeled out diner trolleys to cart the bin bags with their human corpses to the cargo-hold area of the redesigned A380. When the ladies were ensconced safely in the stewardesses' quarters, Jeff headed back to the cockpit.

From there, he operated the switches and jettisoned their unwanted cargo over the Indian Ocean, which in many ways was more apt a final resting place for these extremist Tigerist Puliporeans than any other.

"Where we headed, Captain?" Isa asked for instructions.

"We'll have to head for the only country in these parts that has any real respect for democracy and rule of law, not pretend-democracy and rule by law. First Officer Mohamad Isa, set the course for Chennai, India and move it!" Jeff ordered, grim-faced.

The Holocaust

For once on Tiger Isle, thirteen was an unlucky number. It rained for thirteen days commencing at 0:00 a.m. on December 8, 2012. It rained in the mountains, in the hills and valleys and in the forests, villages, towns and cities. In poured in all four States in sheets till all work and human activity came to a standstill. The life-giving ports, casinos, hotels, resorts, discos, nightspots, brothels, oil refineries and government and private offices, skyscrapers, towers and water-theme parks were empty.

Mudslides and landslides swept away whole settlements, villages and small towns. Animals, birds and creatures died from exposure to continual damp and the cold, or drowned by the millions. River, lake and sea levels rose dangerously. The populace shivered and shook as gale-force winds roared with the combined fury of a million hungry tigers in heat stalking their quarry and in full pursuit of their mates.

Millions fled in panic to Gurunadhapore, hoping to find shelter and protection at the Maha Jagad Tiger Temple and with the presence of Adhi Gurunadha. All, led by Adhi Gurunadha on PNTVS4, read the Tiger Puranam and chanted its verses, hoping against hope for some clues to avert what they clearly perceived was the approach of Armageddon. They prayed around the clock and donated milk, honey and truckloads of beautiful flowers as offerings, especially the rare, brilliant, orange-red variant of Canna

Bengal Tiger, Canna Tiger Isle, deemed the favorite of Ampa and found only in the highlands of Mt. Kailas.

Others gathered at Mt. Kailas at the foot of the gigantic Sivan Lingam and Tiger Thoon. They begged for relief from the fear and mental trauma induced by the matchless, terrifying power of the cosmos. It was all to no avail.

At precisely 0.00 p.m. midnight on the thirteenth day, the downpour ceased as suddenly as it had commenced. The center of Gurunadhapore opened up exactly like the third eye of Siva. Even Google Map's satellite, which passed over that precise spot at that precise moment, could not discern the nature of the vortex that next developed and expanded to double the size of Peninsular Malaysia in seconds. The satellite could identify only its shape.

Later, physicists and cosmologists would swear it was a Black Hole. But they could not explain how a Black Hole could form in inner space on land, let alone the ones in the cosmos! Whatever it was, everything was sucked into it like a giant vacuum cleaner at work. Mt. Kailas, white limestone cliffs, PRIA, the Pulijayam government offices and TV station, Bay of Pigs, Sati Coral Reef, Gurunadha Diving Spot, Tiger Temple, Sivan Lingam and Tiger Thoon, everything slid and tumbled in.

The roof split and collapsed over $65 million Xanadu. Big Porka sank as she was just positioning herself over the seat of her brand-new $250,000 music-playing tankless auto-deodorizing bidet-washlet-toilet, specially imported from Japan. She despaired over going to meet her maker with a full bladder and hair displaced from its usual carefully permed setting, exposing the almost fully receded hairline. Most of all, she despaired over having to make that journey, destination unknown, without the companionship of a couple of the latest two-hundred-thousand-dollar Birkin handbags "donated" to her by the scions of a couple of "corpo rat captains of industry" or fraudtrepreneurs.

His unholiness Adhi Gurunadha was not spared either. But he accepted it stoically. The good, the young and the old perished together with the scum. It was now clear that the stain of grievous sin on Tiger Isle, as in the five towns of Sodom near the River

Jordan possibly some five millennia ago, was beyond redemption, irretrievable. No one was innocent.

Thirty million people vanished in the blink of an eye, never to be seen again, swallowed into a chasm that drilled its way beneath the very ocean floor that had once churned and spat Tiger Isle out. The awesome energy of the tallest, widest and most terrifying tsunami ever seen by human eyes was channeled and dissipated by some miraculous winds north, then west and then south toward Antarctica, thousands of miles away. Aceh and Sumatra were spared the fury of yet another monster tsunami.

Tiger Isle sank back into the mysterious abyss from which it had suddenly risen almost two thousand years ago, never to be seen again.

Last to disappear were the original Tiger Puranam Sanskrit and Tamil texts which burst into flames by spontaneous combustion, as there arose from the depths of hell an almighty roar of a wounded tiger.

Nothing and no one was spared.

It was exactly 00.15 a.m. when the ocean settled back calmly over the spot where Tiger Isle had once existed.

The date was 21.12.2012; unless of course it's North America, where they write down the month first when someone asked you for the date.

Rekha's premonition was thus fulfilled. Her seven friends and the minimum of five she had bargained for survived in the end. She had not consciously bargained for Jeff and Isa. Perhaps Jeff was her subconscious gift to her best friend Simran, so that she would not be alone and Isa because, without his first-officer A380 flying expertise and skills, none could not have escaped to safety.

Over the years they pondered over a thousand such questions. It was easy to answer why innocent babies and young children perished with the rest. They would not have survived anyway, and sudden, instantaneous death was kinder.

Why was Kirpal not spared? After all, he had sacrificed so much for so many and suffered. He had embraced the right principles and lived it. Perhaps he had to pay for neglecting his wife and children. He had never been a real father to his wards. A man has to find the right balance between family and career, or choose one over the other.

Why Maitreya? Without Tiger Isle he would have been a rebel without a cause. It would be too late for him to start elsewhere.

An entire nation of thirty million wiped out? Can we buy Rekha's First Law of Thermodynamics? Or was it a timely reminder to humanity for which some religions say there is precedence?

All I know is that life is a gift and survival, more than an instinct.

Epilogue

It was Monday, September 3, 2012. The Special Cleaners arrived at 11:30 p.m. in a jet-black funeral limousine. Never one to leave anything to chance, their leader, Yama Spotted Jaguar Sivan, had police squad cars seal off the entrance to Sherwood Villas for a couple of hours. No one was allowed to leave or enter the estate. They slid out the casket and carried it on tiptoes, mindful not to jostle its contents. All the lights in the house were already switched on. The front door to the house was open. They could hear the loud sobs from the driveway.

They carefully lifted the casket over the entrance steps, trooped in and placed it gently on the carpet in the center of the living room. In three days, the carpenters had done a miraculous job in restoring Roshan and Rekha's house to its former pristine glory. No one would suspect an EATSS team had wrecked it three days earlier. Two EATSS men in full combat gear and armed with machine guns stood guard in front of the house gates. There were two more at the rear.

Much earlier, all the occupants of the houses in the two rows of that block had been instructed to get to bed early and have all the windows in their homes shut and curtains drawn.

They lifted the cover off the casket as two EATSS men held the trembling and tearful Krishnasamy by his arms and drew him forward for a view.

The casket was beautifully made from expensive lacquered rosewood. In it lay the dead body of Rekha, fully immersed in a sea of her favorite jasmine flowers. Only her face was visible. The head was covered with a garland of jasmine and roses, hiding the broken skull and blue-black lumps on her forehead. To be doubly sure against anyone accidentally touching the flowers and exposing raw scarred flesh underneath, the body, from the neck down, was covered in a tight-fitting Dior black gown with full undergarments and cinched at the extremities of fingers and toes. They had spared no expenses or thought in preparing for this finale.

Krishnasamy gazed at Rekha's face. It was much too much to ask any father to bear that kind of grief. Krishna thought of the joy she had brought him and his wife from the day she was born and of how wonderfully she had looked after them in their old age. No father could have asked more of his daughter. Now he could not tell the truth about her even to his brother.

"Listen old man, we have arranged for the priests, who will arrive here at 10 a.m. sharp tomorrow. We have checked. It's a very propitious hour to begin the prayers and start receiving mourners. Don't move the casket in any way or touch the body. The priests will remain with you here until the casket is transported to the cemetery in the evening. All arrangements have been taken care off. So don't interfere with anything. You have been briefed what to say to anyone who asks questions. She died tomorrow morning in her sleep. Got it?" Yama growled as he put his finger vertically over his lips to indicate secrecy.

They escorted Krishnasamy back to the sofa, where he collapsed in uncontrollable grief.

"Here's something for you," whispered Yama kindly, as for once the mask slipped just a little and some human emotion seeped out. For a trained killer who had seen just about every kind of death and its horror, even he had been shaken to the core at the sight and condition of the three bodies he found in the IR. It was a check for $1 million.

After they had left, Krishnasamy went berserk and furiously tore the check into a million pieces and flung them out the window.

Did Bhairav and Kapalin think he would succumb to their "can you help me, you scratch my back, I'll scratch yours, got it?" sick, unprincipled and immoral philosophy?

For in the end, Tiger Isle was undone not by black holes, undersea earthquakes, tsunamis, or divine displeasure. It sunk from the unbearable heaviness of being inhuman, alien, putrid, stinking, filthy and rotting scum. It collapsed under the weight of endemic, entrenched, unrootable vile and evil corruption, cronyism, religious bigotry and racism. Tiger Isle paid the price that awaited every nation and people on Earth whose leaders yet manage to forget their humanity, which is supposedly fused into the very fabric of their flesh and souls.

As she had in life, Rekha Krishnasamy Roshan looked beautiful and serene. Her shell, as presented now to the world, gave no indication of the ordeal she had been through. There wer no signs of her heroic battle in defending truth, honor and justice and sacrificing Tiger Isle to save the world, her family and dearest friends. The Pulirajaputran fundamentalists and Constitutionalist Tigerist extremists, whose fates were interlocked with Rekha's death and did not know about it even in the end, cheered and exulted at news of Rekha's death. But here lay one labeled a "Keling pariah racist lesbian Tamil Indian bitch whore," whom the gods and angels carefully, gladly and lovingly guided into their world with tears streaming down their faces.

When they left, Krishnasamy and Ramasamy removed her gold Thali, passed on from mother to daughter and had it secretly sent through Allies Without Borders' network to Roshan in California. It was six months later when Lakshmi discovered the most intricate and sophisticated of miniature digital-video cameras hidden within the Thali and its pendant. In their eagerness, haste and utter contempt for "immigrants," Kevin and Jude had ignored standard operating procedures and underestimated their quarry by miles.

Four years later, Rekha's precocious son Karthik became the youngest billionaire ever at age eighteen. He developed the most innovative and popular of role-playing computer games devised, which one could download from the web for $4.99.

It was about a civilization that suddenly emerges in 1200 CE and pits tigers, priests, demigods and gods against Americans, Russians, Chinese, Indians, Europeans and other Asians battling for the keys to unlock the secrets of the universe.

It was called EROPILUP.

They key to victory in EROPILUP lay in unraveling the code which first had to be pieced together from those immortal lines uttered so often by Rekha:

"We are all of One Race, the Human Race!"

THE END

APPENDIX

CHARACTERS

Abu Bakar Greyhound Suryan - *Deputy NDPS*
Adhi Gurunadha - *Tigerist founder priest*
Aja Teak Jagged Lightning Sivan aka Mahathevan - *Rhamba's and
    Renga's first illegitimate son and Bhairav's father*
Anantha Chola Brown Bear Sivan - *Fourth Pulipore president*
Angammah - *Ramasamy's wife*
Arjuna Black Falcon Suryan - *Chairman joint chiefs of staff*
Ashwin - *Rekha's nephew*
Azalea Dawn Gazella Chandran - *Kapalin's mistress*
Bhairav Oak Broad Leaf Sivan LLB - *Aja's 1st son*
Bootesh Lin Liong Tan - *President Everich Construction Plc*
Chandran - *Demigod warrior prince three*
Chandrika Morning Glory Chandran - *Member of Rekha's Gang
    of Eight and Bhairav's personal secretary*
Charlie Chan Chin Chai - *President Euramerica Realty Plc*
Compton, Dexter, May and Robert - *Chandrapore law firm*
Devadeva Chola Mountain River Suryan - *Fourth Founding Father
    President*
Drona Red Hawk Sivan - *Director Joint Chiefs of Staff*
Duryodhana Acacia Broad Leaf Sivan - *Bhairav's eldest son*
Fa Hsien - *Fourth-century Chinese Buddhist monk*
Fahrizat Shariff Hamid - *Member of Rekha's Gang of Eight*
Gemini - *Ramasamy's son, Rekha's first cousin*
Gopalsamy - *Rekha's paternal uncle*
Haniff Hassan Foxwolf - *National director of police and security*

Hisham Yellow Leopard Rudra - *President Water Treatment Plant*
I Tsing - *Seventh-century Chinese Buddhist monk*
Ibn Batutta - *14th century Moroccan Muslim scholar*
Jacquelina Roxana Angel Fish Chandran - *Newscaster PNTV 4,*
    Mahamaya's lover
James Cook - *British explorer, founder of Australia*
Janaki Redwood Rekha - *Narrator/last of Puliporeans in 2211*
Jatin Ironwood Agastyar - *Kalagramam village priest*
Jaya Sea Cucumber Black Panther Chandran - *Kapalin's son*
Jesslyn Ho Sai Wan - *Member of Rekha's Gang of Eight and Kapalin's*
    personal secretary
John Milton Bell IV - *U.S. ambassador to Pulipore*
Jude Yellow Python Moraes - *CIO, Special Branch*
Kapalin Blowfish Black Panther Chandran - *Nisha's son, sixth Pulipore*
    president
Karthik Roshan Rekha - *Roshan and Rekha's son*
Kethu Desert Fox Suryan - *Kapalin's nephew*
Kevin Little Deer Pereira - *Chief Inspector, Special Branch*
'Kim" Catherine De Silva-Wong Kim - *Member of Rekha's Gang of*
    Eight
King Kaundinya III - *Early king of Pulipore*
Krishnan - *Demigod warrior prince no.4*
Krishnasamy - *Rekha's father*
Kublai Khan - *13th century Mongolian China Emperor*
Lakshmi Roshan Rekha - *Rekha's daughter*
Lalitha Dewi Sirikit Jagged Lightning Sivan - *Parvathy and Renga's*
    daughter
Lee Wing Yang - *Robert Lee's father*
Lingamraja Jacaranda Jagged Lightning Sivan - *Parvathy and Renga's*
    son
Magellan - *Spanish circumnavigator*
Mahabalan - *Rhamba's/Renga's illegitimate 2nd son*
Mahamaya Lions' Mane Jellyfish - *Leader of PRAKASH*
Mahathevan aka Aja Teak Jagged Lightning Sivan - *Rhamba's and*
    Renga's first illegitimate son and Bhairav's father
Maitreya Blue Dolphin Suryan - *Leader of the opposition DJP*
Marco Polo - *Thirteenth-century Italian traveller to Kublai Khan's*
    court in China
Mastura Mokhtar - *Member of Rekha's Gang of Eight and Sanat's*
    secretary
Mohamad White Rabbit Saiful - *Senior inspector Special Branch*

Mountain River, Chief - *First Chief of Pulipore, 1200 CE*
Muniammah - *Angammah's mother*
Murugaya - *Rekha's paternal grandfather*
Nisha Chola Black Panther Chandran - *Third Founding Father President*
Rhamba - *Renga's mistress*
Omar Bakri Din Grey Field Mouse Chandran - *New NDPS*
Parameswara Jagged Lightning Sivan - *Renga's father-in-law*
Parikisith Sequoia Sivan - *Janaka Redwood Rekha's lover*
Parvathy Lotus Jagged Lightning Sivan - *Renga's second wife*
Peter Weller Brown Mole Suryan - *President EPD*
Rahim Nor Black Bull - *EATSS black-ops commander*
Rakhini - *Ramasamy's daughter, Rekha's female first cousin*
Ramanujam Charya - *TM's cost accountant*
Ramasamy - *Rekha's paternal uncle*
Rambo Jamal Omar - *President Pulirajaputran Airlines*
Ramesh - *Rekha's nephew*
Rasammah - *Rekha's mother*
Ravilochana Chera Wise Owl Sivan - *First Founding Father President*
Rekha Krishnasamy Roshan - *Heroine, Roshan's wife*
Rengasamy Muthu - *Bhairav's grandfather*
Richard Chan, Rubicon & Mother - *Owner of ad agency SSRMI*
Robert Lee Wing Loong - *Lawyer, CDMR law firm*
Roshan Prasad - *Rekha's husband*
Sagara Kingfisher Great Ape Suryan - *President PEC*
Sri Sanatkumar Mutthiah Muralidharan - *Bhairav crony fraudtrepreneur*
Simran/Jess - *Rekha's best friend*
Sita - *Demigod warrior prince one*
Suryan - *Demigod warrior prince two*
Syryani Frangipani Sivan - *Member of Rekha's Gang of Eight*
Uma Oak Broad Leaf Sivan - *Bhairav's wife*
Valiammah - *Rekha's paternal grandmother*
Varuna Pandyan Honet Bee Suryan - *Second Founding Father President*
William Van Tan Trang - *President Feng Shui Gaming, Resorts &
     Hospitality Plc*
Yama Spotted Jaguar Sivan - *Special cleaner, Secret Service (Yama, Hindu
     god of death)*
Zara Mother Hen Sivan - *President Pulipore Federal Reserve*
Zheng He - *Fifteenth-century Chinese admiral*

PLACES

Adigramam - *Angammah's village in Madras*
Chandrapore - *Capital of Pulipore*
Idumbagramam - *Krishnasamy's village in Madras*
Kalagramam - *Village of Chief Parameswara Jagged Lightning Sivan*
Pulijayam - *Government administrative capital*
Suryapore - *West Pulipore Province*
Shivapore - *North Pulipore Province*
Shakthipore/Krishnapore - *South Pulipore Province*
Sati Coral Reefs - *South West Shakthipore*
Agastya Deep Sea Diving Spot - *South East Shakthipore*
Kantha Limestone Hills - *South East Shakthipore*
Peace Hill, Chandrapore - *Police and Security HQ*

ACRONYMS

ACE	Alpha Consulting Enterprise, Singapore
BAS	Biometric Access System
BVI	British Virgin Island off-shore tax haven
CCCP	Chandrapore City Center Plaza
CCSE	Chandrapore City Stock Exchange
CGA	Comptroller of Government Audit
CI	Chief Inspector
CIA	Central Intelligence Agency, USA
CIO	Chief Investigating Officer
DJP	Democratic Justice Party, main Opposition political party
EC	Election Council
EPD	Economic Planning Directorate
EATSS	Elite Anti-Terrorism Stormtrooper Squad
FDI	Foreign Direct Investment
GAD	Government Audit Department
GIA	Government Investment Arm
GLC	Government Linked Company, parodied as Government Losing Concern
GSA	Government Secrets Act
HQ	Headquarters
ICU	Intensive Care Unit
IEP	Independent Electricity Producer
MEARGT	Ministry of Energy, Alternative Resources and Green Technology

MI5	UK spy and intelligence agency
Mossad	Israel spy and intelligence agency
MSM	Mainstream Media
MTC	Ministry of Trade and Commerce
MOTV	Ministry of Transport and Vehicles
NDC	National Detention Center at Shaktipore
NDPS	National Director of Police and Security
NEA	New Economic Agenda
NGO	Nongovernmental Organization
NPST	New Pulipore State Times
NUP	National University of Pulipore
PA	Publications Act 1980
PACC	Pulipore Anti-Corruption Council
PARC	Public Audit Report Council
PCC	Pulipore Chamber of Commerce
PCE	Pulipore Certificate of Education
PHCE	Pulipore Higher Certificate of Education
PEC	Pulipore Electricity Corporation
PAF1	Pulipore Air Force One jet plane
PFR	Pulipore Federal Reserve
PITS	Pulipore Information Technology Service
PM	Prime Minister
PNSP	Pulipore National Service Program
PNTVS4	Pulipore National Television Station 4
PP	Pulipore Police
PPC	Pulipetro Corporation
PPCI	Pulipore Parliamentary Commission of Inquiry
PPCT	Pulipetro Corporation Tower
PRA	Pulirajaputran Airlines
PRIA	Pulirajaputran International Airport
PSA	Patriot and Security Act
PSB	Police Special Branch —
PSC	Pulipore Securities Council
PSE	Pulipore Stock Exchange
PVC	Poly Vinyl Chloride
RFP	Request for Proposal —
SCPE	School Certificate Public Examination
SI	Senior Inspector
SMS	Short Message Service
SS	Secret Service
SBMSP	Suryapore Bay Maximum Security Prison

SSRMI	Scatchi, Scatchi, Rubicon & Mother International, ad agency
UN	United Nations
UNHCR	United Nations High Commissioner for Refugees
UNTA	United National Tigerists Association, Tigerist religious political party
WLCI	World Lobby Corporation International
Xanadu	Kublai Khan's legendary palace, also name of Kapalin's house

TIMELINES

Mahathevan/Aja	born 1904
Mahathevan/Aja	marries age twenty-five, January 1929
Mahathevan/Aja	dies December 8, 1941
Bhairav	born December 8, 1929
Bhairav	becomes president 1980
Bhairav	resigns January 5, 2004
Kapalin	born 1944
Kapalin	took office January 6, 2004, age sixty
Krishnasamy	born 1915
Krishnasamy	left Madras 1933
Krishnasamy	married 1938
Pulipore	holocaust December 21, 2012
Rasammah	born 1918
Rasammah	left Madras 1933
Rasammah	married 1948
Rasammah	died 2005, age eighty-seven
Rekha	born 1959
Rekha	arrested, Friday August 31, 2012
Rekha	died age fifty-three Monday September 3, 2012
Rekha	body brought home Monday, September 3, 2012
Rekha	buried Tuesday, September 4, 2012